Playing With Fire

"Brooke."

Dalton spoke her name in a voice raw and husky with need. When she leaned up against him, offering with her body what she was too shy to speak aloud, he stepped back. His withdrawal from her was both puzzling and disappointing. Though separated by only inches, she felt a chasm stretch between them.

"Don't look so damned hurt."

"I'm not," Brooke said, turning away from him.

He captured the soft flesh of her upper arm, holding on just enough to keep her there. "You're a very tempting woman, Brooke Tyler. So tempting you make me forget myself." The last fragments of hunger fading in his eyes reaffirmed his words.

"Dalton, stay with me. You could run the saloon."

The words burst out with no prior thought on her part, but she didn't call them back, even when he dropped his hand from her arm and stalked to the other side of the room.

"I'm not the staying kind . . ."

FRONTIER FLAME

FRONTIER FLAME

SUSAN MACIAS

DIAMOND BOOKS, NEW YORK

FRONTIER FLAME

A Diamond Book / published by arrangement
with the author

PRINTING HISTORY
Diamond edition / January 1992

ISBN: 1-55773-644-8

Diamond Books are published by The Berkley Publishing Group,
200 Madison Avenue, New York, New York 10016.
The name "DIAMOND" and its logo are trademarks
belonging to Charter Communications, Inc.

PRINTED IN THE UNITED STATES OF AMERICA

10 9 8 7 6 5 4 3 2 1

To my mother, who was there at the beginning.

To Terry, Jolie, and Denise. Their effort and dedication make this victory very much theirs.

And to my wonderful husband, Tony, who believed in the dream and made it all possible.

Acknowledgments

My thanks to the Wyoming State Archives historical research and publications department for generously providing valuable information.

And a special thank you to Karen Pershing, friend, teacher, and very giving mentor. Her endless patience at last came to fruition.

Chapter 1

Spring, 1880

Some gamblers swore that luck was a woman who needed to be wooed and cajoled into granting favors. But to Dalton Reed, she was a capricious spirit with a spiteful temper who had spoiled his royal flush with an unwelcome two of clubs. He cursed softly, then tossed the cards on the table. There was no point in playing when the deck was stacked against him. He rose from his chair and asked to be dealt out of the next hand.

Moving to the far corner of the Pullman car, Dalton drew a thin cigar out of the inner pocket of his black wool coat. The railroad provided plush chairs and ornate wooden tables for the gambling car. Lantern light flickered and danced with the movements of the last car of the train. The chugging of the engine combined with the rumble of male conversation to create a steady din. Cards flashed in the crowded room, and two feet of gray smoky haze hung below the ceiling.

The plump banker with the florid complexion obviously didn't read the omens as well as Dalton, and he continued to play, losing two more hands.

Some men gambled to make the long train ride bearable. Those were the ones Dalton liked best. They were

1

his bread and butter, those patsies who fell into his hands as easily as apples from a tree. They put their money on the table, begging to be taken; Dalton never had a qualm about granting their requests. But for now, until his luck changed, he'd just wait and watch.

A few minutes later the door at the opposite end of the car opened, then quickly closed. None of the cardplayers looked up as a woman scurried through the train, glancing neither left nor right. The oil lamps reflected the red highlights in her brown hair, and its shine caught Dalton's eye. The years he'd spent growing up in a well-to-do Boston home could not be denied, and he stepped over to the rear door to hold it open for her.

She paused before crossing the threshold onto the platform at the end of the train. Tilting her head to look up at him, she spoke softly. "Thank you, sir." Her green eyes sparkled with some secret amusement before she turned away.

Dalton felt his lips tug upward in response.

Ready to try his hand again, he stepped back toward the table he had left earlier. Two cowboys stood arguing over his empty chair. Dalton was about to join the discussion when he saw the banker push himself to his feet. The look on the older man's face told Dalton that he, too, had seen the young woman pass through the Pullman. The red-faced banker pulled his plaid vest down more firmly over his stomach and wove his way to the back door.

He winked at Dalton. "Maybe a bit of fluff will change my luck."

Dalton looked at the last empty chair at the poker table. Despite the fact that all first class passengers were given free run of the train, many men believed that any woman leaving her car was fair game. Don't get involved, he told himself. The tingling in his fingertips told him that his luck had changed and he would win at cards, but his feet carried him to the banker's side.

"I wouldn't do that," he said, leaning one shoulder against the door and drawing his brows together.

Although the banker probably outweighed Dalton by fifty pounds, he was several years older and half drunk. But he was obviously sober enough to recognize the cold, deadly expression in the gambler's eyes. He tugged again at his plaid vest and walked away without a backward glance.

Dalton looked over his shoulder and saw that the last seat at the poker game had been taken. He pulled the platform door open with unnecessary violence. Damned women, he thought. They were all more trouble than they were worth.

Brooke Tyler jumped when the car door swung open. She pressed closer against the railing, uncertain if she was safer facing a stranger or hanging off the rear platform of a speeding train. The wheels below clacked noisily along the rails; the vibrations threatened her balance.

The man touched the brim of his black hat. "Ma'am."

Her heart returned to her chest, having spent the last several seconds lodged in her throat. It was him. The gambler.

Mrs. Gilmore, her self-appointed guardian for the trip, had warned her not to speak to strange men on the train, especially him. But it was all too tempting. There was no one to say "You shouldn't" or "You can't." After twenty-two years of adhering to the rules of Philadelphia society, the freedom was as heady as Christmas punch. A few short weeks ago she'd been servings cakes and gossiping with the neighbors, and now here she was on the Union Pacific Railroad, heading toward a new life in the Wyoming Territory.

She glanced up. The man watched her silently. Her grip on the railing tightened until the cold metal was digging into her hand.

This was just what she'd wanted, she reminded herself. High adventure, like in the novels she read. Say something!

"It's a beautiful evening," she murmured.

"You shouldn't be out here this time of night."

His voice was low, and his accent was an odd combination of sharp eastern consonants and slow southern vowels, as though he'd grown up in cold, still nights and hot, humid days.

She wanted to know all about him. She'd never met a gambler before, nor was she likely to again. The closest she'd come was a man running a shell game at the state fair when she was a girl. And he hadn't been as good-looking as this man. Despite the darkness of the evening, smoky light shone out from the parlor car. She couldn't see his features clearly, but his shoulders were broad and his hips lean.

He struck a match to light his cigar. The flare illuminated his face. Thick eyebrows hid his eyes as he looked down at the flame, and his cheekbones stood out, as though the bones beneath the skin had been sculpted by a master craftsman. His lips were full and firm.

He looked at her for a split second. Dark eyes bored into her own, freezing her in place; then he blew out the match and she was released.

"Well?"

"Well, what?"

"You shouldn't be out here alone," he repeated.

"I'm not alone."

The sound of his muffled curse indicated he didn't appreciate her sense of humor. "There are plenty of men on this train who wouldn't think twice about seeing if a few minutes with you would change their luck at poker."

"I certainly wouldn't object to having a conversation with . . . Oh!" She bit her lip at the sudden realization of what he had meant. "I didn't . . . I mean, I . . . Oh."

"I guess you're not used to traveling, but you need to be more careful."

The exasperation in his voice was tempered by patience. She bristled at his assumption of her ignorance. "I am not a child," she told him in her most chilling tone.

"That's part of the problem."

Brooke opened her mouth to respond, but words failed her.

"I'll escort you back to your car."

He stepped next to the door, but she touched his arm. "No, wait. Can't we stay out here a little longer?" His forearm shifted under her hand and she withdrew, but the texture of his wool coat lingered on her fingertips. "It's so stuffy in the sleeping car, and Mrs. Gilmore . . ."

Her voice trailed off. She knew it would be unkind to speak ill of the nice lady who had appointed herself guardian, but it was difficult to endure the older woman's incessant chatter. Although the journey from Omaha to Cheyenne wasn't overly long, Mrs. Gilmore had already gleaned the most personal of details about her fellow travelers, including Brooke.

The gambler smiled, his teeth gleaming white in the dim light. "Ah, yes. Mrs. Gilmore. I met her last year on my way to Horse Creek. She wanted to know my life story, until she found out what I am."

His smile had faded with the last few words and she felt him withdraw from the conversation as clearly as if he had stepped off the platform.

When he spoke again, his voice had changed. All pretense of friendliness had faded away, leaving him sounding harsh and judgmental. "You have no business speaking with me. Do you have any idea what will happen to your reputation if we're seen together? If you think the rules of propriety are rigid back east, wait until you get a load of a western town's gossip. There's not a lot of entertainment in the territory, and everybody's business is fair game. Women like Mrs. Gilmore can strike faster than a snake, and they're twice as deadly."

She took a deep breath and smelled the smoke from his cigar. The aroma reminded her of her father. For a moment she wished she were a little girl again, back home in Philadelphia, sitting on the floor at his feet, her head resting on his knee. But the rhythmic clatter of the train broke into her memory, reminding her that her father was long since buried and she was alone in the world.

She picked at the cuff of her wool traveling dress. "Mrs. Gilmore said you were going to Horse Creek. If we're all going to live in the same town, how can we avoid meeting?"

Brooke was just beginning to congratulate herself on her use of logic when the gambler tilted his head back and roared with laughter. She was torn between being offended by his response and noticing how the sound vibrated through her layers of clothing to rub up against her skin. The sensation was not unpleasant.

"I'll be in town for a few weeks and I'm interested only in the poker tournament. Unless you plan on visiting me in Horse Creek's finest saloons, I don't imagine we'll have much contact."

"Oh. I see."

"Anyway, I doubt your husband would appreciate your greeting me on the street."

"Husband?" What was he talking about?

He drew in on the cigar, causing the end to glow in the night. "Aren't you moving to Horse Creek to marry some poor rancher?"

Her spine stiffened, and she straightened her shoulders. "I assume you mean poor, as in 'not wealthy.' You don't know me well enough to insinuate that marriage to me would be an unpleasant experience." Her words carried more bite than the crisp April night.

"I don't remember well-bred women having so much spirit." The lazy drawl in his voice was much more pronounced than before.

"How would you know? I don't imagine you've spent much time having tea with the governor's wife." She felt rather than saw his eyes flicker over her, and she pressed back against the railing of the platform until the metal was digging into her bustle. Despite the apprehension trickling down her spine, she was defiant to the last. "I'm moving to Horse Creek for reasons of business. I have no need of a husband."

"Just as well. Not that you're not pretty enough."

She had puffed up her chest with righteous indignation, but now she exhaled, her anger deflated by his compliment. It had been a long time since a man had noticed her looks. "I'm . . . Thank you."

He dropped the glowing cigar to the floor of the platform and crushed it out with the toe of his boot.

"Are you ready to go in quietly or do I have to carry you over my shoulder?"

His tone was merely curious and not at all threatening. Brooke bit the inside of her lip, imagining the look on Mrs. Gilmore's face if he were to make good on his threat. "I'll go quietly."

They walked through the gambling car. Brooke kept her head down, careful to avoid glancing at the male passengers. The gambler's warning was uppermost in her mind.

At the far end of the car, he held the door open for her. She moved past him, onto the connecting plate allowing the pleats of her gray skirt to brush against his trousers. As she turned back, she hesitated; brief words of thanks hovered unspoken on her lips.

He was standing next to an oil lamp and, for the first time, she saw him in clear detail. A well-cut black coat molded the broad shoulders she had noticed earlier. His face was lean and angular, but pleasant to look at. His thick hair curled over his ears and the top of his white shirt collar.

But it was his eyes that caught and held her attention. They were dark—a darker brown than his hair. When he looked at her it was as though he could see past who she pretended to be and into the secrets she had kept hidden from a cold world for almost three years. The flame of the lamp was reflected in the depths of his eyes.

"I don't know your name." They swayed as the train rumbled around a bend.

He shrugged. "I can't see that it matters. We'll never see each other again."

"You'll be on the stagecoach day after tomorrow. Mrs. Gilmore told me."

The right corner of his mouth quirked up as if he conceded that the infallible Mrs. Gilmore was correct. "We won't speak."

"But I—"

The breath he exhaled carried with it the sound of expired patience. "You're determined to keep me from winning tonight, aren't you?" He shook his head. "Women."

Irritated at him for his attitude and at herself for caring, Brooke stepped back. "Excuse me for detaining you."

She had walked the two steps to the door of the next car and placed her gloved hand on the handle when she felt his fingers brush her arm.

"Reed. Dalton Reed."

She turned her head and smiled. "Brooke Tyler. It's a pleasure, Mr. Reed. Was that so very difficult?"

"No." He didn't smile in return, but she saw the humor reflected in his eyes. "Now get inside before a search party comes looking for you." He moved toward the gambling car, then turned to face her. "Don't forget what I said. We've never met, and don't try to speak to me."

She shut her eyes at his harsh tone. When she opened them a second later, he was gone, having moved with the swiftness of one who was well acquainted with the night.

"Good night, Mr. Reed," she said, addressing the memory of the man. She turned the handle and let herself back into the sleeping car.

"There you are, my dear."

Mrs. Gilmore swooped down the narrow aisle, her duster flapping about her slight body like the wings of a bird. Her face, thin and aged more by the elements than by time, was filled with concern. Small eyes darted left and right as she twisted her hands together. "I've been very worried. Where have you been, Brooke? Not wandering around, I hope. It wouldn't do for a well-bred young lady like you to be strolling through the train at this time of night."

She gripped Brooke's elbow with surprising strength and herded the younger woman toward her sleeping berth. "It was providence that we should meet in Omaha. You on your own for the first time, and me, a lonely widow returning to my home. You would have been lost without me, I shouldn't wonder." She shook her head, but the tightly curled ringlets barely swayed. "Providence," she repeated.

Brooke glanced at the older woman, but closed her ears to the ongoing chatter. Mrs. Gilmore meant well, but sometimes she was such a bother. She was tempted to mention her conversation with the gambler, but the brief moment of savoring Mrs. Gilmore's shock wouldn't have been worth the tirade she would have had to endure.

"Have I made myself clear, dear?"

"Perfectly," Brooke responded and then wondered what she was agreeing with.

The two women sat down on one of the few remaining benches. Around them, the porters were making up the berths for the evening, and most passengers had already retired. Mrs. Gilmore preferred hers to be made up last. She had told Brooke, in a hushed whisper, that she didn't like people watching her get into bed. Sounds escaped from pulled curtains: the muffled conversation of two children telling stories; the soothing murmur of a mother comforting an infant.

"Are you sure I can't persuade you to stay with my sister while we're in Cheyenne?" Mrs. Gilmore asked.

"Yes, quite sure." Brooke struggled to keep her impatience from showing.

The train would arrive in Cheyenne in the late afternoon, but the stage to Horse Creek wasn't scheduled to leave until the following morning. Mrs. Gilmore had repeatedly invited Brooke to spend the night with her and her sister, but Brooke had tactfully refused. The last thing she needed after a journey of over a thousand miles was to spend the night with two Mrs. Gilmores. She'd get more sleep sitting upright on a bench at the stage station. But that wasn't going to be necessary, Brooke thought smugly. She had wired ahead and reserved a room at the Inter-Ocean Hotel. The only difficult part of her plan would be escaping Mrs. Gilmore's watchful eyes.

"Your tea, ma'am."

"Thank you."

Mrs. Gilmore took a tray from the porter and set it on the table between them. The last passenger turned in, leaving them alone. She poured two cups and handed one to Brooke. "Will you be meeting with your lawyer as soon as we reach Horse Creek?"

Brooke wasn't fooled by the casual tone of her voice. Ever since they had met, Mrs. Gilmore had tried to find out the reason for Brooke's move to the small town.

"I would think so." What could be so mysterious, Brooke wondered, that the lawyer would request that she be discreet about her trip? But his instructions had been very clear. Aunt Mattie's bequest required that she not be told any details of her inheritance until she arrived in Horse Creek.

Despite having to sidestep Mrs. Gilmore's questions, Brooke enjoyed having a little mystery in her life. It was a far cry from the monotony of endless charities and teas with well-meaning friends back home. Aunt Mattie had been an accomplished seamstress, a skill her niece had inherited. There was no doubt in Brooke's mind that the "profitable establishment" mentioned in the lawyer's correspondence was a dress shop, and she was looking forward to owning her own business.

"What does your young man have to say about all this?" Mrs. Gilmore asked.

"I don't have a young man." She formed the words automatically, having answered similar questions a hundred times before. One didn't reach the advanced age of twenty-two without people wondering about a man in one's life. Although not a beauty, Brooke wasn't plain enough that people would keep quiet on the assumption that no one had ever been interested.

"My husband died five years ago," Mrs. Gilmore said as she placed her teacup on the table between them. "I still miss him every day."

Her voice droned on, but her companion shut her out. Brooke, too, remembered the loss of a love, but it wasn't by death. Her cup rattled on its saucer, and she steadied it with her other hand. As always, the memory of that day brought a flush of shame to her face and a leaden feeling to her heart.

Joe MacAllister had been a cold, unfeeling fool, she reminded herself. Good riddance. She took a sip of tea and waited for the familiar sensation of humiliation and failure that followed any remembrance of that time in her life. Strangely, she felt nothing. Not embarrassment. Not anger. Nothing. Perhaps she was finally beginning to heal.

"There aren't that many eligible young men in Horse Creek, dear, but we'll have to find someone for you. There's that nice Arthur Franklin, the lawyer's clerk. He's clever, with a fine sense of honor, although he's been known to be slightly impetuous. And I believe a single rancher or two." Mrs. Gilmore leaned over and patted Brooke's arm. "We'll get you married yet."

Brooke placed her cup on the table and rose from her seat. She opened her carpetbag and pulled out a duster, then slipped it on over her gray wool traveling dress. "I'm not interested in getting married, Mrs. Gilmore."

"Nonsense. By the time I was your age I already had two babies and a third on the way. You just haven't met the right man yet."

The porter had finished making up Mrs. Gilmore's bed. Brooke climbed up to her berth. The space between the thin mattress and the ceiling wasn't big enough for her to do much more than turn over. She adjusted her duster to provide as much protection as possible from the soot and cinders that hung in an ever-present haze inside the train. She had barely finished arranging the yards of fabric when the back door of the car opened, admitting someone from the gambling car.

Early that morning Mrs. Gilmore had complained about the men walking past the sleeping berths at all hours of the night. The porter had been sympathetic but unwilling to—as Mrs. Gilmore had suggested—lock the gamblers in their den of sin until morning.

Brooke leaned toward the edge of her berth, hoping the man striding down the center of the car was Dalton Reed.

"Good night, Brooke."

She glanced down at Mrs. Gilmore and smiled. "Good night."

Dalton watched Horse Creek's most persistent gossip settle into her sleeping berth. Beady eyes met his; then she pulled the curtains closed, shutting him out without even acknowledging his existence. He smiled, knowing how much happier she would have been to have a door to slam in his face. Tipping his hat to the swaying wall of fabric, he took a step down the aisle.

The sensation of being watched halted him in midstride, and he looked up. Brooke Tyler smiled her greeting. He wanted to move past her, pretending that he hadn't seen her, but his feet wouldn't cooperate. Covered by the voluminous folds of the duster, her body looked shapeless, but her face was arresting enough to entice any man.

He should know: The pale skin, the pointed stubborn chin, the rose-colored lips had imprinted themselves on his mind. The fifty dollar poker chips had been the exact green of her eyes and he'd spent the last half hour betting recklessly, just to rub the smooth wood against his fingers.

Although he'd won, Dalton was disgusted with himself for allowing a woman to interfere with his concentration. He'd made his fortune gambling, but he wouldn't hold on to it for long if he continued to yield to distractions, however delightful they might be.

He gave Brooke a polite but dismissive nod and took a step toward his bunk in the next car. As if she guessed his intention to leave, she struggled to sit up, but succeeded only in bumping her head on the ceiling of the train. A soft gasp escaped her lips before she covered her mouth with one hand while rubbing her bruised scalp with the other. Her eyes, more almond-shaped than round, laughed over her hand.

He rubbed his own head and mouthed a question, asking her if she was all right. She dropped her hand and nodded.

One knee slightly bent for balance on the moving train, Dalton continued to watch her, all the while telling himself to leave. He had no business being near a woman like her. But he could no more walk away than he could give back the three hundred dollars he'd won at poker.

He reached inside his vest pocket and fingered the round poker chip. There was no logical reason why he had kept that last fifty dollar chip. It would have no value once he left the train. But he had palmed the disk when no one was looking and then had slipped it into his vest pocket.

Brooke looked down, and her long lashes cast shadows on the smooth skin of her cheeks. A slight flush stained the pale skin, and he tried to remember the last time he'd seen a woman blush. When she raised her gaze to him, her eyes were dark and wide. With a start, he realized he had been staring at her for quite some time. He shrugged an apology, curling his lips into a half smile.

He mouthed the word "good-bye." She rolled to face him, supported her head on one hand, and waggled the fingers of her other. Although Brooke was dressed as modestly as a nun, her posture was as seductive as that of the most skilled courtesan he had ever encountered. Her eyelids half concealed the welcoming glow in her velvet green eyes, and her lips were slightly parted. He fought the sudden urge to join her on her pristine pillow and teach her the ways of the world.

With a mumbled curse, he stalked off, alternately vowing never to speak to Brooke Tyler again and trying to remember the name of the redhead who had brightened his last trip to Cheyenne.

Brooke struggled to secure her long hair in its simple style, but the swaying and jerking of the train made the most familiar movements awkward. After adjusting the last pin, she checked her coiffure in her hand mirror. Not perfect, but it would just have to do, she thought as she climbed down from her sleeping berth.

"Good morning, Brooke. Did you rest well? I didn't. Oh, I hate to travel. I'm so looking forward to sleeping in my own bed." Mrs. Gilmore pulled her skirts aside, making room on the bench. In front of her, a small table was set with a light breakfast.

Brooke smiled as she remembered the genteel snores that had drifted up from the older woman's bunk the previous night. Long after the lamps had been dimmed, Brooke had lain awake recalling Dalton Reed's lazy smile.

She had tried to tell herself it had been wrong to acknowledge him; he was a gambler, after all. But he had made her feel curious and pretty and alive, and she hadn't felt that way in a long time. Associating only with members of polite society was no magical talisman against pain and suffering, she reminded herself. Hadn't Joe MacAllister left her practically standing at the altar three years before? It seemed unlikely that a sharper could have behaved worse than Joe had. Besides, there was something about Dalton's eyes. They were deep brown, filled with impatience and humor, and perhaps the slightest trace of interest. No matter his profession or the rules of society, something told her they were the eyes of a man she could trust.

Brooke pushed the thoughts of the handsome stranger from her mind and spent the morning evading Mrs. Gilmore's probing questions. She didn't want to offend her only friend in Horse Creek, but the older woman was a skillful inquisitor and it was becoming more difficult to avoid outright rudeness. She sighed in relief when at last the train pulled into Cheyenne.

"Are you sure you won't come stay with my sister and me? There's plenty of room, and the three of us would have such a grand time together."

Brooke turned back from the window and shook her head. "Thank you, no. Someone is expecting me." She hoped the reservations clerk at the Inter-Ocean Hotel counted as someone, so that her statement wasn't an outright falsehood.

The two women stepped off the train and into the pandemonium of the station. The platform stretched on endlessly, and it looked as though all the residents of the city had turned out to greet the train. Either that or the town of Cheyenne was much larger than Brooke had imagined. The April afternoon was cold, and her breath came out in wispy clouds.

The train creaked and hissed, contributing to the general noise. Crates and trunks were being unloaded from the middle cars, while horses were led off from the back. Hawkers pressed forward, offering food to those continuing on the journey west, and stage drivers called out for fares.

Brooke allowed a family to walk between Mrs. Gilmore and herself, separating the women in the milling crowd. She felt a moment of guilt for refusing the other woman's invitation, but excitement took its place when she spotted the stage for Inter-Ocean Hotel. Her older brother had traveled with her as far as Nebraska, so this was her first moment of independence.

Clutching her carpetbag, she pushed her way through the throngs of people. The Union Pacific Railroad would deliver her steamer trunks to the stage station in the morning. Her small bag contained enough to see her through the night. All she wanted was a clean room and a tub full of hot water to soak away the grime from the journey.

"Afternoon, ma'am. You planning on staying at the hotel?" The expression on the young driver's face matched the questioning sound in his voice.

Brooke straightened her shoulders and drew in a deep breath. "I have a reservation and—"

A hand reached out and seized her arm. "What the hell are you doing?"

She twisted out of her assailant's grasp and turned to look up at familiar brown eyes. "I'm trying to get to my hotel, Mr. Reed. Not that it's any business of yours."

The friendly teasing of the night before had vanished from his face, leaving behind the cold countenance of an angry stranger. "You shouldn't be allowed out unescorted."

She tightened her grip on her bag, stumbling slightly as a tall gray-haired porter brushed past her. She stepped away from Dalton's steadying hand. "I am perfectly capable—"

He cut her off. "Capable? Of what? Did you plan on waltzing into the hotel and requesting a room?"

"I have a reservation." Her voice shook with indignation. Did he think she was foolish enough to not plan ahead?

"Perfect," he said. "The innocent miss from the East made reservations at a gambling house."

"Gambling?" Her voice was weak.

Dalton took the valise from her hand and steered her to the other side of the station. "Yes. It's a very popular hotel. Cowboys, gamblers, all the best people. You would fit in perfectly."

"I . . . I . . ." His look of exasperation cut off any further attempts at conversation. Her mind raced wildly as she wondered how she would find a decent hotel in this strange city.

Dalton stopped abruptly in front of a small black stagecoach and opened the door. Brooke was swept up into a waiting carriage, too stunned to listen to the instructions he gave the driver. What was she going to do?

She barely noticed when the gambler sat beside her, and they traveled several blocks before she realized that she was in a moving buggy. "Where are you taking me?"

He glared down at her, his brown eyes chilling her to the bone. "To a respectable boardinghouse."

His tone indicated he wouldn't welcome any more conversation. She turned away from her hostile companion and stared out of the cab. Although it was a far cry from the sophistication of Philadelphia, Cheyenne did have a sort of rustic charm. The buildings were mostly wood and brick. A few were several stories high. Storefronts advertised every imaginable good and service, although saloons were by far the most common type of establishment.

A cowboy rode up next to the stage. From the toes of his dusty boots to the top of his worn hat, he looked like an illustration on the cover of a penny dreadful. But her tentative smile faded and she drew back against the seat when the cowboy turned toward her, exposing a toothless grin and a patch over one eye.

Dalton's chuckle filled the small compartment, but Brooke refused to meet his gaze.

The carriage pulled up in front of a modest brick structure. The steps were lined with bushes, brown and bare in the April air. A rawboned woman stepped out onto the stoop, her iron-gray hair pulled back in a tight bun.

Brooke took the hand Dalton offered and stepped down. She tried to speak, but he cut her off with a quelling glance.

"Margaret, you look lovely." He climbed the three steps and embraced the other woman. "I've brought you a guest for the night. Brooke Tyler, this is Margaret James." He bent over the older woman and whispered into her ear.

Brooke climbed the steps awkwardly, one hand clutching her bag, the other holding her long skirt. "How do you do?"

Margaret smiled, her face creasing into friendly lines. "Welcome, Miss Brooke. Come on inside before the chill freezes your blood."

Brooke gratefully relinquished her luggage and followed the woman into the heated foyer, but hesitated when she heard Dalton slam the carriage door. She stepped back out onto the stoop. "Where are you going?" she called after him.

He stuck his head out the window. "To the hotel where I always stay—the Inter-Ocean."

Chapter 2

Dalton glanced down at his cards and resisted the urge to smile at the two ladies nestling up against three kings. Luck was on his side tonight. If he won the game with a twenty dollar bet, he would cover the hotel charges and any other entertainment he might choose to fill his night.

He cast a practiced glance around the table and separated the novices from those experienced at cards. Only one of the nine other men at the table met his look with a cool determined stare. Dalton gave a mental shrug and placed his cards face down on the table, waiting for the dealer to throw the last card.

Every hotel and bar across the country used its own distinctive poker chips. Some were stiff cardboard; others were intricately carved wood. The Inter-Ocean Hotel prided itself on providing only the best for its patrons. The thin disks were painted bright colors, their smooth surfaces reflecting the glow of the lanterns and candles.

A man leaned over the table, blocking the light for just a second. The brief shadow made it appear that the chips resting in the center of the round surface had blinked. Dalton stared at the stack and saw a hazy outline of Brooke's eyes. Without even thinking, he passed over the twenty dollar chips and tossed a ten dollar token onto the pile. The bright chandelier was mirrored in the shiny green finish of the carved disk. He suppressed a curse when he realized what he'd done. Even winning the hand didn't alleviate the frustration gnawing at his gut. He collected his money and left the table, then stopped at the bar for a stiff drink.

Just forget her, he'd told himself a hundred times since leaving Brooke at Margaret's boardinghouse. Women like her were bad news, and he'd already had plenty of that for one lifetime. But the advice wasn't working. It wasn't enough that he'd gone and spoken to a lady like Brooke Tyler—now the memory of their brief conversations haunted him. He was worse than a green schoolboy after stealing his first kiss. What the hell had happened?

"You're looking mighty fierce about something, Dalton. Want to talk about it?"

The husky feminine voice dripped with invitation. Dalton slid his gaze up her tight red dress, past her partly exposed breasts, to her smiling lips and bright blue eyes. The redhead. Just the woman he'd been looking for. She ran her fingers down his upper arm, but the movement only reminded him of Brooke's tentative touch on the train. He shook off the thought.

The woman leaned forward. "I remember you from last year. We had a great time together. The memories alone kept me warm all winter."

He touched her cheek and waited for the familiar heat that would boil his blood and settle in his groin. There was a mild stirring, like a bear in winter waking up just enough to turn over and then going back to sleep. He finished his drink and set the glass on the bar with a thump.

"Come on." He stood up, grabbed her arm, and pulled

her toward the sweeping staircase leading to the private rooms.

"Slow down, honey. We've got all night."

Dalton raised his foot and placed it on the first step. He looked up toward the second floor, then back at the waiting woman. The light flickering in her eyes promised him a fulfilling but sleepless night. He'd be a fool to turn her down.

He reached into his pocket and pulled out a fifty dollar gold piece and tossed it in the air. It turned over and over, shining in the brightly lit saloon. He caught the coin and slipped it into the low-cut bodice of her red gown, ignoring the sensation of her warm skin against the back of his hand. "Maybe next time."

As he climbed the stairs, Dalton felt her curious eyes boring into his back. He hoped she wouldn't call out a question, because he sure didn't have an answer. Although more than generous with women, he never gave money away and he rarely turned down such an enticing invitation. He must be getting old or soft, he thought as his right hand toyed with a green ten dollar chip.

The sun was barely peeking through the sparkling windows of the boardinghouse, the rays of light making faint patterns on the dining room walls. Brooke's toe tapped out a staccato rhythm as she pushed her eggs around on her plate.

"There something wrong with my cooking?" Margaret's voice was teasing, as if she knew no one could find fault with anything leaving her kitchen.

"No, of course not." Brooke smiled at her hostess. "I'm a little excited this morning."

"Can't say that I blame you. Moving to a new town and all." The tall woman reached over and removed

Brooke's untouched breakfast. "I'll pack some food up for the journey to Horse Creek. If I know Dalton, he's been too busy playing cards and chasing women to eat a good meal at *that* hotel."

The older woman's wrinkled features softened into an indulgent expression, but Brooke felt her own mouth straighten into a thin line. She still hadn't forgiven Dalton Reed for his high-handed treatment of her the afternoon before. Not that she didn't appreciate Margaret's clean boardinghouse, she reminded herself as she smoothed her gray wool traveling dress.

Margaret had provided a steaming hot bath and a soft mattress. She had also taken Brooke's dress outside and had beaten and brushed away the dust and dirt of the journey. But all those comforts hadn't driven the gambler from her mind. She had awakened several times in the night wondering what he was doing back at the hotel.

"I'm sure it's in the Inter-Ocean's best interests to keep the patrons well fed."

If Brooke's voice was sharper than it needed to be, Margaret gave no indication that she'd noticed. "That might be true, but I'll give you a package to take to Dalton all the same."

"Take to him? Isn't he taking me to the stage? I just assumed he'd . . ." Her voice trailed off as she realized she was beginning to sound like Mrs. Gilmore.

"Now, don't you fret. The station is two blocks away. I'll walk you there myself as soon as you're ready."

Brooke left the dining room and ran lightly up the stairs. In her room, she checked for any belongings she might have forgotten, then closed her valise. The jittery feeling in her stomach was a reminder that her journey was almost over. Soon she would be in a new town, ready to start living her brand-new life.

* * *

The Cheyenne and Black Hills Stage station was much smaller than the platform owned by the railroad company. The coach used for the journey to Horse Creek held six people, but there were only half that number milling around in the cold April morning.

"Brooke! Over here, dear."

Brooke cringed, then turned and waved at Mrs. Gilmore, who was standing next to the stage. In her wool dress and matching jaunty hat, she looked like a perky black wren. "I'll be right there," Brooke called, then turned back to her hostess. "Thanks for everything, Margaret."

The taller woman smiled. "No thanks necessary. I enjoyed having the company. I don't usually get many boarders until May."

Boarders! Brooke's cheeks flamed as she realized she hadn't paid the woman for the room. She reached for her small drawstring bag. "I'm so sorry. How much was the room last night?"

Margaret patted her arm. "It's all taken care of."

"But how?"

Margaret's face was wreathed in smiles. "Dalton paid me. Now run along." She handed her a muslin bag filled with food. "Don't forget to give him my best, but not in front of that busybody, Mrs. Gilmore."

Surprised by the sudden turn of events, Brooke stood rooted to the spot and was only able to watch helplessly as Margaret moved off with a purposeful stride.

"Brooke, who was that woman? Did you have a pleasant evening? Oh, we did. My sister and I sat up most of the night talking. There were so many things to tell her about my trip east. I'm sorry she had to return home before you two could meet. The stage is ready to leave.

Are you all right, dear?" Mrs. Gilmore wrapped her arm around Brooke's shoulder. "We'll be home soon enough. The trip's only about three hours. Maybe you should try to rest."

Brooke nodded at the other woman's chatter as she handed her valise up to the driver. She had lifted her wool skirt with one hand and reached up with the other to grab hold of the stage when two masculine hands appeared from inside, gripped her under her arms, and pulled her on board.

"Thank you very . . ." She lost her train of thought as she met Dalton's dark brown eyes. Lurking in their velvet depths was a smile that reached inside her and lit a candle in her heart.

He was as handsome as she remembered. The lines of his face were strong in the early morning light. She opened her mouth to greet him, but he hushed her with a quick shake of his head.

Leaning forward, Dalton extended his hand and assisted Mrs. Gilmore into the stage. Brooke bit back a grin as the other woman wrestled with her conscience, battling her need to recognize the courtesy with her refusal to acknowledge the gambler's existence. Politeness won as Mrs. Gilmore tilted her head.

Brooke adjusted her skirt and settled back in her seat as the stage set off.

"Are we the only travelers?" Mrs. Gilmore wondered aloud. She shot a wary glance at Dalton. "At least we won't be bothered by strangers talking about themselves."

Brooke kept her eyes firmly turned toward the window. If her gaze met Dalton's, she knew she would give in to the laughter that threatened to erupt. Mrs. Gilmore would never understand, or forgive, for that matter.

"Did you meet up with your friend?" Mrs. Gilmore asked.

"Friend? Ah, yes I did, thank you." Brooke cleared her throat and hoped the other woman would drop the subject. Mentioning meeting someone in the city had been a ploy to avoid spending the evening with Mrs. Gilmore and her sister. She hadn't planned on having to support her falsehood with actual details. Mercifully, conversation ceased.

The thundering of the horses' hooves combined with the rocking of the coach to create a hypnotic ride. The occasional dip of the stage as it bounded over deep ruts attested to the recent rains.

Brooke stared at the bare trees and frozen ground. Winter lingered in the Wyoming Territory. Back home the first flowers of spring had been making their presence known. Were there flowers in Horse Creek? she wondered. Was it a wild place with gunfighters and thieves? Would she be able to make it on her own? The miles of alien scenery stretched on without offering an answer.

"Did you find Margaret's house acceptable?"

Dalton's low voice startled her, and Brooke jumped in her seat. She glanced at her companion, but Mrs. Gilmore had fallen asleep. Her head, leaning against the stage wall, pushed her hat askew.

"Yes, thank you." Her soft tone was as quiet as his, but she felt the irritation from yesterday return. "Although your concern seems a little belated. I didn't appreciate being passed off like an unwelcome delivery."

Cool brown eyes regarded her, their expression unfathomable. "Would you have preferred me to spend the evening with you?"

The very thought sent a heated blush up her cheeks.

"Of course not. I was merely protesting your—"

He cut her off. "Let me get this straight. You had a nice time with Margaret. You were fed and given a very comfortable bed at a well-respected establishment, and you're angry at me for arranging everything for you. Do I have all the information correct so far?"

"I . . . I . . . Oh, fiddle." She leaned back in the seat and ignored his amused smile. How had he twisted her words around so that his actions now seemed reasonable? Something Margaret had said whispered in the back of her mind. "Thank you for paying for my room," she mumbled.

He raised one dark eyebrow. "I'm sorry. Did you say something?"

"Thank you for paying for my room." She enunciated each syllable clearly and in a loud voice. "How much do I owe you?"

"Shh." He nodded at the stirring Mrs. Gilmore. Brooke held her breath until the other woman settled back to sleep.

"Nothing."

She nervously twisted her drawstring bag. "I can't allow you to provide for me, Mr. Reed. It isn't proper."

"Fine time to bring up what's proper. First you prance through the gambling car in the middle of the night; then you plan to stay at one of Cheyenne's wildest hotels. And I can't pay for your room for the night. Women."

He made a noise that was a cross between a snort and a laugh. Leaning his head back, he tilted his flat-brimmed black hat so that it covered his eyes.

He folded his arms across his chest, the motion stretching the wool coat tightly across his broad shoulders. He extended his long legs in front of him, the toe of his boot inches from her gray skirt. The steady rise and fall of his chest told her he was determined to go to sleep.

An hour passed slowly as the stage continued its journey. Brooke found herself occasionally jolted toward the opposite side of the coach. Her calf brushed against that of the gambler and the touch warmed her even through the heavy layers of clothing. The human contact, however impersonal, gave her courage.

Each rotation of the wheels brought her closer to a future that was both frightening and exhilarating. Although she had handled her own financial affairs since her father's death, she'd never traveled or lived alone before. At the beginning of the journey, her excitement had helped her through the scary times, but now, with Horse Creek less than two hours away, her nerve began to falter. She needed to hear a friendly, reassuring voice.

"Dalton?" she whispered. He barely stirred.

"Dalton?" She reached out to touch him, but all acceptable points of contact would require her to rise from her seat. She cast a worried glance at Mrs. Gilmore, but the woman slept on. Leaning forward, she pushed up from the seat and touched his arm, then lowered herself down. "Dalton, wake up."

He sat up and pushed his hat back. "Exactly when did we pass from the formality of 'Mr. Reed' to first-name familiarity?"

She bit her lip and stared down at her lap. "I'm sorry."

"Don't be. I like the way you say my name. You kind of roll it around in your mouth like you're trying it on for size. I think the fit is perfect."

She felt her jaw drop open, but couldn't seem to summon the appropriate muscles to clamp her lips shut. It wasn't that she didn't understand the words he'd said; she just wasn't sure what they meant.

"I've brought you some food from Margaret." She pointed at the muslin bag on the floor by the door.

He grinned, his teeth shining white against the slight tan of his skin. "She's a mighty fine woman. Never known one better."

As he sorted through the contents of the bag, Brooke remembered the older woman's words about him being too busy with cards and women to eat. "Was your evening enjoyable?"

He took a large bite out of a meat pie and chewed thoughtfully. "No."

"Unlucky at cards?"

His eyes narrowed. "What are you getting at?"

She shrugged. "I've never met a gambler before. What exactly do you do when you go to a saloon?"

"You woke me up to discuss gambling?"

"No, of course not."

Dalton watched as Brooke glanced around the stage, her blush bringing soft color to her skin. Despite the time she'd spent on the train, she looked as fresh as the day he had first seen her, back in Nebraska. Her eyes reminded him of a drawing he'd seen once in a book. They were wide, almond shaped, and tilted up at the corners—the color of fresh spring grass, bright and alive and vibrant. With a start, he realized that the color was enhanced by tears that threatened to overflow at any second.

The meat pie turned to sawdust in his mouth, and he struggled to swallow his last bite. Had he said something to make her cry? The possibility twisted his gut like a rein caught in a buggy wheel. "Don't cry. I was only teasing you. We can talk about whatever you'd like."

"I'm not crying."

The single tear that slipped down her smooth cheek

contradicted her words. She brushed it away with a quick self-conscious movement, and he longed to offer her comfort. But the cramped bouncing stagecoach and Mrs. Gilmore sleeping nearby restricted his inclinations. He leaned forward, elbows resting on his knees, hands clenched in frustration.

"I'm scared." He looked across at her, but she stared out the window. She blinked frantically, trying to hold back tears, and her fingers twisted the cord of her reticule. "You already think I'm incapable of taking care of myself, but there's no one else for me to talk to."

"I think . . ." He cleared his throat. "Oh, hell, Brooke. I think you're doing fine."

He reached into his pocket and pulled out a linen handkerchief. As she took the offered square of cloth, their hands touched. The urge to pull her into his embrace was sudden and unexpected. He stiffened and pulled back.

The memory of his last encounter with a well-bred woman still lingered, the incident forever branded on his soul. Don't get involved, he told himself.

"I've never been on my own before."

Brooke's comment penetrated his dark thoughts and recalled him to the present. "Mrs. Gilmore will be more than happy to assist you in any way she can."

She rewarded his teasing words with a slow smile. "But what a price to pay. She'd want to know every detail of my life, and then some."

"An innocent girl like you. What secrets could you have?"

A shadow flashed across her eyes, hinting at sadness. For a second he was tempted to inquire, but he held back. When the stage reached Horse Creek he was going to walk away from Brooke Tyler and never look back. He didn't dally with ladies—no matter how temptingly they were packaged.

Her expression cleared. She tossed her head, causing a single strand of brown hair to escape from under her hat and brush against her neck. "You're right. My life has been ordinary, until now. But all that's going to change. I'm going into business."

He tore his eyes away from the curl that was caressing her neck like a wayward lover. "What kind of business?"

"I don't know."

Dalton opened the muslin bag and passed Brooke a cookie and a small jar of lemonade. "Are you going to decide when you reach Horse Creek?"

"No." Her delighted laughter filled the coach. Mrs. Gilmore stirred for a moment, and they both held their breath. When a snore shattered the silence, their eyes met in shared amusement and Brooke continued in a softer voice. "My aunt left me an inheritance. I'm not supposed to talk about what it is, but the lawyer didn't tell me anything, so there isn't much of a secret to keep."

She shrugged one slender shoulder in a gesture of resignation, drawing his gaze to the snug fit of her traveling gown. The gray wool hid the dust of the journey while the fabric molded itself to the gentle curves of her body. The long row of buttons, from her hips to the high collar against her neck, tempted him with endless possibilities. Although the dress was as good as any he'd seen in New Orleans, Brooke wore it with an air of innocence that was lacking in the other women of his acquaintance. And those women had concerns other than fashion when they chose their wardrobes.

As she regarded him over the lip of the glass jar, he tried to imagine her shock and dismay if she knew what he was thinking. She'd probably slap him and call him a cad. But then again, she might—

"Why are you looking at me like that?" she asked.

"Like what?"

"Like the cat that ate the canary. Did I spill something?" She brushed away imaginary crumbs.

But the motion of her hand across the fitted bodice of her dress caused his blood to race with an excitement that had been noticeably lacking the previous evening. He regretted having turned the redhead away. Well, Cheyenne was only a three-hour ride, he reminded himself grimly.

He glanced out the window and recognized the landscape, then took the empty lemonade jar from Brooke and placed it back in the muslin bag. The stage would pull into Horse Creek within a half hour, and he had to warn her away. She was so trusting and naive that she would probably invite him to her hotel room for dinner.

"Brooke—"

"Dalton—"

They spoke simultaneously. There was an awkward moment as they avoided each other's eyes. "Ladies first."

She stared down at her lap, restlessly twisting her hands together. "I . . . I want to thank you for being so nice to me. I've been a bother since we met, and I . . . Thank you."

Her last words were barely a whisper, and he had to lean forward to catch them. Her face, a picture of embarrassed beauty, touched him deep inside in a place he'd long thought inaccessible to emotion. It only made what he had to say even more difficult.

"Once we get to town, you must never speak to me

again or acknowledge me in any way." Green eyes met and held his. The confusion and hurt in her expression threatened his resolve, but he knew what he was telling her was for her own good. "Do you understand?"

She nodded, her shoulders drooping with dejection. He cursed silently, calling himself ten different kinds of fool. Trouble came in all sizes, but when it appeared in the shape of a woman, he knew enough to stand clear.

Brooke stared mutely at Dalton's set face. His callous words battered against her heart like rain on a tin roof. Despite his obvious exasperation at her innocence, he'd twice come to her rescue. She'd spent little time in his company, but he had a strength that made her trust him. She hadn't known how much she missed having someone to rely on until she was about to lose him. Why had she thought being on her own would be easy?

"Oh, we're almost there." Mrs. Gilmore's voice broke the silence. "Are you all right, dear?"

Brooke glanced up at Dalton, but he was staring out the window. "I . . . Yes, thank you."

Mrs. Gilmore sniffed, as though the scent of conversation still lingered in the air. "I'm so sorry I dozed off like that. I was up most of the night with my sister. I trust everything . . ."

Her voice trailed off, but her implied question brought a heated blush to Brooke's cheeks. What would Mrs. Gilmore think if she told her that she had tried to make friends with the gambler, only to have him rebuff her advances? Brooke tried to think of something appropriate to say, but faltered under the other woman's beady stare.

The stage came to a jarring halt, almost tossing the two women from their seats.

"We're here. I'm so excited to be able to show you

your new home, Brooke. In fact, you must visit me this very evening for dinner. I'll walk you to the hotel and then tell you how to get to my house."

Dalton stepped off the stage and helped Mrs. Gilmore down. The older woman continued speaking, ignoring him as though he were a stair banister.

When Brooke placed her hand in his, the warmth of his palm seeped through her glove. "Thank you."

He nodded and turned to walk away. She reached out to hold him back, but his long stride carried him out of reach. As the coach porters unloaded the luggage, directed by Mrs. Gilmore's authoritative commands, Brooke watched Dalton move up the street and enter the nearest saloon without ever once looking back.

Chapter 3

Although Horse Creek boasted two hotels, only one was acknowledged by the proper women of the town. Mrs. Gilmore had explained that and many other tidbits about the area in the short ten-minute walk from the stage station. The trip had been nine minutes too long for Brooke. She had assured Mrs. Gilmore that she was perfectly capable of checking into the hotel on her own and had renewed her promise to join the other woman for dinner that evening.

As Brooke stared at the small space that would be her home for the next few days, she wondered if the other, less reputable establishment had larger rooms. A medium-size four-poster bed took up most of the chamber. The remaining space was filled with a dresser, topped with a pitcher and washbasin, and her luggage, which was piled up in the corner. A straight-backed chair butted up to the plain white wall next to the window overlooking the street.

Brooke wrestled with one of her steamer trunks, struggling to carry it over to the bed. She had decided to unpack a few things. Even if her aunt's lawyer agreed to see her today, it was unlikely that she would be able to move into Aunt Mattie's house right away.

There was a soft knock on the door. Her eyebrows

drew together. Who could it be? she wondered. She'd sent a boy with a message for her lawyer, but he couldn't possibly have returned so soon with a reply.

As she walked across the room, Brooke glanced in the mirror hanging over the dresser and checked her appearance. Every hair was in place.

"Yes, may I . . ."

The sight of Dalton Reed, standing in the hall and holding a piece of her luggage, robbed her of the power of coherent speech. "I . . . How did you . . ."

His brown eyes glinted with amusement. "You're the one who was so insistent we continue our acquaintance. Having second thoughts?"

Despite his mocking voice, she felt her spirits begin to lift at the sight of his handsome face. She stepped back to invite him into her room, then looked up at him hesitantly. With a start she remembered she wasn't at home inviting a caller into her parlor. She was in a strange city, staying at a hotel. She couldn't let a gambler into her bedroom!

The sound of a door opening, followed by faint laughter, drifted up the stairs. Dalton glanced over his shoulder, then brushed past her and into the room. He turned the key, the lock making an audible metallic thud as it shot home. Her eyes flew to the bed and the open trunk resting on the quilted spread. A blue dress lay on top with a lacy camisole peeking out from underneath.

Every instinct screamed for her to hurry and cover up her undergarments, but to do so would have required her to step between Dalton and the bed.

The bed. The piece of furniture grew in her mind until she felt it had pinned her to the wall and was forcing the air out of her lungs.

"Are you all right?"

Dalton watched Brooke press herself against the wall, wondering if he was angry at himself or irritated with her. It was her fault he was here in the first place. If she hadn't looked so damned hurt when he walked away from the stage, he might have been able to forget her. But the expression on her face had made him feel like a heel, or worse.

He tossed the valise he was carrying on the bed beside the open trunk. "The stage driver accidentally put one of your suitcases with mine. I thought I'd better return it."

"Thank you."

Her response was automatic, he noted as he followed the direction of her gaze. Her eyes seemed to be focused on the contents of the open trunk. He glanced down and saw an edge of lace poking out from under a blue dress. Looking back at her face, he saw by the sudden blush she knew he had noticed.

The cool logical mind that helped him to win at cards heated up as specific erotic pictures snapped in and out of his imagination. Did she own other lace-trimmed garments, and were they now on her body? Were her breasts caressed by frothy white trimming?

The hotel room was suddenly cramped and hot. Dalton moved to the window and rested his hand on the cool pane of glass. Why was she doing this to him? he wondered. He'd been on his own since he was sixteen. In all that time, he'd avoided women like her, women who made a man think about responsibilities and family.

He had to get away before all his promises and defenses crumbled to dust. Hadn't he learned anything from the past? For an instant he was back in Boston, hearing a young girl's harsh sobs, the pain in her voice as she pleaded, then threatened. He clenched his jaw and forced himself to return to the present.

"Do you like the hotel?" he asked, hoping a neutral conversation would divert his attention from the visions in his mind.

"It seems very nice, thank you."

He glanced over his shoulder. Brooke had moved from the corner and was standing by the dresser. In the afternoon light her hair seemed more red than brown.

He remembered the redhead from Cheyenne. Brooke wasn't nearly as curvy or as pretty, but her green eyes drew him the way a shell game drew suckers.

He turned and sat down in the chair under the window. The temptation to spend time in her company was too powerful to resist. In a few minutes he would leave her, but not just yet.

"Are you staying here?" she asked.

He nodded.

"Oh?" Her lips parted slightly, indicating her surprise. "But there's another hotel . . ."

He raised one eyebrow. "Now, how did a respectable woman like you learn about that other hotel?"

She blushed but didn't look away. "Mrs. Gilmore told me."

"She does know the whole town's secrets. What else did she have to say?"

Brooke shrugged, attempting to appear casual while trying to avoid looking at the bed. It was hard to believe that she was chatting with a man in her bedroom. But she wasn't afraid of him.

"What do you think of Horse Creek?" he asked.

"I've only been here half an hour."

"Sometimes you only need a short time to form an impression of a place."

Or a person, she added silently as she studied Dalton. Leaning back in the straight chair, he stretched his long legs out in front of him. His body was lean yet powerful; it reminded her of a stallion her father had once raced. Even though he was sitting still, she sensed within him a coiled energy throbbing just below the surface, ready to spring at the slightest provocation.

She should feel afraid, and she should order him from her room, she told herself. Mrs. Gilmore would be outraged.

Dalton ran his fingers through his hair, the curls springing free of his touch and falling back into place. "I'm sorry about what happened at the stage station." His low voice vibrated, filling up the room and pressing against her skin.

The sincerity in his eyes caused hers to moisten. "I know why you walked away, but I was a little surprised."

"Did you expect that we would exchange addresses?"

Her gaze dropped from his teasing smile, the curve of his firm lips distracting her. "No, but I . . ." She was unable to continue, not sure enough of her feelings to explain them to herself, let alone Dalton. "I thought you'd at least say good-bye."

"Brooke." He rose from the chair and crossed the small room in two long strides. Stopping directly in front of her, he raised his hands to her shoulders as if he were going to touch her, but dropped them back to his sides.

Tilting her head back, she looked up at him. The room was still except for the muted noises from the street—the sound of a wagon rumbling down the road and a shout or two of children playing. Beneath his black jacket and embroidered vest, Dalton's chest rose and fell with each breath.

She was close enough to see the shadow of whiskers darkening his strong jaw. It had been several years since she had been near enough to a man to notice such details. The tiny hairs on the back of her neck stood on end. Was the room getting warmer?

"I took your valise."

His words startled her with their abruptness as much as their content. "I don't understand."

"I took your bag so I'd have an excuse to see you again."

Why? she wanted to ask. But her reserves of bravery had been used up when she invited him into her room.

Dared she assign some meaning to his action? Did he also feel the pull between them? Her hands twisted together until he stilled the motion by clasping her fingers within his.

Their hands were a study in contrasts. His skin was tanned, hers pale; his fingers long, his palms broad; her fingers slender, her palms delicate. But there was as much life in his hands as there was in hers; the warmth of his flesh seared her with a combination of sensation and heat. His thumb brushed against her skin, and the tenderness of his caress was enhanced as she both saw and felt the movement.

Her heart had never raced like this when Joe had touched her, her fingers hadn't trembled, the room had never swayed. She raised her eyes to Dalton's face, seeking an answer, an explanation. But his brown eyes had darkened to black, the bottomless pools drawing secrets from her soul and not revealing any in return.

The grandfather clock in the hallway chimed the hour and broke the spell. Brooke pulled her hands back at the exact moment Dalton released her.

"I'd better go."

She nodded, afraid her voice would fail if she tried to speak.

He turned away. "I won't see you again."

"I know."

She knew he was doing the right thing, for both of them. But that knowledge didn't make her feel any better, she realized as a pebble of pain rubbed up against the corner of her heart.

He walked to the door and unlocked it. When he placed his hand on the knob, she touched his arm.

"Thank you, Dalton. I want you to know that I appreciate everything you've done for me."

He swallowed and closed his eyes. Brooke sensed that a war was being waged within him. She wondered what he was battling and who would win.

He stepped close to her side and bent down, brushing his lips against her cheek. The kiss was brief, but she felt the touch of his mouth all the way to her toes. Before she could react, he'd left. The valise he'd tossed on the bed and the tingling on her face were the only proof he had been there at all.

Brooke strolled listlessly around the room. The space that had seemed so small during his visit expanded until the vastness threatened to engulf her in a tide of loneliness. In an effort to distract herself from her confused thoughts about Dalton, she moved over to the bed and started to unpack.

In a corner of the trunk was a round box. She opened it and pulled out a gray cloth hat trimmed with a vivid teal-blue feather. Her sister-in-law had offered the finery as a going-away gift. Brooke went to the mirror and adjusted the fit until the feather stood up at a jaunty angle several inches above her left ear.

There was a knock. She flew to the door and pulled it

open, but her joyous greeting died unspoken. Her visitor wasn't the handsome gambler she had pictured in her mind; it was the freckle-faced ten-year-old she had sent to contact her lawyer.

"I brung you a note," he announced proudly. "Mr. Gannen said I should wait for you to read it."

Brooke took the offered paper and wondered how the parchment could have become so wrinkled and soiled during the short journey from the lawyer's office. The boy's brown eyes watched her with a curious but innocent stare that gave no hint of his activities while on his mission.

She opened the letter and smoothed the paper. Mr. Gannen wrote that he would be happy to see her that very afternoon if she was willing.

"Can you take me to Mr. Gannen's office?" she asked the boy.

He nodded. "Yes. He told me to take good care of you, ma'am."

The respectful touch of his hand to his cap was marred by the licorice whip clutched tightly in his fist. Brooke hid a smile. "I could never refuse such a gallant escort, now, could I?" She picked up her reticule and shawl, locked the door, and followed the boy down the stairs and through the hotel lobby.

Although the streets of Horse Creek weren't paved, the recent rains had washed away the dust and turned the dirt to a hard-packed surface. The sidewalks were made of wooden planks; the uneven construction caused Brooke to watch her step more than her surroundings. Several storefronts lined the main street, and she was pleased to note there wasn't a dress shop among them. Aunt Mattie's business must be booming, she thought smugly.

An older woman exited the dry goods store just before Brooke walked past. Her hair must have been solid black once, but now two silver wings sprouted from her temples and were woven into an intricate design. Tall and spare, the woman carried herself with the air of royalty. Her dress—three or four years out of style, but made with the finest fabric—was the exact blue of her eyes.

The woman waited until Brooke was standing in front of her, and then she nodded. Brooke had the impression that she was being examined, judged . . . and found wanting. It took every ounce of self-control not to scurry away. Her young escort showed none of her apprehension.

"Howdy, Mrs. Prattly," he said, coming to a stop and pulling off his cap.

"William." Mrs. Prattly smiled. Her face creased with the motion, like fine linen folding into well-used lines. "How is your mother?"

He shrugged. "Still sick, along with the baby."

"Has the doctor been to see her?"

"Naw. We don't got the money. Besides, she's always sick."

Brooke was startled by the child's matter-of-fact answer. He looked too young to be so aware of life's hardships. Before she could offer assistance the other woman bent down and touched the boy's cheek.

"Tell her not to worry. I'll send him by later today. Can you remember that, William?"

"Yeah." After scratching his ear, he put his hat back on and fiddled with the brim.

"Hands at you sides, young man."

He dropped his arms and stood straight. "Yes, ma'am." The respect in his voice was belied by his irresistible grin.

"Ma says she 'preciates them chickens you brung us."

The tall woman glanced at Brooke as if she'd just remembered her presence. A bright flush stained her hollow cheeks, and she quickly looked back at William. "Tell her she's welcome and that I'll be by tomorrow to check on her and your sister." Mrs. Prattly cleared her throat. "Now I really must be going," she said, addressing no one in particular. "Good day."

Despite her obvious haste to be gone, she walked away with studied and regal grace.

Brooke stood staring after her for several seconds. The incongruity of the other woman's severe appearance and softhearted actions was quite amazing, she thought as she studied the retreating figure.

William tugged on her arm. "Come on. Mr. Franklin said I wasn't to dawdle."

A hundred questions spilled into Brooke's mind. It would be ill-mannered to question a child, but . . .

"Mrs. Prattly seems very nice," she offered as they moved down the street.

"I guess. She and ol' man Prattly have the best fishin' hole around. Me and my friends go there in the summer. She don't mind none. Once she even brung us out dinner. But *he* don't like nobody on his land. Last year he run us off with his gun." The boy grinned. "The creek won't thaw soon enough for me."

Brooke's laughter faded as they turned the corner and crossed the street, then stopped in front of a small brick building. Most of Horse Creek's structures were made of wood, but this establishment was built in a style more common in Boston and Philadelphia.

The windows were large and sparkled in the late afternoon light. The steps were meticulously clean, and the door gleamed with a fresh coat of paint.

The boy climbed up the stairs and pushed the door open. As Brooke followed him, she saw that the inside was as well kept as the outside. Hardwood floors shone under her feet, and the two desks facing the entrance were large and ornate.

"I brung her, like Mr. Gannen said," the boy announced.

"Brought, Willy," a masculine voice replied.

Brooke looked up over the boy's head and met the eyes of the man standing behind one of the desks. He was in his early twenties, with pale blue eyes and light brown hair. His face was handsome in a bland sort of way, and he instantly reminded Brooke of her older brother and his banker friends.

"You must be Miss Tyler. I'm Arthur Franklin, Mr. Gannen's law clerk. Won't you please sit down?"

He stepped around the desk and held out a chair for Brooke. He was only an inch or two taller than she, but his wide shoulders and air of authority made him seem much larger. She returned his smile as she took the offered seat.

Willy grabbed the coin Arthur Franklin held out and shot Brooke a grin before racing from the room. Remembering the licorice whip in his hand, she smiled as she imagined his very next stop.

"Did you have a pleasant journey to the Wyoming Territory?"

"Yes, Mr. Franklin, I did. In fact, I met one of Horse Creek's finest citizens on the train."

Arthur sat down in his chair on the other side of the desk and raised a questioning eyebrow.

"Mrs. Gilmore," she said.

"Oh." Arthur stiffened visibly, then tugged on the too-short sleeves of his coat. "I see."

Brooke tried to keep her face from showing any expression, but a giggle burst from her lips. Arthur's blue eyes met hers, and he smiled. "Apparently you've already encountered Mrs. Gilmore's favorite pastime."

"Yes. She gave me a complete history of the town and almost every resident."

He leaned forward, his expression serious. "Did she happen to mention me?"

Brooke shifted in the wooden chair, the seat suddenly hard and unyielding. The look in Arthur Franklin's eyes was as troubling as the memory of Mrs. Gilmore's statement about Arthur being an eligible man.

Brooke wasn't looking for a husband; she wanted to begin a life of independence. The first step would be running Aunt Mattie's business. Her limited experience with men had not been pleasant, and Joe MacAllister's parting words could still bring a flush of shame to her face.

"I don't recall her saying anything about you," she lied smoothly.

Arthur shrugged. "Perhaps I'm not yet important enough to warrant her attention."

His light blue eyes continued to regard her quizzically. Brooke was becoming concerned that her face was dirty or that her hair was coming down. "Is there something wrong?"

Arthur surprised her by flushing. "No. I'm sorry I was staring, but you're very lovely."

Now it was her turn to feel a blush creep up her face. Perhaps coming to Horse Creek had been the best idea of her life, she thought. After three years of feeling inadequate, she had been complimented by two men in two days. Maybe Joe MacAllister's brain had been addled by city living, a wicked voice in her head whispered.

"Thank you for your kind words, Mr. Franklin."

He leaned back in his chair. "Please call me Arthur."

His voice had dropped to a deeper pitch, but that only made her uncomfortable. "I hardly know you, Mr. Franklin." She fidgeted with her bag and stared at the door to the inner office, pleading silently for it to open and for Aunt Mattie's lawyer to rescue her.

"I didn't mean to offend you, Miss Tyler. We could rectify the situation and dine together later this week."

"I couldn't. But thank you for the invitation." She balked at his suggestion. Arthur Franklin reminded her too much of the men in her own family—quick to praise, but probably equally quick to control. Besides, she barely knew the man. Dalton would have been very proud of her response, she thought.

Dalton. Even thinking of his name brought her a measure of comfort and security. Now if only he had issued that dinner invitation, she would have gladly accepted. The thought of spending the evening in the company of Dalton Reed sent a shiver of excitement racing through her body. Her cheek tingled where his lips had brushed against her skin, and she clenched her fists, trying to recall the sensation of his hands holding hers.

"Perhaps another time," Arthur said.

The inner door opened, and Brooke rose from her seat, grateful for the interruption. A man in his late forties stepped into the outer office. He was tall, with wavy white hair and eyes the color of the late morning sky. Their deep, brilliant blue made him seem both intelligent and kind.

"You must be Brooke Tyler. Welcome to Horse Creek, my dear. I am Edward Gannen." He took both her hands in his and led her into his office. "I knew your aunt very well. She was a lovely woman. I see a little of her in your smile."

His words made her feel at home, and she took an immediate liking to Aunt Mattie's lawyer.

His office was as plush as any Brooke had ever seen. Leather-bound lawbooks filled the shelves that extended from floor to ceiling. The rich Oriental carpet felt thick under her feet. After seating her in a comfortable wing chair, Mr. Gannen poured two cups of tea from a cart on one side of the room.

"Are you all settled at the hotel?" he asked.

"Yes." She sipped her drink. "I was telling Mr. Franklin that I met Mrs. Gilmore on the train and she escorted me to the appropriate lodgings."

A smile curved his lips and made him look much younger. "I'm surprised that Mrs. Gilmore would even acknowledge the existence of the other hotel in town."

"Well, she did whisper when she mentioned it."

They shared a moment of laughter, and then Mr. Gannen's face became serious. "Before I tell you about your aunt's legacy, I'd like to find out a little about you." He glanced up at her face. "If you don't mind?"

"I . . . No, of course not." Although his request seemed unusual, Brooke placed her cup and saucer on the edge of his large oak desk and folded her hands in her lap to await his questions.

"When was the last time you heard from your aunt?"

"Last year sometime. Probably during the summer. I remember I didn't hear from her at Christmas, but I assumed the mail was delayed because of snow."

"Did she ever tell you why she came to Horse Creek?"

"Why, no, she never did." Brooke stared down at her fingers, trying to recall exactly what she knew about Aunt Mattie. "She left Philadelphia when I was a girl. Despite the age difference, we were great friends before she went away. There was a story about her losing her fiancé during the war, but I never knew much about that."

The lawyer leaned back in his chair and rested his elbows on the leather arms. "Someone is interested in buying Mattie's business, Miss Tyler. He's offering a fair price for the establishment itself, and he will also buy the grazing land she owned a few miles outside of town. He's willing to pay for all of it in gold. I think you should consider his offer."

Brooke felt as though someone had punched her in the stomach. She didn't recall exhaling, but suddenly her lungs were empty of air and she couldn't breathe. *Sell?*

"No." The word came out with a gasp.

Mr. Gannen continued as if she hadn't spoken. "It would take a few days to complete the paperwork. Then you'd be free to return to Philadelphia."

"I'm not going back." Brooke closed her eyes as she recalled the last three years of her life. Never again would she have to endure the knowing looks and the pity of well-meaning friends—not to mention the humiliation of running into Joe MacAllister's wife every time she went to the shops.

"You would have enough money to live anywhere."

She opened her eyes and stared at him. "Why are you doing this? All I want is to start a new life, running Aunt Mattie's business."

Although his face remained pleasant, his eyes hardened as though they had been coated with a layer of ice. "What exactly do you know about running a business?"

She straightened up in her seat. "I don't see that my financial expertise is any of your concern, Mr. Gannen."

He sighed. "You're quite right, Miss Tyler. I am merely trying to look out for your best interests. Mattie Frost was a remarkable woman, and I don't mean to insult you by saying it would require someone very"—he cleared his throat, his voice thick with emotion—"very special to take her place."

Brooke stared at the older man. He had averted his face, but she could tell he was distraught. Apparently Aunt Mattie and Edward Gannen had been more than simply lawyer and client.

"I can understand that you still miss her," she said.

"I do. But it's more than that, my dear. I feel responsible for you. I don't want you to make a decision that may ruin your life." Having regained control, he looked back at her. "How does your family feel about your move?"

"My parents are both dead. My younger brother is away at school, and quite frankly, my older brother was very happy to see me move out of the house. He recently married, and his wife and I didn't get along." What an understatement, Brooke thought. Her sister-in-law had spent most of her time complaining about how awkward it was having to live with an old maid.

Brooke leaned forward and placed her hands on the edge of the desk. "Mr. Gannen, I'm an excellent seamstress. I've brought patterns and supplies with me. I've seen a few of the women of Horse Creek, and I'm sure they'd love to wear more stylish clothes. I'm quite good with money. In fact, I've been running my own financial affairs since my father died. I'm here to make a fresh start for myself. Please don't try to discourage me."

She had hoped that her impassioned speech would soften his position, but if anything, he seemed even more remote and unapproachable.

Edward stood up and crossed the room to the window. "Mr. Prattly, the prospective buyer, is well respected in this town and—"

"Did you say Prattly?"

He turned back to face her. "Yes, why?"

Brooke shrugged, embarrassed that she had spoken out loud. "Does his wife have dark hair with a silver streak on either side?"

"Yes. Have you met her?"

Brooke remembered William's story about Mr. Prattly and the fishing hole. "William pointed her out to me earlier. Why does her husband want Aunt Mattie's business?"

Edward folded his arms across his chest. "To be honest, I don't know. I was sufficiently grateful to have found a buyer so quickly that I didn't inquire as to his motives. Does it really matter? Gold is gold."

The urge to scream with frustration had been building for several minutes. Brooke took a deep breath and tried to explain one more time. "Mr. Gannen, I have no intention of selling Aunt Mattie's business. Why can't you understand that?"

He walked away from the window and stopped directly in front of her chair. He bent down, gripping the armrests, until his face was inches from hers. "You're the one who doesn't understand, Miss Tyler. This isn't Philadelphia. Wyoming isn't even a state. There are situations here that you can't even begin to grasp."

He straightened up and ran his fingers through his thick white hair. "Your aunt didn't leave you a dress shop."

His obvious agitation was beginning to make Brooke nervous. What was he talking about? "If it's a millinery shop, I can learn to make hats. I'm not afraid of hard work, Mr. Gannen."

He cast his eyes up as if he were appealing to the heavens for guidance. "Miss Tyler, your aunt left you a saloon."

Chapter 4

Brooke stood at the crossing of Horse Creek's two main streets, staring down the deserted road. She wasn't sure how she had gotten there, and she didn't even remember leaving Mr. Gannen's office. She hoped she had at least said good-bye.

A saloon! How had Aunt Mattie ever come to own a place like that? No one in the family had ever guessed.

Brooke closed her eyes and tried to picture her aunt. There was a blurry memory of a loving woman whose smile had never quite reached her eyes. She had generously remembered birthdays and Christmases, and after Mattie moved, her letters had contained witty accounts of her travels. But not once had she mentioned a saloon.

The cold evening air seeped into Brooke's bones and reminded her that she had been standing on the corner for quite some time. The sun had almost completely set, and the street was getting dark. She tugged her shawl more firmly about her shoulders and struck out for Mrs. Gilmore's house.

The widow lived on the far edge of town in a two-story home. There were plants by the single step, but in the fading light Brooke couldn't tell if they were flowers or vegetables. A welcoming light shone through the front window, and she hurried to the porch.

Her knuckles had barely brushed against the wooden surface when the door was opened from the inside.

"There you are, my dear. I was wondering if you'd gotten lost. Come in, come in. You must be frozen. Let me take your things."

Brooke handed her shawl and reticule to the older woman, then accepted the offered seat by the fire. Blazing warmth chased away the chill. The house was small but well kept. Brightly printed fabric covered the handmade furniture, softening the rough edges. All the pillows were edged in lace, as were the curtains. Any masculine influence had been erased long ago, and Brooke wondered if Mr. Gilmore had ever lived there at all.

Mrs. Gilmore darted about like a bird, fluttering to and fro, loading the maple table with delicious-smelling foods. She had changed from her traveling suit to a simple gray day dress. The dull fabric didn't detract at all from the lively gleam in her eyes. "Are you all settled in?"

"Um, yes. Thank you." Brooke suppressed a guilty feeling as she remembered that she hadn't yet unpacked her suitcases. Between Dalton's visit and her trip to the lawyer's office, there hadn't been time to put her things away.

"I unpacked immediately," Mrs. Gilmore said, flicking an imaginary fleck of dust off the pale pink tablecloth. "Everything in its place, my mother always used to say."

Her words flowed over Brooke like water over a fall. She was too caught up in her recent discovery to appreciate any truisms espoused by Mrs. Gilmore's relatives. Why had Aunt Mattie never told anyone about her business? Brooke wondered. But she knew the answer. The Tyler family would have disowned her, much as

Brooke's own brothers would cease to acknowledge her if she didn't sell the establishment.

What was she thinking about? Of course she was going to sell. She could no more run a saloon than a brothel.

She held a hand up to her face, conscious that her bold thoughts had brought a flush to her cheeks. In an attempt to cover her embarrassment, she tried to concentrate on Mrs. Gilmore's conversation.

" . . . the best butcher. Don't you agree?"

"Oh, yes. Most definitely."

Brooke rose and moved to the table, then seated herself where Mrs. Gilmore indicated. "The supper looks wonderful, Mrs. Gilmore. Thank you so much for your kind invitation."

The older woman fairly beamed with pride, and Brooke chided herself for not having been more attentive. Mrs. Gilmore's inordinate interest in other people's lives probably stemmed from having nothing exciting in her own. *Wait until she finds out about my inheritance*, Brooke thought, holding back a smile.

It was as if the other woman could read her mind. "Tell me, dear, did you learn anything from your lawyer?"

Brooke almost choked on the stew. When she had finished coughing, she spoke weakly. "Lawyer?"

Mrs. Gilmore nodded. "I ran into a friend of mine who had chatted with Edna Prattly. It seems you were spotted going into Mr. Gannen's office. Did everything go well? Did you meet that nice Arthur Franklin? He's a very honorable young man with an excellent future ahead of him. Mr. Gannen won't live forever, you know. Horse Creek will need a young attorney. Why, the way Mr. Gannen keeps to himself these days, you'd think he was mourning his wife all over again."

Her tone sharpened considerably on the last few words, and Brooke wondered if there was trouble between the lawyer and the widow. She dismissed the thought. She didn't have the strength to deal with local gossip just now. After reviewing Mrs. Gilmore's list of questions, she decided to answer the safest first. "Yes, I met Arthur Franklin. He seems very nice."

"Oh, he's more than nice. And I imagine he was quite taken with you?" Mrs. Gilmore arched one eyebrow.

"I'm sure I don't know what you mean."

"Don't be coy with me, young lady. I have a daughter who's older than you, and I know what a young man looks for in a girl."

Perhaps Mrs. Gilmore had meant to goad her into a confession, but the ruse failed. Although Brooke had one or two secrets that would stir any gossip's blood, Arthur Franklin wasn't one of them. He had been pleasant at best and, at worst, too much like her own brothers back home. Now if the question had been about Dalton . . .

What did *he* look for in a woman? she wondered. She tried to picture him with someone, but the vision only made her angry and she banished it from her mind.

Mrs. Gilmore continued to chatter on about various events that had occurred in Horse Creek during her absence. Brooke listened with half an ear. It wasn't until her hostess was clearing away the table that Brooke decided to seek her counsel.

"Did you ever know Mattie Frost?"

Mrs. Gilmore stared at Brooke, her eyes suddenly enormous. She placed the plates in the metal sink, then absentmindedly brushed her hands against her cotton skirt. "What a question, child! Know Mattie Frost indeed! I'd be insulted if you weren't new to town and didn't know what you were asking. Now, where did you hear a name like that?"

"Did you know her?"

Mrs. Gilmore added another piece of wood to the stove in the corner of the room, then turned back to Brooke. "I knew who she was, but we were never introduced." She glanced over her shoulder as if afraid someone might be eavesdropping on the conversation, then spoke in a confidential whisper. "She ran a saloon here in town. The Garden Saloon, up on Main Street." Her eyebrows drew together. "Why do you want to know, Brooke? Don't tell me you . . ." Her voice trailed off as her face took on an expression of horror. "You didn't *know* her?"

Brooke toyed with the tablecloth, bunching the fabric between her fingers and then smoothing it flat. The night was still. The pools of light cast by the lamp didn't extend very far into the room, and Brooke had the sensation that she and Mrs. Gilmore were the last two people left on earth. She raised her head and looked at the older woman, silently pleading for understanding and guidance. "Mattie Frost was my aunt. I heard from Mr. Gannen that she had left me an establishment, and I came here expecting to inherit a dress shop."

"Your aunt . . . The saloon . . . Oh, my!" Mrs. Gilmore clutched her thin chest as though she could not catch her breath. "How unfortunate for you. The shame! You must be shocked." She scurried across the room and sank into the chair next to Brooke's. "How ever can you bear it?"

Although Mrs. Gilmore only echoed what Brooke had been thinking, the other woman's patronizing tone made her stiffen her spine. "There is no need to speak as if someone in my family is suddenly a murderer," she said tartly.

"No. No. I didn't mean that. But still. A saloon. Did you know there were"—her voice dropped to a whisper—"dancing girls there? And gambling?"

Dancing girls? Brooke felt her eyes widen. She had never been completely clear about the purpose dancing girls served in a saloon. Were they there to provide a show, similar to what she had seen on her visits to the theater, or did they provide a more private entertainment, the kind that had only been hinted at by her married friends?

"What are you going to do?" Mrs. Gilmore asked.

"I'm not sure."

"Can you sell the saloon and be done with it?"

Brooke remembered Mr. Gannen repeatedly mentioning an interested buyer. "Yes. There is someone who wants to purchase the building."

"Then you are saved."

The relief in Mrs. Gilmore's voice would have been comic if it hadn't been so sincere. "Yes, I suppose I am."

"You don't sound convinced."

Brooke looked up, her eyes meeting her hostess's. "I can't help wondering if it would be wrong to sell. The saloon belonged to Aunt Mattie, and she left it to me for a reason. If she'd just wanted to give me money, she would have instructed her lawyer simply to send me the proceeds after it was sold."

"Those two were certainly close enough that he would have received the message," Mrs. Gilmore mumbled.

"What?" Brooke asked, not sure she had heard right.

"Just thinking out loud, dear. Pay me no mind."

Brooke would have followed her instructions except that she noticed two spots of color high on Mrs. Gilmore's cheeks. What could have brought that on? she wondered.

She remembered Mr. Gannen's sadness when he'd spoken of her aunt. Perhaps her initial speculation had been correct and there had been more than a business relationship between him and Aunt Mattie. Judging from Mrs. Gilmore's pained expression, she, too, must have made a bid for the successful lawyer's company and lost out to Brooke's aunt.

The thought brought a slight smile to her lips and helped lift the mantle of confusion and indecision that had settled on her shoulders when she'd first heard mention of the saloon.

She pushed back from the table and rose with a graceful, fluid motion. "It's getting late. I really must be going."

"Are you sure you're all right? I can arrange for one of my neighbor's boys to walk you back to the hotel." For once Mrs. Gilmore seemed driven by genuine concern.

On the train Brooke had thought the other woman was nothing more than a busybody, but now she felt a growing affection for Mrs. Gilmore. "I'll be fine. The walk will help me clear my head. Thank you for a lovely meal, and especially for listening." Impulsively she reached out and hugged the older woman. Although Mrs. Gilmore's bony structure was very different from Brooke's memories of her mother's ample curves, the contact was reassuring.

"I'm sure you'll do the right thing," Mrs. Gilmore said as she opened the front door.

Brooke stepped into the chilly night air without replying. If only she knew what the right thing was.

Dalton strolled along the deserted sidewalk wondering if the local doctor had a cure for absentmindedness. He had almost lost at cards tonight, and for no good reason other than being distracted. Even if the doctor didn't have a potion, Dalton knew the cause of his malady.

Asked at another time in his life, he might have mocked the idea of a single event changing a man's destiny forever. But his becoming a gambler had been brought about by an isolated episode, and it seemed as though Brooke Tyler had all the markings of another calamitous turning point. The poker tournament would start in a couple of days, he reminded himself. When it was over he'd take his winnings, and ride out of town, and never look back.

"Dalton?"

At first he thought his mind was playing tricks on him, but when the sweet, soft voice was accompanied by footsteps on the boardwalk, he stopped and turned around.

"Brooke? What are you doing out this time of night?"

She stepped closer to him, her pale features blurred in the dark night. "I had dinner with Mrs. Gilmore."

He swore under his breath. Even the town busybody should have had more sense than to let an innocent young woman walk out alone at night. "She should have arranged for an escort for you."

"Don't be angry with her. She did offer to call one of the neighbor boys, but I wanted to be alone. I needed to think."

"We better get you back to the hotel before some drunken cowboy takes a liking to . . . you."

He drew her hand through the crook of his arm, pulling her tightly against his body. The top of her head was level with his chin and the ridiculous feather from her hat tickled his ear. He swatted at the offending decoration. But his irritation was pushed away by the memory of the fragile lace he had seen peeking out of Brooke's steamer trunk. The corner of his mouth lifted up in a smile. Not all feminine frills were annoying.

She trembled against him. "You must be freezing," he said. "You should be wearing a coat. Where's your good sense?"

"Stop yelling at me."

Her voice quavered and he immediately regretted his sharp tone. What was it about her that brought out the protective side of him? He'd known lots of women, both younger and older than Brooke Tyler, but never before had he felt so responsible for someone.

"You keep turning up where I least expect you," he said softly. "I didn't mean to yell."

She tilted her head so that her cheek rested against his shoulder. The movement pushed her breast against his upper arm, and he caught his breath. The contact was as electric as turning up the last needed ace in a high-stakes poker game. Damn. Why did she have to touch him, all trusting like? Why did he have to care?

They turned the corner and crossed the street. He halted half a block from the hotel. "You go on ahead. I'll watch and make sure you get inside safely." He gave her a little push, but she continued to cling to him, her small fingers digging into his upper arm.

"Dalton? I need to talk to you. Can I—" Her voice broke. She cleared her throat before plunging on. He sensed what she was going to say before she said it, but that didn't stop the sudden tightening in his gut and his groin. "Can I come to your room?"

With a single movement he twisted his arm out of her grasp. "I've told you before. We can't—"

She pressed her fingers against his lips to silence him. He could feel the heat of her skin through the supple leather gloves and hated himself for wishing her fingers were bare. His mouth watered as he imagined the taste of her flesh and the sensation of running his tongue across the sensitive pads of her fingers.

"It's important."

He wanted to refuse her, but her words and the tone of her voice could not be denied. When he nodded his agreement, she dropped her hand. For a moment he wished he could turn back time and savor her intimate touch. His lips still ached with awareness of her, and he was filled with a sense of loss.

"There's a private entrance on the side of the building," he said. "We can get inside without being seen."

"That's fine."

There was a question hidden within her agreement, as if she wondered how he had come to learn about the side door. He wanted to tell her it had been something innocent—a prank played on a friend—but held back. Better for her to picture a secret rendezvous. Brooke's own imagination might be his best weapon for keeping her at bay.

The far side of the hotel was lit by a single lamp. Even knowing there was a secret door, Brooke wasn't sure she could have found it. Dalton pressed firmly against the wall, and a small opening gave way. She followed him up the narrow staircase and through a second door leading to the landing. He held up a palm to halt her on the stairs and she waited until he motioned for her to follow him.

They crept silently down the hall toward the main staircase. Two rooms shy of the open landing, he stopped and quickly opened a door. Brooke slipped inside. There was the sound of the bolt shooting home, then the scratch of a match. The lamp flickered and caught, casting a gentle glow over the room.

As he removed his greatcoat and hung it on the brass rack by the door, she shrugged out of her shawl. He took it and placed the garment next to his. The delicately woven cloth clung to his coat sleeve as though seeking the memory of his warmth and strength.

She had never seen Dalton in any setting but public areas or her own hotel room, and she was curious about the secrets his private quarters might contain.

Dalton's chamber was much larger than her small room. She stood in the middle of a sitting area. Two wing chairs flanked a flagstone fireplace. A few feet away, pressed against the opposite wall, stood an armoire. He pulled open the cabinet and took out a decanter and two glasses.

"Have a seat," he said, pointing to one of the chairs.

Brooke sat gingerly on the stiff brocade upholstery. Although the visit to his room had been her idea, now that she was here she was having second thoughts. She kept her eyes firmly fixed on Dalton pouring them both a drink and tried to ignore the large four-poster bed that stood just inside the range of her peripheral vision.

"Thank you." She took the glass he offered and sniffed at the amber liquid.

Brandy! Was he trying . . . He couldn't possibly think that . . . She swallowed.

Dalton sat in the other chair and placed his glass on the small table between them. "Dammit, Brooke. I'm not going to attack you, so get that look off your face. You're the one who wanted to talk, not me. And take off that ridiculous hat."

Her apprehension had faded with each sentence until she was able to laugh at his last request. "I'll have you know that this is the latest style." She reached up and pulled out the hatpin securing the gray fabric to her head. His dark eyes followed her every movement. His gaze dropped briefly to her chest, where the cloth stretched across her breasts, and then his eyes returned to her face. She thought she had imagined the flicker until she saw the lines around his mouth tighten. Fear and elation warred within her.

She set the hat on her lap and brushed her finger against the jaunty feather. The sound of a clock ticking reminded her of the lateness of the hour and the reason she needed to see him. He had to help her. There was no family member to ask, no trusted friend. Funny how the one person she felt she could turn to was a gambler she'd known for only two days.

"I saw my lawyer today." She glanced up, but Dalton's face was impassive, the emotions carefully hidden behind a mask of flesh and bone. How did he do that? she wondered. "My aunt's inheritance is . . ." It was so awkward even to talk about. What if he was shocked as Mrs. Gilmore had been?

"It's all right. Take your time." His voice, low and powerful, encouraged her, while his steady gaze comforted her.

"Have you ever run a saloon?" she asked.

Dalton leaned forward and picked up his glass. Swirling the brandy, he stared over her shoulder into a past she could only guess at. "Once. In New Orleans."

"Is it difficult?"

He grinned, his white teeth gleaming in the subdued lighting. "You thinking of looking for a job?"

But the smile faded as she stared at him. She took a deep breath to make her voice strong, but wasn't surprised when her throat closed and the only sound that emerged from her mouth was a croak. "I . . ."

He rose from his seat and leaned over her chair, then set his glass on the table and took one of her hands in his. She hadn't known that she was trembling until she saw her pale hand quivering against his palm. His free hand brushed against her cheek with a soothing motion.

"Do you need money?" he asked. "Is that why you want a job?"

His face was close to hers, almost as close as it had been earlier, in her room. Her eyes fixed on his lips, and she remembered the brush of them against her skin. She wanted him to kiss her on the mouth, the way Joe MacAllister had. Only this time she wouldn't shut her teeth against his probing tongue as she had with her former fiancé.

Dalton looked into her green eyes and wondered if he'd burn in hell for the thoughts in his mind. Tightening his fingers around her hand, he continued to gently stroke her cheek. He knew he should step back. The comforting touch he'd offered was rapidly becoming an erotic game. Brooke needed him for help, not for seduction.

He pulled his hands away and straightened up, then moved to the armoire and took a slim cigar from the simple wooden box. "I'd be happy to give you enough money to return safely to Philadelphia." He was proud of his speech, proud that he hadn't betrayed his mounting passion. If his fingers weren't as steady as usual with his cigar, there was no one to comment on the fact.

Brooke's sigh filled the room. The sweet sound of innocence and pain touched him like a ghost from the past.

"I don't need money; I need advice."

"About?"

"A saloon."

Brooke watched as Dalton carefully closed the cabinet. He moved with the studied movements of someone not quite sure of his place in a room. When he finally faced her, she almost burst out laughing at the pained expression on his face.

"I'm sure I didn't hear you correctly."

"I'm sure you did." Teasing him lightened her spirits, and she grinned saucily at him.

"Brooke."

The warning growl did nothing to dampen her growing humor. "Why, sir, I'm merely trying to experience life in the West to its fullest. I felt sure you'd approve." She glanced at him from under her lashes, but her smile faded when she saw that she had angered him.

"I thought you had something important to discuss, Miss Tyler. If I had known you were only interested in playing games, I would have left you on the street where I found you."

Brooke pushed herself up from the chair, her temper flaring to match his. "I found *you,* if you will recall, *Mr.* Reed. And as for playing games, I was simply trying to lighten the end of a very difficult day. I do have something to talk about, but I . . ." She was angered by the burning behind her eyes. "No!" She blinked frantically. "I'm not going to cry. Damn!"

Brooke gasped, then clapped her hand over her mouth and stared at Dalton. His dark eyes brightened, and the corner of his mouth twitched.

She dropped her hand and pointed her index finger at him. "Don't you dare laugh," she warned.

He tried to hold back, but the laughter overwhelmed him. His broad shoulders shook, and he clutched the armoire for support. "I'm . . . sorry," he gasped.

"I can see that."

"No . . . really." He took several deep breaths and regained control. "If you could have seen the look on your face when you said—"

She cut him off. "I know what I said, thank you."

He stubbed out his cigar in a tray and crossed the room to stand next to her. "I'm sorry, really. Now why don't we try this again?" He took the hat from her and dropped it on the seat behind her. Holding her hands in his, he looked deep into her eyes. "How can I help you?"

"My aunt left me a saloon."

A sliver of emotion slid across his face, but it vanished quickly and she couldn't be sure what he was thinking.

"And?" he prompted her.

"What do you mean, 'And'? I own a saloon. Isn't that enough?"

He smiled. "If that was the only problem, we wouldn't be having this conversation."

She glanced at the floor, unable to continue staring into his face. He was right. The saloon wasn't the problem; she was. "What should I do?"

"Sell it."

She had known what his answer would be, but even so, she felt disappointed. "That's what everyone says I should do."

"Then listen to them, Brooke. A saloon is no place for a lady like you. Gamblers and cowboys go there, not green-eyed women in ridiculous hats."

She stared at the top button of his vest, aware of her hands still caught in his grasp. Warm strength and courage flowed from him to her. "I'm not ready to make a decision yet. Aunt Mattie left me a saloon, and I need to know why. I can't go back to Philadelphia a failure."

"You won't be. I'm sure you'll realize a tidy profit and you can set yourself up with a shop or anything you want."

She looked up at him. "I want to see it."

He briefly closed his eyes, as if in defeat, but didn't pretend to misunderstand. "When?"

"Do you have any plans for tomorrow?"

"I have a poker tournament at two o'clock."

"Fine. Why don't we meet in the lobby of my hotel at ten? That should give us plenty of time."

Dalton's eyes darkened to glowing onyx. There was a message for her hidden in the deep color, but she couldn't decipher it. He released her hands and walked to the far end of the room. One broad shoulder rested against the entrance to the alcove containing the bed. Her glance took in the thick spread covering a mattress big enough—she swallowed—for two.

"Make sure you think this through," he warned. "Once you accept ownership of a saloon, there'll be no going back."

His words contained just enough authority to send a shiver of apprehension slithering up her spine. She tossed her head to dispel the feeling. "I'm not moving in, Dalton. I just want to go look."

Chapter 5

———

"Miss Tyler, what a pleasure to see you again." Arthur Franklin beamed as he rose to greet Brooke.

"Thank you, Mr. Franklin." She placed her hand in his, but resisted his attempt to raise it to his mouth. A smile twitched at the corner of her lips as she imagined what Dalton must think about the law clerk's action. "I don't believe you've met Mr. Reed." She turned toward Dalton while pulling her hand out of Arthur's. "Dalton, this is Arthur Franklin, Mr. Gannen's law clerk."

Although the two men shook hands, Dalton's arched eyebrow and Arthur's pained expression both informed her that she had committed another in her long list of social errors. Well, she no longer cared anymore, she told herself. So what if Arthur Franklin knew she called Dalton by his first name? Compared to owning a saloon, it seemed a minor infraction.

"Is Mr. Reed your business adviser?" Arthur asked.

Brooke glanced up at Dalton. Was he? His gaze met hers, and she nodded, indicating he could answer the question.

"I am here to assist Miss Tyler." Dalton's voice was smooth, giving nothing away.

She studied the two men. Arthur was indeed handsome, in a mild sort of way. But his blue eyes bordered on pale, and his stature, although not short, compared unfavorably to the gambler's long, lean lines.

"And what is your occupation?" Arthur asked.

Brooke sensed a subtle but growing antagonism between the two men, and she stepped between them. "Dalton is a gambler. As I have recently inherited a saloon, he seemed to be the best person to ask for advice. Don't you agree, Mr. Franklin?" She removed her gloves and slapped them against the palm of her left hand. "If it wouldn't be too much trouble, I'd like the key to my aunt's establishment."

"But . . . I thought . . ." Arthur cleared his throat. "Mr. Gannen mentioned that you would be selling the saloon. I've already drawn up the papers." He indicated the stiff legal sheets strewn across the surface of his desk.

His face had paled, and she wondered why she had ever thought Arthur Franklin attractive. The more time she spent in his company, the more he reminded her of her older brother, always assuming things were going to turn out exactly as he wanted them to, never asking her opinion on anything. Gentleman or not, no one was going to tell her what to do.

"Mr. Gannen advised me to sell, but I have not yet made a decision." Righteous anger stiffened her spine. Dalton's powerful presence gave her courage and, at the same time, made her feel protected. "My key, Mr. Franklin."

Arthur's blue eyes pleaded with her, but she would not be swayed. He blinked his concession. "As you wish."

He left the outer room, entered the lawyer's office, and returned a few seconds later with an envelope. "Here."

As he dropped the packet onto her open waiting hand, she noticed he was careful not to touch her. "Thank you."

Dalton took her elbow and steered her toward the door, but before they could leave the building, Arthur called her back.

"Miss Tyler? If I could have a word?"

She glanced over her shoulder and then up at Dalton. "I'll just be a minute," she told him. Dalton hesitated, as though he might not leave her alone with Arthur, but then he shrugged and stepped outside.

Brooke turned back to the desk and waited expectantly. Arthur cleared his throat several times, seeming unable to form words or a sentence. While she waited, she saw that he was more nervous than at their first meeting. The studied charm had faded, leaving him looking as vulnerable and as rumpled as his half-undone tie.

"Miss Tyler, I am indeed sorry if I offended you in any way. I had been assured that you were selling, and I . . ."

His voice trailed off, but she didn't have the heart to let him continue floundering. "Mr. Franklin, I quite understand. There's no need to apologize."

"Thank you." His smile was wide and genuine, reminding her that he was a nice man, in an ordinary sort of way. His open face held none of the hidden shadows and nuances that molded Dalton's expressions.

"Good day, Mr. Franklin." Brooke opened the door.

"Miss Tyler?"

She turned back to Arthur and raised her eyebrows. "Yes?"

"Would you allow me to call on you?"

Brooke glanced out the open doorway and saw Dalton waiting for her on the sidewalk. When he caught her eye and smiled, Brooke felt her heart jump; she turned back to Arthur to refuse his request. But the lawyer's clerk stood by the desk, leaning forward expectantly. She remembered Mrs. Gilmore's claim that Arthur was a young man with a future. She remembered Dalton's constant reminders that he would prefer to have nothing to do with her. "If you'd like, Mr. Franklin."

As soon as the words left her lips, she longed to call them back. But Arthur looked so happy that she couldn't bear to say anything. Perhaps he'd forget all about her.

"Brooke, are you planning to spend all day here?" Dalton stood in front of the open door, glancing impatiently at his gold pocket watch.

"No. I'm ready now." She nodded at Arthur Franklin and followed Dalton down the steps.

They walked to the saloon the same way he'd suggested they walk to the lawyer's office: Brooke in front, Dalton several paces behind. Despite her claims that it made her feel like a fool, he had insisted. He was adamant about preserving her reputation. Some help that would be if she decided to keep the saloon, Brooke thought.

The Garden Saloon. With its windows boarded up, the building looked abandoned, but the sign warmly reflected the rays of the midmorning sun. The letters were painted in elaborate gold script with vines and flowers twining around the words. What a lovely sign for such an unsavory establishment, she thought.

Brooke stood across the street and waited for Dalton to catch up with her. On the outside, the saloon looked about the same as any other business on the street; only the wide, ornately carved double doors hinted at the mysteries within.

"Have you been inside before?" she asked.

He adjusted his dark hat. "Yes. I stopped by a couple of times last year."

As the blood drained from her face, she clutched his sleeve. "Then you knew my aunt. Why didn't you tell me?"

"I never met the owner." He turned and glanced up the street. Two women were rounding the corner and heading their way. "Come on." He grasped Brooke's hand and pulled her across the street. "We'd better get inside before someone sees us together."

The heavy metal key turned easily in the lock. The door swung open silently, admitting them into the dim stillness of the saloon. Brooke hadn't known what to expect, but the sound of their footsteps echoing in the large room seemed anticlimactic after all of Dalton's concern about her reputation. Somehow she had expected a townswoman or two to leap from the corner and accuse her of having loose morals.

So this was a saloon. She stood just inside the doorway, trying to take everything in. The building had been closed for over a month, since her aunt's death, and dust was everywhere. Three round tables huddled together along one side of the room, with a small stage on another.

The entire right wall was taken up by the bar. She walked over and ran her fingers across the smooth birchwood, tracing the dents and grooves—tokens of old disputes or forgotten good times.

The backbar was as long as the bar, but it stretched almost to the ceiling. On either side of the main rectangular mirror was a smaller diamond-shaped beveled mirror. She looked up and saw Dalton's reflection.

He belonged here. Moving with the confidence of someone comfortable with his surroundings, he circled the room. His dark coat contrasted with the bright green and ivory wallpaper. Apparently Aunt Mattie had taken the name of the saloon very seriously. All the paintings hanging on the walls were of plants and flowers.

"This was a great place," he said as he continued his inspection.

"It's not as large as I had imagined. How did you ever gamble here? There are only three small tables."

He smiled. "I'll show you." When she made no move to follow, he stopped in the center of the floor and crooked his finger at her. "Come on."

She trailed after him to the back of the room where a carved wood and beveled-glass partition stood. Pushing open one of the swinging doors, he motioned for Brooke to enter. Although this room was slightly smaller than the main bar area, there was no doubt as to its purpose. Four tables, each of which could seat at least ten people, stood in the center of the room. Various gambling devices lined the back wall. A smaller table on one side was piled high with unopened decks of cards and boxes of poker chips.

Dalton watched as Brooke picked up some of the poker chips. Mattie Frost had ordered her playing disks from the finest companies in Europe. Even from across the room, he could see the intricate designs carved into the wooden counters.

She opened her hand and allowed the chips to flow through her fingers like water. "Am I rich?" she asked, her green eyes filled with laughter.

He pulled a cigar out of his coat pocket. "Only if she left you some money. Chips are tokens for cash only when you gamble."

He leaned against the doorsill and struck a match. While he lit his cigar, she moved to the back of the room and toyed with the wheel of fortune. She pushed against the upright brass pins, setting the wheel in motion. The sun shone through the high windows, illuminating the cloud of dust while the wooden disk slowed and the clacking sound wound down.

Brooke bent down and read off her fortune. "One hundred dollars!" She clapped her hands together and spun to face him. "Oh, I *am* rich now. Dalton, this is fun!"

Her face was pink with excitement. Rose-colored lips parted in a wondering smile he couldn't help but return. The air of playfulness and innocence about her was contagious, and he longed to hold this moment forever in place. In her light blue dress with her hair pulled back in a simple braid, she looked like a schoolgirl on a holiday adventure.

She crossed the room to his side. "Why didn't anyone tell me that a saloon could be so exciting? I never imagined what could possibly keep men trapped inside for so many hours at a time, but now I understand."

Dalton frowned. Although he was pleased that Brooke was having a good time, he had expected the visit would show her that she couldn't possibly keep the saloon. Selling was the only reasonable alternative. If she was too stubborn to figure that out for herself, he'd just have to help her see reason.

"Brooke," he growled. "There's a lot more to running a saloon than playing the games. It requires a cool head and a great business sense. Not to mention the ability to keep drunken men from killing anybody who gets in their way."

"I'm aware of that." The light in her green eyes flickered and died.

"I'm sorry. I didn't mean to dampen your enthusiasm, but you've got to see the impossibility of the situation. You can't run this place on your own."

"But, Dalton . . ."

She was standing too close. The hem of her skirt was only inches from his boot, her breast a scant breath from his arm. The dusty air was suddenly filled with the subtle smell of lilacs and that mysterious fragrance a woman creates to draw a man. He'd smelled it before, when he was a boy, and it had forever altered his life. Brooke contained the same power within her innocent self, the power to mold a man's destiny like a child playing with mud. But the same force that might build a castle could also destroy it with the careless flick of a hand. He'd never allowed a woman close enough to touch his soul, and he wasn't about to start now.

Yet all the logic in the world couldn't prevent him from searching her eyes for a wanting that matched his own. He saw the question on her face. Untutored, untouched, she didn't know what he was asking. The response was there, without her knowledge, as she swayed toward him, her breathing quickening, her lips slightly parted.

Dalton dropped his cigar into the brass spittoon next to him. Every part of his mind commanded him to walk out of that room and keep going till he reached Cheyenne, or maybe New Orleans. But the rest of his body, especially the throbbing need between his legs, had been denied too long. With a deliberate motion, as though to warn her of his intentions, he placed his hands on her shoulders and drew her close. Her arms hung limp at her sides.

Brooke stared at Dalton's face. The heat of his hands burned through the thin cotton of her dress until she knew she would carry the scars for the rest of her life. Slowly, tentatively, she placed her palms against his chest. Through all the layers—jacket, vest, and shirt— she felt his heartbeat. The rhythm matched her own, as if they had both run a hundred miles. She wondered that they didn't explode.

His eyes darkened to black, the color of coal just before it flares with a bright, blinding light. When his hands slipped down and across her back, she allowed him to pull her close. Her world stopped and waited, breath held, until his lips touched hers.

She had thought she'd be afraid, but the urgent pressure of his firm mouth on hers was tender. The trembling within her body was a reaction to the feelings awakened by his kiss. He was still, allowing her to become familiar with the feel and texture of him. When she slid her hands up over the back of his neck, he flicked his tongue across her bottom lip.

Brooke gasped at the soft contact, instinctively pulling her head back. Their eyes met. She swallowed, then slowly moved her fingers through his soft hair. The curls felt alive, like springy coffee-colored silk. His mouth descended again, and she licked her lips in anticipation. But before she could withdraw her tongue, he had touched it with his. The moist contact sent a river of heat coursing down her spine. When he nudged against her mouth, she opened to receive him.

As his tongue touched and swirled, he pulled her closer. She didn't know which brought the most pleasure, the pagan dance between their lips, or the hard masculine pressure of his body against her suddenly aching femininity.

She had never felt this way before. Joe MacAllister's kisses hadn't heated her blood to the boiling point. She had never longed to rub against him in an effort to relieve a tension she didn't quite understand.

When Dalton tensed and put her away from him, she wanted to protest. But his burning eyes robbed her of the power of speech. Her mouth felt swollen and lonely, and she ached to relieve the sensations with a tender kiss.

"Brooke."

He spoke her name in a voice raw and husky with need. When she leaned up against him, offering with her body what she was too shy to speak aloud, he stepped back. His withdrawal from her was both puzzling and disappointing. Though separated by only inches, she felt a chasm stretch between them. Had she done something incorrectly?

"Don't look so damned hurt."

"I'm not," she said, turning away from him and walking toward the main room of the saloon. It was a wonderful kiss, she told herself. She wouldn't let Dalton's foul mood spoil the memory.

He captured the soft flesh of her upper arm, holding on just enough to halt her progress without bruising. "You're a very tempting woman, Brooke Tyler. So tempting you make me forget myself."

She opened her mouth to speak, but couldn't think of anything to say. His compliment, perhaps the most honest she had ever received, stirred feelings she had never felt before. The last fragments of hunger fading in his eyes reaffirmed his words.

"Dalton, stay with me. You could run the saloon."

The words burst out with no prior thought on her part, but she didn't call them back, even when he dropped his hand from her arm and stalked to the other side of the room.

"I'm not the staying kind."

His words were a slap in the face, and she jerked her head as if she had been physically struck. "I see."

He studied the bar, as if viewing it for the first time. "No, you don't. There are things from my past that you couldn't begin to understand. Places I've been, things I've done. Anyway, you aren't looking for a business partner; you're looking for a husband."

"I am not—"

He looked over his shoulder and cut her off with a glance. "Deny it all you want, but I've known women like you. Brooke, you deserve a good life. One that I can't give you, however tempted I may be to try. Save yourself for the Arthur Franklins of the world."

Dalton admired the way she clutched her tattered composure around herself like a cape. A lesser person would have denied the truth of his statements or tried to change his mind, but Brooke just tilted her jaw defiantly and stepped across the room.

"I'm sure you have other business to attend to, Mr. Reed. I shall not detain you any further. Thank you so much for your kind assistance."

Watching her walk back into the gaming room was the hardest thing he'd ever done. Damn you to hell, Joanna, if you're not there already, he thought bitterly. It had been thirteen years, and he was still paying for his mistake. The price hadn't seemed so high before, but now, with Brooke weaving her way into the fabric of his life, the debt was as heavy and dark as his despair.

The taste of Brooke's sweet mouth still lingered on his lips, and yet he knew he had to let her go. Everything he'd told her was the truth, and the sooner she started to understand that, the sooner she'd get on with her life.

"Excuse me. I'm looking for a Miss Tyler."

Dalton glanced up at the tall man who had entered the saloon. In his early fifties, he dressed and walked like a man accustomed to getting his own way. His clothes had been tailored to conceal his bulky form, and his dark hair and beard were neatly trimmed.

Dalton walked over to him. "And you are . . . ?"

"Prattly. Samuel Prattly. I'm here to see Miss Tyler about purchasing her aunt's saloon."

Dalton told himself that the feeling in his gut wasn't disappointment. He offered his hand. "Miss Tyler is in the gaming room. I'm sure she'll be happy to discuss your offer."

Prattly's handshake was firm and strong. "I certainly hope so. I own all the other buildings on this block, and I want to tear them down and build one large store. Sell everything under one roof." He lowered his voice to a confidential whisper. "My wife thinks I'm crazy, but I keep telling her, it's the way of the future. Yes, sir." He grinned and thumped Dalton on the back.

Dalton was slightly taken aback. He didn't usually respond to strangers, especially the overconfident kind. In his profession, he'd found that the more he kept to himself, the more easily he slept at night. Still, Prattly seemed like a regular sort. "Why don't you go on back and talk with Miss Tyler? She's a little shy, but I'm sure you can persuade her to sell."

"Much obliged." Prattly winked at Dalton and headed toward the back of the saloon.

Dalton watched the older man leave and wondered why he felt a nibble of uneasiness. Perhaps Brooke had gotten to him more than he realized. Who was he kidding? She had gotten to him in places he had thought were sealed up years ago.

He walked behind the bar and sighed. What a day. And he still had the poker tournament that afternoon. He needed a drink.

Brooke opened the ledger sitting on her aunt's desk. She had found the door to the small office in the hall off the gaming room and had stepped inside, intending to stay hidden until Dalton left. Her cheeks still stung with the heat of a blush as she remembered his accusations. A husband! How dare he tell her what to do with her life! He was nothing but a no-account gambler. Someone who made his living taking from others.

He was also the most wonderful man she had ever met. And as much as she hated to admit it, she could hardly wait until he kissed her again. If he kissed her again.

"Miss Tyler?"

Brooke jumped in her seat. "Yes?"

The man standing in the doorway wasn't Dalton. She swallowed against sudden fear and prayed that the gambler hadn't left her alone in the closed-up building.

"I'm Samuel Prattly, and I'd like to talk to you about purchasing your saloon."

"Got a whiskey for me, son?"

Dalton looked up at the short, husky man strolling toward the bar. The man moved with the rocking motion of someone more used to riding than walking. His trousers and shirt had seen better days, but the star on his chest gleamed like a bride's best silver.

Dalton reached under the bar and pulled out a second glass. "Always plenty for the sheriff." He poured an inch of amber liquid into the squat glass. "I'll make it a short one, seeing as you're on duty."

"That I am. I'm Hank Morgan. The law in these parts." He chuckled. "I always get a kick out of saying that."

"Dalton Reed."

The sheriff's face was tanned and wrinkled from hours spent in the sun, but the lines fell into a kindly pattern.

"What brings you here, Sheriff?" Dalton pulled another bottle from the backbar and poured himself a drink.

The sheriff folded his arms on the wooden bar and leaned forward. "Saw the door open and thought I'd come have a look-see. Didn't know who'd be running this place, now that Mattie's gone."

Dalton took a sip from his glass. "Her niece is here, looking around. She asked me to come with her."

Hank Morgan raised one scraggly white eyebrow. "You some fancy-pants lawyer? We already got one in this town and that's one too many in my mind."

Dalton threw his head back and roared with laughter. "No, Sheriff. I'm a simple gambler by trade."

"A gambler, eh? Well, then, you must be here for the tournament." Morgan's eyes narrowed as he surveyed the room. "I sure hate to see this place torn down."

"You mean if Prattly buys the saloon?"

Morgan looked back at Dalton. "You sure know a lot about this town for someone who just rode in on the stage in the last day or so."

Dalton placed his hands on the bar in plain view and with the palms down. "Prattly is here right now, talking with Miss Tyler, Sheriff. He's the one who told me about his plans."

"I guess I can buy that." He finished his drink and put his glass on the bar. "Are you sure Mattie's niece is fixin' to sell?"

"Gold, Miss Tyler. I am willing to pay in gold."

Brooke glanced down at her hands and wished she could throw Mr. Prattly all the way back to his prize fishing hole. "You've already said that. I understand that you're offering a more than fair price. But I must say, yet again, that I am not sure I want to sell the saloon."

She looked across the desk at him and immediately regretted the action. His light eyes shot icy daggers as he leaned forward. "May I remind you, Miss Tyler, that Horse Creek is a very close-knit town. I am of some influence here. If you wish to be accepted by local society, you might want to reconsider your position as a saloon owner."

He uttered the word "saloon" with the same contempt used by ministers during their most fiery sermons. Although she knew he spoke the truth, something about him got her back up, and she continued to defy him.

He was very different from his wife, she thought. If her actions were anything to go by, Mrs. Prattly's intimidating facade hid a heart of gold. Brooke had a feeling that Mr. Prattly's heart was solid stone. "I am not afraid of you or your town, Mr. Prattly." She stood up. "Good day."

When he rose from his seat, he towered above her like an avenging angel. She held her breath and tightened every muscle in her body to keep herself from trembling.

"Miss Tyler, I didn't mean to offend you or to imply that I would use my vast power to undermine your respectability." He spoke as though to a wayward child, causing Brooke to stiffen her resolve all the more. "Perhaps I've been a tad harsh with you. I hope you will forgive me, dear. Gannen told me that your parents are gone, and Mattie would have wanted me to look out for you. Can we start over?"

Every pore of him oozed sincerity, she thought with disgust. And she hated herself for almost believing him. She wouldn't have at all, except for the way his voice had softened when he spoke of Aunt Mattie.

"Did you really know my aunt, Mr. Prattly, or are you simply trying to sway me?"

He had the grace to look ashamed. "I really *was* a friend of Mattie's. If I am overeager to buy the saloon, you must excuse me. I'm driven by my dream to build the largest store in the Wyoming Territory, maybe in the West."

He sounded as if he was telling the truth, but she couldn't be sure. He might be taking her for a fool. Still, two could play at that game. She hadn't spent her life in the company of businessmen without learning a trick or two. "Of course, Mr. Prattly, I understand. I'll think about your offer," she purred. "But now I must ask you to leave. All this talk of buying and selling has tired out my feeble female brain." Her laugh was false, and she was relieved when he joined in.

"Of course, my dear. Perhaps in a day or so." He nodded, then left the room.

Brooke collapsed on the chair. She felt as if she had lived two lifetimes already that day, and it wasn't even noon.

"Any luck?" Dalton asked as Prattly strode across the saloon.

The older man smiled confidently. "I should be able to start construction by the end of the week." He walked to the door. "Gentlemen."

"Glad to hear the lady decided to sell," the sheriff said.

"Why?" Dalton poured him a second drink.

"Strange things been happening around here the last few months." He glanced over his shoulder as if to make sure Prattly had left the room. "I'll tell you, boy. But you've got to keep this news to yerself."

Dalton swallowed, his throat suddenly thick and dry. "Go on."

"Somebody was trying to shut Mattie down long before she died."

"Are you saying she was murdered?"

"No." Morgan sipped his drink. "I'm saying someone was going pretty far outta their way to make her life mighty difficult. My guess is that ain't gonna change if the saloon reopens."

Chapter 6

"Are you sure?" Dalton asked.

The sheriff shrugged. "As sure as I can be. I was a mite worried about Mattie's niece. But now that she's planning to sell, everything should be fine."

"I don't know that she will. Brooke is a stubborn woman." Dalton thought about the way she had asked him to stay and help her run the place. She was just fool enough to consider managing it by herself. "Were you concerned about someone trying to . . ."

Dalton set his glass on the bar. He couldn't even say the word. It was difficult to imagine anything bad happening in this sleepy town. Horse Creek was a good size, but it was far enough off the beaten track to have escaped the attention of the riffraff that passed through Cheyenne. Still, the thought that Brooke might be in danger set his stomach to churning like horse's hooves thundering through a muddy field.

"Prattly usually gets what he wants. She'll be safe now, what with him tearing down the building and all."

Dalton remembered the well-dressed man who had left a few moments before. He'd been very confident about buying the saloon. "Did you ever find out who was responsible for giving Brooke's aunt trouble? Could it have been Prattly? He wants to own this place."

The sheriff removed his hat and brushed his palm across the few wispy strands of white hair lying against his pink scalp. "You ain't the only one in this room with that thought, son. But Prattly wouldn't have hurt a hair on that pretty lady's head. He might have wanted to buy this saloon, but he was also in love with the owner. He and Mattie had kept company for quite some time before she died." He set the worn felt hat back on his head. "In fact, he and the doc were with her when she slipped on the ice and fell. Both men blame themselves for not saving her, but it couldn't be helped."

There was a sadness in Morgan's blue eyes that told its own story. He, like Prattly, must have cared for Brooke's aunt, Dalton thought. "I never met her, but I'm beginning to see that Mattie Frost was a very special woman," he said.

"That she was." The sheriff smiled briefly. "Mattie sure thought the world of her niece. Talked about her from time to time, saying she was mighty bright." He drained his glass. "Too bright for some."

The pitch of his voice had lowered, becoming almost challenging, but Dalton ignored the gauntlet. "I imagine strong women run in the family."

He met Hank Morgan's eyes, allowing the older man to take his measure. This wasn't the action of a law-man looking over someone new in town; this was the action of a man who had loved a woman. A man performing a duty to Mattie's kin. Dalton knew that the sheriff would find an excuse to throw him in jail if he harmed so much as one hair on Brooke's beautiful head. The thought should have angered him, but instead he was comforted by the knowledge that someone else was watching over her.

"You leaving after the tournament?"

Dalton hesitated. Of course he was leaving. There wasn't anything or anybody that could keep him in this town a day longer than he had to stay. "I don't know."

That answer seemed to be the one the sheriff was looking for, because he smiled at Dalton and touched the brim of his hat. "I'll be seein' you around, Reed."

Brooke stared at the ledger, but the numbers danced unintelligibly before her eyes. It wasn't that she didn't understand the record-keeping system in the saloon—she'd always been good at ciphering and could add a column of figures faster than anyone she knew—but the faint sound of Dalton's voice in the other room shattered her concentration. She wanted to go out and send away whomever he was talking to; she wanted to see him and have him hold her in his arms; she wanted to feel his lips pressed against hers one more time before he walked out of her life forever.

"Brooke?"

The nearness of his voice startled her, and she jumped in her seat. The brush of his boots on the wooden floor told her that he was standing in the doorway to the office, but she didn't look up. Despite her fantasies of a moment before, facing Dalton Reed after he'd told her he wasn't interested in a woman like her was more humiliation than she could stand. "Yes, Mr. Reed?"

"Brooke, I have to leave now. I want you to lock the door behind me, and make sure you get back to the hotel before dark."

She toyed with the quill pen, her gaze never straying from the rectangular confines of the scarred oak desk top. "Thank you for your concern, Mr. Reed. I'll be sure to comply with your requests."

She heard three angry steps. Then two large masculine hands appeared in the center of the desk. She studied the well-groomed nails, the long fingers, and the light covering of hair on the backs of his hands. White cuffs led to dark sleeves, but she couldn't force her eyes any higher than the powerful forearms.

"Stop calling me Mr. Reed as though I'm some young pup you met at your mama's house for tea. I'm concerned about you and I . . . Dammit, look at me when I'm talking to you."

He crooked a finger under her chin and forced her head up. She considered keeping her eyes closed, but the small gesture of defiance seemed childish and cowardly. She had come out west to start a new life and to take care of herself; she might as well begin right now.

But Dalton's dark eyes didn't contain the anger and disdain she had expected. The smoky depths were alive with solicitude and some other emotion she couldn't quite decipher. The lean lines of his face were drawn and stiff, as if he was trying to hide his thoughts behind a mask of normalcy but hadn't quite succeeded.

His mouth was a straight line, and she wondered if she had simply imagined the full lips pressed against hers in a moment of passion. But the tingling in her chest reminded her that there had been more between them, more than his dark eyes were willing to admit.

The warm fingers cupping her chin moved against her jaw, creating greater heat than the gentle friction warranted. Each stroke brought her closer to pleading with the tall man before her. But she wouldn't. He'd made it clear that whatever emotions had passed between them would be ignored, if not forgotten. Every moment with Dalton had been recorded in her mind and her heart. Years from now she would be able to recall them and relive each wondrous second. But what would Dalton remember?

Brooke drew a deep breath, determined to leave him with a memory of her that was proud, not pleading. "I'm not trying to anger you. I know that you have a tournament to attend, and I was simply trying to cooperate."

She wrenched her head away from his tender hold and rose. "I doubt that we will see each other again, so I'd like to thank you for all your efforts on my behalf." She smiled tightly.

The farewell speech that she had planned was supposed to go on for a few more sentences, but she knew that her control was slipping away with each rapid beat of her heart.

Brooke was so beautiful as she stood before him mouthing correct little words of thanks and farewell. In a day or two he would be grateful that she'd finally come to her senses; no doubt she'd sell the saloon and return to Philadelphia. But right now, in the dusty office, he was sure that he would never be the same. The pain in her green eyes accused him, and he knew that disrupting her life was a great crime. Not, however, a greater crime than the one that had driven him from his home when he was little more than a boy. When would he learn?

He had sought Brooke out, had tutored her innocent lips, had seen the passionate fire glowing in her face. His punishment would fit his deed. Somehow in a short span of time, she'd found her way into a crevice within his heart.

"I'll be . . ." Dalton drew in a deep breath before trying to speak again. "I'll be in town for a few more days. The tournament's at the Cattle Run Saloon, across town. I'll either be there or at the hotel, if you need me." He walked away. When he reached the doorway, he spoke without turning around. "Be careful, Brooke. Don't go out at night alone. Sell this place and get the hell out of town. And lock the door behind me."

Brooke listened to the sound of his footsteps as he walked through the saloon. There was a brief silence; then the slamming of a door echoed and died. She waited for sadness or torment, for some emotion to spring up and overwhelm her, but her body was strangely numb. Her limbs felt heavy and cold, as though she'd stayed outside too long in a freezing rain. The chill crept into her heart. She turned down the lantern in the office and went toward the front of the building.

Brooke had thought that she might be afraid after Dalton left. But the empty saloon seemed lonely rather than eerie, and it welcomed her. She locked the door and pocketed the key, then walked toward the bar.

An open bottle of liquor rested on the scarred surface, and she was tempted to serve herself a drink. She could even get drunk and forget all about the gambler, she thought with a smile. Wasn't that what men did? But instead of pouring the amber liquid into a glass, she replaced the cork. She didn't know how much one had to drink to achieve drunkenness and wasn't even sure she would recognize the state if and when it happened. Better to explore the rest of the building.

Behind the gaming room, next to the office, was a staircase. Brooke lit the lantern hanging on the wall and carried the light up the stairs. The landing was long and wide, with two doors at one end and one at the other. She stepped toward the single door.

The knob turned easily in her hand. Brooke crossed the threshold and held the lamp up high, illuminating the large area. The room was dusty and dark, as the rooms downstairs had been. Thick burgundy drapes hung from floor to ceiling against one wall. Only a sliver of light cut across the woven carpet, shining through a small gap where the heavy curtains met.

After setting the lamp on a table next to the door and crossing the floor, she pulled the drapes open, holding her breath when a cloud of dust rose into the air.

Sunlight flooded the room. A canopy bed, built of rich mahogany and covered with a velvet and brocade spread, stood against one wall. Clothes were strewn haphazardly across the two rocking chairs in front of the cold fireplace, and papers littered the rolltop desk. Except for the musty smell and waiting silence, it was as though her aunt might return at any moment.

A tarnished silver frame on the desk caught her eye, and she picked it up. Contained within the first oval was a picture of Brooke herself, taken three years before. In the second was a portrait of a young man in a Union uniform. Even though she didn't recognize the face, she had no doubt that the man was Mattie's long lost love. That her aunt had cared for her enough to place her likeness next to his made Brooke feel unworthy. Tears slipped down her cheeks until the room was a watery blur. She sank onto the bed, clutching the photographs to her breast, and sobbed.

When she had no more tears left, Brooke lay back on the coverlet and closed her eyes. She must have slept, for when her eyes next opened, the room was in shadows and her stomach was growling.

There was an open door to the left of the bed. She walked into a tiny storage room. One side contained racks of dresses and dozens of shoes; the other was a sort of kitchen, with a dry sink and several cupboards. She found some tins of biscuits and a couple of bottles of mineral water.

As she munched on the food, she wondered what her brothers would think about her situation. No doubt they'd scold until their faces turned red and order her back to Philadelphia. But the thought of returning to a place where she'd spent the last three years feeling like a failure was more than she could bear. Sadness settled on her slim shoulders and made her heart tighten almost as painfully as it had when Dalton had left.

"I won't think about it," she said aloud and then giggled when the sound of her voice startled her.

Brooke glanced out the window. Judging from the long shadows on the street, it was close to four o'clock. Time to head back to the hotel if she wanted to make it before dark.

She was halfway down the stairs when she stopped, one foot hanging in the air, not quite touching the next step. She didn't want to go back to the hotel. There was nothing waiting for her there—only a solitary meal in the dining room and then a cold night alone in her room. No doubt Dalton's memory would rise up to torment her until the sun appeared at dawn.

After all, she was Mattie's heir, she thought as she turned around and climbed up the stairs. The least she could do was to go through her aunt's papers and get everything in order.

Wood was stacked by the fireplace. In a few minutes the logs were crackling; the cheerful heat chased away the musty smell. She turned to tackle the rolltop desk.

Most of the cubbyholes contained requisitions and receipts that related to the saloon. There were a few personal notes from people whose names Brooke didn't recognize.

In the right-hand drawer was a box containing all the letters she had written to her aunt. She flipped through the envelopes, smiling as her handwriting evolved before her eyes; from her childish flourishes at ten, to a very ornate stylized penmanship at fourteen, to its current adult script. She put the box aside, determined to read the letters later. She pressed against the drawer to close it, but the rich wood hesitated as if something was caught. She pulled the drawer all the way out and found another box of correspondence, similar to the one that held her letters, but these were addressed in a very masculine hand. Her eyes flickered from the box to the picture and back.

The envelopes were worn from frequent handling, and the ink had faded with age. A pressed rose lay on top of the letters; its dried petals were crumbling and fragile, and yet it had endured as long as Mattie's love for her soldier. Brooke longed to know what the young man had written, but couldn't bring herself to intrude into their romance. Perhaps another time she would feel welcome, but not tonight.

The last area she explored was the slim drawer in the center of the desk. It was empty except for an untitled leather-bound book. When she opened the cover, she saw that she had found her aunt's journal. Most of the entries were short, and the dates indicated that Mattie had written sporadically.

Brooke flipped through the pages until the sight of her own name caused her to stop and scan the entry. The date was from three years before.

I received Brooke's letter today. News of my family brought its usual feelings of relief and longing. I can never go back, nor do I want to, yet sometimes I find myself missing everyone. I have always found the heart to be a very contrary organ.

Brooke says that she is no longer planning to marry
Joe MacAllister. There is no mention of the reason
for ending the engagement, and I worry about her.
I see so much of myself in the girl. In a way, I'd
like to invite her here, to stay for a while. But that is
unthinkable. I couldn't stand to see the disillusionment
in her eyes when she learned that her favorite aunt
runs a saloon. No. Better to keep the secret to myself
and my relationship with my family intact.

I miss Roger more today than I have in a long time.
Perhaps it is because of Brooke's broken engagement.
Perhaps it is because today is the anniversary of his
death. Perhaps it is because I'm an old fool.

I've been thinking of drawing up a will. Edward
pleads with me not to speak of such things, but I
refuse to listen. I shall leave Brooke the saloon. I
expect to live a good many more years, but if I do
not, she might find the same comfort in Horse Creek
that I have.

Brooke closed the diary and put it back in the drawer.
The reason for her inheritance was now clear. Somehow Mattie had known of her niece's suffering and had
sought, in some small way, to alleviate the pain.

The sun had completely set, leaving the bedroom dark
and cold. She brought water and tea up from the bar.
While the water heated, she began picking up the clothes
that had been scattered around the room.

Aunt Mattie's taste leaned toward the elegant and
expensive, if not modest, Brooke thought as she held
up an intriguing ornate silk dress. The deep green fabric was sewn in tiny tucks across a scandalously low-
cut bodice. The skirt cascaded down from the waist in
drapes and ruffles and bows, and Brooke secretly hoped

that she and her aunt still wore the same size. Shoes and
ribbons and delicate lace shawls were heaped together
in tangled piles on the floor. Between the garments
thrown around the bedroom and those in the closet,
there were enough clothes so that Mattie could have
gone two months without wearing the same dress twice.

Brooke carefully hung up the green silk gown, brushing
her hands against the cool fabric. None of her things was
half as fine, or a third as lovely.

She crossed to the fire and poured the water into a
cup. While her tea brewed, she sat in the rocker and
stared into the flames. There were so many questions
she longed to ask her aunt. The journal made it clear that
she had never forgotten her first love, nor had she ever
married. Will it be that way for me? Brooke wondered
as she thought about Dalton. What was it like to find
a love that could never be replaced? Certainly she had
recovered from Joe quickly enough.

Her mind traveled back to that horrible day three years
before. She still remembered the smell of the roses from
the garden. She'd been deciding which flowers would
decorate the house the following Saturday for their wedding reception. Joe had walked up the path, his normally
smiling face drawn into a frown.

"I must speak with you," he'd said in that banker's voice she'd always hated. "I want to call off the
wedding."

She remembered how her world had ground to a halt
and crashed, then continued to turn with everything all
bent and disarrayed.

"Why?" She'd barely been able to force the word past
her lips.

"There's someone else." He looked at his pocket watch,
polishing the crystal cover the way he always did when

he was nervous, then glanced back at her. His normally pale face was flushed, and he looked ashamed. "I've been seeing Polly Baker for several weeks now, and she's agreed to be my wife."

"Polly Baker? But she's so . . ." She'd been unable to continue speaking. Polly had always had her eye on Joe, but Brooke had never considered the other girl a threat. There had been whispers that Polly had ways of pleasing a man that an unmarried female shouldn't know, but Brooke knew that wasn't the reason Joe had chosen her. Polly wanted a man to be the center of her universe, and Joe wanted to be worshiped. Although Brooke had thought she'd loved him, in her eyes he didn't have many godlike qualities.

"I never meant to hurt you. I kept hoping my feelings for Polly would go away. But they haven't." He reached out to touch her, but she stepped back. "It wouldn't be fair to you, to either of us, to go through with the wedding. I'm sorry," he said. "I hope you can forgive me and . . . I'm sorry."

He'd walked away without looking back.

The days that had followed had been an endless parade of well-meaning but pitying friends and smug ill-wishers, culminating in the marriage of Joe and Polly.

There were few things a close-knit community enjoyed more than a scandal. And if all the participants continued to live in the same area, the story never died. After three years people had still referred to Brooke as "that poor girl Joe MacAllister practically left at the altar." Aunt Mattie's bequest had been her salvation.

A log broke in the fire and recalled her to the present. Her legs had grown stiff from being tucked under her in the rocking chair, and she stood up to stretch her muscles. A sword hung on the wall above the fireplace, and she went over and ran her fingers along the edge of the cool steel. A token of love and a token of war.

Did you find this blade a comfort, Aunt Mattie? she asked silently. But there was no answer. Just the snapping of the flames and the distant cry of some animal in the night. And yet the room contained a comforting essence, almost as if her aunt was pleased she was here.

Brooke slipped out of her dress and slid between the cotton sheets on the bed. The pillow was musty, but an exotic scent lingered, the faint perfume bringing to mind faraway places and people.

The morning would bring her an answer, she thought as her eyes drifted shut. A solution that would make Mattie proud of her.

"Mister? Mister?"

"What?" Dalton barely glanced at the young boy tugging on his sleeve.

"You Dalton Reed?"

"Raise you twenty." Dalton tossed the coin on the table and turned to face the child. "You've got no business being in this saloon, boy. Does your mama know where you are?"

The youngster smiled engagingly. "No, but I don't think you're goin' to tell her, are ya?"

"That all depends on why you're here."

"I got a letter. From a lady. She gave me a penny to deliver it." The boy handed him the note, then stuffed his hands in his trousers pockets, pleased with his day's work.

"You playing poker or minding the kid, Reed?"

Dalton glared at the man sitting at the opposite side of the table. "I'm in." Another chip joined the large pile in the center of the table. He turned back to the child. "Here's a dime for your trouble, son. Now get along before we both get thrown out."

Dalton clamped his cigar between his teeth and stared at his cards. One more nine would give him four of a kind, an unlikely but virtually unbeatable hand. He rubbed the note once for luck and nodded at the dealer. The brown-haired man tossed the card in a perfect arc, and it landed face up on the table. Nine red hearts gleamed in the afternoon light and Dalton raked in the pot.

Thank you, Brooke, he thought to himself and read her message. After hours of forcing his facial muscles into a carefully neutral expression, it felt awkward to frown, but the expression was involuntary. She wanted to meet him at the saloon, later that day. Leaving or staying, her news was bound to be bad.

He heard the piano music from the street. The gentle melody wasn't normal saloon fare, but it drew him in all the same. As he stepped inside, he realized that the windows were no longer boarded up and the sunlight spilled onto the freshly swept floor.

One of the small tables had been set with two glasses and a bottle of bourbon; a pot of flowers rested on the apron of the stage. Thick velvet drapes provided a perfect backdrop for the delicate blooms.

"Good afternoon, Dalton. Thank you so much for joining me."

Brooke rose from her seat at the piano. As the last note of music died, Dalton became aware of his heartbeat thundering in his ears. She must have raided her aunt's wardrobe, for Brooke was dressed like a saloon girl.

Her thick hair was piled high on her head, with a few artfully arranged curls brushing against her shoulders. A long-sleeved rose-colored gown clung to her breasts and waist, the lace-edged bodice revealing more of her gentle curves than it concealed. The center of the skirt cascaded to the floor, but the sides were caught up with bows and exposed more lace and ruffles.

He wanted her. His fists clenched and unclenched as he imagined the pleasure of ripping the gown apart and feasting his eyes on her creamy skin. No doubt her corset would slow things down a bit, but releasing the restrictive garment, lace by lace, would only heighten his pleasure.

"Dalton?"

Reluctantly he drew his gaze from her bodice and looked at her face. The almond-shaped eyes that had so entranced him with their laughter looked uncertain, almost afraid. The half smile on her lips reminded him of his promise to himself. There was to be nothing between them.

He raised one eyebrow. "You look lovely, but this isn't your normal style, is it?"

"I don't know what you're talking about." Brooke tilted her chin, but then betrayed her confident pose by tugging up on her bodice. "Won't you join me for a drink?"

She led the way to the table, without checking to see if he followed. Dalton hesitated. He knew what she was going to say, and he wasn't sure he could take the news. He should leave right now and never look back. But if Brooke stayed in Horse Creek, her life might be in danger. He had to persuade her to return east. He walked over to one of the chairs and held it out for her.

"You've decided to keep the saloon." Dalton took the opposite seat, shifting it to the right when his knee brushed hers.

She poured two drinks, but didn't touch her glass. "Yes. Last night I found my aunt's journal. She wanted to leave me this place so I could have something of my own. I can't sell it now."

Dalton drained his drink in one long swallow, then poured another. "And what do you know about running a business? Have you ever dealt a card game, ordered supplies, mixed a drink? What happens when one of your patrons gets out of hand and starts shooting up the place? Think you're up to bouncing out a drunk twice your size?" He leaned forward, across the tiny round table, until he was so close that he could smell her freshly washed hair. The scent enraged him, and he deepened his voice to a growl. "What if some high-spirited cowboy decides that your services come with the price of a drink? What are you going to do then, my little virgin miss?"

Two spots of vivid color appeared on her cheekbones, highlighting the pallor of her skin. She swallowed, the motion drawing his eyes to her bare throat. The long lines from her jaw to the lacy bodice of her dress were an invitation that no mortal man could ignore, and Dalton called upon a higher power for restraint.

"How would you stop *me*, right now?" he asked.

She wouldn't. He saw the response in the fiery green of her eyes. The silence in the room cracked as loud as thunder, while the bands of control that held him firmly in check began to snap, one by one.

"No." He hit the table with his fist, causing her to jump and look away. "All right, Miss Tyler. You said you wanted to talk to me. You better explain yourself quickly before I do something we'll both have cause to regret."

She gazed at him for a moment, her expression blank, as if she had forgotten the reason for his visit. "I, um . . . I've decided to keep the saloon." She held up her hand when he started to interrupt. "I'm aware of my limitations. I have a head for figures, but I don't know anything about the business. Therefore I'd like to make you an offer. If you'll stay for six months and teach me everything I need to know, I'll give you two-thirds of the profits accrued during that time."

He tried to stare her down, but she continued to meet his gaze, her green eyes unflinching. She cleared her throat. "Do we have a deal?"

Chapter 7

"You'll stay, even if I don't agree to help you."

Brooke knew he wasn't asking a question but she answered all the same. "Yes, of course. I'm not afraid."

Dalton looked torn between frustration and amusement. "You're very stubborn."

"Yes."

"And foolish."

"Perhaps."

He stood up and walked to the far side of the saloon. His long strides were restless, his body moving for motion's sake rather than with the need to be somewhere else. As always, he took her breath away.

She'd sought to combat her incapacitating reaction by wearing one of Mattie's dresses. The rose silk had given her confidence, even if the bodice dipped so low that she was afraid to take a deep breath for fear of tumbling out the front. But the knowledge that she looked her best hadn't neutralized Dalton's effect on her. The raw hunger she'd seen etched in his face had only weakened her further. If she had not read her aunt's journal, she would have scurried from the room and abandoned her plan to run the saloon.

"I won't marry you."

His words cut through her, piercing her heart. Only pride deflected the fatal thrust. She took a slow breath to steady her voice. "I don't recall asking you to."

He spoke from the bar, his back to her, their eyes meeting in the backbar mirror. "Just so we understand each another."

Her neck ached from holding her head at a haughty angle. "Then you agree to my offer?"

"Yes."

Relief made her weak. Who would have thought that he'd agree? When she'd awakened with the idea of keeping the saloon, she hadn't dared to hope that Dalton would help her. She wanted to believe he was doing it for reasons other than money, but one glance at his cold dark eyes informed her that attributing his actions to any other motive would be foolish. And she was no fool.

"Well, there's much to be done. I must see the lawyer and inform him of my decision." She stood up and glanced around. "The rooms must be cleaned and supplies ordered."

He turned to face her. "Time enough for that tomorrow; it's almost four. I told you not to be on the streets after dark." He looked so serious, his expression as dark as his black jacket.

"Whatever you think is best," she murmured as she walked to the piano and picked up her reticule and one of Mattie's heavy shawls. "I'll visit my lawyer in the morning, then meet you here. I'd like to return to my hotel now, unless you have any other questions?"

Dalton crossed to the door. "You're wearing that dress out?"

She glanced down at the gown, then back at him. "Yes. Why?"

His lips moved, but no sound emerged. Finally he coughed. "Nothing. You look lovely. I imagine your server at dinner tonight will be most attentive."

Brooke brushed past him and out the door. She would have asked him to clarify his statement, but Dalton was laughing too hard to be capable of rational speech.

"Miss Tyler."

Arthur Franklin breathed her name as if in prayer, and Brooke had to fight back the urge to slap him. However eligible Mrs. Gilmore might proclaim him to be, Brooke had always found fawning to be an irritation.

"Mr. Franklin," she said crisply. "Is Mr. Gannen available this morning?"

"I believe so. I'll tell him that you wish to speak . . ." Arthur's voice trailed off and she noticed that his eyes seemed fixed on her chest.

She had appropriated several of Mattie's gowns for her own use. One of her earliest memories of her aunt was a Christmas years before. Brooke had received a length of cloth and Mattie several yards of ribbon. Each had wanted what the other received. That night, right before Mattie left, they'd traded presents. After that, when her aunt had visited, there had always been a flurry of exchanges. Despite the difference in their ages, their tastes had complemented each other. Now, with Mattie gone, Brooke drew comfort from wearing her clothes, even though she was sure she'd never get used to the plunging necklines.

Arthur continued to stare at her exposed skin.

"Is something wrong?" she asked.

"I . . . ah . . . no, Miss Tyler." He cleared his throat and backed up toward the door, bumping into his chair, sending it tumbling to the floor. After righting it, he gave her a tight smile and disappeared through the lawyer's door.

A minute later Edward Gannen appeared and ushered her into his office. Brooke brushed past Arthur without meeting his eyes. Once seated, she shook her head at the offer of refreshments. "Mr. Gannen, I've decided to keep the saloon."

The white-haired gentleman stared at her, his expression unreadable. "Are you sure you want to do that, Miss Tyler?" He took his seat behind the desk.

She nodded.

"Then I'll inform Mr. Prattly that you won't be selling." He leaned back in his leather chair and folded his arms across his chest. "May I ask what changed your mind?"

"Aunt Mattie."

He raised an eyebrow. "How? A visitation perhaps?"

He looked perfectly serious, but she saw the humor sparkling in his blue eyes. "Not exactly, Mr. Gannen. I found her journal, and in it she explained why she left me the saloon. In a way, she was hoping to provide me with security and a place to call my own. I can't turn my back on her generosity." She shrugged. "I have nothing waiting for me back east."

"May I call you Brooke?"

She nodded.

"Brooke, you have no experience in business. You freely admitted that to me. Forgive me for saying so, but a refined young woman such as you will find it very difficult to run a saloon." He leaned forward, resting his hands on the desk. Concern threaded through his voice and wrapped itself around the words. "Have you thought this through?"

"I've hired someone to show me the ropes, so to speak. He's a gambler by trade."

Edward looked at her exactly the way her father had

when her first beau came calling. "And what do you know about this man, my dear? He may be a criminal, or worse. He may try to rob you or take advantage of you . . . ahem . . . physically."

"Mr. Gannen, I appreciate your interest in my welfare, but Dalton Reed has proven himself a gentleman on more than one occasion. I trust him implicitly."

Edward toyed with the letter opener on the desk. "I knew Mattie Frost quite well, but I never did agree with her about the will." He smiled at her. "May I give you some advice, Brooke?"

"Of course."

"This town is quite small, and it is the women who determine who is socially accepted. It can be lonely outside that circle. If you must run a saloon, I suggest you find a way to appease them. You have spent your entire life in the company of good people. I doubt that you would enjoy mingling with the riffraff of Horse Creek."

He was right, she thought. But how did one make a saloon acceptable? Somehow the idea of holding a ladies' night didn't seem appropriate. "I'll give your suggestion some thought, Mr. Gannen. And I want to thank you for your advice and for caring." She smiled at the older man and rose from her seat.

"The saloon will be operating in a few days. May I expect you for the opening?"

"Of course. And, Brooke . . . ?"

She stopped at the door and turned back to face him. "Yes?"

"I remember your aunt wearing that dress. She was a handsome woman, but you possess a radiance that I haven't seen in many years."

"Mr. Gannen, you are a shameless flatterer. Now I

know why my aunt wrote so fondly of you in her journal." Her smile grew wide as she watched the lawyer blush. "Good day, sir."

Brooke pulled the door closed and stepped into the outer office, only to bump into Arthur Franklin.

"Miss Tyler."

He put his hand on her arm, as if to steady her. His touch was neither pleasant nor distasteful, but she moved away, not wanting to give him any encouragement.

"Will you be staying in Horse Creek?"

She looked up at the young man, but he stared at a point somewhere over her left shoulder. If only she hadn't said that he might call on her, she thought. But this wasn't the first time she'd taken pity on someone, only to regret it later.

"Yes, Mr. Franklin. I've decided to keep the saloon." Perhaps that announcement would discourage him.

He swallowed, his Adam's apple bobbing like a bar of soap in a tub on washday. "Would you care to go for a drive with me on Sunday?"

Even though she wasn't the least bit tempted by his invitation, an outright refusal would have been rude . . . and foolish. Edward Gannen's advice about finding a common ground with the women in town remained in the front of her mind. If she failed to appease those who made the rules, she would be very much alone. And despite Dalton's occasional lapses into passion, he'd made it painfully clear that he wasn't interested in any type of permanent relationship. How had her life gotten so muddled?

"I'm afraid I'll be quite busy this Sunday, Mr. Franklin. Perhaps I could accept your kind invitation another day?"

"Oh, yes, Miss Tyler. I'm sure we'll run into each

other from time to time." He fairly beamed with anticipation.

Invite him to the opening, an evil voice whispered in her ear. Brooke smiled. If Arthur was as respectable as Mrs. Gilmore claimed, he'd probably die of apoplexy if he saw her in the saloon.

"Good-bye, Mr. Franklin," she said, then left the lawyer's office. It was almost noon. She hurried toward the saloon, eager to see Dalton again.

"Excuse me, sir. We're looking for the new owners."

Dalton stood up from behind the bar where he had been sorting bottles and looked at the couple standing in the doorway of the saloon. They were an odd pair, both with wide hazel eyes and light brown hair liberally streaked with gray. He might have taken them for brother and sister if not for the differences in their forms. The woman's cheekbones were set high in her pale face and she was tall and quite thin. The man barely came to her shoulder. He had a face like a chipmunk, with pudgy cheeks and a bushy mustache. The bright colors and stylish cut of their clothes seemed out of place in the small town of Horse Creek.

"You might say I'm running this place," Dalton said, stepping around the long wooden bar and rolling down the sleeves of his shirt. "Name's Dalton Reed. How can I help you?"

The man stepped forward. "I'm Caleb Barns, and this is my wife Elizabeth. We used to work for Mattie, till she passed on." He brushed his fingers against the worn brown hat he was holding. "We'd like our old jobs back and maybe our room. If that's possible?"

His request was music to Dalton's ears. He'd been hoping the former employees would get wind of the saloon opening up. He'd gathered enough information from around town to know that Mattie Frost had run a fair establishment and had treated her help well. Without some assistance, he and Brooke didn't have a prayer of making the business work. Despite her claims to the contrary, he was sure she was going to be more hindrance than help.

Dalton slipped into his black jacket. "What were your positions here?"

Elizabeth stepped toward the piano and grinned. "I played that beast over there, just for music or to accompany the girls when they danced. I also cooked for Mattie and the help, and oversaw the cleaning and laundry. Caleb here, he tends bar. The man knows every drink ever invented, and some that ought not to be served to God-fearing people."

"Elizabeth, mind your tongue." Caleb swatted his wife playfully on the rump, but looked pleased with her praise, all the same.

Dalton found himself smiling with them. "I don't see any reason you can't have your old positions back, but we're all new to each other. Let's see how it works out for, say, three weeks. That'll give us time to take each other's measure."

Caleb nodded. "Sounds like a right sensible plan." They shook hands. "Now, about our room upstairs?"

"I can't make any promises there. Brooke Tyler is the owner. I imagine she'll be moving into the saloon. I expect her any time now."

Elizabeth placed her cape and bag on the piano stool. "While we wait, I'll help you clean up. This place is as dirty as a hen house."

In the next hour the saloon began to take shape. Ned, a gangly freckle-faced adolescent, showed up to reclaim his job as the stock boy. While Elizabeth cleaned and polished the windows, Dalton and Caleb took inventory and made a list of supplies to be ordered. Dalton had just checked his watch for the third time in ten minutes when the saloon's door opened.

"About time you decided to show up, Brooke. You can't expect—" He drew in a quick breath and stared at the three women standing in the doorway. None of them was the green-eyed innocent who was tormenting his life, but he felt a grin stretch across his face all the same. He'd wondered if they'd return.

"Ladies."

The woman in front stepped forward. She was of medium height with strawberry-blond hair and a snug-fitting low-cut yellow dress that left very little to the imagination. She moved with a swaying walk, kicking out the front of her skirt with each step.

"You must be Dalton," she said, her voice low and husky. When she reached the bar, she leaned forward, inviting him to look upon her cleavage.

Dalton allowed himself a moment of indulgence before returning his gaze to her face. As she batted her lashes, he saw that she had outlined her eyes with a thin dark line and her cupid's-bow mouth was stained redder than a perfect midsummer strawberry.

"I'm Lily," she said with a wink. "And these two girls are Rose and Violet." The two brunettes by the door grinned coquettishly and waggled their fingers in greeting. "We've come about our jobs. We've been working cross town, but the conditions aren't what we're used to. Mattie knew how to treat us girls. You look like you might be of the same mind."

Lily's brown eyes promised him untold delights if he confirmed her statement. But Dalton ignored the invitation; he couldn't wait to see the look on Brooke's face when she met "the girls."

"I don't think the owner has any plans to hire dancing girls, Lily," he said truthfully. The grin he was holding back caused his jaw muscles to ache, and he cleared his throat as he wondered when he'd last had this much trouble trying to keep a straight face.

"Now, Dalton, of course you need us. Why, we bring in half the men in this town. They just love to see us up on that stage." She picked up a bottle of whiskey from the bar, took his arm, and led him over to one of the tables, which he had moved to the middle of the room. After pushing him into a chair, she sat on his knee. "Now, what do I have to say to convince you, honey?"

He was sure that her act had worked on better men than he was. Despite the feel of her knee brushing against his inner thigh and her fingers tracing the buttons on his vest, he could feel the laughter building in his chest. "Lily, you've got this all wrong."

Elizabeth came into the room, carrying a fresh bucket of soapy water. When she saw Lily, she came to a halt, splashing the floor with water and suds. "Child, what are you doing to that defenseless man?"

"That's what I'd like to know."

Dalton recognized Brooke's voice and tried to stand up, but Lily seemed to sense his intent and clung to him tenaciously with her hands and legs. He managed to rise, but caught his foot in her skirt and lost his balance. He stepped back, hit the chair, then fell across the table, splintering it and taking Lily to the floor with him. Elizabeth leapt forward to offer assistance, but succeeded only in drenching him and Lily with the soapy water. The dancer's screams mingled with Elizabeth's apologies, but the part of the room where Brooke was standing remained coldly silent.

As he rubbed the water out of his stinging eyes, Dalton wondered why he couldn't have spent the summer in New Orleans. "Brooke—"

"I'd love to hear your explanation, but first I think you'd better get out of those wet clothes. And your lady friend as well."

"She's not my—"

"I assure you—"

He and Lily spoke at the same time. The saloon girl glared at him, then used his shoulder to push herself to her feet. With both hands, she pulled her wet hair out of her face, then straightened her dress.

"I am an entertainer, and Dalton is my employer, not that it's any of your business." Her eyes narrowed. "You don't look like a dancer. What do you want here?"

Dalton groaned when he saw Brooke's lips thin with anger. She was half a head shorter and several pounds lighter than Lily, but he knew she wouldn't hesitate to defend herself and her property, regardless of the odds.

He struggled to his feet. "Brooke, don't be hasty."

She glared at him. "Hasty? Why you . . ."

Just then, Caleb made a belated appearance in the saloon, his arms laden with bottles from the storeroom. He took one look at the situation and started to back out of the room. But Elizabeth had spotted him. "Caleb, show Dalton to his room so he can get out of his wet things. Lily, you come with me. You can wear one of my dresses until yours dries."

Brooke stood rooted to the floor watching Dalton and that brown-eyed hussy being led away. His room? Who had given him a room in her saloon? And who were those other people? And why did that woman have clothes here? "Would someone please tell me what's going on?" she said aloud.

"It's really very simple."

Brooke jumped, having forgotten the two women she had brushed past when she'd entered the room. "And who are you?" she asked as she turned around.

"I'm Violet, and this is Rose." The girl who spoke had blue-black hair that gleamed in the morning light. Her companion was a little shorter, and her hair was a medium brown. Their dresses were simply styled, yet cut so low that Brooke felt positively demure by comparison.

Violet smiled tentatively. "We used to work for Mattie, as dancers. We wanted to get our old jobs back, but Lily felt that asking wouldn't be good enough. She was trying to persuade Dalton to hire us all." Violet glanced at the wet floor and the broken table. "I don't think her plan worked."

"I never liked it from the beginning," Rose said. "But Lily needs to be showing off all the time. Besides, we're desperate. We all hated having to leave after Mattie died. She was the best. But the sheriff and her lawyer wouldn't let us keep this place open."

Brooke sat in the chair that Dalton had vacated. "Dancing girls?" she asked weakly. "Do you do anything . . . else?"

"Oh, no." Violet shook her head until three ringlets sprang free and bounced against her shoulder. "We never entertained upstairs. Mattie ran a decent place." Her eyes got very wide. "If they plan to provide the other type of entertainment here, I'm afraid we won't be wanting our jobs back. Isn't that right, Rose?"

"That's right." Rose nodded emphatically and pulled on Violet's arm. "We better be going. You know how

Mr. Hadley hates it when we're late."

"Wait!" Brooke leapt from her chair and ran to the two women. "I'm not going to ask any of you to, ah, do anything you don't want to do." She smiled, suddenly self-conscious. "This is only the third time I've been in a saloon, and several things weren't clear to me. If Mattie had dancing girls, I guess I can, too."

Violet placed her hands on her hips. "Well, who are you? I thought Dalton was in charge. Just 'cause you got some claim on him don't mean he's going to do everything you tell him to. Men get stubborn that way. We're not going to give notice at Hadley's till Dalton says we're hired."

Brooke grinned. Part of her was embarrassed that they would think she was some . . . some plaything of Dalton's, but another part of her was pleased to be in charge. After living for twenty-two years as the only girl in a family of boys, being the boss gave her a heady feeling.

She walked to the partition at the back of the room and held open the door to the gaming room. "Ladies, my name is Brooke Tyler. Mattie Frost was my aunt, and she left this saloon to me." She gestured toward the hallway beyond the gambling salon. "If you'd care to step into my office, we can negotiate your salaries."

Dalton clutched the blanket around his waist as he paced in front of the fire. The silence from the room below was more ominous than screaming would have been. Who knew what Brooke was doing to the dancers or, worse, what they were doing to her? He'd suspected that at least a couple of the women would come to talk to the new owner. He cursed himself for not warning Brooke about them. He'd wanted to see the look on her face when she was confronted by what she would no doubt consider fallen women.

Hell of a price to pay for a laugh, he thought. Brooke was furious, the saloon wouldn't have any dancers, and he was stuck upstairs wearing some flea-bitten blanket.

But what bothered him more than the anger was the hurt he'd seen in Brooke's green eyes. By agreeing to run her saloon, he'd become a part of her life, if only for a short time. Even though he would never claim her as his own, he cared for her enough not to flaunt other women in her face. He'd shamed her, and that betrayal left a bitter taste in his mouth.

"Clothes don't dry any faster with you wearing a path in the floor like that." Elizabeth walked into the room and set a tray on the table next to the fire. "I brought you some hot tea and biscuits." She felt the clothes hanging on the screen. "You should be able to get dressed in a few minutes. But don't worry. Your little friend's doing just fine with Rose and Violet."

He shot her a questioning glance. "How did you know?"

She smiled. "I got eyes. I saw the way you looked at her and how angry she was. Oh, my, if she'd had a blade in her hand she would have sliced you open from belly to jaw, for sure."

He choked on his tea. "That's very colorful, Elizabeth, thank you. But it's not what you think. Brooke's the owner of the saloon. I'm just an employee."

"But I thought you said you were running the place."

"I am, but I'm running it for her. She's Mattie's niece."

Elizabeth sat in the chair next to the fire and smoothed her apron over her lap. "Imagine that. Why, Mattie used to talk about that girl all the time. Sometimes she'd read parts of her letters aloud to me, at breakfast." She glanced up at him. "She's from a fine family back east, isn't she? What's she doing in Horse Creek?"

The older woman's worn face reminded him of his grandmother in Virginia. Elizabeth's turn of phrase and big heart were straight out of the farm belt, and she made him feel like a boy again. "You're a fine woman, Elizabeth Barns, and I'll feel better knowing you're here to look after Brooke."

She brushed his compliment aside with a wave of her hand. "You gamblers are all slick-talking devils. I just won't pay you no mind." She stood up and walked to the door. "Lily's things are probably dry by now. I better help her dress so she can go make her apologies to her new employer." She shook her head unbelievingly. "Mattie's niece. Imagine that."

Dalton stared into the fire long after Elizabeth had left. Memories of his family rose up from the flames to haunt him. If he recalled only the simple times of his youth, he was safe. Games played with his brother, trips taken with his father, the warmth of his mother's embrace—those memories brought a smile to his lips. But the later recollections were stained with shame and anger and desolation. And the common thread that held all the dark emotions together was the knowledge that he could never return home.

A faint sound drifted up through the floorboards. He dropped the blanket on the floor and reached for his still-damp clothes as he realized that Lily was probably making her way downstairs to confront Brooke.

He had barely finished tucking his shirt into his trousers, when he burst into the saloon. But the main room was empty; only the damp floor and the broken table attested to the earlier disaster. He looked around as if he might find the women hiding in a corner, then turned and headed toward Brooke's office.

The dancing girls met him halfway down the hall. Their smiling faces gave him reason to hope everything had gone well.

"Good-bye, Dalton," the two brunettes said in unison.

He nodded.

"Sorry about the mix-up," Lily said as she sashayed down the narrow corridor. "See ya on Saturday." She winked as she passed him.

He straightened his tie and walked into the office.

Brooke was bent over the desk, reviewing a page covered with numbers. The glow from the lamp highlighted her ringlets, turning the soft brown curls into a warm reddish gold. Her chin cast a shadow across her chest, accenting the delicate hollow between her breasts. His mouth grew dry as he imagined the taste of that sweet valley. In the space of a second and without any effort, she had rendered him hot with wanting. He tried to picture what she could accomplish if she set her mind to arousing him, but his groin hardened painfully at the prospect. He sank into the chair across from her desk.

She looked up, startled. "I didn't hear you come in. Have the girls left?"

He nodded.

She smiled. "Did you realize they were all named after flowers? Lily told me Mattie picked out their names so that they all matched the theme of the saloon. Quite clever, I think." She looked back at the ledger as a blush stole up her cheeks. The flush of color entranced him. "Lily and Elizabeth explained what happened earlier. I'm sorry I got angry."

"You had every right to be, Brooke. I should have told you about the dancing girls."

She stared at him. "You knew? But how?"

He laughed. "What did you think the stage was for?"

"I never gave it any thought." She smiled, the gentle curve of her lips more erotic than Lily's most practiced pout. "I've given Elizabeth and Caleb their old room back. I'll be taking Mattie's room."

She stood up and made a great show of closing the ledger and storing it on the bookshelf behind the desk. Her spine was stiff. At first he thought she was still angry, but when she continued to speak without facing him, he realized she was embarrassed.

"There's a third bedroom upstairs. It's yours if you'd like. I imagine it would be convenient for you to stay here, and I, um, wouldn't expect you to pay rent or anything. The fact that Caleb and Elizabeth sleep on the same floor should prevent any talk in town."

She sat back at her desk, still avoiding his eyes. "Was there anything else you wished to discuss?"

"You're planning to run a saloon, and you're worried that people will talk because there isn't a chaperon upstairs?" He leaned forward and brushed his index finger across her cheek. The brief contact was a spark that set off a fire in his heart and his groin. "You're quite a woman, Brooke Tyler."

"Miss Tyler?"

Brooke looked up from the table she was polishing. She was alone in the room; everyone else had gone into the kitchen for the midday meal.

Standing in the doorway was a tall, dark-haired woman. Although they'd never been formally introduced, she recognized the town's leading citizen. Edna Prattly was

the last person she'd ever expected to see standing inside
a gambling establishment. Brooke wanted to ask about
William and his mother and the fishing hole, but her
guest didn't look especially approachable.

"Yes, I'm Brooke Tyler. Mrs. Prattly?" Brooke brushed
her hands against her skirt and motioned for the other
woman to take a seat.

"I prefer to stand, thank you." Her cultivated speech
was accompanied by a polite smile that didn't reach
her eyes.

If she wouldn't sit down, chances were she wouldn't
accept the offer of refreshment either. "What can I do
for you?"

Mrs. Prattly looked around the room, her thin mouth
drawn into a straight line. "I've come to make you an
offer for the saloon."

Brooke sank into the closest chair. "Excuse me?" She
couldn't have heard her correctly.

"I'd like to buy your establishment. Name your price."

Why did everyone in the Prattly family want to purchase her business? "It's not for sale."

The older woman set her reticule and gloves on the
table. "Everything is for sale, Miss Tyler. Or haven't you
learned that yet?"

"Mr. Prattly has already made me an offer. I'll tell you
what I plan to tell him. I'm not selling—at any price. I
know he wants to build a big store, but I—"

"That man and his dream." Mrs. Prattly sighed heavily
and pulled out a chair. She sat down without seeming to
realize what she was doing, then looked at Brooke. "This
isn't about what Samuel wants. I don't intend to give
him the land. I simply need this saloon torn down and
every stick of wood carted away until all that remains
is dirt." There was an edge of bitterness in her voice

that had nothing to do with anger.

Tear the building down? She couldn't be serious. "I don't understand."

"You don't need to." Mrs. Prattly studied her. "I mean to have my way, Miss Tyler. You can't stop me."

Was this all a very bad joke? But Edna Prattly looked completely serious. Brooke kept remembering the kindness she'd seen in the other woman's face when she'd spoken with William. Hadn't she offered to send the doctor to the boy's mother . . . and at her own expense? Were there two Mrs. Prattlys?

"Are you threatening me?" Brooke asked.

"Hardly. Do I look like the sort of person who would return with a gun and shoot the place up?"

For the first time since walking in, Edna Prattly smiled. Instinctively, Brooke felt herself drawn to the woman. "No, of course not. But why—"

"Don't doubt my resolve, Miss Tyler. And be warned. One way or the other, the Garden Saloon must go."

She stood quickly and gathered her possessions. Without a backward glance, she swept from the room.

Brooke stared at the front door for several minutes. "Well, I never . . ." She rose and stood with her hands on her hips. "That was the most irritating, maddening . . . Oh!" After throwing the dustcloth on the table, she stomped into the kitchen.

Elizabeth looked up from the stove and smiled. "The menfolk are all done eatin'. You hungry yet?"

"No." Brooke walked to the square table and pulled out a chair, then kicked the bottom rung. "Do you know what that woman just told me? She announced—quite politely, I might add—that she intends to buy the saloon. And if I don't sell, she's going to shut me down."

"You're not makin' sense. What woman?" Elizabeth

ladled out a bowl of stew and stuck a couple of pieces
of bread on a plate. "Sit down, child. You're more het
up than a chicken after a spring rain. Eat this. Then tell
me what happened."

"I'm not hungry." But she plopped down on the seat
and picked up a spoon. "I saw her being nice to a boy
in town. His mother was sick or something. And now
this. I don't understand anything at all." She looked up
at Elizabeth. "What do you know about Edna Prattly? Is
she dangerous?"

"No, child. But she's . . . different." She poured a cup
of coffee and sat down opposite Brooke. "I knew Edna
even before she married Samuel. She weren't a pretty
girl. Not plain, exactly, but nothin' special. The family
had money, though, and that made her popular enough.
The first time she saw Samuel, she set her cap for him.
Didn't care a lick that he was the handsomest boy in the
whole territory. Didn't even seem to mind that he told
everyone he was marryin' her for her money."

The older woman sighed and sipped her drink. "Samuel
was always full of them dreams of his. Dreams cost
money, and that was somethin' Edna had plenty of. So
they got hitched. Samuel got his cattle and horses, and
Edna . . . well, I'm not sure what she got."

Brooke propped her elbows on the table. "She loves
him? And he doesn't care about her?"

Hazel eyes met hers. "That about sums it up."

"How sad." The story tugged at Brooke's heartstrings.
Caring about someone who didn't care back was something she was familiar with.

"Don't waste too much time on pity. If Edna Prattly
wants to get rid of you, or the saloon, there ain't many
people to tell her otherwise."

"There's something I don't understand. If she loves

her husband so much, why did she tell me she doesn't intend to give him the land?"

"I can't rightly say." Elizabeth leaned forward. "But be warned. Edna Prattly always gets everything she wants."

"You're wrong, Elizabeth. She never got her husband to love her."

Chapter 8

"I'm simply asking you to explain the difference between Jamaica rum and Santa Cruz rum, Dalton. After two or three drinks, I suspect no one can tell one from the other. I don't see the point of stocking all these brands."

Dalton sighed. Although Brooke was catching on much more quickly than he had expected, she still had trouble understanding that bars had to cater to a variety of tastes. The needs of the patrons couldn't be satisfied by a few kegs of beer and a bottle or two of whiskey. And if that wasn't enough, she had taken to wearing Mattie's dresses. For the past couple of weeks, he'd had to explain everything from the intricacies of the pneumatic foot pump behind the bar to the proper glass used when serving a brandy fizz, all the while trying to ignore plunging necklines and exposed shoulders. He couldn't take much more.

"Would you use maple syrup in a recipe calling for molasses?" he asked.

"Of course not."

He leaned over her desk until their noses nearly touched. "Then order both rums."

He was so close that Brooke could see the flecks of amber and chocolate brown that gave his eyes their glowing color. His breath fanned her face, and she wanted to lean forward the last inch that separated her lips from the promise waiting on his. But he withdrew and resumed his seat.

"We need to find a farmer to supply us with dairy products," he said.

She blinked at the sudden change in subject. Her thoughts had definitely not been on bar supplies. "For what?"

"We need fresh eggs and cream delivered daily. Eggs are used in several drinks, mostly flips, and cream has countless uses. We'll also need ice, syrups, spices, and sugar."

She bit back a groan. "Tell Caleb to make up a list. I'll have the store in town start an account for us. I think one of Ned's relatives has a farm nearby, so talk to him about the eggs and cream. Anything else?"

Dalton leaned back in his chair. The April morning was unseasonably warm, and he'd taken off his coat and rolled up the sleeves of his white shirt. A sprinkling of dark hair covered his forearms, and she watched the muscles in his arms bulge and retract with each movement of his hands.

"Yes, I do have one or two other things."

He sounded serious; the playful teasing of a few moments before had disappeared, leaving his emotions hidden behind a blank stare. "Do you have enough money? Between the cleaning and the stocking, not to mention new costumes for the girls . . ." He cleared his throat. "I don't want you to use up your whole inheritance. If the business doesn't make it, you'll need something to live on."

A week ago his neutral expression might have frightened her, but Brooke was beginning to understand her gambler. While his eyes and lips gave nothing away, his voice was filled with concern. He was worried about what might happen to her. Perhaps he cared for her just a little. Her heart skipped a beat at the thought.

She leaned forward over the desk and smiled. "Thanks for asking, but Mattie left me more money than I could ever have imagined. If I'd known that a saloon was so profitable, I would have come west years ago."

"Bold talk for someone who hasn't even served a single customer. You may change your tune in a week or so when your ears are ringing from the noise and your eyes are burning from the cigar smoke and your—"

"Stop." She held up her hand. "I get the idea. But it's too late to scare me off."

He folded his arms across his chest. "Elizabeth told me you plan to close the saloon on Wednesday afternoons and Sundays? Do you want to explain that?"

"Sunday we all go to church."

"All of us?"

The growl in his voice made her nervous, but she didn't back down. "Yes. I'll have to live in this town long after you've gone. The least you can do is to make my adjustment easier."

"I don't think a little churchgoing will be enough to change the minds of any of the good folks here."

"I know. Wednesday afternoon is my ace in the hole."

He raised his eyebrows. "Your what? Have you been taking lessons at the other saloons behind my back?"

"Brooke." Elizabeth stepped into the office; her hazel eyes fairly blazed with anger. "That woman is here, hovering out in front as if she'll damn her soul just by crossing the threshold. I don't like her or her kind and I don't take to being scorned by a woman wearing an ugly hat."

"Who is it, Elizabeth?" Brooke asked. She glared at Dalton as he threatened to erupt into laughter.

"That Mrs. Gilmore, the old busybody. Says she knows you."

Dalton coughed. "You're in trouble now, Brooke."

She rose from her chair and touched her hand to her head, checking that her hair was in place. "Nonsense. I was hoping she'd call. She's exactly the person I need to help me with my plan. Elizabeth, would you prepare some tea and a few slices of that wonderful cake you made this morning?"

"Humph." The older woman stalked off, muttering as she went. "Don't see no reason to be feeding the likes of her. If we had fewer of *them* around, the world would be a better place, if you ask me. In fact . . ." The rest of her comments were lost when she slammed the kitchen door behind her.

He stood up. "I can't wait to hear this."

"You're not going to hear anything. Now go upstairs or into the gambling parlor or wherever, but stay out of my way."

When he continued to stand beside her desk, she put her hand on his chest and gave him a gentle shove. "Get out of here."

"I'm going."

She stood in the doorway until he walked up the stairs, each step slower than the one before. "And don't listen at the stairwell," she called after him. "Morally upright people don't eavesdrop."

His mumbled complaints faded away. Brooke drew in a deep breath for courage and headed for the front of the building.

"Mrs. Gilmore, how good of you to call. Won't you join me for tea?" Brooke pulled the slight woman into the saloon and seated her at one of the small tables. "I've been meaning to stop by to visit, but I've been so busy lately. How are you?"

"Brooke," Mrs. Gilmore began as if she could barely catch her breath, "I came because I'm concerned about you. What are you doing here in a . . . a . . . this place?" Her dress was the lightest shade of gray and the hat resting at a perky angle was a bizarre combination of yellow flowers and pale straw. One bud rested close to her left ear as though constantly whispering secrets. "I heard that you were planning to run this business, and I came to talk some sense into you."

She was perched on the edge of her chair, poised for flight at the slightest provocation. She reminded Brooke of a sparrow in a houseful of cats.

"Don't worry about me, Mrs. Gilmore. I'm fine. Aunt Mattie has left me well provided for. I'll be reopening the saloon soon."

"I . . . I . . . My dear, have you taken leave of your senses? You'll be shunned by everyone." Her entire being quivered with indignation, from the top of her hat to the toes of her sensible shoes. "It's him, isn't it? He's led you astray."

"Who?"

Mrs. Gilmore glanced over her shoulder, then leaned forward and whispered, "That gambler fellow. I saw him watching you on the train. He took a fancy to you, and now you're ruined."

Brooke took the other woman's hand in hers. "No one's ruined. I made this decision all on my own."

The older woman pulled her hand back and sat up straighter in her chair, her dark birdlike eyes flashing. "If you truly won't change your mind and that's your final decision, there's nothing I can say, except good-bye. I'll miss you, but I'm sure you'll understand that I can't continue our acquaintance."

"But, Mrs. Gilmore." Brooke lowered her eyes demurely and sent up a quick prayer. Her plan just *had* to work. "I'd hate to think of us not being friends. You were so kind on the train, and then inviting me to dinner."

"Thank you, dear. But this"—she indicated the bar and shuddered—"isn't right. No lady would ever run a saloon."

"Why?"

"Excuse me?"

"Why can't a lady run a saloon?"

"Because . . . That is to say . . ." Mrs. Gilmore opened her mouth twice more, as though words failed her. "It's simply not done," she said finally.

"Oh." Brooke sighed. "It was my aunt's dying wish that I make a place for myself here." She mentally crossed her fingers. The journal had mentioned Mattie's desire for her to find comfort in Horse Creek. That was almost a dying wish.

"I didn't know that," Mrs. Gilmore said. "Were the two of you close?"

"Yes."

The older woman seemed to be considering the new information. Before she could state her conclusion, Elizabeth came into the room and set her tray on the next table. The smell of tea and fresh-baked cake filled the air.

"Could you at least stay for one cup?" Brooke asked as she poured the rich liquid.

"Well, I really shouldn't," Mrs. Gilmore said, sniffing the air. "But I suppose no real harm would come to me. It's unlikely that any of my friends will walk by."

Brooke leaned forward and whispered, "I won't say a word."

While they chatted about various goings-on in town, Mrs. Gilmore darted surreptitious glances around the room. She was probably gathering enough information to keep her gossiping for a year, Brooke thought. She encouraged the other woman to keep talking and waited for the right moment to play her ace.

" . . . so few things to keep one occupied in a small town, don't you agree, Brooke?"

"Yes, I do." She set her cup on the table and folded her hands in her lap. "In fact, I've been giving that some thought. What I miss most about Philadelphia is the lending library."

"You're so right. We've tried to establish one in town, but the men don't see the need." She touched Brooke's arm. "They are more interested in outdoor activities, but a lady needs something refined to occupy her time."

"I've arranged for some books to be sent to me, about thirty titles to start with, then ten or so each month. But now that I think about it, it wouldn't be neighborly to keep them to myself. Perhaps I could arrange for the ladies in town to borrow the books informally." She sipped her tea, trying not to smile.

Mrs. Gilmore clapped her hands together. "A literary society! I've heard about the ones in New York and Boston. Imagine, the Horse Creek Literary Society! But where would we meet?"

Brooke took a deep breath. "Perhaps at the school? No, that won't work. The children use the building during the day. Is there a restaurant in town that would be agreeable? Or we could meet here. I plan to close the saloon on Wednesday afternoons anyway." She looked around the room. "I could hang a drapery to cover the bar, and we could have sandwiches and cake. What do you think?"

Watching Mrs. Gilmore wrestle with her conscience was almost painful. No doubt the older woman had figured out that accepting the saloon as a meeting place was a condition of gaining access to the books.

Mattie's diary had mentioned that boredom was the real enemy in the West, especially in the winter when the snow kept people housebound for days. She was gambling that Mrs. Gilmore's habit of gossiping would spread the word and that the books were enough of an enticement to draw in the townswomen. Even if only a few came to the meetings, she'd have a chance to get to know people.

The older woman tilted her head as if she were listening to the advice of the flower on her hat. "I'll mention it to some of my friends," she said after a long moment. "And I'll report back to you on Sunday." She stood up and fixed her eyes on Brooke. "You are planning to go to church, aren't you?"

Brooke released her breath with an audible sigh. She hadn't won the battle, but the troops were in place. "Of course. The entire staff will be there. And the saloon will be closed."

Mrs. Gilmore nodded. "Till Sunday, my dear."

She stayed in her seat long after the other woman had left. The strain of her performance had drained all her energy, and she wasn't sure she could even climb the stairs to her room. But the results had been worth the effort, she thought. Mrs. Gilmore had the influence and social contacts to make sure Brooke was accepted into the fold of society. If only the books arrived in time.

"I applaud you. If you gamble as well as you toyed with Mrs. Gilmore, you'll be even more extraordinary than I imagined." Dalton leaned against the doorjamb, one leg crossed in front of the other, the toe of his boot touching the floor.

She glared at him. "I thought I asked you not to listen."

"I never claimed to be morally upright."

"That's fine for you, but if Mrs. Gilmore questions *my* character, the plan is ruined. So I haven't succeeded yet."

"But you will. You have the most at stake. I've always done my best when my life was on the line."

"No one's going to murder me if the ladies don't approve of my plan." She picked up the tray and carried it across the room. As she walked past him, he touched her arm, bringing her to a halt.

"If those women reject you, Brooke, you'll wither away, the same as if they had killed you."

She started to shake her head and deny the truth of his words, but she could not. Dalton watched as her eyes grew wide, the emerald depths sparkling with emotion.

"How did you know it was so important to me?"

Because she haunted him day and night, never giving him a moment's rest. Because her scent invaded his sleep, and when Elizabeth had accidentally brought him lilac soap, he'd saved it in a drawer. Because he was afraid he was beginning to love the one woman he could never have. Because, no matter what, he was going to walk away from her when their time together was over.

He shrugged. "I knew." He took the tray from her hands and carried it into the kitchen. "Come on, I want to teach you to play cards."

It was as though he had asked her to take off her clothes and parade naked down the center of town in broad daylight. "I couldn't," she said, hiding her hands behind her back. "It wouldn't be right."

He took her arm and tugged her into the gaming room. "You can't run this place if you can't gamble. I'll need you to deal some games. Besides, if you don't know how to play, how do you expect to know if anyone's cheating?"

Her jaw dropped. "Do *you* cheat?"

He pushed her into a chair. "Never ask a man if he cheats. That question is a direct route to a pine box." He sat next to her and broke open a fresh deck of cards. "And no, I don't cheat. I don't need to."

She watched the way he shuffled the deck, his hands moving faster than her eyes could follow. The room was dim; only two lamps hung on the wall. When she had complained about the lack of windows, he had explained that they didn't want the men to know what time it was. That way they usually stayed and gambled longer.

"There are fifty-two cards in a deck and four suits. Hearts, diamonds . . ."

"Dalton, stop. I'm too tired to learn right now. Can't I just watch?" She rested her hand on his forearm and enjoyed the rough texture of the hair and the strength beneath his skin.

He swallowed and pulled his arm away. "Sure, but you're going to have to learn soon."

"I will."

The large room was still; the sounds of the others in the building seemed far away. Dalton shuffled and dealt, then gathered the deck back together and repeated the process. He toyed with the cards, manipulating them between his fingers, cutting the deck with one hand.

She'd noticed before that he kept his hands well groomed. The nails were clean and neatly trimmed.

He would often rub the pads of his fingers with fine sandpaper. When she'd asked him why, he'd explained that he needed to keep his fingers sensitive so he would know if someone was using a marked deck.

Her brothers' hands were also free of calluses, but their palms were pudgy and soft. Every part of Dalton was lean and powerful. As she watched him practice, she wondered how those sensitive fingertips would feel against her skin. Her breathing grew shallow as the boned corset seemed to tighten around her rib cage. Her breasts throbbed with something between an itch and an ache. She knew that he could relieve the pressure with a single stroke.

The bold image in her mind made her flush with embarrassment, but she continued to study his hands. The world disappeared until only the table, the cards, and the man remained. One of the lamps hissed and went out, the last of its oil consumed. The room darkened.

Brooke stared at him. Half his face was in shadow, but his eyes glowed. The cards slipped out of his grasp and spilled across the table. Her body burned with fire, but her hands were as cold as ice and her fingers trembled. In the background, Elizabeth called out that supper was ready.

"You'd better go on and eat," he said, looking away from her.

"Aren't you coming?" she asked.

"I'm not hungry."

But the taut lines of his body belied his statement. She wanted to protest being sent away.

"Go," he commanded.

She didn't see him for the rest of the evening. That night, while she lay in her bed reading Mattie's journal, she listened for him. As she had every evening since they had moved into the saloon, she waited for his slow measured tread on the stairs. Only when his door had clicked shut did she turn down the lantern and close her eyes. Knowing he was close made her secure enough to finally rest.

"How are you holding up, honey?" Elizabeth asked.

Brooke leaned back in her chair and moaned. "This has been the longest morning of my life. I don't know how much more I can take."

"The menfolk are sure having a good time of it, though," the older woman said.

Brooke nodded ruefully and glanced around the room. Five young women, each in a different costume, stood beside the stage. Caleb and Ned were working behind the bar. Hard to believe it could take them two hours to clean and dry the glassware, she thought. But with auditions being held for the fourth dancing girl, the men's attention to a task that would keep them in that particular place was not unexpected. Dalton strolled into the room, a cigar clamped between his teeth.

"Are we ready for the next girl?" he asked as he took the chair next to hers.

"I guess."

The words came out like a sigh, and he shot her a grin. "Want to give up? I'd be more than happy to choose the dancer all by myself."

"Thank you, no. I've seen what you consider important when choosing an entertainer, and I don't agree with your taste." She nodded at Elizabeth.

The tall woman walked over to the piano. "All right, ladies. Who's next?"

A curvy blonde in a skintight blue gown handed her a tattered sheet of music, then stepped up on the stage.

The girl's dress clung to her from shoulder to thigh, then billowed out in the shape of a bell, and her legs were bare almost to the knee.

Brooke felt a flush spread up her face. She had blushed at each girl's audition and was beginning to wonder if her face would be red permanently.

Dalton leaned over and whispered in her ear. "Her legs are nice, don't you think?"

"Stunning," she hissed back. He continued to watch her, and she tossed him a quick, tight smile.

Elizabeth began to play the piano, and the girl sang along. Her voice was pleasant. Certainly she couldn't make her living doing theatricals, but she was the best Brooke had seen that day. Horse Creek was not overrun with talented singers and dancers. Most of the others had been tone deaf or worse.

Dalton hadn't been much help, either. He was willing to forgive a multitude of sins if a woman "filled out a gown the way God intended." She would have slapped him if she hadn't been so sure that he was teasing and testing.

The song ended and Lily joined the girl on stage. She demonstrated a simple routine, and then the two women performed together. Brooke was pleased when they completed the dance without a single mishap.

"I like her," she said to Dalton.

"Fine. Hire her."

"But aren't you . . . I mean, is it the right decision?"

He looked at her, his dark eyes unfathomable. At times like this, she hated his skill in assuming a poker face. "It's your call. If you want to be the boss, you have to accept the responsibility. Ladies." He grinned at the women and walked out of the room.

Brooke stood up and stared at the group before her.

The last girl was still on the stage. "What's your name?"

The blonde stepped forward. "Suzanne."

Brooke turned to the other applicants. "Ladies, thank you for your time. The opening has been filled. I'll let you know if we need someone else."

For a moment she was afraid they were going to refuse to leave, but the women gathered their things together and moved toward the door. She heard a few grumbled complaints about the blonde and about herself, and one girl raised a rather colorful question about Dalton's manhood. She coughed to cover her chuckle.

Elizabeth whispered in her ear. "I think you picked the best one, honey. Seems real nice, too."

"Let's keep our fingers crossed. I don't think I could endure more auditions any time soon." She walked over to the stage. "Suzanne, why don't you come with me into the office? We can decide when you're to start and what your stage name is going to be. The other girls are named after flowers. Do you have a favorite?"

Although she was tall and very pretty, Suzanne shyly avoided Brooke's eyes. "My mama's name was Magnolia. She died when I was little, and I don't recall her very well. Would it be fittin' to use that? I've never been a dancer before. I took some lessons in Cheyenne, but this is my first job." She blushed. "I guess I shouldn't be tellin' you that, but I figured you'd want to know."

Brooke led her into the office and motioned for her to sit in one of the chairs. "What were you doing before?"

Suzanne looked down at her lap, then up. "My daddy left home 'bout three years ago. I tried to get a decent job. For a while I took in laundry. I did some baking. But sometimes . . ." She cleared her throat. "I couldn't always find work. I, um, I entertained gentlemen from time to time, but I swear it wasn't my choice." Her lips quivered, and tears spilled out of her blue eyes. "Then I got beat up real bad, and I swore I'd never do that again."

"Of course you mustn't, my dear." Brooke felt herself trembling. She wanted to comfort the other girl but didn't know what to say. The life she described was so foreign, so unimaginable. A shudder racked her body. Suzanne couldn't have been more than eighteen. "Where are you staying?"

"I don't have a place," she said, avoiding Brooke's eyes.

"Here." She opened the cashbox and withdrew several bills. "Consider this an advance on your salary."

She saw that the dancer wanted to refuse. Pride was evident in the rigid set of her shoulders, but there was gratitude in her eyes. "Thank you, ma'am. I haven't been eating regularly of late."

"Oh, my . . . that's horrible." Brooke stood up and walked to the hall. "Elizabeth?" she called.

"Would you fix Suzanne some dinner?" she asked when Elizabeth appeared. "Then have Caleb or Ned escort her to the boardinghouse where Lily and the others stay. Tell them to take care of her." She smiled at Suzanne. "You eat up and regain your strength. You begin rehearsals tomorrow. The saloon opens in less than a week."

"So, which one did you hire? The tall blonde with the great legs or the redhead with the big—"

"Dalton!" Brooke cut him off. "I hired the last girl, Suzanne. And yes, she's the one with the stunning legs." She continued to count the bottles in the shipment of liquor from Cheyenne. The storeroom was cold, and she pulled her shawl more firmly about her shoulders. "Did you know that poor girl was abandoned by her father when she was barely fifteen? She's had to make her way by doing whatever she could. It's shameful."

Dalton stepped into the smaller room, took the papers from her hands, and set them on a crate. "It's life. Most people who work in saloons aren't there because they want to be. Lily loves to perform, but I'm sure Rose and Violet would rather be married to some decent farmer and raising a dozen kids, instead of dancing on that stage six nights a week. Not everybody was born in a three-story brick house complete with servants. Most of us were driven here by forces beyond our control."

She remembered her own dark secret. "I suppose you're right. But I was still appalled by what she told me."

"She'll be safe now, thanks to you. And if you feel that bad, maybe we should hold auditions again and hire another dancer."

She started to consider his suggestion, but then she saw the twinkle in his eyes. "Oh, you'd like that, wouldn't you? Another morning spent ogling the girls. 'This one's too thin; that one's not curvy enough,' " she mocked.

He grinned at her. "If I didn't know better, I'd say you were jealous."

She drew in a breath. "Jealous? How like a man to assume that! I didn't realize how much you were going to enjoy your work."

"The time did fly."

"I have things to do."

She raised her arm to push him out of the way, but he caught her fingers in his. "Your hands are like ice."

They were caught immobile in a moment of time. She couldn't pull away—didn't want to, really. He'd been so careful to avoid touching her that she'd begun to wonder if she'd imagined their kiss.

Dalton rubbed her smooth skin, then pulled her close and slid her hands under his vest. She caught her breath when she felt the warm shirt against her palms. His heart was pounding.

"Dalton, I . . ."

"Shh, don't move." He held her forearms firmly against his body, the fragile skin and bone the only barrier between them. Her elbow rubbed against the buckle of his belt.

His eyes blazed with a passion that matched the raging in her blood. He was going to kiss her. She read it in his eyes, felt it in the brush of his fingers across her neck and down her back.

She freed her arms so that she could wrap them around his shoulders. The broadcloth of his coat was scratchy beneath her touch, a rough contrast to the smooth, hot lips that pressed against hers. He explored slowly, as if measuring . . . remembering. When his tongue nudged for entrance, she opened her mouth and tasted him.

The air around them was cool, yet the heat created by their bodies was enough to consume the room. She slid her hands under his coat and stroked the vastness of his back. His hands rested at her waist, a band of fire that made her breasts ache.

He drew his lips from hers and traced the territory from jaw to ear. The nibbles against her sensitive earlobe both tickled and aroused, and she giggled a trifle nervously.

"Do that again," he murmured against her neck.

"What?" Her voice was so low and husky she barely recognized it as her own.

"Laugh for me. I like the way it sounds and what it does to me. It makes the hunger bearable."

He licked the hollow of her throat; the moistness

caused her to moan. "I-I can't."

"I've dreamed of this."

His words were muffled as he ran his lips to the very edge of her gown. His hands slid up from her waist and cupped her throbbing breasts. The ache intensified. She leaned into his touch, wanting, needing, but not knowing exactly what to say, what to ask for. "Dalton?"

He didn't answer. His tongue probed the valley between her curves, his thumbs brushed against her sensitive nipples. Flames of pleasure consumed her.

"Yes," she breathed. She clung to him, threading her fingers through his hair.

Dalton wondered if he had the strength to rip her dress open or if he should struggle with the buttons. The hard buds of her breasts taunted him through the layers of fabric, and he feasted again on the smooth lines of her throat.

Her soft cries of pleasure made him long to unbutton his trousers and bury himself in the silkiness of her moist warmth. Pressure built in his groin until he was afraid for her. He dropped his hands to her hips and pulled her as close as he could.

But the yards of material offered him no relief, and the sound of Elizabeth in the kitchen reminded him where they were. Brooke's eyes were wide and unfocused as he claimed her lips for one last kiss.

This time her tongue met his and followed back into his mouth. He groaned when she explored and teased all the crevices between his lips.

"Ah, stop." He pulled back and tried to slow his breathing. Brooke blinked slowly and swayed toward him, her palms rubbing teasing circles on his chest.

"I don't want to stop," she said softly. She ran her fingers up his shirt and tugged on his collar. "Dalton, I know you want to kiss me again."

"Don't tempt me." A slender rope of control was all that held him from plunging them into a vortex of hungry passion. Her pleading words began to unravel that cord.

Brooke stared at the grim line of his lips and dropped her hands. "You're serious. I don't understand. Why would you kiss me like that and then stop?"

"Did you want me to take you like this?" he asked bluntly. "Here, in the storeroom, with Ned and Elizabeth walking around outside?"

She covered her flaming cheeks with her hands. "No, but—"

He grabbed her arm. "I was wrong to kiss you, Brooke, but don't compound my error with one of your own. I'm not some youth you can toy with, like a cat with a mouse. There is nothing between us. I won't allow it."

"*You* won't?" The passion in her breast had been replaced by anger. White-hot fury burned her soul until it was raw with pain. He was rejecting her, just as Joe had. "You dare to touch me so intimately and then scorn me?"

She looked around the room, searching for a weapon, anything with which to hurt him as much as he'd hurt her. She spied an open crate of liquor and went to grab one of the bottles.

"Brooke, stop it."

Her fingers closed on the heavy bottle, but he wrenched it away. "Do you really need to punish me for a simple kiss?"

"It's not . . . the kiss—" Her voice broke.

"Hush, love." He cradled her in his arms, smoothing her hair and rubbing his palm against her back. "Sweet Brooke, I'm sorry, so sorry. I never meant to hurt you."

"What's wrong with me?" she pleaded as she clutched the rough lapels of his coat. "No one wa-wants me."

Dalton stood in the darkening room and looked heavenward, praying for guidance. Her reaction to his withdrawal was more than the pique of an unsatisfied woman. Somehow he had touched a wounded portion of her heart. He had callously trampled on the one person he cared about. Would he never learn?

He led her to a crate and eased her down. Her face was pale. Taking her hands in his, he sat beside her. The dark green of her eyes probed into his being and forced the words from him. "There are ghosts from my past I can't begin to explain. I'm not the man you deserve. I'm sorry I hurt you. It was never my intent. There's nothing wrong with you. If it makes you feel better, know that I burn for you."

"Then . . ."

"No. There's no other choice—I *have* to do this."

She glanced away and he caught his breath. She held his fate in her hands, and he had no reason to hope for mercy. When she turned back, her eyes met his and she smiled her forgiveness.

Chapter 9

The white clapboard church stood near the edge of town, about three blocks past the saloon. A small sign attached to one wall announced that Pastor Stephen Bolt held services at ten-thirty on the first three Sundays of each month. On the fourth he traveled to other villages in the countryside.

Dalton walked up the plank steps. This frontier chapel with its plain wood exterior and simple rectangular door was a far cry from the awe-inspiring stone cathedrals he'd grown up attending. In Boston his family had been generous with the neighborhood church. Several ornate pews and two stained-glass windows bore a dedication to the Reed name.

But once inside the small building, the air of serenity was the same as he remembered, he thought as he slid into the roughly hewn pew. The low murmur of voices and the quiet expectancy soothed his troubled spirit, and he gave Brooke a mental note of thanks for forcing him to accompany her.

She sat in front of him, Suzanne on one side, the Barnses on the other. He was behind, with Ned and the other dancers. While Brooke had lingered upstairs dressing, he had held a whispered meeting about who was to sit with whom. He hoped that the sight of Brooke flanked

by a respectable married couple and a yet unknown
woman would be enough to allow the women in town
to acknowledge her, but, so far he'd been wrong. All
around them, couples joined in quiet conversation, dis-
cussing beef prices and babies. Despite the surreptitious
glances in her direction, no one spoke to Brooke. Dalton
had expected her lawyer to be of some help, but Edward
Gannen was speaking with a young man at the front of
the church.

Dalton craned his head to look for a gray-haired old
padre, but didn't see anyone who fit his preconceived
notion. Mrs. Gilmore happened to look up, and he nodded at her when their eyes met. She jerked her head
away and stared straight ahead. Her thin cheeks were
stained with color, and the bird on her hat quivered with
indignation. Dalton stifled a grin as he stretched his legs
out in front of him.

In the far corner of the room, Arthur Franklin was
deep in conversation with a tall, spare woman. She
was much older than the law clerk and had that air
of frontier town society about her. Franklin was probably staying in the good graces of the law firm's most
profitable client.

Edward Gannen took his seat. Dalton stared as the
young man the lawyer had been talking to walked toward
the front of the room. *He* was the minister? Dalton raised
an eyebrow. The young man was in his middle to late
twenties and looked more like a rancher than a man of
the cloth. His dark suit emphasized his sandy hair and
tanned face.

Dalton clenched his fingers around his hat as the man
stepped up to the pulpit and surveyed the assemblage.
His blue eyes seemed to linger on Brooke, and Dalton
fought back the urge to jump up and strike him.

"Good morning, everyone. I see some new faces, so let me introduce myself. I'm Stephen Bolt, the pastor here in Horse Creek. After the service, I hope I get a chance to meet our new members."

The man's smile was much warmer than Dalton would have liked, and he fidgeted on the suddenly hard seat. "Making cow eyes in church," he muttered to himself. It was ungodly. His temper was flaring when Brooke glanced over her shoulder and smiled at him. Her dress was a deep rust color, and the matching hat dipped low over one eye. He admired her soft skin and the curve of her lips. The last drop of his anger evaporated when she gave him a flirtatious wink.

The day before, they had worked together with their usual teasing camaraderie. The fiasco of their most recent kiss had been ignored, if not forgotten. He still remembered the fire that had burned within him, but he pushed the embers aside. At the end of the six months, he was leaving. Nothing could happen between now and then to change his mind. He cared about Brooke more than he had ever cared about a woman before, and he wouldn't taint that affection by leaving her with the false hopes their mating would surely spark.

Brooke watched Edna and Samuel Prattly take the pew across the aisle. She waited to see if the older woman would acknowledge her in any way, but there wasn't the slightest flicker to indicate that they had previously met. Mrs. Prattly picked up a hymnal and offered it to her husband. As he took the book, she removed an imaginary piece of lint from the sleeve of his jacket. The wifely gesture caused Brooke to smile . . . until Samuel shook off the friendly touch and glared at Edna. The rebuff was clearly and painfully public. Edna faced front, her shoulders stiff and proud. But Brooke saw the flash of hurt before the brittle mask slipped back in place.

The congregation rose to sing a hymn. Suzanne leaned over and whispered in Brooke's ear, "I never seen a man so fine before. And he sounds just like an angel from the Lord."

Brooke glanced up at the man in question and saw that Pastor Bolt seemed equally entranced by Suzanne. For a moment she was pleased, but bit her lip when she realized that any budding romance would be cut off when the minister found out that the statuesque blonde danced in a saloon. And then there were the Prattlys—a perfect social match, and yet they were unhappy. Why did life have to be so complicated?

She had been in Horse Creek only a few weeks, but she already felt as if she'd never lived anywhere else. The hopes and dreams of her new friends were much more vivid than anything she'd experienced before. Her life in Philadelphia was almost a dream; her brothers and their wives seemed like the characters in a play or a penny dreadful.

But Dalton was real. He was the most powerful force in her life. And he was going to leave her. She tightly clutched the hymnal, afraid it would slip from her trembling fingers.

She had to stop him from going, convince him that he belonged with her. If she could find a way into his heart and unlock the dark secret buried there, perhaps she would be able to hold him next to her forever.

When the services ended, Pastor Bolt led everyone out of the church. Brooke sat with her friends until the building had emptied, then gathered her shawl and reticule.

Dalton put his hand on her shoulder. "Are you up to this? I'm sure the church has a back door."

She shook her head. "Thanks, but I'll manage. I'm the one who wants to fit in, so I can't back out now. I guess I'd better—what's the expression?—beard the lion in his den." She straightened her hat, squared her shoulders, and started down the aisle.

The spring morning was cloudy and cool, but Brooke's face felt hot when she walked down the steps. Although she didn't meet anyone's eye, she had no doubt that every woman in the churchyard was watching her. The next few minutes would tell if her literary society had been enough of a bribe or if the women of Horse Creek would simply snub her.

Mrs. Gilmore stood several feet away, studying her hands. Her hunched shoulders and pursed lips made it clear she wasn't going to be the first one to speak. The low murmur of conversation died, and the crowd shifted to make room for Brooke as she walked through. She held her head high and her back stiff. I've done nothing wrong, she told herself.

"Brooke, my dear. How wonderful to see you again."

Edward Gannen took her hand and smiled. His warm blue eyes had never been so welcoming and she felt her heart swell with gratitude "Mr. Gannen, good morning."

"I don't believe you've met Pastor Bolt." He led her to the pastor. "Brooke Tyler, Stephen Bolt."

"Pastor Bolt." She nodded politely.

"Miss Tyler."

He took both her hands in his and leaned over and kissed her cheek. She pulled her hands back and blinked, surprised by the friendly reception.

He chuckled. "You must forgive my exuberance, but I feel that I already know you like a cousin or a younger sister. Mattie Frost was a great friend of mine and of the church." His face grew sober. "I've missed her these past weeks. We often talked long into the night about God and man and"—he leaned over and whispered in her ear—"the difference between Jamaica and Santa Cruz rum."

She laughed, looked at the lawyer, then back at the pastor. "It seems that my aunt was blessed with many wonderful friends, and I thank you both for your kindness."

"Morning, Pastor." Elizabeth gave Brooke an encouraging wink. "You've always dined with us on the second Sunday of the month. I'm planning your favorite roast for next week. May we expect you?"

Stephen glanced at Brooke. "I would not wish to presume."

She smiled. "Of course you're welcome. Is two o'clock acceptable?"

"Yes, thank you." He patted her arm and then turned to greet another worshiper.

Brooke linked her arm through Elizabeth's. "What a wonder you are. Imagine thinking to invite him to lunch in front of everyone. Thank you, Elizabeth."

The older woman brushed aside the praise. "Just doin' my job and what Mattie would have wanted me to do. Well, we better be gettin' back. The stove probably needs more wood."

Brooke held back, hoping someone else would approach her. The sea of people shifted around her until she felt like a tiny boat tossed by the current.

They had chosen to ignore her. Defeat was a bitter taste on her tongue, but she was determined not to let them see her pain. She had thrust her jaw forward and taken a step toward the main road when a woman touched her arm. "Miss Tyler?"

Brooke turned. "Yes?"

"I'm Amanda Carson. My husband and I own the dry goods store." She was as short as Mrs. Gilmore, but rounder, younger, and prettier. Her dress wasn't stylish, but it suited her ample curves. "I wanted to thank you for all your business. I'm sure you know there is another store in town, and I appreciate you choosing us."

"My aunt bought her supplies from you for several years, Mrs. Carson. I saw the name of your store in the records. I've no reason to question her good judgment."

An older woman rushed over and clutched the shopkeeper's arm. "Amanda! What are you doing? You can't—"

"Hush, Mother. I'm introducing myself to Miss Tyler." She smiled at Brooke. "This is Betty Smith, my mother."

"How do you do?"

Mrs. Smith's eyes darted around. "Please, Amanda. People are staring. What will they think? You can't address a woman who owns a saloon." She spoke the last word in the merest whisper.

"Yes, I can. I've heard about the literary society, and I'd like to attend." She tilted her chin up at the last word, daring anyone to find fault with her decision.

Relief flooded through Brooke's body, making her knees quiver. "That's wonderful. I've been notified that the books have left Philadelphia and will be arriving at the end of next week. Perhaps we could plan the first meeting for the following Wednesday?"

Mrs. Carson nodded. "That would be fine. I look forward to seeing you again."

Stephen Bolt approached the little gathering. Brooke saw the young minister detain Betty Smith, despite the woman's frantic efforts to get away. "Mrs. Smith, Amanda. Are you two the first to sign up for the literary society?"

Amanda nodded, but Mrs. Smith just looked uncomfortable.

"Very commendable," he continued. "I expect the leaders in my church to be examples in the community. Keep up the good work, ladies."

Mrs. Smith underwent an instant and rather comical transformation from dour and disapproving to friendly and fawning. The older woman beamed under the young man's praise, while Brooke and Amanda exchanged smiles.

Dalton stood behind Brooke and watched the townswomen, one by one, greet her. Some of them seemed more sincere than others, but he knew that all of the women would show up for that first meeting. A few would come solely to see the inside of a saloon, but enough would return to give Brooke a chance at a decent life here. As much as he hated to admit it, he owed his thanks to that young minister.

He pulled his hands out of his pockets and walked over to the man. "Pastor, I'm Dalton Reed." They shook hands.

"Call me Stephen, please."

Dalton was irritated to discover that the minister was as pleasant-looking close up as he had been at a distance. No doubt he'd soon be sniffing around Brooke.

"I understand you work at the saloon."

Dalton adjusted his hat. "You heard right."

"I was wondering. Do you know that young woman over there? She was sitting beside Miss Tyler, and I don't recall seeing her before."

A slow smile split Dalton's face as he looked down the

road. "That's Suzanne. A lovely girl, don't you think? And very sweet. I understand she's pretty much alone in the world. Brooke has taken her under her wing."

Stephen's blue eyes met his. "Will she be joining us for supper next Sunday?"

Dalton pulled out a cigar. "I think that can be arranged."

"I look forward to that, sir." Stephen grinned.

"Dalton, let's go home."

Brooke stepped up next to him and slipped her hand through the crook of his arm. He wanted to draw back, to deny her claim to him in front of all these people. Couldn't she see that she wasn't helping her cause by clinging to him? But in truth, he couldn't resist the gentle pressure of her body leaning against his. She smelled of lilacs and spring and promises. He wished he were weak enough to forget about the consequences of giving in or strong enough to face the demons that forced him to leave.

Mrs. Gilmore approached them. Her small eyes darted toward Brooke's hand resting on his arm. She ignored him and addressed Brooke. "You have been accepted, my dear. The first meeting of the Horse Creek Literary Society will be held on Wednesday next."

Brooke leaned over and kissed the woman's cheek. "I owe it all to you."

"Well, I . . . Thank you." Mrs. Gilmore blushed. "I simply did what any friend would do."

Dalton started to laugh, but Brooke's fingers bit into his arm. The little birdlike woman smiled her good-bye and turned to leave.

"Good day, Mrs. Gilmore," he called out.

She froze in mid-stride, as if making a decision. Then her hat dipped with the barest of motions.

"I think she likes me," he whispered in Brooke's ear.

"You would."

They walked past the last couple in the churchyard. Dalton recognized Samuel Prattly standing next to the dark-haired woman he'd seen talking to Franklin. She must be Prattly's wife, he thought. She had a pinched, narrow face, and her nose was tilted up in the air as if the odors of common people were too much for her to bear. He felt anger course through him as he remembered she was the woman who had made the threats. Brooke had told him that she didn't believe Mrs. Prattly meant her any physical harm. Elizabeth and Caleb agreed with her, but Dalton wasn't so sure. If Mrs. Prattly wanted the saloon that badly, one stubborn, naive, beautiful woman wasn't going to be much of a deterrent to her.

"Prattly." Dalton touched his hat.

"Reed." Mr. Prattly stepped forward and looked at Brooke. "Miss Tyler, I've heard that you've decided not to sell."

Dalton felt Brooke tense, and her fingers dug into his arm, but her voice was firm. "That's right, Mr. Prattly. I believe my aunt meant for me to keep the saloon."

Mrs. Prattly sniffed audibly. "So Mattie Frost corrupts from both sides of the grave?"

"Edna!" Prattly shot her a quelling glance, then turned back to Brooke. "I apologize for my wife. She is not feeling well today. If you change your mind, Miss Tyler, I'm still willing to buy."

She shook her head. "I won't. Horse Creek is my home now."

Brooke tried to catch Mrs. Prattly's eye, but the other woman stared past her. She gave no hint that they'd met or spoken before. It was obvious her husband knew nothing of the encounter . . . or of her determination to prevent him from buying the land.

Samuel Prattly stroked his beard. "The offer stands." He stepped away and then turned back. "I understand you're starting a literary society?"

His light eyes twinkled, but Brooke didn't trust his charm anymore. She'd seen him deliberately hurt his wife. Edna Prattly might not be the easiest person to live with, but as always, Brooke found her heart going out to the injured party.

"Yes," she said. "The first meeting will be on Wednesday next." Brooke looked questioningly at Mrs. Prattly, but she didn't acknowledge the glance. Not that she expected her to attend the meeting. More than likely she'd be trying to figure out a way to have her lawyer draw up eviction papers.

"Smart girl," Prattly said. "Mattie would be proud of you, Brooke Tyler." He took his wife's arm and led her away.

Brooke stared after them. "I don't understand that man. He talks as if he knew Mattie. When he stopped by to discuss a selling price, he said they were friends."

Her comment caught Dalton off-guard, and he started to laugh. "They were, in a manner of speaking."

"What do you mean? That he came to the saloon?"

"It would be best for you to leave it alone, Brooke."

She pulled her arm away. "Stop treating me like a half-witted child. Tell me."

Dalton studied her stubborn expression. She'd stay in the middle of the road until her curiosity was satisfied, and he'd be stuck standing with her. His stomach growled, protesting the possibility of missing one of Elizabeth's meals. "Mattie and Prattly were close."

She narrowed her eyes. "How close?"

"They were lovers."

Her jaw dropped.

He took advantage of her surprise and pulled her toward the saloon.

"But he's married!"

"Yes."

She sighed. "Now it all makes sense. His wife doesn't want him to have the saloon because it once belonged to Mattie. The poor woman."

"Brooke, she's trying to close down your business."

"I know, but"—she bit her lip—"she loves him. It must have hurt when she found out he was seeing my aunt."

"I doubt that he kept his wife informed about his . . ."

"Affairs?" Brooke offered dryly. "Wait a minute. Are you sure about your information? I thought Mattie and Mr. Gannen were . . . had been . . ."

"Yes."

She blinked several times. "Two men? Imagine that."

"You sound as if you like the idea."

"Maybe I do. Why should men be the only ones to have a little freedom?"

They stepped into the saloon. "Don't get any ideas, little one," he growled. "You can hardly handle me."

Brooke adjusted the wick on the lantern then slipped into bed. As she had every night since moving into the saloon, she picked up one of Mattie's journals. She had found several leather-bound books chronicling her aunt's life from the time she'd left Philadelphia. Brooke had been reading them in order, but this evening, she flipped ahead until she found the first reference to Samuel Prattly.

June 2, 1878. I met a man today. Even as I read the sentence back, I want to laugh at my own fanciful imaginings. I've met many men since arriving in Horse Creek, but none of them made me feel as though my insides were quivering like jelly.

His name is Samuel Prattly. I've heard tell of him, of course, but today was the first time he came into the saloon. He bought a bottle of champagne, and we shared it. I don't know much about him. I know he has a wife, but Samuel claims they are estranged. At times like this I regret being cut off from the good women in town. There is no way for me to find out gossip about this man. Lizzy hides the truth when it suits her. I shouldn't be cross; I know she does it to protect me. Samuel says he will return at the end of next week. I find myself counting the days.

June 11, 1878. He came back today. As I write this entry, he sleeps a few short feet from my desk. It is late, almost dawn. But I'm not sleepy. I haven't felt this way since . . .

Oh, Roger, why did you have to die? We were supposed to live the rest of our lives together.

Brooke closed the diary. So Mattie and Samuel Prattly *had* been lovers. When had Edna Prattly found out? Somehow Brooke doubted that Samuel had gone out of his way to be discreet. She picked up the journal and flipped forward a few pages.

February 1, 1879. There is no estrangement between Samuel and his wife. I've seen much of the world, but the news still shocked me. I am an old fool who wanted to believe in love a second time.

I was shopping at the Carsons' store yesterday when
I overheard two women talking about Edna Prattly.
Apparently the poor woman is suffering badly. She
has loved Samuel from the time they were children.

He lied to me. I don't know which is more surprising, his lie or the ease with which I was taken
in. Never again will I allow my emotions to rule
me. I have neglected my male friends badly these
past months, but not one has complained. They are
an honorable lot. Only Samuel is a cad. After tonight
I will never see him again.

Brooke set the book down and drew the covers around
her shoulders. So many lives tangled up together. How
could anyone make sense of the muddle? For the hundredth time, she wished Mattie were alive and able to
speak of life and love and men.

"Shuffle the deck."
Brooke glanced at Dalton and then reached for the
cards. "I don't want to do this," she grumbled, trying to imitate his dexterity with the cards. She split
the deck and picked up half in each hand. Her fingers
slipped, and the cards went flapping across the table like
birds taking off in flight. She folded her hands together.
"Sorry."
He clamped his cigar between his teeth and scowled.
"Try it again. Slower this time. No need to rush."
This was the third evening they had practiced gam-
bling. She'd mastered the intricacies of the faro table
and the fortune wheel, but manipulating the cards with
Dalton's skill and agility continued to elude her.
"My hands are smaller than yours," she complained.
"Some of the best dealers I've seen were women."

"Thanks for telling me that." How nice for him, she thought. But a discussion about mysterious females from his past was not her idea of inspiration. She gathered the slippery cards together and began to shuffle. When she had smoothed the last card into place, she smiled. "All done."

"Not quite. Now you have to learn to play. We're going to start with a simple counting game the French call vingt-et-un. Twenty-one."

He spread the deck on the table and pointed. "Four suits, thirteen cards each. Face cards worth ten, number cards worth their face, aces are one or eleven. The object is to get as close to twenty-one as you can, without going over."

She nodded. "I remember. How much shall we gamble for?"

"Nothing." He dealt. "What do you have?"

"Twenty."

"I have seventeen, you win."

She wrinkled her nose. "Now I know why you didn't want to play for money."

They continued to practice. Brooke glanced around the room and tried to imagine it filled with people. The lantern on the table cast more shadow than light, but when the saloon opened, the room would be as bright as day. The heavy chandeliers held thirty candles each. She knew; she'd polished every crystal prism until the glass sparkled and her shoulders ached.

Brooke picked up the second deck and dealt. This game wasn't much fun, she thought and looked at her cards. A ten of clubs and a seven of diamonds. Not a great hand, but there was still hope. She reached for a third card.

Dalton shook his head. "You shouldn't do that. You'll

probably bust. Better to stand on seventeen."

She looked up at him and pushed a strand of hair out of her eyes. "But you said to get as close to twenty-one as possible. There are only a dozen cards left in the deck, and we've used up all the high numbers. With only one eight and two fives remaining, the rest are four or smaller. I have a very good chance of getting the right card."

He stubbed out his cigar and stared at her. "You know which cards are left?"

"Yes," she said slowly, not sure what the big deal was. "This game is boring. Keeping track of what's been played gives me something to do."

He leaned across the table and kissed her hard on the lips. "Amazing! I've never known anyone to just start counting cards."

She didn't know why he was so happy, but if a simple thing like that would make him kiss her, she was pleased. "I've always done well with figuring."

"Teaching you the rest of the games will be easy. We'd better move on to something more difficult." He got up from the table and picked up a worn black case that he'd left by the door. After setting it on the table, he pulled a key out of his vest and unlocked it.

Brown eyes held green, as if he were taking her measure. Her brief flash of elation faded and she was afraid.

"Don't look scared, Brooke. I need to show you the seamier side of life in a saloon."

He held out his hand, and she allowed him to pull her to her feet in front of him. One palm rested on her shoulders, reassuring her with its weight and warmth as he pawed through the case. "Stripped decks, bugs, holdout devices, and shiners. The number of ways to cheat are limited only by the human imagination, and you have to be aware of as many as you can." He handed her a deck of cards. "Can you feel anything different about them?"

She ran her fingers along the tops and the sides. She thought they didn't seem quite even. "Are some smaller?"

"Yes. It's called stripping. The dealer cuts a sliver of the paper away on certain cards. That way he can make sure he gets the best hand."

She put down the cards and picked up a pipe. "What's this?"

"Look inside it."

She glanced into the bowl and saw a tiny reflection of herself. "A mirror?"

He shrugged. "When his stake's gone and his belly's empty, there's not much a man won't do to stay alive."

She turned away from the table and buried her face in his strong, broad chest. "I can't do this."

"Yes, you can. You have to." He lifted her chin with the tip of his index finger. "A lot of people are depending on you for their livelihood. There's time for you to learn what you need to know. I'll be here for a while yet."

If he meant to reassure her, he'd failed miserably, she thought. Just the mention of his leaving was enough to make her ache with loneliness and pain. But she wouldn't let him see that she cared. Surely he knew of her feelings, but if she didn't say anything out loud, she could pretend her affections were a secret, a treasure to be savored in private.

Dalton stowed the trunk in the corner and led her out of the room. "We'll practice some more tomorrow. Come on, I'll buy you a drink."

They stopped in the hall, and she smiled up at him.

"The bar's not open yet. Besides, you know I don't drink."

He didn't tease her back. She sensed something unfamiliar about him, as if the wall of protection around his heart had cracked, allowing the feelings inside to slip out. His brown curly hair gleamed in the lantern light, but his eyes were dark, the flashes of emotion too brief to be absorbed. He stood stiff, and his mouth was a grim line.

"Stay with me."

He ground out the words as if he cursed her, and yet she wasn't shocked. She took one of his hands in hers and raised it to her face. Cupping his fingers and palm about her jaw, she smiled against his warm skin. "I'm here."

She tugged on his hand. He resisted at first, then followed her up the stairs. Elizabeth and Caleb were already in their room for the night, and the building was still. Brooke opened her door and led him to one of the rockers by the fireplace. She added a couple of large logs to the fire and put water on to heat for tea. After lowering the wick in the lantern, she sank to the floor. The flames warmed her as she leaned against Dalton's knee.

"Tell me what's troubling you," she said.

He brushed his fingers across her head. "Take your hair down. Please." His voice was husky.

She looked up at him. There wasn't any desire in his face; the set of his mouth was troubled, not passionate. Moving of their own accord, her hands pulled the pins from her curls and smoothed the tangled tresses over her shoulders.

He gathered her hair in his hands and spread it across his thigh. She rested her head by his knee as she leaned against his leg.

"I love the color of your hair," he said. "In the darkness, like this, it's almost red. A liquid fire that doesn't burn my hands, but singes my heart."

His words painted a vivid picture that stirred her senses. The pot on the fire began to boil, but she didn't move a muscle. The tea could wait . . . everything could wait. This time was for Dalton.

"Today's my mother's birthday," he blurted unexpectedly.

"What—"

"She thinks I'm dead."

Brooke drew in a breath. "When was the last time you saw her?"

He didn't answer for so long that she wasn't sure he was going to speak at all. "Nine years ago," he said finally. "I was twenty, and I went home to make things right. But nothing could be done. I left and never went back."

Dalton saw the pain in his mother's eyes as clearly as if she stood in front of him. All his feelings of hope and promise had faded with her carefully worded sentences. He was too late, she'd told him. Joanna was dead.

But his mother had been wrong. Joanna lived on in his mind. He could still hear her high-pitched voice taunting him with her plans. She'd sworn to have him . . . or die trying. She hadn't cared that he didn't love her, or even like her. All she'd wanted was the Reed name and a chance to live in the big house on the corner. He'd refused to go along with her, had ignored the wishes of his family. Just as she'd promised, Joanna had died trying. And he was the one who killed her.

"I could write your family, if you'd like," Brooke offered. "Knowing you're alive would probably be the best present your mother could have."

She felt his pain as if it were her own . . . and in a way it was. As she grew to care about him more, the boundaries between them blended and merged until his feelings were hers. She longed to ease his suffering.

"No. It doesn't really matter anymore."

His voice was hollow and empty, as if he spoke from a long way away. But the distance was measured in time, not space. He had returned to the past, a place of pain and torment, where she couldn't reach him or help him.

She stood up slowly, then lowered herself onto his lap. Dalton cradled her as if she were a child, and yet he was the one being comforted. The fire snapped and the logs crackled; the smell of burning wood mingled with the scent of her perfume. If he held her close enough and slowed his breathing to match hers, somehow the pain couldn't reach him.

Chapter 10

"You planning on spending all day abed, girl? There's work to be done if you want this place to open tomorrow." Elizabeth's voice faded away as she thumped down the stairs.

Brooke rolled over and stared at the clock above the desk. The normal ticking was noticeably absent, a silent reminder that she had forgotten to wind it the night before.

She stood up and stretched, only to halt in mid-motion when she caught sight of herself in the mirror. She was still wearing her dress from last night. But what . . . ? She looked at the bed. The coverlet was in place; only an imprint of her body marred the smooth surface.

Dalton. She remembered that he had not wanted to be alone. They'd talked in front of the fire. *That* she remembered. And she had sat on his lap. But she recalled nothing beyond the feel of his arms holding her tightly against his chest. She must have fallen asleep.

Her cheeks flamed, and she covered the warm skin with her hands. He didn't . . . They couldn't possibly have . . . No! She shook her head. Dalton was an honorable man. He would never have taken advantage of her like that. And if their kisses were any indication, there was no way she could have slept through his attentions.

She changed her clothes and brushed her hair. She was still pinning up her curls when she walked onto the landing.

"Good morning."

She froze, arms above her head, three pins still in her mouth. "Morning," she mumbled, avoiding Dalton's gaze. The blush returned, and she hoped he wouldn't mention last night.

"Did you sleep well?"

So much for that wish, she thought. "Uh-huh." She secured the last lock of hair and lowered her arms. "And you?"

"Fine."

She wanted to walk past him and down the stairs, but he was standing by the railing. To get around him she would have to step close to him—too close. His face was freshly shaven, and he smelled of bay rum. The teasing glint had returned to his eyes, and she was forced to look down at the rich brocade of his vest and the crisp whiteness of his shirt.

Elizabeth appeared at the foot of the stairs. "Brooke, there's somebody here with more supplies. You want to pay the man?"

"I'll be right down," she called. "Well, I'd better go." She smiled at Dalton and started to move around him. Just when she thought she'd escaped unscathed, he touched her arm.

"Thank you for last night."

The simple words danced through her head, fluttered in her stomach, and lodged in her heart. "I'm glad I could be a comfort to you."

"So am I."

She wanted to look at him, to read the emotion in his eyes, to see if it matched the huskiness in his voice, but she was suddenly shy. It was as if they had become intimate, but through a joining of the spirit rather than the body. She wondered if anything could possibly be sweeter.

He nudged her. "Get to work. We open tomorrow."

The day, which had begun with Dalton's gentle words, rapidly spun out of control: "Brooke, I can't find a nutmeg grater." "Brooke, there aren't enough cigars for the cigar apartment." "Brooke, the newspapers aren't here." "Brooke, Suzanne's costume don't fit right."

Brooke slumped at her desk and wished she'd never heard of Horse Creek. Her back ached, her neck was stiff, and she was tired to the bone. The only thing that kept her from boarding the first train east was the knowledge that everyone else had worked just as hard as she had. Especially Dalton. Every time she looked up, he was there, lending a hand, settling a dispute, tossing her a casual smile that never failed to lighten her mood and catch in her heart.

She'd lost count of the times he'd told her to make the necessary decisions whether she wanted to or not. Sometimes she chose correctly and sometimes she didn't, but she was learning more each day. He could have ordered the supplies in half the time it had taken her, but she knew he was training her for the future . . . after he was gone.

Caleb Barns stepped into the office. "The newspapers just arrived on the stage, Miss Brooke. Some boxes came, too. The driver said they was there yesterday, but they forgot to bring 'em."

She rose and smiled. "No harm done, Caleb. Let's go have a look."

The main room of the saloon gleamed in the late

afternoon sun. The birchwood bar was as smooth and shiny as sanding and several coats of varnish could make it. The new stage curtain was made of heavy red velvet, and the piano had been tuned. Bottles of every imaginable brand of whiskey, rum, and gin lined the backbar. Fresh kegs of beer and ale had been laid below the bar, ready for their contents to be pumped into the customers' glasses.

Dalton sat at one of the tables, sorting through the newspapers. "Here." He tossed her a magazine.

She read the cover. "*Harper's Bazaar*. I didn't order that."

He smiled. "I know. I did. Thought it might make you feel more at home."

She touched his arm. "Thank you. Look at these clothes." There was a sketch of a woman wearing a beautiful morning dress. The modest neckline and long sleeves made her aware of her own low-cut gown. "I guess I won't have much opportunity to wear things like this anymore."

Brooke remembered how awkward she'd felt after Joe had called off the wedding. But even though she'd been the object of gossip and speculation, she'd still been a part of society. Here in Horse Creek, she didn't fit in. Neither all "bad" nor all "good," she was struggling to make a place for herself. There was a narrow gray area between the moral judgments of black and white—an area in which it would become more difficult for her to maneuver without Dalton's support and understanding.

She tried to understand the emotions coursing though her. She wasn't sad, exactly. More resigned than anything. There wasn't any going back at this late date.

As always, Dalton read her mind. "You can still go home."

She glanced at the magazine, then tossed it on the table. "No, I can't."

He captured her arm before she had taken two steps. "I never meant to upset you. I thought you'd be happy to read the stories and see the latest fashions."

His brown eyes held her next to him long after his hand had released her.

"I'm not upset," she said, "but sometimes I feel lost. You've spent most of your life inside a saloon or a gambling hall. I haven't. I don't miss Philadelphia, and I'm not sorry Mattie left me the saloon. It's just that things have changed so quickly. I don't know if I'm coming or going."

"You're doing fine." He flashed her a smile, the one designed to turn her knees to butter and start her heart pounding against her ribs. It worked, too. She felt her spirits brighten.

"Well, lookee here." Caleb held a glass up in the air. "I'd forgotten that Mattie'd ordered these honeys. Why, aren't they the prettiest things you ever saw?"

Brooke moved over to the bar and drew a glass out of the open box. "What are these for? Oh, my." She stared at the tumbler, convinced that her eyes were deceiving her. Painted on the glass was a picture of a woman . . . a naked woman with a translucent scarf draped around her waist and arms. But her breasts were . . . definitely not covered. And they were so big.

"I, um . . . um . . ." She swallowed and tried again. "And what are these for?" she asked brightly, looking at the floor.

"Display," Dalton said in a mock whisper.

"In the storeroom?"

He laughed. "No, on the wall above the bar. But if they bother you . . ."

After placing the glass on the counter, she risked a glance at Caleb. "Not at all. They're lovely. Go ahead and put them up."

Lily strolled into the room, her red and black costume draped over one arm. "I need a needle and thread. One of the buttons came loose. Oh, the glasses are in." She picked up the tumbler and studied it. "Sure are pretty. And look at those—"

"Lily," Brooke warned.

"What?" The dancer looked up, her face a picture of confusion. "I was just going to say they're mighty big."

"Thank you for sharing that with us, dear. Now come with me and I'll find you a needle and thread."

Brooke had taken a step forward when she felt, more than heard, Dalton start to laugh. She turned back to him. "Did you want to say something?"

He choked for a second. "No. Not a word." His face muscles twitched.

She took two steps, then looked back, but he didn't smile. "Are you sure?" she asked.

"Quite sure." He coughed.

When she reached the doorway, she spoke without turning around. "I know how many glasses were in that box, gentlemen, and I expect to see that number on display. Do I make myself clear?"

There was a mumbling noise behind her that she took for a yes.

Lily glanced at her with admiration. "You sure know men, don't you?"

"Not yet. But I'm learning."

"I can't believe this corset," Brooke grumbled as Elizabeth laced her up the back. "It doesn't even begin to cover me." She stared in the mirror at the lace and bone garment that hugged her ribs and pushed up her breasts. The ruffled trim barely concealed her nipples.

"That green silk dress is cut real low, honey. Besides, you want to dazzle Dalton, don't you? Ain't no quicker way to gain a man's interest than showin' a little cleavage."

"Really?" Brooke bent down and picked up her petticoat, hoping Elizabeth wouldn't notice her blush. She did recall, in minute detail, Dalton's attention to that very part of her body when he'd kissed her last week. The mere memory was enough to cause her stomach to tighten and her nipples to throb.

Elizabeth tightened the waistband of the undergarment until Brooke was gasping. "I won't be able to breathe," she complained.

"Hush, child. Tonight's special. You want to look your best, don't you?"

She ducked her head under the layers of green silk and slid her hands through the armholes of the dress. "I want it to be over. I dread tonight. Walking into that saloon full of men, knowing that they're all staring at me." She stood still while Elizabeth hooked the back of the gown. "I won't have a thing to say to them. I don't know about cattle and farming and mines. Besides—"

"Hush. You'll be fine. And those men don't want to talk to you about any of those things. They jest want to look." She adjusted the ruffles on the skirt. "And maybe touch a mite."

Brooke rolled her eyes. "That's it. I'm not going downstairs. Forget it."

She started to sit on the bed, but her friend pulled her up. "Don't you crush that silk. I spent over an hour ironing that for you, girl." Elizabeth's hazel eyes flashed with a warning not to disobey.

"Yes, ma'am," Brooke said meekly.

"That's better. Now let me look at you." She studied the dress and shook her head. "Something's missing. Oh, the emeralds. Stay put, I'll be right back."

Emeralds? Brooke grinned. Things were looking up. She stepped into her shoes. They were covered with the same fabric as the dress and were decorated with small green silk roses. The fit was perfect.

"Did someone here order jewelry?" Dalton entered Brooke's room, but whatever else he'd planned to say went right out of his head when he saw her.

She was the most beautiful creature he had ever seen. She wore her hair pulled back in an intricate braid. Silk flowers and bows were woven among the shiny tresses. Her dress was cut so low that he was torn between wondering how it stayed up and hoping it might slip down. The soft fabric, the exact color of her eyes, clung to her breasts and ribs like the touch of a familiar lover. If he had thought he would leave Horse Creek with his heart intact, her gentle smile made a mockery of his plan.

"Don't you look impressive," she said.

He glanced down at his black suit and white ruffled shirt. "Not nearly as wonderful as you, my dear." He held out the box he was carrying. "You will outshine these poor trinkets."

She opened the case and gasped. "I think you're mistaken. Look."

He glanced down at the jewelry. Emeralds and diamonds winked up at him, their brilliance almost blinding. "Mattie had excellent taste," he murmured, picking up the necklace. "May I?"

Brooke turned around and lifted up her hair. He fastened the emeralds around her neck. The green stones, each one surrounded by small diamonds, encircled her throat and caressed her bare chest, the last jewel resting just above the curve of her breasts. She put on the earrings.

"How do I look?" she asked.

He stared at her for a moment, wondering what he'd ever done to deserve her, then took her hand and raised it to his lips. "As I suspected, your beauty is unsurpassed."

She laughed. "I know you're telling a falsehood, but I forgive you."

He offered his arm. "Shall we?" Her eyes grew wide, and he knew she was afraid. "I'll be with you, for as long as you need me."

The words had hardly left his lips before he wanted to call them back. Of all the stupid things to say, he berated himself. Adding "I meant for tonight" would only have made matters worse. She looked away from him, but not before he saw her lips quiver.

"Brooke, I—"

"Not another word, Dalton Reed, or I shall embarrass us both. Come, our guests are waiting."

The rooms that had seemed so large when she had swept and scrubbed the floors now appeared much too small to contain the crowd of bodies pressing against the bar. The sound of male voices and laughter, the clink of glasses, and the piano music rose to the ceiling and mingled with the cigar smoke. But when she and Dalton entered the room, a hush fell over the crowd. If it had been snowing she could have heard each individual flake settling on the roof.

A sea of faces gazed at her expectantly, but she didn't

know what the men wanted. Dalton squeezed her hand, then stepped away, and she stood alone.

"Gentlemen, I am Brooke Tyler, and this is my saloon." Her voice held a faint tremor, and she swallowed before continuing. "Mattie Frost is no longer with us, but her spirit lives on, within these walls and in my heart. I will do my best to live up to her expectations, and it is in her honor that I offer each of you a drink . . . on the house."

There was a moment of silence; then a cheer rose up and shook the rafters. The crowd surged toward the bar.

"Well done," Dalton said quietly.

"Thanks." Now that no one was watching her, she felt her body begin to tremble. "I hope I can make it through the rest of the evening."

"You'll be fine. In fact, here comes your first admirer to pay his respects."

Brooke looked up and saw her lawyer walking toward them. "Mr. Gannen."

"Brooke." He raised her hand to his lips. "You are stunning. A charming, radiant woman is a joy to behold."

His bright eyes and stiff speech told her that the upright lawyer had chosen to relax with one glass too many. "Perhaps you'd like some coffee," she suggested.

He brushed her offer aside. "I'll be fine, my dear. A man needs to let go once in a while. Tonight we drink to Mattie." He drained his mug. "And to you, sweet Brooke."

She guided him toward a chair. "Tomorrow you're going to feel as if you were run over by a bull, Mr. Gannen. But it's your head."

She left him at the table and looked around for Dalton. He was entering the gambling area accompanied by a white-haired man. She walked over to the two of them. "I don't believe we've met. I'm Brooke Tyler."

"Ma'am." He tilted his worn hat. "Sheriff Morgan. Are you aware that gambling is illegal in the Wyoming Territory?"

She felt the blood drain from her face. "I . . . I . . . Dalton?" She turned to him and was astonished to see him laughing. "Is this a joke?" she asked weakly.

Morgan shook his head. "No, but don't worry about it. The circuit judge comes through Horse Creek once or twice a year. As the sheriff, I will arrest you on those occasions for having gambling on the premises. You'll pay a fine and be back in business the following day."

"You're kidding?"

"Nope." The white-haired sheriff glanced around the room. "That's how it's done out here. Well, I think I'll try my hand at faro. Mattie's table was always real good to me. Reed, Brooke." He strolled away.

"I can't believe he's going to gamble here and then arrest me."

"That's life in the West."

"Jail . . . how charming. Something else I can look forward to." She clutched Dalton's arm. "Are there any other surprises you've forgotten to tell me about?"

He cocked his head as if considering her question. "None that I recall, right now."

"If you think of any others, save them for the morning. I've had about all I can take."

"I know how to take your mind off your troubles."

She glared at him suspiciously. "I'm not sure I'm going to like your suggestion."

"How would you know? I haven't even said anything yet."

"Call it a lucky guess."

"Come on. You'll love it."

He took her hand and pulled her farther into the room. The tables were all full and doing a brisk business. Dalton tapped one of the dealers on the shoulder and whispered in the man's ear. He nodded and stood up.

"Brooke, why don't you deal the next hand?"

Dalton held the chair out for her, but she stood frozen to the floor. He couldn't mean it, she thought frantically. She could barely shuffle a deck. "I can't possibly . . . I mean, I'm sure the gentlemen would prefer someone more experienced to deal their card game."

An old man with an eye patch smiled at her. "Your first time, honey? Don't worry, we'll be real gentle like . . . won't we, boys?"

She felt her cheeks flush, and she glared at Dalton. "If you insist." She sat down amid cheers and whistles of approval. When Dalton leaned over and handed her the cards, she gripped his arm. "I'll get you for this," she murmured.

He whispered into her ear, his warm breath tickling her skin. "Just play poker and count the cards. You need to win back the price of that free round."

The cards felt awkward at first. But after a couple of false starts, she was able to shuffle and deal without mishap. Even with eight players, including herself, she found it easy to keep track of the cards played, and she was as surprised as the men when she won hand after hand. When the men began to shift uncomfortably, Dalton passed her a new sealed deck, and the game began again.

Dalton stood behind Brooke's left shoulder, alternately watching her hands gain speed and sureness and enjoying the enticing view down the front of her dress. The shimmering silk exposed the tops of her breasts, and he imagined he could see the barest sliver of her rose-colored areolae. He swallowed, his throat dry and tight.

He touched his finger to her shoulder. "I think that's enough for tonight. We don't want to wear you out or take all the money in one sitting. Right, gentlemen?"

The chips in front of her were stacked several inches high. She returned five of them to each of the men, then rose with a fluid motion. "I know you were being kind and allowing me to win. Next time you won't be as gentle, and neither will I." She smiled and followed Dalton from the room.

He cornered her in the hall. "They didn't let you win; you did that all by yourself."

She laughed. "I know. Isn't it wonderful? I knew what the cards were going to be almost before I dealt them. It was as if they were talking to me. And the looks on the men's faces. They wanted to spit with frustration." She clapped her hands and spun in a graceful circle, her skirt billowing out around her. "Oh, Dalton." She touched his arm. "I'm having a lovely time. Thank you, for everything."

Her eyes darkened as the excitement changed to something more powerful. Her breasts rose and fell with her rapid breathing, and the motion mesmerized him. He knew he could take her right now with no protests, no qualms from either of them.

Footsteps sounded on the stairs, and Elizabeth came into view. "Show's about to start," she said, brushing past them.

Brooke stared at Dalton; the regret in her body matched that in his eyes. "Maybe my good timing relates only to cards," she whispered.

His wry grin was a poor substitute for his arms, but it warmed her all the same. "I know what you mean."

"Have you seen Samuel tonight?" she asked as they walked toward the main room.

"No. I checked with the sheriff earlier, and he told me the Prattlys have left to spend several days in Cheyenne. It seems Mrs. Prattly's threats don't include disrupting opening night."

Dalton's sharp tone almost made her regret having confided in him about the other woman's visit. "She didn't exactly threaten me."

His eyes grew dark. "What would *you* call it?"

"A warning."

"It's really the same thing. Be careful. That woman could be dangerous."

She thought of Mattie's diary. "I don't think so. She's frightened and angry, but not at me. To her the saloon represents her husband's affair. She loves him, and he doesn't love her back. I understand that . . . even if you don't."

Brooke hadn't seen the dancers' show all the way through yet. While the girls had been rehearsing for hours every day, she had been busy with other tasks. Dalton took her arm and led her to a reserved table near the stage. The men gathered close around them, and the room was filled with hushed whispers.

The red velvet curtain opened, and suddenly the stage was alive with red and black frilly costumes and flashes of arms and legs. The musical revue lasted about twenty minutes and would be performed several times each night. It consisted of several dances interspersed with songs. The girls sang together and individually, and Brooke found herself blushing at many of the earthy lyrics. Some of the phrases were confusing, but she didn't dare ask Dalton what they meant. There were playful references to the size of certain male parts, and she found herself wondering what Dalton would look like without his tailored black suit. Brooke had grown up with two brothers, so the male body wasn't a complete mystery to her, but her married friends had hinted that a part of it got bigger . . . at night, under the covers. She had always wondered why.

As the girls cavorted on stage, she studied her gambler. His brown hair curled around his ears and onto his collar. She remembered the feel of those curls, soft and springy against her hands. He was the perfect man, she admitted silently. Perfect for her. She recalled a poem she had read once, something about having only one day to live. *I would live it at your side*, she thought as she stared at him.

She felt his hand brush against her thigh, the brief touch sending fire racing through her body. A small smile curved his lips, and she knew it was only for her.

They locked the doors shortly after midnight. Brooke looked ready to collapse at any moment. Dalton resisted the urge to carry her up to her room and place her on that wide bed. This time he wouldn't cover her with a blanket and leave. This time he'd undress her and love her until her moans of ecstasy shattered the wanting in his soul.

"My feet hurt," she said as she slipped off her shoes and limped to the hall. "I may never walk again."

"Come on." He pressed against her back, forcing her to climb each step. Elizabeth and Caleb followed behind them. He was grateful that the presence of the older couple prevented him from giving in to his desire. However sweet the night, the morning would no doubt bring tears and recriminations.

Brooke paused in front of her door. "Good night, Dalton." She smiled wearily.

He crossed the landing and into his room and lit the lantern by the door. He was tired as well, he admitted to himself as he slipped off his coat and unbuttoned his vest. Pulling the shirt from his trousers, he moved to the bed.

The sound of shattering glass followed by a scream cut through the night.

He flew across the landing and flung open Brooke's door. "What happened?"

She stood in the center of the room, staring at the floor. The cold night air blew in through the broken window, and a rock lay on the floor surrounded by shards of glass.

"I turned on the l-lantern, and that came through the window." She was shaking so much she could barely speak.

He gathered her in his arms as Elizabeth and Caleb entered the room. "We heard a crash," Caleb said.

"Someone threw a rock through Brooke's window."

Elizabeth bent down and picked up the stone. "That's not all." She unwrapped something and handed it to Dalton.

He glanced at the paper. It was a note: "Leave Horse Creek now, or you'll be sorry." The childlike script didn't detract from the menace in the message, and Dalton felt icy tentacles of fear wrap themselves around his heart. Someone had played pranks on Mattie Frost, and now someone was trying to hurt Brooke. Everything she'd told him about Edna Prattly's threats came back to haunt him. Brooke had said she didn't believe the other woman would hurt her. Apparently she'd been wrong.

Chapter 11

"What does it say?" Brooke asked, as she trembled in his embrace.

He shook his head at the older couple, warning them not to say anything. "Nothing, love. It's just a prank, probably played by one of the boys in town. Come on." He led her from the room. Elizabeth and Caleb trailed behind.

"Where are we going? I need to clean up the mess."

"I'll take care of it." He led Brooke into his room and sat her on his bed, then turned to the other woman. "Would you make her some tea and pour some brandy in the cup? Caleb, check in the storeroom and see if you can find some wood to board up the window."

Brooke stared at him, her green eyes dark with confusion and hurt. "Why would someone throw a rock at me? I haven't done anything to bother anyone."

Dalton added a couple of logs to the fire, then returned to the bed. Her hands were cold and he rubbed them between his. "Let it go. There's nothing we can do tonight. Whoever threw the rock is long gone. We'll talk to the sheriff in the morning and see if he knows who might have done it."

If Morgan didn't have any ideas, Dalton sure had a couple of his own—starting with Edna Prattly.

He'd never met Mattie Frost. Even though her death had saddened him, the news hadn't evoked the dark fear and cold anger that the threat on Brooke's life produced. And if the note was simply a joke, he'd find that prankster and beat him until he walked like a three-legged dog, regardless of who he—or she—was.

Brooke shivered in the late night chill. Gooseflesh dotted her soft skin, and he drew a blanket around her bare shoulders. Elizabeth returned with the tea.

"Caleb's covering the window," she said as she set the tray on Dalton's desk.

"Thanks." He smiled at her. "Would you get Brooke's night things? She can stay here, and I'll sleep in her room."

He handed the tea to Brooke. "Drink this," he ordered.

She sniffed the cup. "You're always pouring brandy down me, Dalton Reed. If I didn't know any better I'd say you were trying to get me drunk and have your way with me."

If the smile on her lips didn't quite reach her eyes, he wasn't about to comment on the fact. Her attempt at humor, however small, relieved him. Brooke was a strong woman; she'd probably outlive them all. Unless someone . . . He pushed the thought away.

Dalton leaned forward and whispered in her ear. "You know that's all I dream about." As she chuckled softly, he realized that his admission was a two-edged sword. While he had meant to tease her into feeling better, his confession had also been completely truthful.

"I'm perfectly capable of sleeping in my own bed," she protested when Elizabeth returned with her night-gown and robe.

"You'll stay here if I have to tie you to that bed. Do I make myself clear?" Dalton stood up and tried to act fierce, but he had a sinking feeling that he only looked concerned.

"Yes."

She smiled at him; the sweet gentle curve of her lips made him long to climb under the sheets and pull her soft body next to his throbbing need. He stalked away without looking back.

When Dalton entered Brooke's room, Caleb was nailing a board over the window. "Need someone with a mighty powerful arm to throw all the way to the second floor," the older man said. The pounding of the hammer punctuated his sentence.

Dalton found a broom, then swept up the glass. "I'll talk with the sheriff tomorrow. Probably just some kids, though." He didn't want to say anything about his suspicions until he'd spoken with Morgan.

Caleb spoke without turning around. "Think the same feller did this as tried to shut Mattie down?"

Dalton dropped the broom with a clatter. "How did you know about that?"

The bartender shrugged. "Don't take much in the way of brains to figger it out. Shipments got lost or the orders were never placed. One time somebody let loose a couple dozen mice in the buildin'." He faced Dalton, his hazel eyes clouded with concern. "I know you think it's Miz Prattly, but this ain't her style. She'd be comin' in with her fancy lawyer, spoutin' them big words of hers."

"I hope you're right," Dalton said, but he still had a bad feeling about the woman and no one could make him think otherwise.

"That little girl in there . . ." Caleb nodded toward Dalton's room. "She done weaseled her way into Lizzy's heart, and mine, too. I won't take kindly to anything happenin' to her."

"I won't let anyone hurt her."

Caleb picked up his tools and an extra piece of wood, then headed for the door. "From what I hear, you ain't gonna be around all that long. Who's goin' to look out for her when you're gone?"

"She's all settled," Elizabeth said as she met Dalton in the hall. "No hysterics for that one. She's tough, like her aunt." She hesitated, as if she wished to say more, but then patted his arm and walked toward her door. Dalton took a deep breath and entered his room.

Brooke looked as demure as a nun, the collar of her white nightgown covering her throat clear to her chin, the sheets pulled up over her chest. But she was still sitting in his bed, with her brown hair flowing across the very pillow that had caressed his face. The fire reflected its brilliance in her eyes and cast haunting shadows across her cheeks.

"How are you feeling?" he asked quietly as he walked into the room.

She shrugged a slender shoulder, the slight rise and fall of the coverlet hinting at the womanly curves hidden below. "Foolish. I shouldn't have screamed. And I think it's silly for me to sleep in your room when I have a perfectly good bed in my own."

"But tonight I'll be in it, sweet Brooke. Surely you don't mean to imply that you wish to share it with me?"

She glanced down at her hands and twisted her fingers together. "I don't always know when you're teasing me, Dalton. Was that an invitation or an attempt to make me feel better?"

He sat next to her, his weight dipping the mattress until she was pressed against him, thigh to thigh. Smoothing a curl away from her forehead, he savored the satin softness of her skin. "Would you be shocked if I said both? You're a beautiful woman, Brooke Tyler, and I'm as vulnerable to your charms as any man." The corner of his mouth curved up. "Be gentle with me."

She laughed. "Now I know you're teasing. Leave me be. I'm tired."

He banked the fire, then lowered the lantern wick. The room was bathed in firelight. She settled back in the bed and turned to face him. "Good night, Dalton."

The muscles in his body contracted with need, his throat too tight to allow breath or words to flow. He left her without saying anything.

But if he had thought that leaving her side would alleviate his desire, he hadn't figured on the unique torture of sleeping in her bed. The light of the half-moon illuminated feminine frills and treasures, each a haunting reminder of her. The very cotton fabric of the sheet was suffused with her fragrance, and her gentle voice echoed from every corner of the room.

He tossed and turned, seeking sleep rather than comfort. But fear and need laced together, making peaceful rest a hazy illusion.

"Hard to say who wrote this," Sheriff Morgan said as he studied the note. "Almost looks like a child, or a right-handed adult using his left hand. One thing's fer sure: He don't want us to know who he is."

"I'd thought of that as well, Sheriff," Dalton said, struggling for patience. He had faith in Morgan, but he had also hoped for something substantial. "I think Edna Prattly wrote it."

"I heard tell you had an idea like that. Care to tell me why?" The lawman's eyes were suddenly piercing and direct.

Dalton repeated what Brooke had told him about her conversation with Samuel's wife. "She told Brooke that she'd see the Garden Saloon torn to the ground, one way or another. Mattie Frost owned the building and land outright. If Mrs. Prattly can't find a legal way to get rid of Brooke, what's to stop her from using force?"

Morgan opened his bottom desk drawer and pulled out a file. He dropped the note on top of the papers. "Guess I'll go have a talk with the woman as soon as she gets back in town. I jes' can't see her harmin' anyone, but I won't deny what you've said."

Dalton took off his hat and ran his hand through his hair. "I'm coming with you."

"Thought you might." He drew a cigar from his coat pocket and turned it over in his hands. "I'll let you know when I'm headin' out. In the meantime, I'll do my best to keep an eye on that little lady."

"Thanks." Dalton set his hat on his head and adjusted the brim. His lips pulled into a straight line. "I'll hire a bouncer for the saloon." He walked to the door. "Let me know if you find out anything, Sheriff."

"I will. And, son?"

"Yes?"

"What about Brooke protecting herself?"

He grinned. "I've got a couple of ideas about that, too. Let's hope I can convince *her*."

General stores always looked the same, he thought. Twice the goods crammed into half the needed space. The result was a jumble of kitchen supplies, bags of seed, and other necessities all competing for attention. Dalton bypassed the rows of merchandise and walked straight to the front of the shop.

He recognized the plump woman behind the counter. She had been the first to approach Brooke at church, and he had chosen her store deliberately.

Mrs. Carson gave him a tentative smile, studying him as if he was familiar enough to tug on her memory, but not familiar enough to place. "May I help you?"

"Dalton Reed, ma'am. We saw each other at church last Sunday. I work for Brooke Tyler."

"Oh, of course." Her slight smile blossomed until it transformed her plain features into friendly beauty. "What can I do for you, Mr. Reed?"

"I'd like to buy a few items, if you have them. And I also need some advice on how to get something made to measure, in leather."

She nodded. "I'll be more than happy to oblige. What are you looking for?"

Brooke crept down the stairs and headed for her office. She hoped to reach her desk without being detected. Once there, she could pretend that she had been hard at work for several hours . . . or a few minutes, at least.

Between the effort of getting the saloon ready to open, the excitement of the first night, and the trauma of the vandalism, she had been exhausted. When she'd finally opened her eyes that morning, it had been after twelve.

She tiptoed across the hall and pushed against her office door.

" 'Bout time you showed yourself, girlie. Shall I make you some lunch?"

She sighed heavily and hung her head as she turned to face the other woman. "Elizabeth, I'm so sorry for sleeping late. I—"

"Now, don't you fret none. Everything's fine. Come on. I've saved you some of the cinnamon buns you like so much. Dalton's gone to talk to the sheriff, but he should be back right quick."

Brooke had barely finished licking the sticky icing from her fingers when Dalton strolled into the kitchen. His paper-wrapped package drew her attention immediately, but he placed it on the table without batting an eye.

"Did you sleep well?" he asked.

"Yes. I've only been up for a short time."

He poured a cup of coffee from the pot on the stove and took the seat across from her. "I checked on you before I left, and you were snoring like a baby."

She felt a flush creep up her face. "I don't snore."

"How would you know?"

"I . . . I . . . Well, I don't."

His tolerant laughter brushed up against her ears, tickled the fine hairs on the back of her neck, and generally added to the brightness of the day. She should have been angry that he'd watched her while she slept, but she wasn't. In fact, picturing Dalton standing over her bed started her stomach to tightening around the breakfast she had just eaten.

"I spoke to the sheriff."

His businesslike tone was the antithesis of his teasing laughter of a moment before. "What did he say?"

"Not much. He said it was probably kids, as we thought." He traced random circles on the pine table with his cup. The coffee perking on the stove and distant laughter from the saloon were the only sounds. "You willing to sell now?"

His question came from nowhere, and she sat in stunned silence.

"You might want to heed this warning. It could be a joke, or it could be something deadly." His eyes met hers. The dark pupils were filled with seriousness and purpose. Hidden in their depths was the smallest trace of an emotion she hesitated to identify. Fear. Not for himself, but for her.

"I won't leave, Dalton. You can't make me."

He rose and picked up the package. "I thought you'd say that. You're a predictable woman, I'll give you that. And stubborn as hell. Come on." He pulled her to her feet.

"Where are we going?"

"To teach you to use a gun."

"But I don't want to shoot anyone," she protested for the third time, steadily avoiding looking at the paper-wrapped box between them.

Dalton turned the rented buggy off the main road and into a small clearing. "I never said you had to like it, Brooke. But if something happens, I want you to be able to protect yourself."

She folded her hands in her lap and stared straight ahead. Her mouth was drawn into a stubborn frown. "I couldn't hurt anyone deliberately."

He placed a finger under her chin and turned her until she was looking at his face. "You don't have any trouble picking a fight with me," he teased.

His grin was irresistible, and she felt her lips curving in response. "I won't like it," she promised.

"You don't have to," he agreed as he helped her down from the buggy.

The ground was rocky underfoot, and she gripped Dalton's arm to maintain her balance. The tall grasses and plants clung to her skirt. The sweet smells rising from the earth were a pleasant reminder that spring was finally ready to cast off the last traces of winter.

"This looks good enough." Dalton stopped about ten feet from a lone plains cottonwood tree and placed his package on the ground. "Have you ever used a gun?"

"I shot a rifle, once." She wrinkled her nose. "My father took me hunting when I was about eight. Mama was visiting family; otherwise I would never have been allowed to go." She smiled as she remembered pleading for weeks to be allowed to accompany her older brother. "When my father brought down a buck, it broke my heart." She met Dalton's compassionate glance and turned away, suddenly embarrassed. "I'd never realized that hunting meant killing. When I saw that proud, handsome animal die right before my eyes, I started to cry. You can imagine how my mother felt about the whole thing. I don't think she spoke to Papa for a week."

Dalton gave her arm a reassuring squeeze. "No one's going to make you shoot at any animals. Just a piece of paper."

He walked to a tree and attached a sheet about one foot wide and two feet long. When he returned to her side, he bent down and opened the brown package. Inside the box was a small but deadly-looking weapon. He handed it to her. "This is a derringer pocket pistol. It's small, but it can kill a man, the same as any other gun."

At first she thought the metallic weapon looked like a toy. But as she realized the responsibility and consequences of using it, her hand and wrist quivered under the increased weight. "Dalton, I can't." She tried to give him back the derringer, but he refused to take it.

"I'm doing this for your own good. Do you think I *like* the idea of you carrying around a loaded weapon? As mad as you get at me sometimes, I'll be lucky to live out the summer."

As always, he knew the perfect words to say to put her at her ease. "All right," she agreed. "I'll learn to use it, but I doubt that I could ever shoot anyone."

"I can't tell you how happy that makes me."

He showed her how to load the pistol, then demonstrated how to fire it. She covered her ears at the loud pop.

"Now you try."

She held the gun gingerly between her thumb and index finger, as if it were a poisonous snake. The walnut grip was still warm from his palm, and the heat gave her comfort. She took aim at the tree and pulled the trigger.

Her arm jerked up, and she almost hit herself in the forehead. A loud squawking accompanied the flapping of wings as a large bird was frightened into flight. The paper attached to the tree fluttered unscathed in the breeze.

"What happened?"

"I think you scared ten years off the life of that sage chicken."

She glanced at him over her shoulder, and her eyes narrowed. "If I were you, I don't know that I'd find this situation humorous. After all, I am holding a loaded weapon."

He brushed his right index finger against her nose. "Not any more. The derringer only holds two bullets. Remember that." He reloaded the gun, then handed it back to her. "Try again."

Lifting his arm until it was level with hers, he placed his hand beneath hers to steady her. "Look down the barrel and sight on the tree. Squeeze the trigger slowly. You don't have to kill anybody. Even if you miss the head or chest a single bullet in the leg is usually enough to slow a man down so that you can run away."

His chest vibrated with his words, and she felt the rumblings against her back. His left arm circled her waist; the contact comforted as much as it excited. The strong muscles of his forearm were inches below her breasts, and she longed for the courage to raise his arm until that band of steel pressed against her aching curves.

He smelled like a man. The scent of his soap, spicier than her lilac bars, a trace of cologne, the tobacco from his cigars—they all swirled together, fused by the heat of his body. The result was a heady mixture that made her throat dry and the secret place between her legs damp.

When she fired the gun again, she felt a matching explosion somewhere in her stomach. The target fluttered, revealing a puncture mark.

"I hit it!" She thrust the gun into Dalton's hands and ran to the tree. "Look at this. I actually hit it." She rushed back to him, pointing at the proof.

"Lucky shot," he muttered.

"Spoilsport," she countered.

They continued to practice for almost an hour. On the way back to the saloon, Dalton stopped at the general store and picked up a package.

"Another exciting gift for me?" Brooke asked.

"Yes, as a matter of fact." He held it out of her reach. "You have to wait until we get back home."

"Dalton, I want to see it now." She thrust out her lower lip and blinked. "Please?"

He picked up the reins and snapped them. "I admit you're very tempting, but I can't be convinced."

She pulled her hat lower on her forehead. "I could change your mind."

"You sound like a petulant child. And you're right; you could deliberately tempt me. But how would you stop me from taking all of you?"

He asked the question so casually that it was several seconds before she understood what he had said. She wanted to deny what he accused her of, but she could not. Enticing Dalton with a brush of her hands, the touch of her lips, had been her intention. Her cheeks flushed more from her tactics being exposed than from his question.

She sulked the last three blocks of the journey. Dalton wondered if she knew how appealing he found her lower lip. He longed to draw the tender flesh into his mouth and suck on it until she pleaded for mercy. A flash of desire ripped through him, causing him to tighten his hands on the reins until the horse tossed its head restively.

When they reached the saloon, Brooke jumped off without assistance. By the time he had returned from the stable, she was nowhere to be seen. He climbed the stairs two at a time, then knocked on her door.

"Open up, Brooke, or I won't give you the present."

"I don't want it," she called back.

"All right. If you insist."

He stood on the landing and waited. Within three seconds she flung her door open. "No, wait . . ." Her voice trailed off when she saw him standing in the doorway. "You tricked me."

"I know." He stepped into her room and closed the door behind him, then handed her the package.

She took the box and gave him a wary glance. "This isn't another gun, is it?"

"Not exactly."

She pulled the string and the paper fell away. "A knife?"

He nodded. "And a sheath to wear around your . . . leg." He coughed.

Brooke picked up the thin leather thong. One side was of the softest suede. There was a small buckle and a sheath for a knife. "You expect me to wear this?"

"Always."

She thrust the gift into his hands. "That's ridiculous. I'm not an outlaw. I don't need to walk around armed."

"I insist." His voice was low and firm. This was one argument he was determined to win.

She walked to the fireplace and stared at the cold grate. "You can't tell me what to do."

"If you refuse to wear the knife, I'll leave Horse Creek right now." He hated threatening her, but knew no other way to make her understand.

Her shoulders stiffened, and she raised her head. "What about our deal?"

"I'm changing it."

"Do you want to leave so very much?" Her voice was so quiet he barely heard her; yet the pain in her words filled the room.

"I just want you to be safe."

"I see." She crossed her arms over her chest, as if to ward off a chill. "So you do care for me a little?"

He didn't remember moving, but suddenly he was behind her, his hands on her waist, the leather sheath pressing into her dress. "You know I do."

"Very well. I shall wear this contraption." She turned and pulled it from his grasp. "Where does it go?"

"I'm not sure." When he had sketched what he needed for Mrs. Carson, he had tried not to think about the item actually being on Brooke's leg. "Above the knee, I think."

She crossed to the bed. "Turn around, Dalton."

He complied, only to find a reflection of her in front of him, in the mirror above the dresser. She lifted her skirts and buckled the sheath halfway up her thigh. The fine fabric of her undergarments clung to her and left very little to his imagination. Her long legs were more perfect than he had pictured in his mind, and he cursed himself for ever having spoken to her that first night on the train.

"You may turn around."

But instead of moving, he looked up and met her gaze in the mirror. Her eyes widened as understanding dawned. She raised her chin. "I can see that Mrs. Gilmore was right. One can't trust a gambler."

"Haven't I been telling you that all along?"

Brooke sat in the buggy, tucked between Dalton and the sheriff. She smiled, careful not to let him see. They'd had an argument at the saloon about whether or not she'd accompany them to the Prattly ranch, but she'd refused to be left behind. Short of tying her to the door in her office, Dalton had been given little choice.

As they rounded the bend in the road, she drew in a gasp of surprise. The house was two stories tall and much grander than any she'd seen since leaving Philadelphia. A perfectly manicured lawn stretched out in front, a testament to what money and hard labor could accomplish in the wilds of Wyoming.

The sheriff stepped out of the buggy and secured the horses. Even as Dalton helped her down, she could see he was still angry. His dark eyes met hers, but the fire flickering inside wasn't from his hands holding her waist.

"You're being very narrow-minded," she murmured softly so that Morgan couldn't hear. The sheriff was carefully looking around the outside of the house.

"I'm worried about your safety," Dalton said, pulling her hand into the crook of his arm. "Something that doesn't seem to concern you at all. Have you given any thought to the fact that you're entering the home of the one person on earth who'd like to hurt you?"

"Nonsense. Mrs. Prattly doesn't care about me, she just wants the saloon shut down."

He looked at her and shook his head. "Not just shut down—torn down. We could head back and wait for her to set the place on fire."

There was no talking to Dalton when he got in this sort of mood, she reminded herself. What her handsome gambler didn't understand and what she couldn't bring herself to explain was that she understood Edna Prattly.

Brooke knew what it felt like to be rejected by a man. Joe MacAllister had at least had the decency to tell her before the wedding, but that was his only saving grace. And it hadn't made the pain or embarrassment any more tolerable.

Edna had lived her whole married life with a man who only wanted her money. If the incident at the church was any indication, Mr. Prattly didn't go out of his way to be kind. "What you don't understand, Dalton, is that—"

"You two gonna stand there jawin' or do you want to go on in?" Morgan stood on the porch and knocked loudly.

By the time they'd climbed up the three steps, the door had been pulled open. A young girl of about fifteen stepped out. She was dressed in a black uniform, complete with a starched apron and a frilly white hat.

"May I help you?" she asked.

Morgan nodded. "Tell Mrs. Prattly that Sheriff Morgan would like to speak with her."

The young woman moved back and motioned for them to follow her. The entryway was spacious, with tiled floors and vaulted ceilings. If she didn't look out the windows, Brooke could have sworn she was in New York or Boston. Elizabeth hadn't been exaggerating when she'd said Edna Prattly had money.

The maid continued down the hall and stopped in front of an open arch. "You may wait in here."

The sheriff led the way into the room, glanced around once, then removed his hat. Even Dalton gave a silent whistle of appreciation.

Floral fabrics draped the windows and covered the furniture. Family portraits—the richness of the jewels worn and the haughtiness of their expressions bespoke the subjects' wealth—competed with tall cabinets and bookcases for wall space.

She shook her head when Dalton motioned for her to take a seat. The chairs looked dangerous. They were deep and soft, not conducive to rising easily after one had been seated. She perched on the corner of a small settee instead.

Morgan was not accustomed to such furniture. He plopped down in one of the chairs, only to have to struggle to his feet when Mrs. Prattly swept in seconds later.

"Sheriff, Mr. Reed, Miss Tyler." She nodded graciously. "What an unexpected pleasure. Nelly"—she turned to the maid hovering in the archway—"please bring tea for our guests."

"Yes, ma'am." The girl curtsied, then swiftly moved away.

"Gentlemen, please be seated."

Edna joined Brooke on the couch, leaving the men to the mercy of the chairs. If she hadn't been concerned about the outcome of the meeting, Brooke would have dared to smile at the older woman. But Samuel's wife didn't look at all amused by the visit. Her blue eyes snapped with annoyance and some small flicker of what might have been fear.

Sheriff Morgan cleared his throat. "Mrs. Prattly—"

"Please." She held up her hand and smiled graciously. "Why don't we hold off on business until the tea is served?"

He coughed. "I thought you might want your husband to be present while we, ah . . ."

"Are you planning to arrest me?" Edna's voice was steady, but Brooke saw the slight tremor in her hands.

"No. Of course not." The sheriff coughed again.

Brooke stifled the urge to pat Edna's arm. She knew neither Dalton nor the other woman would appreciate her sympathy.

The gambler glanced at her. He was stubborn, she thought. Nothing would convince him that Mrs. Prattly meant her no harm. Still, she wasn't offended that he thought so much of her safety. If only his concern spilled over into the rest of their relationship, perhaps she could get past the carefully constructed wall he kept around his emotions.

"How are you enjoying Horse Creek?" Mrs. Prattly asked Brooke.

"It's very nice . . ."

Dalton held back a sound of disgust. The social chit-chat was irritating, to say the least. Why didn't Morgan arrest the woman and question her from a jail cell? She was responsible for the rock through the window. He didn't know how she'd accomplished it when she'd supposedly been out of town, but the feeling in his gut had saved his life more than once. When he felt that clenching, he didn't ask questions; he just pulled out his gun and rolled for cover.

"Here we are." Mrs. Prattly motioned for Nelly to place the tea cart in front of her, then excused the girl. She poured the tea and smiled tentatively at Morgan. "Sheriff, I believe you had some questions for me?"

"Don't you want Samuel to—"

"I'm very comfortable speaking with you three alone."

"Someone threw a rock through Miss Tyler's window the other night. I was wondering if you knew anything about it."

She turned to Brooke. "You poor child. Are you all right? Was anyone hurt?"

"Just the window."

"I assure you, Sheriff, that I know nothing about the crime. I've heard rumors since my husband and I returned, of course, but that's all. We were in Cheyenne that night . . . at a party with several friends. I can give you their names if you'd like to verify that I was there."

Dalton narrowed his eyes and studied her. He could spot a bluff a mile off—she wasn't lying. Damn. He'd been so sure she was behind what had happened. Glancing at Brooke, he frowned at her "I told you so" smile.

Morgan stumbled over himself to assure Mrs. Prattly that wouldn't be necessary. They spoke a few more minutes, then were shown to the door. On the ride home, Brooke chattered on about how pleased she was that Edna had been exonerated. What she didn't seem to realize and what Dalton didn't have the heart to tell her was that if Mrs. Prattly wasn't responsible, someone else was. And that person was still out there . . . waiting.

Chapter 12

"But none of my dresses are right," Suzanne wailed as she threw another garment onto the already impressive pile on the bed.

Brooke stepped over and pulled out a light blue gown. "What about this one?"

"It's so plain," the blonde fretted. "I want him to notice me."

"So wear something low-cut," Lily suggested as she glanced through her magazine.

"Lily, he's a minister, not a customer at the saloon," Rose said. "If you can't say something helpful, then go read in your room."

Violet brought a pale pink gown into the crowded bedroom. "What about this one?"

"I just don't know which to wear. Brooke, what do you think?"

Brooke stood up and walked over to the dress Violet was holding. "I like this. It's pretty, yet demure. It will complement your blue eyes and light skin. And I'll let you borrow Mattie's pearls for the afternoon."

"Are you sure?"

Brooke nodded. "Mattie loved a great romance more than anyone else I know. She would have wanted you to wear them."

"Oh, thank you. I won't forget this."

Brooke found herself pulled into an enthusiastic hug and crushed against Suzanne's ample bosom. She disentangled herself and laughed. "I'm sure I'll need the favor returned sometime in the future."

Lily raised one perfectly plucked eyebrow. "I can't imagine why. Dalton already thinks the world of you, Brooke. He's just waiting for you to say the word, if you know what I mean." She gasped when three pillows were simultaneously hurled in her direction. "What did I say?"

Rose glared at Lily. "You are so insensitive sometimes. Miss Brooke doesn't need her private affairs blabbered all about, you fool."

"It's all right, Rose." Brooke smiled at the sweet brunette. "I can take care of myself. And as for needing advice about clothes, that time will come soon enough." She met four pairs of troubled eyes. "Didn't Dalton tell you?"

Lily stood up, her magazine falling unnoticed to the floor. "Tell us what?"

"He's only going to be here for six months. He'll be leaving in the fall."

"But why?" Suzanne clutched the pink gown until the sleeves were crushed. "I know he cares about you."

Their genuine concern caused Brooke to smile with a brightness she didn't feel. "That may be, but he's still leaving. Now you all need to rest for tonight's shows, and I have to get back. I'll see you at the saloon."

As Brooke turned to leave, Lily touched her arm. "I'll walk you out."

The boardinghouse, across town from the saloon, started out as a luxury hotel, but when the gold rush fizzled, it had been converted into private apartments.

The rooms were large and reasonably priced. And the owner, Mr. Peterson, was a big burly man who protected his boarders with a meaty fist and a ready rifle.

The two women walked down the stairs. Brooke waited for Lily to begin the conversation. Although she was the unofficial spokeswoman for the dancers, Lily tended to stay out of Brooke's way. Brooke wasn't sure if it was because of how they had met, or if Lily didn't like her, but either way, she respected the other woman's right to privacy.

"I'm worried about Suzanne," Lily said when they reached the bottom of the stairs. "I think she's settin' herself up for a lot of pain, and I'd like you to do something about it."

Brooke stared at her. "I don't understand."

Lily shrugged, her silk dress whispering with the rise and fall of her shoulders. "You're having her over to dinner tomorrow with that minister fellow. I saw him making eyes at her in church, but he ain't goin' to do much more than that. She's going to start thinkin' that she has a chance of being something more than she is. But when one of his self-righteous church ladies gets a whiff of what's goin' on, he's gonna dump Suzanne faster than a farmer totin' manure."

"I doubt that Mr. Bolt would be—"

"You don't know nothin', Brooke Tyler." Lily's eyes were filled with scorn. "You come from your fancy East Coast city and start to run a saloon like it's a lark. When things get rough, you can just run home to your family and your servants. But us"—she jerked her head toward the rooms—"we've got nothin' else in this world but the bodies given us by the good Lord. And I'll be damned if any of us are gonna earn our keep by entertaining upstairs."

Lily's eyes glistened with unshed tears, and her harsh words cut Brooke to the heart. "I'd never deliberately hurt any of you. And I'd never abandon you, either, but if Suzanne wants to see Mr. Bolt, we don't h. ∍ the right to stand in her way. She's your friend. I should think you'd want to encourage her."

Lily turned away, her hands clenched into fists. "You would think that. But who's going to pick up the pieces when he marries a rancher's daughter instead? And what about you?" She spun back and faced Brooke. "If what you say is true, if Dalton is leaving, then you're just the same as us. Trash. No one's going to want to marry a saloon owner any more than they want to marry a dance hall girl. We're all trapped."

Lily raced up the stairs, the pounding of her feet matching the rapid thumping of Brooke's heart.

"You're wrong," she called after the woman, but there was no response. Her words lingered in the air until they rang in her ears and made her wonder if Lily had been correct.

I'm here because I want to be, she told herself as she set out for the saloon. But her thoughts were more of a question than a statement.

In Philadelphia her life had been carefully defined by the mores of society. Here she made her own rules. She wasn't trapped; that she knew. There was enough money in Mattie's account to keep her in comfort for the rest of her life. Despite her concerns about Mrs. Prattly's threats to shut her down, she wasn't going anywhere. She had grown to love the Garden Saloon. Still, she had to admit the best part of her day was Dalton. Once he was gone . . .

She shook her head. Time enough to think about that when it actually happened. And if there was a grain of truth in what Lily said, then Brooke was even more determined to help Suzanne snare the handsome minister. A marriage between the two would certainly turn Horse Creek on its ear, she thought with a grin. It might be just what the town needed.

"Miss Brooke, there's a gentleman here to see you."

Brooke glanced up from her desk and tried to smile at the tall, heavyset man standing in the doorway to her office. But her lips refused to cooperate. Evan Jones made her nervous.

Although she had agreed that they should hire a bouncer, she didn't like having Jones on the premises. His beady eyes seemed to follow her wherever she went; yet if she watched *him,* he never once looked at her directly. Even his slow, measured tread gave her the jitters. He had a habit of moving silently into a room, then startling her when he spoke.

"I'll be right there, Evan."

He touched his hat, then walked away without making a sound. She suppressed a shudder as she rose from behind the desk.

"Caleb, did the stage bring this week's newspapers yet?" Brooke asked as she entered the saloon.

"No, ma'am. But I was just on my way to the station."

"Fine. Would you stop at the general store and bring me some . . ." Her voice trailed off as she noticed the man sitting awkwardly at one of the small tables. "Mr. Franklin? You're the one who wanted to see me?"

"Miss Tyler." Arthur stood up and smiled at her. His face was pale, and his eyes darted nervously about the room as if he expected naked women to appear at any moment. "I was wondering if"—he cleared his throat—"if you would care to dine with me on Monday night."

He turned his hat in his hands, spinning it faster and faster until she was afraid it was going to fly out of his fingers and crash into the glasses displayed above the bar. A refusal of his invitation hovered on her lips, but she bit it back. Lily's words were still ringing in her ears.

Arthur Franklin might not be the greatest catch in town, but he was respectable, she thought as she glanced at his well-cut but out-of-style suit. No doubt the evening would be a complete bore, but perhaps not a total waste if it made Dalton jealous. She found it very irritating that the gambler constantly pointed out that he couldn't be interested in her, but glared at any customer who got a little too friendly.

Arthur watched her with a touchingly hopeful look in his eyes, and she didn't have the heart to turn him down. "What time should I expect you, Mr. Franklin?"

He beamed so brightly that she was tempted to shield her eyes. "I shall call for you at six, if that is convenient."

"Fine. Good day, Mr. Franklin." She started to return to her office, but he called her back.

"Miss Tyler?"

"Yes?"

"I was wondering." He cleared his throat several times, his face flushing bright red. "Would you call me Arthur?"

Dread twisted her insides, like an apple eaten green. She didn't want to call him by his first name. She didn't even want to go out with him. "Certainly, Arthur, but only if you'll call me Brooke."

* * *

Brooke placed the last pearl in Suzanne's hair. The gleaming pins matched the baubles at her ears and throat. "There. You look perfect."

"Oh, Miss Brooke, how can I ever thank you?" Suzanne leaned forward and stared at herself in the mirror. "I look like a real lady. You think Pastor Bolt will notice?" She glanced anxiously at Brooke.

"I'm sure he'll think of nothing else. Now hurry downstairs. He's due any minute."

Suzanne fled the room in a cloud of pink silk, her blond ringlets bouncing against her shoulders. Brooke looked down at her brown cotton gown. She had deliberately dressed plainly and had asked Elizabeth to do the same. This was Suzanne's day. The young dancer was to be the shining jewel at dinner.

"Matchmakers inevitably get their fingers burned."

Dalton's voice teased as much as it warned. She caught a glimpse of him out of the corner of her eye, but refused to acknowledge him. Although she continued to check her appearance in the mirror, she was conscious only of his tall masculine body leaning against the door frame.

"I see you've reverted to East Coast prim in your attire. Could it be that you want to make sure the very eligible, very handsome Stephen Bolt only has one thing on his mind?"

"I'm sure I don't know what you're talking about, Dalton. I merely tried to dress appropriately for a visit from the clergy."

He crossed the room in two angry strides and gripped her arms. "You're playing games with people's lives. It doesn't become you."

His words hurt more than his hands, but she still twisted free of his grasp. "What are you so afraid of?

That Suzanne and Stephen might find something in common? That they might get married? I thought your ghosts haunted only you, Dalton Reed. Or do you object to anyone finding happiness?"

He stared down at her, his eyes wide, his lips drawn into a straight line. No twitch of a muscle or flicker of a lash betrayed his feelings, and she resented him for that. Whatever regret she might have felt for speaking harshly slipped away through the cracks in her composure.

"Well, say something," she demanded.

"You're making a mistake."

"Why?"

He turned away. "There are things you can't understand."

"Don't walk away from me." She gripped his arm and forced him to face her. "You're always saying that, as though life is this great mystery that only you have experienced. Well, I've lived, too. I've seen suffering; I've been hurt. You aren't the only one with a secret."

"You're a naive child." His calm voice was a marked contrast to her shrill tone.

"What does that mean?"

He pulled her hands away from his jacket and held them tightly together. "It means that Stephen Bolt is the minister of a small-town congregation and Suzanne is a saloon dancer, and they can never find happiness together. You'll only hurt them both by trying to make things work between them."

"But he wouldn't care about her being a dancer."

"He would care that she used to be a prostitute."

He'd left her without a defense. His logic had battered at her rationalization until there was nothing left to do but open the door and allow her hopes to steal away. She walked to the window and stared out over the street. Her arm brushed against the wood covering the broken pane.

"Brooke, I'm sorry."

"Why? Because I'm a dreamer? Because you spoke the truth? You've nothing to be sorry about. As always, you have all the answers and I'm a fool. Do you ever grow tired of the game?"

"Don't."

She heard him cross the room, then felt the touch of his fingers on her arm. The gentle pressure made her eyes burn, and she blinked frantically to hold back the tears. "I need them to be happy together," she said. "But everyone tells me that can't be. Just yesterday Lily demanded that I prevent it."

"She's right." He wrapped his arms around her waist and pulled her back against his solid frame. "I don't want you or Suzanne to be hurt."

But it's too late, she thought to herself as she inhaled his familiar fragrance. Pain had become a part of her destiny the moment she boarded that train in Nebraska. For whatever reason, Dalton had decided he would never allow himself to be close to a woman. He'd love a woman with his body, no doubt, but he'd keep his heart carefully out of reach. He'd warned her a hundred times. And she'd listened, too. But somehow the message hadn't sunk in. And now it was too late.

She turned in his arms and placed her cheek against the rough fabric of his coat. The steady thumping in his chest reassured her that he was with her at that moment in time. The brush of his hands on her spine, the scent of his body, the soothing murmur of his voice, would stay with her always. She would live out her days repeating the tragedy of her aunt's life. Two Tyler women who loved men they could never have.

Dalton glanced around the table. Suzanne and Stephen Bolt were holding an animated conversation, the intensity of their voices belied by the smiles on their faces. Caleb attacked his meal as if he suspected the couple might suddenly discover there was food on the table and take the choicest pieces for themselves. Elizabeth bustled about, filling bowls and checking on her pies. But it was Brooke who held Dalton's attention.

She sat straight in her chair, the very picture of lady-like deportment. Her left hand rested in her lap; her right delicately held the fork she was pushing around on her plate. Her eyes were downcast, her expression polite.

He willed her to look up at him, to say something saucy, to toss her head and smile engagingly . . . to forgive him. But she did not. There were dark shadows under her eyes, physical proof of his betrayal. He'd cared for only one other woman in his life and he'd disappointed his mother, too.

With a blink of an eye, he was back in the past. Joanna sat next to him in the old family buggy. Her shrill laughter proclaimed her victory. Hatred filled him until all attempts at rational thought were burned away by the rage.

He still remembered the look on his mother's face when he told her he was leaving. She'd begged him to stay, reminding him that he was only a boy of sixteen, but he'd tossed her concern aside. When pleading hadn't worked, she'd spoken of the family honor. But at sixteen, "honor" and "duty" had been empty words. He'd found out their meaning later on—the lesson had cost Joanna her life. And when he'd returned four years later, ready to make amends, it had been too late.

That torment had forced him to leave his home a second time, and he had never gone back. He didn't want to leave Horse Creek under the same circumstances.

"Caleb, can you come in here, please? The stove is giving me some trouble," Elizabeth called from the kitchen.

Caleb glanced at Dalton and shrugged his shoulders. "She don't let nobody near that stove but her."

"Caleb?"

Elizabeth's voice had increased in volume and pitch. Her husband practically stumbled over his chair in his haste to get to the other room. Dalton knew that Elizabeth was trying to give Suzanne and Stephen a chance to be alone. No doubt she and Brooke had planned the whole incident down to the last detail. Then he had come along and ruined everything.

"Brooke?"

She glanced up at him. "Yes?"

He winced at the chill in her eyes. He would do anything to return them to their laughing warmth. Anything. "I, um . . . I have a couple of things I need to discuss with you. Could you join me in your office for a moment?"

"Now?" she asked, looking around the table.

"Yes." He turned to the other couple. "If you'll excuse us?"

Stephen glanced up and winked. "Of course."

Dalton led Brooke to the office. She stood near her desk and stared at him. "I don't see what couldn't have waited. It was very rude to leave our guests alone like that."

He touched her cheek. "Wasn't that the plan?"

"Yes, but I thought . . ." She smiled as understanding dawned. "You mean you're trying to help? But didn't you say that—"

"Shh." He covered her mouth with his index finger, enjoying the tempting pressure of her lips against his skin. "I'm willing to admit I might have been a little hasty with my decision."

She pulled her head away. "You mean you were wrong?"

In his heart he knew he wasn't. No doubt the budding relationship in the dining room was headed for disaster. But he would go to any length to see once again the teasing light in Brooke's green eyes. "Yes, I was wrong."

" . . . and then he turned the buggy off the road, and we drove into a field of flowers just beginning to bloom." Suzanne leaned back on the bed and sighed. "It was the prettiest thing I ever saw. He was so handsome, with his blue eyes. And that smile . . ."

"And?" Brooke prompted as she pinned up her hair.

"Well, he didn't kiss me, if that's what you're askin'. But he looked at my face and told me he liked me very much."

Brooke smiled. "That's wonderful. Are you going to see him again?"

The tall blonde turned to face Brooke and propped her head up on her hands. "I don't know. I want to o' course, but . . . I told him."

Brooke sat on the corner of the bed. "About your . . ."

Suzanne nodded. "Yes, about entertaining upstairs. I knew I had to tell him the truth. I was afraid he'd take me straight home, but he didn't. He was still for a long time." She grimaced as she remembered. "When he finally spoke, he was so angry his voice shook. I was scared he was goin' to beat me like my daddy used to, but he didn't. He said it wasn't my fault, that I was a victim of cir-cum-stan-ces." She stumbled over the unfamiliar word. "Ain't that the greatest thing you ever heard?"

"I hope he wants to call on you again, Suzanne," Brooke said, and started to stand up. But the dancer touched her arm.

"I gotta tell you something else." The young girl looked down at the coverlet. "I'd like to look for another job. I'll stay here till I can find one, but I—"

"Hush. You don't have to explain to me. I understand. In fact, when the literary society meets this week, I'll find out if anyone needs some help."

Suzanne looked up, her blue eyes filled with tears. "You are the best friend I've ever had."

Brooke laughed as she felt moisture on her cheeks. "Don't get me started crying, too, or we'll both be sobbing up here for hours and Arthur will wonder what's wrong with me."

"Arthur Franklin? Why are you letting him call on you? Dalton Reed is twice the man he'll ever be, and in love with you, to boot."

Brooke shook her head and stood up. "No. Dalton's still leaving and I'm still staying."

"But you love him?"

She picked up her reticule and walked to the door. "Of course."

Brooke's meal with Arthur wasn't worse than she had imagined, but it certainly wasn't better, either. The food at the hotel dining room was as unimaginative as she'd remembered from her short stay, and a far cry from Elizabeth's wonderful cooking.

Arthur had gone out of his way to make everything perfect, but fate was against him. The rented buggy had lost a wheel, so they'd ended up walking to the hotel. Their table was close to the kitchen and unbearably hot. The meat was undercooked and the vegetables cold. By the time they were served dessert, Brooke was afraid that the poor man was going to burst into tears.

At Edward Gannen's office, Arthur had appeared forthright and in control. But here, alone with her, he seemed almost unable to speak. They sat in uncomfortable silence for several minutes until she tried, for the third time, to engage him in conversation. "Were you born in Wyoming?" she asked.

He smiled gratefully. "Oh, no. I'm originally from a small town in New York State."

"What drew you to Horse Creek?"

He stared at her as if she'd whipped out a deck of cards and started to deal a hand of poker. "I . . . I . . ." He took a sip of his drink and choked on it. He coughed until she was forced to pound on his back several times.

"Are you all right?"

"Ye-yes," he sputtered.

As he continued to clear his throat and wipe his eyes, she studied him. He was attractive—some might even say handsome, she thought. There was something familiar about the shape of his head and the placement of his eyes, as though his clear image had been traced from somewhere else. He continued to remind her of her oldest brother, as much in attitude as in appearance. Poor Arthur, she thought. He was trying so hard to please her. He'd be crushed if he knew of the unfavorable comparison.

"Would you care to take a stroll or do you have to be back at . . . to work soon?" he asked.

The thought of spending any more time with Arthur Franklin was enough to make her plead for mercy, but she wasn't one to do things by halves. "Of course I have time for a walk, Arthur. I can think of nothing I'd like better."

Dalton paced restlessly in the saloon. It was after eight. What could be keeping Brooke? No, he thought as he passed in front of the main doors for the third time. Not what—who? That pasty-faced law clerk was out there with her. Probably staring at the moon and telling her lies . . . kissing her lips. His hands clenched into tight fists. He wanted to strangle Arthur Franklin with his bare hands.

"Excuse me. Do you know where I could find Mr. Prattly?"

Dalton glanced at the tall man standing in front of him. He was mean-looking, with hair as red as the scar across his right cheek. "I don't want trouble," Dalton said as he reached under his jacket for his gun.

The man stared at him. "I work for Prattly. His prize mare is about to deliver her first foal, and he told me to come tell him when it was time."

"He's in the back." Dalton jerked his head toward the gaming room.

"Much obliged."

The tall man strolled away. Dalton continued his surveillance of the saloon entrance, cursing Arthur for courting her, Brooke for allowing it, and himself for caring so damned much. He was so preoccupied with his anger that he barely noticed her when she walked through the wide double doors. She pushed through the crowd, then slipped into the hallway. He went after her.

When he climbed the last step, she had already reached her room. His boots sounded out on the wooden landing as he crossed to her closed door. "I want to talk to you, Brooke Tyler," he called out.

"I'm changing my clothes."

"Just because I agreed to teach you how to run this place doesn't mean you can spend all your time gallivanting about town playing with your little friends."

She opened the door a crack and glared at him. He was torn between watching the anger flashing in her eyes and staring at the robe she had clutched to her breasts. Both were exciting.

"It isn't even eight-thirty, Dalton. I seriously doubt that two hours spent eating dinner constitutes 'all my time.' "

She tried to close the door, but he stuck his foot in the crack and forced it open. "Get out of my room," she ordered.

"Not until we get this settled."

"There's nothing to settle, except the fact that you're imagining things."

"What were you doing with him?" The words were out before Dalton even knew what he was going to say. There was no way to call them back.

"What do you want to know?" Brooke looked confused as she clutched her wrapper more tightly around her. But instead of offering more protection, the thin fabric clung to her body, clearly outlining her tempting curves . . . curves that Arthur Franklin might have touched. Fury surged within him; white-hot heat burned through his civilized veneer.

He held her, digging his fingers into her soft upper arms, wishing he could brand her as his own. "Did his kisses make you feel like mine do?" he asked as he lowered his mouth near hers.

"How would I know?"

If she had struggled, he would have taken her right there. But her quiet response, her lack of fear, her gentle half smile, shamed him.

Brooke watched the emotions chasing across Dalton's features. For once, his poker face failed him, and she saw into his soul. His anger faded, leaving behind contrition and self-disgust.

"I'm sorry," he said as he released her arms. "I don't know what got into me."

I do, she thought. The realization that her handsome gambler could be jealous of someone like Arthur Franklin was enough to make her laugh . . . or cry. But she did neither. "I have to get dressed," she said, pushing him into the hall.

"Oh." He looked around, a frown of confusion furrowing his brow. "Of course."

He spoke as if he were in a trance, and she supposed he was. It wasn't every day that someone like Dalton discovered a whole new set of emotions.

"I'll see you in a few minutes," she called as he headed down the stairs. He nodded without turning around.

But she didn't speak to him again that evening. By the time she had greeted her customers and watched the new dance routine, Dalton had disappeared. When she found him, he was slumped down in a corner chair, an empty bottle of their best whiskey resting by his feet.

Chapter 13

Brooke stood on the bar, trying to lift the heavy curtain onto the ceiling hooks, which were maddeningly out of reach. She stretched up on her toes and managed to toss the fabric over the hooks. When she lowered her weight back onto her heels, she felt her feet slip on the varnished surface. She reached for the drape, but the canvas slid through her fingers and she tumbled off the bar . . . and into Dalton's waiting arms.

"Good morning." He smiled down into her eyes, his strength a warm band of protection. "Is this a test to make sure that my reflexes are in working order?"

He looked wonderful. She hadn't talked to him since Caleb and Evan had carried him to his room on Monday night. He'd spent most of Tuesday glassy-eyed and pale, walking around as if his head were about to fall off.

Her heart pounded in her chest, more from his proximity than from her near-disaster. "I was just putting up the draperies." She placed a hand on his vest, partly for balance, but mostly to make sure he was really there.

He carried her over to a chair, then sat down, pulling her onto his lap. "Would you be hurt if I told you they're very ugly?"

"They aren't a decoration. I'm trying to disguise the

room." She shifted and turned so that her head was
resting on his shoulder. Convention told her that she
should get to her feet, but it felt too good to be close to
him. For the last several days they had seemed to spend
all their time being angry with each other. She had been
lonely without their closeness, their teasing.

"Ah, the first meeting of the eminently respectable
Horse Creek Literary Society. When do the dragons
arrive?"

"At one. So there's lots to do."

He smoothed her hair away from her face and brushed
his lips across her forehead. "I'm here to serve."

The tender contact gave her courage. "I've missed
you, Dalton," she whispered into his collar. "I'm glad
you're feeling better."

"Me, too. I'm old enough to know better. Whiskey
can be meaner than a tarred bear."

Dalton felt her giggle, her side vibrating against his
chest, her breath tickling his neck. He was about to draw
her closer when she stood up.

"Come on, it's time to work."

She started to climb back up on the bar, but he stopped
her. "Allow me."

After the draperies were hung, he tried to sneak out
of the room, but Elizabeth blocked the exit. She glared
at him. "Wash or sweep?"

He glanced down at the soapy water. The bucket
looked familiar. "I'll sweep."

The three of them worked together, Elizabeth and
Brooke chatting, Dalton listening with half an ear. When
she'd told him that she'd missed him, he'd felt as if
a horse had kicked him in the chest. She gave her
affection so freely that he was left feeling miserly by
comparison.

There was nothing like spending the better part of a night staring into a bucket to make a man see the error of his ways, he thought. His time in Horse Creek was slipping away faster and faster, and he wanted to leave with good memories, for both of them. If he could leave at all.

She'd crept inside him when he wasn't looking, and now he couldn't imagine being without her. But his pain was the least of his concerns. There was still the matter of someone harassing Brooke . . . and Edna Prattly's threats. Just the thought of Brooke being hurt was enough to make him blind with rage. Hiring Jones should have made him feel better, but it didn't. He swore to himself that he'd make sure Brooke was safe before he left for good.

Caleb walked in carrying a large box. "Here are them books you wanted. But I don't know why you're going to all this trouble for them old biddies. Seems to me they should be home tending to their husbands instead of running off to a saloon." He dropped the box on the floor.

"Caleb Barns!" Elizabeth set her dustcloth on the table and stepped menacingly toward her husband. "I can't believe you said that, let alone thought it. Why, you old coot! I ought to . . ."

But the terms of the threat went unsaid as Caleb winked at Dalton, then sprinted out of the room and up the stairs, his wife at his heels.

"You don't suppose she'll really hurt him, do you?" Brooke asked. Her green eyes were wide, her lips parted.

Dalton grinned when he heard their bedroom door slam shut. "No. But I don't think they'll be down for a while yet, either."

Brooke looked confused, but he chose not to enlighten her. When she murmured a soft "oh" and left the room in a hurry, he laughed out loud. She was back in a few minutes, carrying a stack of linens.

"Here," she said, putting them on a table. "You can fold the napkins for me."

He sat down and frowned. "I don't know how to do this, and I'm not very keen on learning."

"Nonsense. You can shuffle a deck with one hand, Dalton Reed. These little squares of fabric will hardly give you pause."

She demonstrated the technique, then stepped away. "Now you do the other nineteen."

He grumbled as he picked up the starched linen. Brooke started on the tablecloths. He watched her shake out the lace, then let it float back to the table. She adjusted the corners and smoothed out the wrinkles. When she lifted her arms, the bodice of her dress tightened; when she leaned over the table, the cooperative blouse gapped slightly, just enough to tease him with a view of the very tops of her breasts. The fluid movements of her body were a graceful dance and reminded him that there were only four people in the building and two of them were already upstairs, probably . . .

Brooke brought in a tray containing cups, plates, and several teapots. As she arranged the china, he realized that he had never witnessed her performing domestic duties. He'd seen her angry, defiant, laughing, and passionate. He'd watched her shuffle a deck of cards, pour a drink, and add a column of figures. But he'd never seen her cook a meal, do laundry, or tend to a child.

The vision was clear in his mind. He could see her holding a baby close to her. The green-eyed, brown-haired infant would suckle at her breast, and he . . .

He swore under his breath and walked to the window. Stop it, he told himself. Thinking about marrying Brooke was an exercise in futility. He could never be what she needed—hell, what she deserved.

He glanced over his shoulder and saw her polishing the crystal glasses. If only . . . if only what? he asked himself. If he had not committed the crime that made him unable to claim her, he would never have met her in the first place. He remembered reading, many years before, about Greek and Roman gods. No doubt his circumstance had been arranged by similar creatures intent on their own amusement.

"Dalton, are you all right?"

He turned to face her. She stood before him holding a bouquet of flowers in her arms. Her beauty caused a physical pain in his chest. When had he first loved her? When she admitted she missed him? When she had asked him to help her with the saloon? When she'd smiled at him on the train?

He leaned down and touched her mouth with his lips. A flash of fire, a touch of velvet . . . Then he straightened. "What can I do next?"

"Brooke! Where are you, dear?"

Brooke recognized Mrs. Gilmore's voice and stepped into the saloon. The slight woman gave her a warm smile. "You've done wonders with this room. No one would guess where one was at all." She chattered on happily, inspecting the place settings, glancing over the books.

Her hat was true to character. A jarring combination of rust fabric and black feathers rested at a perky angle on her head. The snug-fitting gown made her look like a brown wren dressed up to go calling.

"Mrs. Gilmore, don't you look lovely." Elizabeth bustled into the room carrying a plate of desserts. "Let me pour you some tea. And you must have a slice of my pie. I've got a piece right here." Elizabeth beamed at the smaller woman.

Brooke stared. What was going on? Elizabeth hated Mrs. Gilmore. She leaned over and whispered in her friend's ear. "Are you feeling all right?"

"Never better." Elizabeth patted her arm, then returned to the kitchen.

Brooke smoothed her hands nervously over her skirt. She'd tried on most of Mattie's wardrobe and all of her own, searching for the perfect garment. She'd finally settled on a slightly out-of-style green morning dress she'd brought with her. The high neck and long sleeves made it the most conservative that she owned.

"Hello?"

"Mrs. Carson, how good of you to come," Brooke said, drawing the plump woman into the room.

"I've been counting the days. And you must call me Amanda."

Brooke returned the other woman's smile and knew that she had found a friend.

Women continued to arrive in twos and threes. Brooke moved among them, trying to match names with faces. She called upon the tactics she'd seen Dalton use in the gaming parlor to make guests feel at home. When everyone had found a seat, she walked to the front of the room.

"Good afternoon, ladies. Welcome to the first meeting of the Horse Creek Literary Society. I suggest we begin by electing someone to preside at our meetings. After that, you may choose the books you'd like to read for the next meeting. Mrs. Gilmore, would you—"

"Excuse me. I have something to say."

But the voice didn't belong to the little birdlike woman. Brooke looked up and saw Mrs. Prattly standing in the entrance of the saloon. Her silver-streaked hair was pulled back, exposing the harsh planes of her face. Her eyes were dark and cool, but Brooke could have sworn she saw a hint of satisfaction in the thin line of the woman's mouth. This was it, she thought. Edna Prattly was finally making her move. A chill settled over the room, snuffing out laughter and conversation.

"Ladies," Edna said graciously as she walked into the room. "I'd like to take a moment of your time to talk to you about your husbands . . . if you don't mind?"

Although she had asked permission, Brooke didn't doubt that the older woman would say what she'd come to say, regardless of anyone else's feelings on the matter. What was it Dalton had told her? Better to face the enemy head on than risk being stabbed in the back.

"Why, of course we don't mind, Mrs. Prattly. I'm sure everyone would be happy to listen to you. Allow me to get you some tea."

The older woman flashed her a look of annoyance and admiration, as though she'd expected to be treated badly. Her grudging nod made Brooke bite back a smile. But the smile faded quickly as Mrs. Prattly stepped in front of the group.

"I'd like to talk to you about your lives and the abuses committed against you. How many of us have had to bear the shame and heartache of having food stolen from our children's mouths? I'm talking about the demon liquor. Martha"—she pointed to a pale young woman standing in the back of the room—"your husband gambled away the money for the mortgage. And,

Betty, how many times have the women of this town brought you food so that your children could eat? I'm starting a temperance movement aimed toward shutting down these dens of sin and returning our husbands to the fold."

The women in the room gave a collective gasp. Brooke held on to the teapot and was pleased to see her hands were perfectly steady. Amanda moved to her side.

"Some of us like our husbands being out of the fold for an hour or two. Are you all right?" she asked in a whisper.

Brooke nodded and continued to listen to Mrs. Prattly's eloquent plea. There was no doubt of the older woman's sincerity, but her timing and method couldn't have been worse.

"Here's your tea," she said, handing Edna a cup and saucer. "Cream? Sugar?"

"A little cream, dear. I hope some of these ladies will be interested in joining me. So many of our husbands spend all their time and hard-earned money in establishments such as this." She covered her mouth and glanced apologetically at Brooke, as if suddenly realizing her part in all this. "Does it offend you that I have brought this up? I never realized . . ."

Sure, Brooke thought. And the cows on your ranch fly into the barn to be milked. Edna had planned this attack right down to her fawn-colored gloves. It was a game of cat and mouse, and Brooke didn't much like being the mouse.

"I'm not at all offended, Edna," Brooke purred. "Do you mind if I call you Edna? Do you want to hold your temperance meetings here as well? You could join your husband for a drink after one of the shows, if you'd like. We do serve nonalcoholic beverages."

A small titter swept the room until Mrs. Prattly quelled it with a glance. "How very sweet, child, but no. I've rented a storefront a few blocks down the street. I just wanted to let everyone know the first meeting will be next Wednesday. At this time, actually."

That was one for the cat. So now they were in competition for the ladies of Horse Creek. On alternating Wednesdays, women could attend temperance gatherings and meetings of the literary society. Brooke would have laughed if she hadn't been playing for such serious stakes. No matter. Dalton had taught her how to bluff when she was holding nothing but a pair of deuces.

"Is there anything else you'd like to add?"

Mrs. Prattly walked to the exit. "No. Will we see *you* at the temperance meeting?"

Brooke tried to smile, but her muscles didn't want to cooperate. The literary society hadn't even had a chance to begin and it was already defunct. "I may send a donation instead."

"Good day." Edna smiled her triumph just before she pushed through the doors and left.

Brooke turned back to the group of women. "I certainly understand Mrs. Prattly's concern. If any of you feel uncomfortable continuing with the meeting, I won't feel slighted if you want to leave."

Martha stepped forward. "Miz Prattly's right. My husband did gamble away all our money for the mortgage. Drinking's wrong, and I can't stay here any longer. I'm gonna march with her till I can't move another step." She picked up her reticule and walked out.

Amanda moved next to Brooke and took her arm in a gesture of support. She addressed the group in a loud, clear voice. "I'd like to say that my husband works hard all day. If he wants to go get a drink now and then, or play a game of cards, I'd rather he came here where the tables are honest and the girls don't do more than dance."

"That's true," someone else said. "I told Tom if he could spend his evenings at the saloon, then I could spend my Wednesdays at these meetings. If the saloons are all shut down, I'll be trapped in that house with him and the kids."

Several other women nodded in agreement. Betty, a small woman with a fading purple bruise on the side of her neck, shook her head. "My man spends all our money on liquor and gaming. I just want to keep him home." She smiled softly at Brooke. "I'm sorry. You seem like a real nice lady, and I did so want to read the books, but I"—she cleared her throat and twisted her fingers nervously—"must leave."

"I understand." Brooke picked up one of the novels from the stack on the side table. "Here," she said, pressing the book into the other woman's hands. "Take this and read it. When you're done, I'll lend you another."

The girl looked doubtful. Mrs. Gilmore patted her arm and led her to the door. "It's all right, Betty. No one's going to tell on you." She clucked like a mother hen and watched the young woman go. "Poor girl. You did a nice thing, Brooke, letting her have that book to read." She glanced around the room. "Anyone else want to leave or can we begin our meeting?"

There was a murmur of voices, and gradually the room grew quiet. "Fine." Mrs. Gilmore stepped in front. "The first order of business is to elect a president."

Brooke stared at the empty doorway, unable to turn and face the other women. It had been a draw, she thought with relief, but she still felt overcome by the shocking turn of events.

She felt a touch on her shoulder and turned to look at Amanda Carson. "Come and sit down, Brooke," she said. "You're shaking like a leaf."

"Am I?" She allowed herself to be led to a chair. "I'm sorry," she whispered, her hands trembling around the cup of tea she had been offered.

"Don't think another thing about it, dear. You handled yourself just fine. I would have gone to pieces or thrown her out."

Brooke glanced at her new friend and smiled. "You're very kind."

The hour passed quickly. By the time Brooke had recovered her composure, she found herself assigned to the refreshment committee. Singly and in groups, the women expressed their support. She was invited to tea, a bazaar, and a church social. The warmth and friendliness made her feel more welcome and wanted than she had ever felt in Philadelphia.

After the other women had left, Amanda helped her clean up. "Are you going to be all right?" she asked. "I don't want to worry you, but Mrs. Prattly is a difficult woman." She smiled sheepishly. "I guess you saw that for yourself. But if she's starting a temperance movement, she's bound to march here. After all, Samuel spends most of his evenings at your gambling tables."

Brooke shrugged. "I'm not happy about it, but she can't do anything to hurt me. It's men, not their wives, who frequent saloons. And I doubt her husband will stop coming here because of her."

"Yes, I'd heard something like that."

Brooke's mouth dropped open. "You knew about . . ."

"Mattie and Samuel? Let's just say their names were bandied about." Amanda grinned. "Look at who he's married to. I almost can't blame him."

But Brooke *did* blame him. She remembered reading about Samuel Prattly's lies in Mattie's journal. Despite Edna Prattly's overbearing ways, she didn't deserve Samuel's treatment of her. That was the worst part, Brooke thought, being able to see both sides of the problem. On the one hand, she deeply resented Edna's intrusion and disruption of the meeting. On the other hand, what would *she* have risked to keep the man she loved by her side?

When had life become so confusing? Since Brooke had come to the West, issues and people were no longer black and white. She needed customers to keep the saloon open, but she didn't approve of a man drinking with the money needed to care for his family. Was there any point of compromise?

Amanda placed the last cup on the tray. "I'd better get back to the store, or my husband's going to send out a posse. We're so busy all the time. I've got to find someone to help me." She smiled. "You take care, Brooke."

Brooke stared at her friend. "Did you say you were looking for someone to help in the shop?"

"Yes. Why? Do you know anyone?"

"Suzanne. She's one of the dancers here, but she'd rather do something more respectable, if you know what I mean."

Amanda patted her plump hips and sighed. "And I'd give anything to be a dancer. Tell her to come on in tomorrow and I'll talk to her." She winked. "Gee, that means there'll be an opening here." She gave a small kick and laughed. "I guess I'd better stick to the general store."

Dalton walked into the saloon and smiled. "Care to share the joke, ladies?"

The two women looked at each other and giggled. "No, I don't think so," said Brooke.

"Mrs. Carson." Dalton nodded. "I'm glad you could make it today."

"Please, call me Amanda. I had a lovely time. Brooke is quite a tiger."

"A tiger?" He raised an eyebrow and glanced at Brooke, but she avoided looking at him. "Would you care to explain?" he asked.

"No."

Amanda gathered up her books. "I must get back. Oh, Mr. Reed, did everything, um, fit?"

"Yes. Very well. I'm obliged to you for getting it so . . ." His voice trailed off as he realized he had fallen into her trap. He had no reason to know if Brooke's knife holster fit unless he'd seen it on her leg. "I meant that . . ." He cleared his throat.

Far from shocked, Amanda Carson looked amused. "I'm glad everything worked out. I'll see you soon, Brooke." She kissed the younger woman on the cheek. "If my husband comes to gamble, let him win. Bye."

Dalton climbed on the bar and began unhooking the drapery. "How did it go?" he asked.

"Very well." Brooke turned away and hurried toward the hall.

"You can't hide from me forever," he called after her.

"I know." She hesitated in the doorway. "I have to get dressed for tonight."

Dalton watched her leave. Something had happened in this room. Something bad enough to put a shadow in her eyes. He sent a silent thank-you to Amanda Carson for letting him know. He'd give Brooke an opportunity to tell him herself, but he wouldn't let the issue die.

Anyone who hurt or threatened her would have to answer to him.

"I finished unpacking the shipment, ma'am."

"Thank you, Evan." Brooke leaned against the wall and tried to smile at the bouncer. No matter how many times she told herself Evan Jones was just another employee, she still felt nervous when she was alone with him.

"I'll be in the back if you need me." He nodded his head, then moved away soundlessly.

Brooke released the breath she'd been holding and walked behind the stage.

"Suzanne, may I speak with you a moment?"

The tall blonde stopped buttoning up her shoes and glanced up. "Did I do something wrong?"

Brooke laughed. "Of course not. I have some good news." She sat on the bench in the small dressing area. The other girls had already put on their costumes and were mingling with the saloon patrons. "I spoke with Amanda Carson today at the literary meeting. She owns the general store. She's looking for someone to help her, and I thought of you right away. She's expecting you to stop by tomorrow to talk about the job."

"Oh, Miss Brooke." Suzanne's eyes grew moist and she smiled. "You are the most wonderful lady in the whole world. I can't believe how nice you are to me. A job in a shop . . . I'll be a real lady now for sure."

She bounced up and held out her red skirt as she circled the tiny room. "I'll be able to meet the women in town, and they won't look down on me, neither. And when Stephen comes in to buy his necessaries, why, I can help him. I'll be just like a regular person."

Brooke laughed. "You *are* a regular person. There

isn't a woman in Horse Creek with a sweeter spirit than yours. And if Stephen Bolt hasn't figured that out, then he's not half the man I think he is."

Suzanne collapsed on the bench and hugged her. "I don't know how to thank you. I owe you so much."

Brooke disentangled herself from the yards of ruffles in the girl's costume. "You haven't won him yet."

"But I will." Suzanne stared at the wall, her face a picture of hope and determination.

Brooke rose and walked to the door. If only she could borrow a little of that confidence, she would be as sure about winning Dalton.

Dalton crossed the gaming room, greeting guests as he passed. Brooke was at the far table, dealing her nightly half-dozen games of poker. What had started out as a lark had turned into one of their most profitable ventures. With her ability to count cards, she inevitably won a sizable pot each evening. Yet every night the customers fought over the privilege of sitting at her table. He shrugged his shoulders. She was undoubtedly the first female dealer the men of Horse Creek had ever seen.

Some men played at her table only once, probably to say that they had, but others returned regularly. Tonight Edward Gannen and Sheriff Morgan sat on either side of Brooke. They tossed good-natured insults at each other and paid Brooke extravagant compliments.

The two were part of a group of gentlemen whom Dalton privately referred to as "Mattie's men"—Gannen, the town lawyer; Hank Morgan, the sheriff; Jonathan Holte, a crusty old rancher who rode in once a week; Samuel Prattly, and a couple of others. They all had one thing in common: Mattie Frost.

During the years she had lived in Horse Creek, Mattie had taken each of them into her bed. They were a loyal lot, and understanding. They knew that Mattie had given her heart to the memory of a soldier, but they took the warmth she offered, the friendship, the unconditional acceptance. She had never favored one man over the others. Each had told Dalton that he would look out for Brooke; they all owed Mattie a debt, and that was their payment.

As far as Dalton could tell, Samuel Prattly had been her only error in judgment. If rumors could be believed, she'd broken off with him as soon as she'd discovered the true nature of the man. Dalton regretted never having met Brooke's aunt. She must have been some kind of woman.

But her beauty could not have surpassed her niece's, he thought as he watched Brooke. She sat like a queen holding court. He'd found an ornate chair for her to sit on. The woven back was a tall oval, rising above her head. The arms were carved in the shape of lions, her hands resting on the animals' heads.

Tonight her dress was the palest peach, as though a white gown had been stained by the first rays of the morning sun. The front of the fitted bodice dipped slightly, exposing the valley between her breasts. Cascading ribbons, in colors ranging from the lightest ivory to the deepest peach, held the split sleeves together, secured at the top of her shoulders. She wore no jewelry, except for pearls gleaming in her upswept hair. The pale bareness of her throat was more alluring than any sparkling stone.

But her eyes still contained a disquieting essence. She had avoided him all afternoon and evening, but she wouldn't escape again.

"And the dealer has a full house, gentlemen. My game again."

There was a chorus of groans around the table. Edward Gannen leaned forward. "I swear the cards whisper to you, my dear. How else can you explain your extraordinary luck?"

Brooke smiled. "I use a trick I learned as a child." She leaned forward conspiratorially. The table grew silent. "It's called addition."

There was a moment of silence; then the group erupted in laughter. Dalton stepped forward and brushed his hand against Brooke's shoulder. He felt the spark that leapt between them, but pushed the sensation away. Getting answers from her was more important than the flame of desire, however much he might want it to consume him.

"I must have a word with you," he said, leaning down and speaking in her ear.

Her green eyes reflected the moment of passion. "I know."

He stepped back and allowed her to precede him out of the room.

"We'll need to find another dancer," she said as she sat behind her desk and began rearranging papers. She was trying to avoid looking at him, but Dalton wasn't sure why. There was a stain of color on her cheeks, as physical a reminder of their moment of wanting as the pressure in his groin.

"Oh?" He slipped into the chair opposite her.

"Amanda is looking for someone to help her in the shop and I told her about Suzanne."

"Any word on the budding romance?"

She glanced up at him, as if checking for sarcasm.

"No, she hasn't seen Mr. Bolt since last Sunday. But I'm sure he'll talk to her soon."

Dalton reached into his jacket pocket and pulled out a cigar. The ritual of removing the paper wrapper, clipping the end, then lighting the tobacco, gave him time to formulate his thoughts.

There was no easy way to ask. "What happened today?"

She shrugged one slender shoulder, the ribbons whispering against her satin skin. "I held a meeting. Several women attended, and they were very nice. Oh, I was elected to the refreshment committee."

He inhaled on the cigar, wishing he were tasting her instead of the acrid smoke and tobacco. "And . . . ?"

"And . . . I don't want to talk about it." Her green eyes flashed defiantly.

"That is not one of your choices."

"You have no right to question me, no right at all. You are simply an employee here, Dalton Reed." She leaned forward, her chest rising and falling with each breath. "I'll thank you to remember your place."

He sighed heavily. Tilting his chair back until it was balanced on two legs, he rested his feet on the desk. "Making me angry won't get you out of this conversation any quicker than cooperating, Brooke. And as for keeping me in my place . . . are you prepared to say where that is?"

Late in the evening, when the day had been busy and the hours long, his voice always became smoky and southern. He drew out his words until they lapped against her body like water in a bath. His patience and understanding touched her, as did his desire to be a friend. But to admit the need within her, the need to confide in him, to be with him, was to admit her love.

Her feelings for Dalton were her strength and her weakness. With him, she could do anything . . . except hold on to him. Without him, she could do nothing . . . except remember.

His place was with her. In her saloon, in her life, in her bed. His place was fathering her children, comforting her in sickness, being comforted himself. His place was to grow old at her side, to lie next to her until the end of time.

"Tell me what happened."

The command was whispered in velvet, but it was wrapped around steel. She closed her eyes. "Mrs. Prattly stopped by at the meeting."

"That's a surprise. She didn't strike me as the type to lower herself to the sordid depths of literature."

She glanced at his face, relieved to see his familiar grin. "She's not. She came to . . . to . . ." Her voice faltered. "She's starting a temperance movement. She went on about the sins of gambling and drinking, then invited everyone to join her crusade . . . even me."

Brooke jumped when she heard the thump of Dalton's chair legs hitting the floor. His expression was grim; a muscle in his cheek twitched menacingly. "If she were a man—"

"A couple of women left, but everyone else stayed." She sighed. "I understand why she's doing this. She needs to get back at Samuel for his affair with Mattie. In a way, I can't really blame her. I just wish . . . I'm so confused."

"Do you think she's going to march here? Never mind. I already know the answer." He frowned. "What can I do?"

"Nothing but warn the staff."

Dalton's eye's grew dark. "Brooke, I—"

There was a knock on the office door. "Come in," she called.

Suzanne leaned in and waved a piece of paper. She was beaming. "I got a note from Stephen. He's asked me to go riding with him this Sunday. Ain't that grand?" She clutched the letter to her breast and sighed. "He's the prettiest man I ever met." She winked at the gambler. "Exceptin' you, Dalton."

"I'm flattered, Suzanne."

"I gotta get back to work. I just wanted to tell you the news." She backed out of the room.

Grateful for the break in tension, Brooke stood up and walked around the desk. "We should both be back in the saloon."

He stared at her. "Aren't you going to say it?"

She batted her eyelashes at him. "I'm sure I have no idea what you're talking about."

"Don't you want to say 'I told you so' about the preacher? You told me he'd call on her again."

"I don't have to." She kissed his cheek, then brushed past him. "You've already said it for me."

The temperance marchers didn't appear for almost two weeks. In that time Brooke allowed herself to be convinced that Edna Prattly's threats had been the empty blustering of an injured spouse. But on the thirteenth day after she had announced the forming of the organization, nine women and a half-dozen children collected in front of the saloon.

Mrs. Gilmore provided the first warning. The small woman flew in through the back door of the building and scurried up the hall. Only the sight of men actually gambling at the big tables in the back room halted her progress. By the time Dalton revived her with smelling salts, Brooke was on her way to the front door.

"Good morning, ladies," she said as she stepped onto the sidewalk.

"Brooke." Edna Prattly nodded graciously, then handed one end of a cloth banner to one of her coworkers. The uneven lettering reminded the God-fearing that whiskey was the drink of the devil.

Two men rounded the corner. When they saw the crowd, they quickly changed direction and headed up the street in the direction of the Cattle Run Saloon. Brooke wanted to stamp her foot in frustration.

"Is it safe to assume that all the drinking establishments in this town will receive equal attention?" she asked tartly. "Or am I being singled out?"

"We are starting here. Perhaps next time we'll march somewhere else. The committee hasn't really decided." Mrs. Prattly issued a command, and the ragtag group started walking up and down the sidewalk.

Brooke stood her ground for several minutes, forcing the women to step around her. Betty, the young woman who had left the literary meeting so reluctantly, couldn't bring herself to look Brooke in the eyes. The bruise on the young woman's neck had faded, but a bright bluish mark on her cheek had taken its place. Brooke felt a knot in her stomach.

"Howdy."

She glanced down and saw the boy who had escorted her to Mr. Gannen's office the day she arrived in Horse Creek. "William. How nice to see you again. Have you had a chance to go fishing?"

The boy grinned. "Yup. I was there jest last week. Caught me a mess of fish." His smile faded. "But I'm gettin' mighty tired of eatin' them all the time."

He reached up to scratch his head. Brooke bit back a

gasp when she saw the dirty bandage around his hand. "How did you hurt yourself?"

William shifted uncomfortably, a dull red staining his cheeks. " 'Tweren't nothing."

"Willy!" Betty grabbed the boy's arm and smiled apologetically at Brooke. "Sorry, ma'am. He didn't mean to bother you none. Now, William, git home and watch your sister. She's been coughing again."

Edna Prattly began to lead the women in a song about the glory of drinking pure water, but Brooke ignored the voices and stepped back into the saloon. After locating Evan, she wrote a note and asked the bouncer to deliver it to Amanda Carson's store. By the time Betty returned home, her cupboards would be filled with food and supplies.

Brooke didn't like having the temperance marchers in front of her store, and she was angry at Edna Prattly for using the saloon as a pawn in her fight to gain her husband's attention. But that didn't mean she could overlook the suffering in her own community. She was as much a part of Horse Creek as anyone else. It was going to take a lot more than a couple of dozen temperance marchers to convince her otherwise.

Chapter 14

The mild spring had given way to the languid days of summer. Long hours of sunlight meant that the peak time in the saloon was between nine and midnight. In the high temperatures, keeping ice frozen became the most important order of business.

Brooke calculated the balance in her ledger with practiced ease. The profits were mounting steadily. Every other week she deposited two-thirds of that money into Dalton's account. She tried not to remember that the success of the business would finance his departure.

By the time the ground had frozen over, he would be gone. No doubt the snow would slow her blood, as it did the creek, but there would be no spring thaw for her. She would go on, her heart permanently encased in ice.

No, I won't think about it, she told herself. There would be time enough to mourn after he left. Until then she was determined to enjoy every second they had together and to hold on to the hope that she might break through the wall he had built around his emotions.

"Excuse me, ma'am. Are you Brooke Tyler?"

"Yes." When she raised her head, her eyes were level with a silver buckle in the center of a worn brown belt. Looking up, she saw a snug-fitting sun-bleached shirt straining across a broad chest. A sweat-stained bandanna hung loosely around a tan throat. His jaw was square, his mouth a slight curve, but his eyes were in shadow. "You want to take your hat off, cowboy?"

The man removed the worn felt, then ran his fingers through his light brown hair. His eyes were the color of a muddy pool of spring water, not dark enough to be brown, but not light enough to be green or blue. He was only a few years older than she was. His expression was wary, and yet she felt herself instinctively drawn to the man. He was someone she wanted to like.

"I'm Luke Hawkins." He dropped a small leather bag on the desk, and it thudded against the wood. "My payment for the first half of the year, ma'am."

She opened the bag and turned it upside down, spilling nuggets of gold across her papers. "Maybe you should have a seat, Mr. Hawkins."

"Luke, ma'am, if you don't mind. 'Mr. Hawkins' makes me feel old . . . like I've got one foot in the grave." A grin cut across his tanned face, turning ordinary features into handsome ones.

She smiled in return. "And I'm Brooke. I appreciate the donation," she nodded toward the gold. "But maybe you could tell me what it's for? I doubt that you enjoy our whiskey so much that you pay for it in advance."

He chuckled as he sat on the edge of the chair in front of her desk, his hat hanging loosely in his hands. "I graze my cattle on your land. Mattie and I had an arrangement. I paid her twice a year, July first and January first. If that suits you, I'd like to continue."

Brooke leaned back and laughed. "I can't see why not. I had almost forgotten that I owned the grazing land."

"You've got a couple thousand acres stretched between Cheyenne and the fort."

"The fort?"

"Fort Laramie, ma'am . . . ah, Brooke."

She leaned forward. "Why haven't I seen you in here before?"

He shrugged. "I've been visiting the Cattle Run, across town." His face turned grim. "I thought Prattly'd bought out this place. We had a run-in back about a year or so. One of his men was rustling cattle off my land. I didn't want to buy my whiskey from a cattle thief."

"What happened?"

"His wife came calling at my house one afternoon, all gussied up." He grinned at the memory. "My housekeeper served tea and those tiny little cakes. Mrs. Prattly chatted on about nothing for nearly an hour, then went home. Except she left behind a draft to cover the cost of the cattle her husband had stolen. I never could figure it out. I've seen her once or twice since then, but neither of us says a word about what happened."

"Mrs. Prattly is starting a temperance movement in town. Stick around. You can watch the march."

"You don't say." His oddly colored eyes met hers, sizing her up. "What're you doing about it? Mattie would have stood in front of the building waving a shotgun."

"I confess I've yet to use a gun, or any other weapon, for that matter. Some of the women have joined the temperance movement because of what's happened in their homes. I feel sorry for a wife who doesn't have enough money to feed her children."

Luke nodded. "I knew someone once who used to drink himself into a temper. Took it out on those unfortunate enough to walk within arm's length of his fist." He reached in his trousers pocket and pulled out a five dollar piece. "Give 'em this from me next time they visit you."

"I will." She laughed. "I think I'm going to like you, cowboy."

"Feeling's mutual." Luke grinned.

She was sure that flash of white against his tanned face had set female hearts fluttering from here to the California border. She rose from her seat. "Come on, I'll buy you a drink."

He stood up, but looked uncomfortable. "Don't feel right, ma'am, a lady buying *me* a drink."

She tucked her hand through the crook of his arm. "You forget, Mr. Hawkins, I own this saloon."

Dalton tried not to glare when he saw Brooke escort the tall rancher out of her office. He hated the snake of jealousy coiled in the pit of his stomach. But when she laughed at something the man said, then smiled with her green eyes all lit up, Dalton felt the venom surging through his body. As she looked up and noticed him, her smile softened from playful to tender, and the poison drained away.

"Dalton, won't you join us?" She left her visitor and walked behind the bar. "This is Luke Hawkins. He grazes cattle on some land I own. Luke, this is Dalton Reed."

"Hawkins." Dalton offered the other man his hand. The younger man's grip was strong and sure, conveying confidence in his ability to take care of himself and those around him. "You're in for a treat. Brooke doesn't do that much mixing behind the bar, but anything she serves is bound to leave you wanting more."

Luke placed his hat on the scarred birchwood bar. "I remember Mattie used to get a bee in her bonnet every now and again. She'd throw Caleb out and spend a day or two mixing drinks." He grinned. "Many's the morning I woke up in my own barn without a whiff of a memory of how I got there."

Dalton watched Brooke's small hands as she worked. Her movements were clean and swift. She poured a pony of brandy, an egg, and a dash of sugar into a mixing glass, then added a handful of ice. After shaking, she strained the mixture into a tall, thin punch glass, then filled the cup with cold ginger ale.

"Try this, Luke. It's guaranteed to make you forget the heat of a Wyoming summer."

He took a long drink. "Tastes good. Reminds me of summers back home."

"Where's home?" she asked.

Luke shrugged and looked uncomfortable. "I grew up in Kansas, but I've been here almost three years."

"Would you like a drink, Dalton?" she asked.

Dalton was relieved that Brooke had sensed the other man's withdrawal and changed the subject. "I'm not quite up to your cocktail artistry, Brooke Tyler. Just give me the rest of that bottle of ginger ale."

She laughed and leaned toward the rancher. "A couple of months ago Dalton drank a whole bottle of our best whiskey. He was sick for two days and hasn't touched a drop of liquor since."

Luke grinned. "Been known to overindulge a time or two myself."

"Well, I've learned my lesson." Dalton winked at Brooke.

Elizabeth bustled into the saloon. She carried a tray of sandwiches and several slices of her pie. "I thought I heard a familiar voice out here. Luke Hawkins, you dirty old cowpoke. Where have you been?" She set the food on a table and stood in front of him, her hands on her hips. "I should box your ears for staying away so long."

"You don't want to do that, Lizzy." He pulled Elizabeth in his arms and swung her around. "You're crazy about me." He put her down and kissed her on her cheek. "Always have been."

Dalton was amused to see the ever-confident, ever-in-charge Elizabeth Barns reduced to blushing silence. His appreciation of Luke went up a notch.

"I guess if I was to beat you, you wouldn't be of a mind to eat that food I prepared," she said gruffly.

Luke tugged on one of her apron strings until the bow came undone and the fabric drifted toward the floor. "I want you, Lizzy," he growled.

Elizabeth picked up the apron and used it to swat him across the arm. "You forget yourself. You're just a boy, Luke Hawkins. I'm a hell of a lot more woman than you could handle."

He sighed, looking sad. "Then I guess I'll have to console myself with your wonderful cooking." He grinned at Dalton. "She's the meanest woman in the whole damn country. Every time I see her, I ask her to run off with me, but she never does. Stays with that used-up old man of hers."

"I heard that, boy." Caleb strolled into the room and pulled him into a bear hug. The gray-haired older man barely came up to Luke's shoulder, but the affection flowing between them was as tangible as the creek running just outside of town.

Dalton felt a twinge in his chest as he continued to enjoy the banter between the three people. His own family had often been like that, teasing, caring, loving. But everything had changed when he turned sixteen. He'd shamed them all and then he'd run away rather than face the consequences of his actions.

Brooke wrapped her arms around his waist and leaned her head against his chest. "I like Luke," she said softly.

"Me, too."

They turned and started out of the bar, leaving the three friends to themselves. "He's quite, ah, good-looking," Dalton said tentatively.

"Yes."

He swallowed and kissed the top of her head. "And close to your age."

"I'd noticed that, too."

Her voice gave nothing away. They continued to walk toward the stairs, her arms around his middle, his around her shoulders. But he couldn't see her face.

Maybe Luke Hawkins was the solution to his problem, he thought grimly. He was young and capable. Elizabeth and Caleb obviously thought the world of him. He was a rancher, probably earning a decent living. He was as hard as the land and could take care of himself. He'd protect Brooke. When the fall came and it was time for Dalton to leave, she could take up with Luke.

But the logical solution didn't comfort him as he felt it should. Just the thought of her smiling at the cowboy, touching him, kissing him, was enough to make Dalton rigid with jealousy.

She stepped away from him and climbed the bottom step. "You're probably thinking of setting me up with him, aren't you?"

She spoke without turning around, which was for the best, he thought. He could feel his mouth hanging open. How long had she been able to read his mind?

"I didn't—"

She turned to face him, cutting his words off with a single glance. Her green eyes blazed with emotion . . . emotion he didn't allow himself to read. "You don't get it, do you?" With her on the step, they were the same height. She clutched the lapels of his jacket and pulled him close to her. "I don't want Luke Hawkins. I don't want Arthur Franklin. I want you."

She leaned forward and brushed her lips against his, taunting him with the sweet pressure. But before he could gather her into his arms, she pulled back. "And you're just foolish enough to let me go."

He stared up at her, watching her swaying hips and straight back as she climbed the staircase. Even after the door of her room had slammed shut, he stood frozen to the floor, held fast by his confusion.

The steady clip-clop of the horse's hooves matched the pounding inside Brooke's head. She had spent a restless few days. Between the Fourth of July celebration in town, and her attempts to solve the mystery in Dalton's life, her nerves were stretched to the breaking point. The last thing she needed was to spend the afternoon bouncing in a springless buggy beside a very hot, very sweaty Arthur Franklin.

But here she was. Since that first disastrous dinner, he had continued to call on an irritatingly regular basis. Every other week he appeared at the saloon and invited her out with him. Every other week she promised herself that this time she would say no. And every other week she smiled sweetly and accepted.

Why? she asked herself. Was it because he was her sole link with respectability? But he wasn't. The literary society was doing well. A few of the women had dropped out after the initial meeting, and Mrs. Prattly had persuaded a couple of others to stay away, but fourteen women attended consistently. Their friendliness and generosity were more than Brooke could have hoped for.

One of the carriage wheels bounced in a particularly deep rut and Brooke was thrown against Arthur's shoulder. "Sorry," she mumbled, then scooted as far away from him as the cramped seat allowed.

"Would you prefer to walk for a while, Brooke?" he asked.

"Yes. I think there's a meadow up a little ways. We could stretch our legs."

Arthur tied up the horse under a clump of trees, then helped her down. His hands were slick with sweat, and she fought the urge to brush her palms against the skirt of her gown.

They walked through the field. Larkspur grew as high as her waist, its flowers long spikes of blue. Brooke inhaled the fragrances of summer, the faint smell of bee's honey, the flowers and grasses browning in the heat of the sun—and Arthur, mopping his brow for the twentieth time.

"Why do you continue to call on me, Arthur?" she asked suddenly.

He darted a glance at her, then swallowed. "I, um . . . Because I . . ."

Without warning he grabbed her arms and planted a wet kiss on her lips. The contact was unpleasant, and she jerked away.

"Oh!" Arthur looked as shocked as she felt. "Miss Tyler, Brooke, I . . . please accept my apology. I don't know what got into me. I didn't mean to treat you with such disrespect. Perhaps it's the . . ."

She held up her hand to stop the flow of words. "There's no need to make this an issue."

He bowed awkwardly. "You are too kind."

Kind? Brooke didn't know if she should laugh or get on the first train back east. They walked a little way. She tried to think of something clever to say, but the memory of Arthur's kiss washed everything else from her mind.

"How long are you going to continue to work in the saloon?" he asked finally.

"I'm not sure." She strolled toward the tall trees. "I think about selling, but I hate the idea of Mrs. Prattly tearing the place down." She rubbed her fingers against the cool bark of the cottonwood, then sank to the ground. "If someone would buy the saloon and keep it open, I might sell." After Dalton left, she wasn't sure she'd have the heart to keep the business going.

As much as she had grown to love the town and her new friends, there would be nothing to keep her when the gambler was gone. But she owed her employees loyalty. She still remembered Lily's impassioned statement about keeping the other dancers from depending on entertaining upstairs for their livelihood. There was much to consider.

He picked at a blade of grass, tearing the green shoot into pieces. She sighed. "I need to get back, Arthur. It's Saturday, and there will be a big crowd tonight."

He helped her up, then led the way to the buggy. The ride back to town was accomplished quickly and in an uncomfortable silence. Once again she was trying to think of the words to tell him that she couldn't see him again. Their relationship was a mockery, and despite his kiss, she still hadn't found out why he continued to call on her.

She patted her face with her handkerchief. It was too hot to deal with that today. All she wanted was a cool bath and a cold drink of water.

"Arthur, would you drop me off at the Carsons' store, please?" She would treat herself to a bar of scented soap and chat with Suzanne and Amanda at the same time.

He pulled up in front of the wooden building and helped her down. He looked uncomfortable, as if he wanted to say something but didn't have the courage. Finally he mumbled a farewell and climbed back into the buggy. Brooke was tempted to call after him, but thought better of the idea. Perhaps he would finally give up on her, she thought with a slight smile, and take up with someone who would appreciate him. Maybe Lily.

She was still chuckling when she entered the cool, dark store.

"And what do you find so funny, Brooke Tyler?" Suzanne asked from behind the counter.

"The thought of Lily and Arthur Franklin marrying each other."

"They'd be mighty odd together, I'll grant you that."

Brooke looked at her former employee, pleased by the changes she saw. The young girl was dressed in a conservative gown, the dark blue a perfect foil for her blond hair. The plain cotton garment enhanced the lush curves of her body in a way the low-cut dancing costume never had. But it was Suzanne's face that showed the greatest transformation. The dark shadows had fled from under her eyes. Her cheeks were full and flushed with health, and her ready laugh charmed most of Amanda Carson's customers.

"I came to buy myself a bar of soap."

Suzanne winked. "I don't guess you'll be wanting something in handmade lye?"

Brooke stepped over to the display. "I was thinking more along the lines of English milled, myself." She sniffed. "Um, lilacs, my favorite. I'll take this." She placed the bar on the counter. "And how is the good minister?"

The young girl blushed. "Stephen's fine. He still sees me regular-like." She leaned forward and whispered. "He kissed me last week. After the Fourth of July party

in the main square. It was dark and the stars were shining
so big in the sky. I was afraid, 'cause of what I'd done
before. I was scared I wouldn't like it or I'd do somethin'
too bold." She smiled dreamily. "But it was like my first
kiss. I was all tremblin', and I couldn't breathe. It was
wonderful." She ducked her head. "This sounds silly, I
know. I mean, I've been with almost a dozen men, but
he makes me feel special."

Brooke touched her friend's arm. "It's not silly at all.
You've described a very magical night. It's no more than
you deserve."

"Look at us," she said, brushing a tear away from
her eye. "Gettin' all worked up about somethin' foolish."

"Romance is never silly," Brooke chided. As she
pulled some money from her reticule, her fingers
brushed against the cold metal of the derringer. The
gun went with her everywhere. She oiled it every
couple of weeks. She hadn't fired it since the day
Dalton showed her how, but she kept it near, to
appease him.

"I thought I heard your voice." Amanda Carson bustled into the room. "How are you, dear?"

The two women exchanged a hug. "I've been out
riding with Arthur, but I'm fine anyway."

The plump woman wrinkled her nose. "It's so hot
today. I'd much rather see Dalton sweat than Arthur
Franklin."

There was a moment of stunned silence. Then they all
broke out in laughter.

"I can't believe I said that," Amanda murmured.

Brooke picked up her package and headed for the
door. "I can't either." She turned back and grinned.
"But I agree with the sentiment."

* * *

Brooke had barely finished hooking up her gown when Elizabeth knocked on the door.

"Those marchers are back." The gray-haired woman frowned as she stuck her head out the window. "Damned old biddies. Don't they have somewhere better to be than this saloon?"

Brooke sat in front of the mirror and began pinning pearls into her hair. "Lizzy, don't be angry. Most of those women don't have anything to eat. I don't like them marching here any more than you do, but I can't force them to leave. Did you prepare the baskets?"

"Yes." Elizabeth planted her fists on her slim hips and scowled. "They're tryin' to shut you down, and all you do is give them food. Don't make sense to me."

"It doesn't have to." She smiled. "I can't fix their problems, but I can make their lives a little easier. Have you seen the bruises on Betty and Willy? Not every husband is as good as Caleb."

"Well, that's the truth, although sometimes even he tries my patience." She moved toward the door. "I'll be in the kitchen if you need me."

Dalton met her in the hall. "What are you so riled up about?" he asked.

Elizabeth pushed past him and started down the stairs. "That girl up there doesn't have a lick of sense. She's still feeding those rabble-rousers. Don't seem to matter that all they want to do is shut her down. Some people ain't got the brains God gave a chicken."

Dalton chuckled and walked to Brooke's room. "Are you decent?" he asked as he pushed the door open.

"Ask Mrs. Prattly." She rose from her seat and turned to face him.

The sunlight streamed through the window and high-lighted the pearls in her hair. With her pale dress and even paler skin, she looked like a princess from a book his mother had read to him when he was a child. Only her green eyes, bright with humor and the barest flash of desire, made her seem approachable.

The familiar hunger rose up to consume him, ignited by the warm days and sultry nights. Not to mention her recent buggy ride with Arthur Franklin.

He suspected she continued to see the law clerk to maintain her tenuous grip on respectability. But the thought of her out with another man was enough to make him want to challenge him to a duel . . . or even a fistfight. In time, hot tempers gave way to cooler moments of rational thought. When he was gone and Brooke was alone, she'd need someone to take care of her.

The picture gave him no rest, except the knowledge that one more part of his debt was paid. Perhaps, if he lived long enough, he would be free of the past and able to return for Brooke. Until then, he could only stand by helplessly and watch someone else lay claim to her.

"May I?" He held out his arm. She placed her fingers against the sleeve of his jacket and allowed him to escort her to the saloon.

"Excuse me, sir. Are you Dalton Reed?"

The small woman standing in the hallway looked as frightened as a rabbit cornered by a coyote. Her eyes were much too big for her face, and a bright purple bruise marred her right cheek.

"Yes." Dalton stepped closer to the woman, careful to move slowly and not alarm her. "How can I help you?"

She clutched a small bag in her hands. "Elizabeth said I could find you here. I understand Miss Brooke is in the gaming room, and I didn't want to disturb her. I'm Betty. Miss Brooke—" Her voice broke, and tears spilled down her cheeks.

"Why don't we go into the office and sit down?"

He led the young woman to a chair, then took the seat next to her. Moisture continued to fall freely from her blue eyes, leaving a wet trail over the bruise.

"Miss Brooke's been telling me that I have to leave my man . . . for the sake of my babies if not for myself. She brought me money yesterday, and I wanted to know if you'd tell her thank you. I'm leaving for Cheyenne right now. Mrs. Prattly's going to take me." Betty smiled sadly. "Also, give her my apologies for marching outside the saloon. It weren't right of me. She's a fine woman."

"I'll give her the message."

Betty rose from her seat and walked back to the hall. "Tell her I'll write her when I've found somewhere to live."

Dalton pulled a piece of paper from the desk and quickly wrote down an address. "When you get to town, go to this boardinghouse. The lady who runs it, Margaret, will give you a place to stay and help you find work."

"Oh . . . I don't know what to say." Betty's tears began anew. "Thank you." She rose up on tiptoe and pressed a damp kiss against his cheek. "Good-bye."

The echo of her footsteps on the floor had long since faded by the time Dalton felt ready to return to the gambling room. Brooke was just finishing her poker game.

"I have a message for you," he said softly, pulling her into a quiet corner.

"Yes?" She smiled at him. The love and promise shining in her eyes was nearly blinding.

"Betty's left for Cheyenne. She said to say thanks and that she'll write when she settles down. I gave her Margaret's address. I think they'll do well together."

She touched her lips to his cheek, much as Betty had, but this time the contact caused his heartbeat to quicken and a smoldering heat to lap against his groin.

"What was that for?" he asked.

"For being an honorable man."

Chapter 15

"Brooke, I'm out of sugar. And that shipment from Cheyenne won't be in till tomorrow. I'd use some from the bar, but Caleb don't have enough, neither."

Brooke dropped her pen on the desk. "Don't worry, Elizabeth. I'll run over to Amanda's right now and get some. Anyway, it's high time I paid our account."

"Fine." The older woman headed back to the kitchen. "You tell her that I'm making her favorite pie today, so she might want to git here early for the literary meeting."

Brooke laughed as she leaned over and unlocked the strongbox. She counted out the amount she needed, then folded the bills and put them in her skirt pocket.

"Dalton?" She walked through the hall and into the gaming room. "There you are. I'm running over to Amanda's to pick up some sugar for Elizabeth. Do you need anything?"

He sat at one of the big tables, practicing with the cards. He exercised his fingers for several hours each week. She knew he was concerned about losing his dexterity, but she hated the reminder that he would soon be leaving her and once again earning his living gambling.

"I've got everything I need right here."

His low voice and tender smile made her feel as if he was caressing her skin instead of the cards. She hoped he really meant what he implied because she was finding it more and more difficult to hold back her feelings.

Every afternoon, while they walked among the customers, she longed to announce to the world that he was hers and that she loved him. Every night, when they went to their separate rooms, she longed to invite him into her bed. But she did neither. What if he didn't love her? What if he didn't want her?

"I'll be back in a short while."

She was walking down the hall when Evan stepped out of the shadows, startling her as always. "Ma'am." The bouncer touched his hat. "There's something in the storeroom you need to see."

"What? Did the shipment get messed up again?" She moved into the dark room. "I've told those people in Cheyenne not to send up—"

A large hand clamped over her mouth, cutting off her words. For a second she thought that Evan was playing a game with her, but when he closed the storeroom door, she realized he was serious. Deadly serious.

She began to struggle, kicking, trying to scream, but he held her fast. She flailed her arms in an attempt to knock over a crate or bottle and alert Dalton.

Evan's hand tightened on her face until his thumb and forefinger cut off her breathing. She bit him and tasted blood, his sweaty palm, and her own fear. Still, bands of iron held her tight.

The muscles in her chest knotted and convulsed. He gasped when her elbow connected with his side. Her feet became entangled in her long skirt and she felt herself falling against him. She pulled at his arm, clawing his hand, struggling to breathe.

He pushed her to the floor, pressing one knee between her legs. The fabric of her gown held her trapped. The floor was hard and unyielding, offering no weapon or escape. Her terror mounted, silent cries echoing in her mind. Her heart pounded in her ears. The dark room prevented her from seeing his eyes, but she imagined their coldness.

She tried to roll away from him, but his knee held her pinned to the floor. His hand shifted, and at last she was able to pull air into her agonized lungs. *Help me,* she shouted against his flesh, but the room was still except for their silent struggle and the sound of their labored breathing.

She felt something lumpy under her left side. The gun. Oh, God, let me kill him, she prayed as she dug through the folds of her dress. Her fingers found the thick cord of the reticule. She worried the thong, her fear making her clumsy. He stuffed a bandanna in her mouth. The dirty fabric made her gag. After pinning her down with his leg, he began to wrap a rope around her ankles. Her hands would be next. She had to get that gun.

She felt the fabric slide open and she shoved her hand inside. Relief flooded through her as her fingers closed on the grip of the derringer. She pulled it out and pressed the muzzle into his ribs, then cocked the hammer.

Evan stiffened and grunted with surprise. "You gonna kill me, little girl?" The contempt in his voice was almost as frightening as the attack.

She pulled the cloth from her mouth. "If I have to. Get up. Very slowly."

He rose and stepped back. She tried to untie the rope around her feet, but couldn't. Finally she glanced down at the knot. When she looked back up, Evan had faded into the shadows of the room. Icy fear trickled down her back. She heard a noise and turned.

The wide outside door used for deliveries was sliding open. Sunlight slipped into the room, illuminating Evan. With both hands trembling, she raised the gun. "Stop," she commanded.

He looked back at her and laughed. "You're not going to shoot me, girlie." Then he slipped out the door.

She kicked free of the rope, ran after him, and fired, but he had already mounted a horse and turned it in the direction of the open prairie.

The door to the hallway flew open. "What the hell? Did I hear a gunshot? Brooke? Oh, my God." Dalton crossed the room and pulled her into his arms. "Brooke, what happened? Are you all right?"

She dropped the derringer on the floor and clung to him. Tremors racked her until she couldn't even support her weight. Dalton picked her up in his arms, and she buried her head in his shoulder. "He tried—to kill me." Tears poured down her face.

"Who?"

"Evan."

"I'm going to . . ." Dalton paced in front of the sheriff's desk, his hands clenched into tight fists.

"Settle down, boy. You gettin' all riled up isn't gonna help nobody, especially Brooke. Now, tell me again about Evan Jones."

Dalton leaned against the wide window and stared unseeingly at the street. "He answered the ad in the paper; he rode out here from Cheyenne for the interview. A couple of other men showed up, but Jones seemed the most qualified. He was a good shot and had excellent references. I telegraphed a couple of the people he'd worked for and got back recommendations that he be hired." He'd run the scene over and over in his mind so many times that he recited the sequence of events from rote.

Where had he gone wrong? he asked himself again. Anger, fear, and guilt twisted in his gut like a badger and two coons fighting it out.

His chest tightened as he remembered hearing the shot ring out. As long as he lived, he'd never forget the look of terror on Brooke's face when she collapsed into his arms.

"According to his references, he was working in New York about the time Mattie was being harassed," Dalton said.

"Too bad. His bein' here coulda solved the mystery real easy. But in my experience, that don't happen much." Morgan glanced up at him. "What I don't get is why he attacked Brooke now. Something must have stirred him up. He's been working for you for over two months. Did he get in trouble?"

Dalton resumed his pacing; the rhythm of his boots hitting the floor matched the grinding of his jaw. "Not that I'm aware of. Brooke never had much to do with Jones. She said he made her nervous. God." He sank into a chair and pounded his fists on the armrests. "Why the hell didn't I listen to her?" He laughed harshly. "I told her she was being silly."

"Beatin' yerself to death ain't gonna bring him to justice any faster than not." The sheriff pulled a bottle of whiskey out of the bottom desk drawer. "Have some. Make you feel better."

Dalton glanced at the bottle and shook his head. "No. That's the last thing I need. What do we do now?"

The older man rubbed his hand across his cheek. "I'm gonna talk to people in town and see if'n anybody knew Evan Jones from before. Think I'll ride out and talk to the ranchers as well. If they don't know him, they might come across him on their land. In the meantime, my deputy is bringing by a few men you can hire to protect yerselves. They don't come cheap, but they're the best." He uncorked the bottle and poured himself a generous portion. "I'd trust 'em with my life . . . and Brooke's."

Dalton grimaced. "I'll have to take your word for that."

"I'm doin' it as much for her as for Mattie."

"I know."

The sheriff sipped his drink. "While I'm doin' all that, you try and figure out what triggered Jones. I believe somethin' set him off. If we can figure out what it was, maybe we can figure out the rest."

Dalton sprang out of his seat and leaned over the desk. "We could be talking about two unrelated incidents. We have to worry not only about Evan Jones trying to hurt Brooke but also about the person who threw the rock through the window. Jones wasn't even hired until after that."

Morgan raised a white eyebrow. "Could be."

Dalton felt a rising sense of frustration and anger. He wanted action and a solution . . . *now*. Damn this backwater town. What good was one old man against someone like Evan Jones? He had a sneaking suspicion that Edna Prattly was behind the whole problem—but he couldn't prove it.

By the time another bouncer had been hired and the reports filled out, it was after four. Dalton headed back to the saloon, wondering how Brooke was holding up. He hoped that Elizabeth had sent her to bed with a stomach full of brandy.

But when he stepped into the building, he saw that the front room was still set up for the biweekly literary meeting which had apparently just ended, and Brooke was sitting at a table talking with Amanda Carson.

"What the hell is going on here?" he demanded.

Both women jumped and Brooke blanched. He cursed himself for frightening her. "I'm sorry, but what are you doing up? I told you to go to bed and rest."

She stared at her lap, nervously twisting her fingers together. "I couldn't cancel the meeting without telling everyone what happened, and I don't want to . . . talk about it."

The last three words were a soft whisper. He wouldn't have heard them at all, except that he was already kneeling beside her, stilling the restless motion of her hands. "Hush, love. I'm here."

He glanced at Amanda. "Did she tell you?"

The plump woman nodded; her normally cheerful face looked shocked and afraid. "Yes, just a minute ago. I knew something was bothering Brooke during the meeting, but I had no idea. Did you . . ." Her voice trailed off.

He nodded. "I spoke to the sheriff. He's going to be talking to the townspeople and ranchers to see if anyone knew Jones. He also introduced me to some men we can hire to protect Brooke."

"I'd better get back to the store." Amanda stood up. "Send for me if you need anything, honey."

"I'll be fine."

But Dalton noticed that her lips trembled too much to smile. He turned to the other woman. "Let me walk you out." He squeezed Brooke's hand, then stood up and took Amanda's arm. "Did anyone else notice anything amiss at the meeting?"

She shook her head. "No, I'm sure they didn't. She was quite calm. But if you want me to sit up with Brooke tonight, I'm available."

"Thank you." He smiled at the friendly shopkeeper. "I'm sure we'll manage. Why don't you stop by tomorrow and see how she feels? She may want to talk to another woman."

"I will. Good-bye, Dalton."

He turned back to Brooke, swearing under his breath when he saw the tears rolling silently down her cheeks. The slight swelling around her mouth wouldn't have been noticed by someone who hadn't known what had happened. The darkening bruises had been covered with powder. But as he studied her closely, the imprint of Jones's hand was clearly visible.

Dalton pulled her to her feet, then picked her up in his arms and carried her toward the stairs. "I wish you'd let me send for the doctor."

"I'm fine," she murmured as she rested her head against his neck. "Elizabeth patched up the gash on my leg. I must have fallen against a crate. Nothing really awful happened. Evan didn't do anything but try to tie me up."

"I know, but you seeing the doctor would make *me* feel better."

His teasing was rewarded with a wan smile. He pushed her bedroom door open with his foot, then stepped inside and set her on the bed. "Get into your night things, then get under the covers. I'm going to get you something to drink."

"But the saloon," she protested, clinging to his arm.

He pried her fingers loose, feeling the iciness of her skin. "I think it will survive without you for one night."

"All right."

She started undoing the buttons down the front of her dress, and he quickly turned away. He was halfway across the landing when he heard her call out.

"Don't bring any brandy. I hate that stuff."

Dalton started up the stairs for the third time. On this try, he actually made it to the middle of the staircase. He was trying to gauge the time Brooke would need to get undressed and safely in bed. The last thing he wanted right now was to walk in on her while she was changing. Between his concern over her recent attack and the months of wanting her, his self-control was almost nonexistent.

He knocked on her door with one hand, balancing the tray with the other. "May I come in?"

"Yes."

But Brooke wasn't in the bed with the pristine white sheet pulled up around her throat. She stood facing the window. The drapes were open, and sunlight shone into the room, passing through the delicate lawn nightgown she wore and outlining her slender body.

The white fabric hung straight from her shoulders, pausing only to caress the enticing curves of her behind. The lines of her legs were long and lean, and he pictured them wrapped around his hips.

He gripped the tray until his knuckles turned white, then hastily set it on the desk. "I—I brought you tea with brandy and honey," he said hoarsely. "I think that . . . it will, ah, taste better that way."

The day had been relatively cool for the middle of July, but Dalton felt as if he'd spent a week hiking through the desert. His face was flushed and his palms damp. And there was no disguising the suddenly prominent bulge in his trousers. "Elizabeth is fixing dinner; then she'll be up to sit with you." He turned to leave.

"Don't go," she said softly.

"I can't stay."

"I don't want to be alone."

"You won't be. I just said that—"

"I want *you* to stay with me, Dalton."

She turned to face him. Her eyes were wide, the startling emerald depths glistening with unshed tears. Her hair cascaded over her shoulders, hiding her breasts, but he saw her flat stomach and the dark triangle of hair that protected the soul of her femininity.

"If I stay"—he swallowed—"I'll . . ."

"Yes?" she prompted. "You'll what?"

"I want you, Brooke Tyler."

"I'm yours."

Dalton looked so startled that Brooke would have laughed—if she could have. But somehow she didn't have the strength. The thought that he might walk away from her at this moment in time was more frightening than the memory of the attack.

She stood by the window and held her breath, waiting for him to make the first move. Her fingers twisted the cotton of her nightgown until he crossed the room in two long strides and placed his hands on her cheeks. His touch burned against her skin; heat raced to all parts of her body, and she swayed toward him.

"Are you sure?" he asked. His eyes were as dark and glowing as the night sky with a full moon.

She nodded.

"There's no going back."

"I don't want to," she whispered. "Please."

He silenced her with a kiss. Not the raging, plunging kind she had expected but soft, tender brushes of his lips against hers. He never touched long enough for her to concentrate on the pressure. It was like setting a fire by lighting individual twigs. Within moments the flames were racing out of control.

She placed her hands on his shoulders, enjoying the breadth and strength of him. The brocade of the vest was bumpy compared with the smoothness of his shirt. Her fingers touched the straight line of his jaw, the curve of his ears, before burying themselves in the rich thickness of his dark curly hair.

They stood several inches apart. She longed to bridge the space between them, but didn't have the nerve. Her breasts felt heavy and uncomfortable. They were achy and full, the nipples pushing against her gown. She pressed her thighs together as tightly as she could, trying to alleviate the pressure she felt between her legs—but it didn't help.

He drew her lower lip into his mouth and sucked. She caught her breath at the action, her eyes flying open. His lashes lay across his cheeks like elegant fans, and she lowered her eyelids and gave herself up to his ministrations. When his tongue probed for entrance, she opened her mouth and met it with hers. The stroking, seeking, exploring, was as perfect as she remembered. When he pulled back, she whimpered.

"Hush. We've got all night."

He drew the drapes shut, plunging them into semi-darkness, then took her hand and led her to the bed. He pulled back the coverlet and blanket, leaving the mattress covered by a single sheet. The darkness made her feel more comfortable, and she gasped when she heard the striking of a match.

"I want to see you as well as touch you, Brooke. And aren't you just a little curious about me? Or are you familiar with the naked body of an aroused man?"

His grin flashed white in the lantern light, and she smiled bravely, trying to ignore the heated flush on her face. "I confess you are the first." And only, she said to herself, but pushed the thought away. Tonight was for loving. The remembering, the hurting, would be for another time.

She stood awkwardly beside the bed, suddenly shy. She reached out toward his chest, then let her hand fall. "Tell me what to do."

"Love me." The southern cadence had returned to his voice, making her think of sultry nights and beautiful women. She wanted to be beautiful for Dalton. She wanted to be everything for him.

"I do."

He pressed her shoulders until she sat on the edge of the bed. When he picked up her hand and raised it to his mouth, she held her breath. When he nibbled on the pad of each finger, she swallowed. When he licked the palm of her hand, she moaned.

"Do you feel up to undressing me?" he asked.

She dropped her eyes to his trousers, then immediately looked away from the bulge she'd never seen before. "All of you?" Her voice squeaked.

"Only as much as you want."

The buttons of his vest were large and easy to undo. Good thing, she thought, as her fingers stumbled. The garment fell to the floor with a gentle whoosh.

The shirt was trickier. The closures were smaller and more stubborn, and the crisp fabric continued below the waistband of his pants. She undid the first four buttons, then hesitated. He pulled his shirttail out, then dropped his hands back to his sides. She continued to undo the buttons, meeting his eyes in confusion when she realized the fabric was warm from his skin. He nodded his encouragement.

He shrugged out of the shirt, and it joined its mate on the floor. The lantern glow highlighted the gleaming planes of his broad chest. A patch of hair, as dark and curly as that on his head, covered his skin. The pattern was uneven, wide at the top, but narrowing at his waist.

She touched him. His flesh was warm and alive, the curls as smooth as satin. She ran her fingers up and down and felt his muscles ripple and contract with her touch. He groaned.

"You like that," she said, pleased that she could bring him pleasure.

"Just wait until I do it to you."

Her eyes widened at his half threat, half promise. The ache in her breasts intensified. Her fingers brushed against the hardened nipples buried within his silky pelt of hair.

He stepped back. "I can't take much more. We'd better try something else. Stand up, my love."

He untied the ribbon at the neck of her gown, then slid the garment over her shoulders and down to the floor. Her hair hung down her back, tickling her. She quivered under his gaze, anticipation and shyness battling for control.

Taking her in his arms, he eased her back on the bed. She pressed herself against him, as much to cover herself as to touch. But he guessed her intent and pulled back. "Don't hide from me. You're the most beautiful woman I've ever seen. Your skin is the color of cream. And your breasts . . ." He trailed his fingers across her shoulders.

"I've dreamed about them for weeks."

The ache in her chest had become uncomfortable, pounding in time with her heartbeat. When his hand finally closed over one breast, she thought she might die. But that pleasure was nothing compared to the sweetness of his lips exploring the other nipple. He teased one sensitive bud with the tip of his tongue while his hand stroked the other. Brooke tossed her head from side to side, her breath coming in ragged pants.

Why had no one told her? Was this the mysterious torment that she had been warned about? She had never imagined such feeling. It was as though a feather tickled every nerve in her body.

He abandoned her breasts, but atoned for the loss with a tender kiss. He nibbled and sucked and licked and teased until her lips were swollen and her body was hot. His hand followed the path from her breast to her buttocks, then back, leaving a trail of goose flesh in its wake. When his fingers tiptoed across her thigh, she opened her eyes.

He was watching her, asking her to trust him. A single finger slipped between her legs and buried itself in her moist warmth. He moved back and forth, as if seeking, then he touched some secret spot and she jumped.

"What . . . what did—"

"Did you like it?" he asked.

"I don't remember." She looked away from him.

He touched her a second time.

She swallowed and tried to speak. "It's like being plunged into an icy stream and boiling water, all at the same time." Her legs opened, silently begging him to continue.

While his hand worked its magic below, his lips alternated between her mouth and her breasts. She felt a building pressure within her, and her limbs grew heavy. When he began to slide his lips down her stomach, she didn't have the will to protest. And when his tongue touched the secret place, she knew she was about to die.

She couldn't catch her breath, and yet she didn't need to breathe. "Dalton?" she gasped. His hands touched her in reassurance. She cried out as her body began to explode from the pleasure. Her muscles convulsed into hot flowing lava until every part of her being had been filled and released.

When the last shudder had smoothed away, she felt herself pulled next to his strong body. "What . . . What happened?"

"You had a good time," he teased.

"But I never felt anything so . . ." She buried her face in his shoulder. "Was I supposed to?"

"Yes." He brushed back her hair and tenderly kissed her forehead.

"Do you feel that, too?"

He chuckled. "I'd like to, if you don't mind."

"I'd like to see you with your clothes off."

Brooke felt her face flush with embarrassment, but she didn't call the words back. He stood up and unbuttoned his trousers. Within moments he stood before her naked, proud. She stared at him, the proof of his desire standing free and erect.

"Touch me."

She glanced at his eyes, but he was wearing his poker face, if nothing else. "Would you like that?"

"More than you know."

She reached out and touched the smooth tip. The skin was silkier than she had imagined, and hotter. When he groaned, she smiled. "Maybe you should lie down."

"I think you're right."

He reclined on the bed, all of him relaxed, except that which held her attention. She traced its length and width, discovering the ridges, the places that made him hold his breath, the movements that made him moan. She wanted to take him in her mouth, to pleasure him as he had pleasured her, but she was unsure. He sensed her hesitancy and sat up.

"I need you." Passion blazed forth; the raw wanting in his face made her feel powerful.

"Yes."

He knelt between her legs. His fingers began their dance again, and she felt herself climbing back to that place of release. But before she had peaked, he pressed himself against her. The silky length slipped inside her, inch by inch. She tensed as he withdrew slightly.

"What's wrong?"

He leaned forward and kissed her lips. "You're really a virgin."

"Of course."

"I'm sorry."

She started to ask him why when a pain ripped through her, startling her more with its unexpectedness than with its intensity. He stayed perfectly still.

"Will it hurt again?" she asked tentatively.

"It only gets better," he promised. He began to move within her. She watched the muscles in his arms and chest release and retract in time with the thrusting. A familiar tingling began, and she closed her eyes. But before she could reach the peak, he had stiffened and cried out her name.

She felt the pleasure rippling his body as he lay on top of her. Her love for him expanded until the pressure was too much to bear. Tears slipped from her eyes, falling in a salty river from her temples to her hair. "I love you, Dalton Reed," she whispered in his ear.

"And I love you, Brooke Tyler."

Chapter 16

Dalton pulled on his trousers and gathered the rest of his clothes together. The clock above the desk had stopped—neither of them had thought to wind it last night—but he judged the hour to be past noon.

He paused at the foot of the bed and watched Brooke sleep. Her lips were parted with her gentle breathing. The sheet covered all of her lush curves except one arm and the toes on one foot. Even that view was enough to make him want her again.

They had talked and loved all through the night. He had taken her twice more. They had crept downstairs sometime in the early morning to steal food from the kitchen. When dawn broke, they had finally fallen asleep. His shoulder had been her pillow, her hair his blanket.

He walked across the room and silently opened the door, then stepped out into the hall. After pulling it shut, he turned, and ran into Elizabeth.

" 'Bout time you decided to join the rest of us, hard at work," she whispered. "Or were you planning to lie abed all day?"

Her hazel eyes snapped at him, but her grin was knowing. He felt an unfamiliar heat creeping up his face. "I, ah . . . We, ah . . ."

She patted his arm. "I got eyes and ears, Dalton Reed,

and I know what you've done. But I don't think you know why you did it, do you?" She sighed. "It's none of my business, though. I reckon the two of you will just have to work it out for yourselves."

"Thanks, Elizabeth."

"Don't be thankin' me, boy. I think you've just sealed your fate. Yes, sir. Now, what time did you finally let that little girl in there git some sleep?" She jerked her head toward the door.

He cleared his throat and swallowed. "About six."

Her eyes widened, and she studied him with renewed appreciation. "Is that a fact? Well, I'll be." She turned and headed for the stairs. "I see I need to have a talk with Caleb. Six. Well, I just can't even . . . My, my . . ."

Dalton was still chuckling when he made his way to his chamber. After bathing and dressing, he checked on Brooke. She continued to sleep.

He walked into the saloon and saw Luke sitting at one of the tables. "Morning, Luke."

The cowboy grinned. "Just the man I've been waiting to see. Elizabeth is fixing you breakfast. It's a little late in the day for me. I was up at sunrise, but I let her talk me into keeping you company."

Dalton sat down. "That's very generous of you. And what brings you to Horse Creek? Want to start celebrating the weekend a little early?"

"No. I wanted to talk to you and the sheriff about what happened yesterday."

Luke's words were like dousing a campfire with a river of water. Dalton felt his high spirits flood away until all that remained was an icy fear for Brooke's safety. "You have some news?"

"Yes. Jonathan Holte, one of my neighbors, stopped by yesterday and told me what happened. Evan Jones has been seen on our land from time to time. I have some business up at the fort today. I wanted to get all the information from the sheriff so I can take it to the officer in charge. They do a lot of patrolling throughout the countryside. Maybe they'll come across him."

"I hope so."

Dalton's voice was harsher than he had intended, and the other man shot him a quick glance. "We'll find him, Reed."

"You'd better be right. I can't leave until I know Brooke is safe."

"Leave?" The cowboy's eyes narrowed. "But I thought you and she were, ah . . . Hell, you know what I'm trying to say."

Dalton shrugged. "I know. She hired me to teach her how to run this place. When my six months are up, I'm heading out." He imagined that day in his mind. The picture was lonely and bleak, chilling his body straight through to his soul. But he had no choice. Nothing had changed in the last twenty-four hours.

Liar, his mind whispered. Everything had changed. He had loved Brooke with his body and had cherished her with his heart. He had put that feeling into words and had allowed her to do the same. No doubt she believed things would be perfect between them now. He'd have to tell her the truth. And the truth would destroy her. He was no better than Evan Jones, he thought. But then, he'd always known that.

Luke sipped his coffee. "Did the sheriff have any leads yesterday?"

"No. Nothing." Dalton leaned his elbows on the table. "I wish I knew what caused Jones to act when he did. He'd been working here for several weeks before he attacked Brooke. I don't know." He shook his head.

"I've been over this a hundred times, and it still doesn't make sense."

Elizabeth bustled into the room carrying two plates piled high with food. "Enough bad talk," she ordered as she set the meal in front of them. "I don't want to hear nothin' besides your teeth chewing my food and your lips tellin' me how good everything is."

Dalton took a bite, then murmured the appropriate praises. But the food could have been gravel, for all that he tasted.

"Got any of that grub left for me, woman?" Sheriff Morgan asked as he walked into the saloon and pulled up a chair next to Luke's.

Elizabeth grinned. "I might have a spoonful or two left, Hank. You jest wait right there."

Dalton watched the older man take off his hat and set it aside. "Any news?"

"Nope. I had my boys out most of the evening, ridin' to the ranch houses nearby, but nobody saw nothin'. I talked to folks in town myself. It's like he vanished clean off the face of the earth. I might ride down to Cheyenne and have a look-see."

"I'm heading up to the fort later. I'll take a message there if you like, Sheriff."

Morgan nodded. "Good idea, Luke. Them cavalry boys might just earn their pay for the month."

Elizabeth returned with another plate and a basketful of muffins. "You all right, Dalton?" she asked, staring at the large amount of food still in front of him.

"It's not your cooking, Elizabeth. I'm not very hungry this morning."

She shook her head. "You might want to think about keeping your strength up. Women can be mighty demanding creatures."

Luke leaned back in his chair and patted his flat stomach. "Don't tell my aunt Sarah, but Lizzy's the best cook in the world. Wish I could persuade her to move out to my ranch." He sighed. "No such luck."

The sheriff grinned, his weathered face folding into deep creases. "I think Lizzy's got a couple of nieces lookin' to get hitched. You could marry one of 'em. She'd be out cooking for you so fast your head'd be spinnin' like a dog in a tornado."

"No, thanks. I've had my share of bad luck with women. I don't plan to get tangled again."

Dalton was relieved to hear the cowboy's comment. However logical his idea had been about Luke Hawkins taking up with Brooke, he couldn't stand the thought of her in another man's arms, no matter how upstanding that man might be.

"I better be heading off or I'll get to the fort in time for the first snow." Luke rose to his feet and put his hat on. "Tell that pretty girl of yours that I sent her my regards and I hope she's feeling better."

Their eyes met in a moment of silent communication. Dalton knew that he trusted Luke and that the feeling was returned. It had been a long time since he'd called another man friend. "You take care of yourself, Hawkins. If you find out anything about Evan Jones, the drinks will be on the house from now until spring."

Luke sauntered to the door. "Now, that's my idea of a reward."

Brooke nibbled at the muffins on her tray. She wasn't hungry. In fact she might never have to eat again. The lingering scent of their lovemaking was as satisfying as any meal. As she shifted on the bed, the dull complaints of previously unused muscles made her smile.

In their whispered comments, her married friends had never mentioned it would be so . . . glorious. Even the colors in the room seemed sharper, as if the world had just been nudged into focus.

She heard hesitant footsteps outside her door and smiled. "Come in."

But instead of her handsome gambler, Brooke saw Mrs. Prattly standing in the doorway. They had spoken on occasion, when Brooke had given some of the women marchers a meal to take home to their children. Their conversations had been polite, short, and uncomfortable.

This morning Edna Prattly looked old and defeated. The fine fabric of her gown was wrinkled and stained, and dark circles beneath her eyes told of lack of sleep.

"I came as soon as I heard about the attack," she said softly, moving to the side of the bed. "Tell me, Brooke. Did he hurt you?" Eyes that usually only glared with anger were now filled with concern and more than a hint of fear.

Brooke swallowed. Suddenly, she could feel the bruises on her face and the gash in her leg. Her love for the gambler had chased away all thoughts of unpleasantness, but now, facing Mrs. Prattly, the memory of yesterday's attack crashed in on her world. "Tell me what you know," she commanded.

The older woman pulled the straight-backed chair closer to the bed and sat down. Her glove-clad fingers twisted together in an endless circle of worry. "I can't begin to say how sorry I am. I never meant for this to happen."

"You arranged for Evan to attack me?" Brooke was unable to keep the accusation from her voice.

"No. You must believe me. I . . . Things have gotten

out of hand." Edna sighed and looked her full in the face. "I hired Evan Jones about two years ago. I wanted him to make trouble at the saloon. My instructions were quite specific: no one was to be hurt. After Mattie died and you took over, I found myself losing my taste for the game. I . . . He . . ." She drew in a deep breath. "I told him to disrupt the opening."

Brooke stared at the older woman. "But when we went to your house you said you knew nothing about what had happened."

"I know." She smiled sadly. "I never allowed Evan Jones to tell me what he was doing. That way I could always claim ignorance." She leaned forward and clutched the corner of the coverlet. "I swear to you, that was the last time he worked for me. I told him I wouldn't be hiring him anymore. I had grown . . . fond of you and didn't want anything bad to happen."

A hundred questions swirled through Brooke's head. When had all this started? Was it because of Mattie's affair with Samuel? She remembered the journal entry— the one her aunt had written about Edna Prattly's suffering.

Edna stood up and walked to the window. "You probably can't understand what it's like to love a man who doesn't care for you at all, but I know. From the moment I met Samuel, I knew I wanted him for my husband. He married me for my money. I had no illusions about that. I could bear almost anything, as long as we were together. But then . . ." Her voice broke.

Brooke slipped out of bed and pulled on her robe. "You don't have to tell me if you don't want to." She touched Edna's arm.

"No, I must." The older woman brushed the tears from her face. "When he met Mattie Frost, it was love at first

sight. I remember when he came home that day. There
was something different in his eyes, a light I couldn't
explain. I overheard people talking about the two of
them. I think I was meant to overhear." She smiled
bitterly. "My wealth didn't always ensure that I had
many friends, but plenty of people were always willing
enough to bring me the bad news. I hoped Samuel would
grow tired of Mattie, but he didn't. After about a year he
came to me and said he wanted . . ." A harsh sob racked
her frame.

"Shh." Brooke handed her a linen handkerchief and
rubbed her hand along Edna's back. "Take your time.
It's all right."

"No, it isn't. You see, he wanted a divorce."

"But Mattie didn't want to marry him," she blurted
out. "They weren't seeing each other anymore."

"I know that now. I came to see your aunt and
demanded that she give him up. She told me she already
had . . . months before. She wasn't interested in marrying
anybody, least of all Samuel. But he thought an offer of
marriage would win her back. I was torn by the shame
of what had happened. No one in my family had ever
been divorced. And even though Mattie refused to have
anything to do with him, Samuel never returned to me.
As long as he could come to the saloon and see her, I
knew I'd never have a chance. I hated her as much as
I loved Samuel. I wanted to get rid of Mattie Frost, so
I hired Evan Jones to make her life difficult."

"Did he kill her?"

"Oh, no." Edna turned to face her. "I would never
have killed anyone. I felt bad enough about disrupting
the shipments and the other things Evan was doing. But
I was desperate. I thought if I could tear down this
building, Samuel would return to me."

Brooke crossed her arms over her chest. "But if Evan isn't working for you, why did he attack me yesterday?"

"Because"—Edna hung her head—"he's been blackmailing me. I made the mistake of giving him some instructions in writing. The papers showed I was the one behind the trouble at the saloon. He wanted money to keep quiet. He was very angry that I didn't want to continue hiring him, and he threatened to go to the sheriff. I've been paying him off these last months, but a couple of days ago I told him I wouldn't give him any more money. He said he'd make me sorry. I thought he meant he'd do something to me. I never expected that he'd . . ."

Brooke led the other woman back to the chair and helped her sit down. "Try to relax. I'm perfectly fine. Evan didn't do more than scare me."

"Are you sure? The bruises . . ." Edna touched Brooke's cheek.

"It's nothing. Really."

"I'm so terribly sorry, Brooke. I hope you'll be able to understand what happened, if not forgive me. I just wanted my husband back. I realize now that tearing down the saloon wouldn't have made any difference."

She crouched on the floor and took Edna's hands in hers. "I do understand. And I forgive you." She wasn't so sure she wouldn't have acted exactly the same way if the man in question had been Dalton. It was difficult enough knowing that he might still be planning to leave her when his time was up. Having to deal with another woman would have made things worse. It was a wonder Edna hadn't set fire to the building herself.

"There's something else," Edna said.

"Yes?"

"I won't . . ." She wiped her eyes and tried to smile. "The Horse Creek Temperance Workers are no more. I'm sorry about the trouble I caused. I know you gave Betty the money to leave for Cheyenne."

Brooke frowned. "How did you find out about that?"

"I took her in my buggy."

The two women gazed at each other in silent understanding. "Maybe we should start working together," Brooke offered.

"I'd like that."

There was another knock on the door. "Come in," Brooke called.

Sheriff Morgan stepped into the bedroom. "I got your message, Mrs. Prattly."

Brooke sprang to her feet. "What do you want with her?"

"It's all right, dear." Edna rose and awkwardly patted her arm. "I'm going to answer a few questions for the sheriff and tell him everything I know about Evan Jones."

"But will he . . ."

She shrugged. "I hope not. I don't think I'd do well in jail. And despite our problems, Samuel would never survive on his own, even overnight. I do appreciate your concern. Come out and see me soon. We still have a lot to talk about."

Brooke stood in the center of the room and watched Morgan lead the older woman away. Her legs began to tremble, and she crawled back into her bed. Tears streamed down her face, for Edna Prattly and Mattie . . . and for herself.

Elizabeth tapped Dalton on the shoulder. "She's swearin' she's not gonna spend another minute upstairs in her room. Says she wants to come down and work."

He glanced down at the older woman. The concern in her face filled him with guilt. "I'll go talk to her. I don't want her up and around until tomorrow."

"You been avoidin' her all day. You didn't expect to get away with it forever, did you? Hell, if you're gonna break her heart, do it now and get it over with."

Elizabeth's hazel eyes saw too much, he thought. "I'll speak with her."

His feet carried him up the same stairs that, twenty-four hours before, had led to a night of unforgettable passion. He vacillated between what he wanted to say and what he had to say.

As a boy of sixteen, he hadn't understood about honor. Now all he had left was the echo of his promise not to take Brooke. He couldn't undo what he had already done, but he could swear it would never happen again.

He knocked on her door once, then pushed it open. She was sitting up in her bed, the sheet pulled to her waist, her hair falling over her shoulders and back. "How are you feeling?" he asked.

Brooke smiled when she saw Dalton's beloved face. She had missed him. The memory of their previous evening was enough to make her blush, but she also wanted to repeat the experience. Nothing had prepared her for the rapture she had found in his arms.

"I'm fine." What a bland word to describe the joy still lingering in her body, she thought.

He crossed the room and sat on the edge of the bed. "No soreness? A headache?"

She giggled. "From you or Evan?"

He smiled, but she noticed the humor didn't lift the heaviness she saw in his dark eyes. "Either. Both. How's the cut on your leg?"

A flicker of apprehension touched her skin, like a breath of winter browning the edges of a rose. "I've almost forgot it's there. And my bruises"—she patted her face—"aren't so swollen today. Is there any news?"

"About Mrs. Prattly?"

She nodded.

"I heard that Morgan's releasing her. Apparently he thinks you're not going to press any charges, and as she has no plans to continue her vendetta against the saloon, he doesn't see any point in jailing her."

The gruff tone of his voice made her smile. "But *you* think she should stay there for a while?"

"The woman tried to ruin your business, Brooke. Doesn't that mean anything to you?"

"Yes, of course it does. But I understand why she acted the way she did. Besides, nothing bad happened."

"Nothing?" He raised an eyebrow. "If Jones hadn't attacked you yesterday . . ."

We wouldn't have been together last night, she finished silently. Regret stained his tone. She scrambled forward until she was kneeling beside him. Her fingers shook as she caressed his cheek. "I love you, Dalton."

He stiffened at her touch and resisted her slight pressure to turn his head. Just when she was sure that he was about to push her away, he gave in. His lips claimed hers with all the glory of their last mating. Their tongues dueled, the sweetness of the battle sending desire flaming to all parts of her body.

Dalton raised his hands in an attempt to slide free of her taunting embrace. But instead of resisting, his fingers claimed the curves of her breasts, relearning their weight and texture, the exact size of her erect nipples. Even through the nightgown, he pleasured her, her whimpered moans transferred from her throat to his by their kiss.

He had to stop. He had to tell her it could never be, but his wall of icy resolve melted into a useless puddle in the heat of her innocent seduction. The throbbing need in his groin could not be denied.

He pulled her onto his lap, until she straddled him. With one long movement, he tugged off her gown and buried his face between her breasts. He feasted like a beggar long deprived of food. The taste of her skin was sweeter than candy, more intoxicating than any whiskey.

Her head fell back as he licked her nipples. Her hands moved his head from breast to breast. Then she fumbled for the buttons on his trousers. He felt himself spring free. The cool air whispered against his rigid flesh before he lifted her hips and buried himself into her moistness.

They began to move together. The tight heat tortured him, but he held back until he felt her muscles begin the rapid contractions that signaled her release. Only then did he allow himself to explode inside her, his groans of delight mingling with her cries.

The bath was warm. Brooke lowered herself into the steaming water and sighed with appreciation.

Dalton grinned. "You were walking kind of funny. Something wrong?"

"As if you don't know. I feel like a wishbone, after the wish." Her tone was rueful, but her eyes glowed brighter than any of Mattie's emeralds.

He walked over and dropped a kiss on the top of her head. "I didn't come here to be tempted by you. You have only yourself to blame."

"I'm not complaining." Nor would she. Each time they made love, Brooke discovered new and better pleasure.

Besides, if she kept Dalton happy in her bed, she might
be able to banish the shadows from his eyes.

She wanted to repay him for the pleasure he'd given
her. He had told her he loved her, and she would treasure
that always. But as important and wonderful as that rev-
elation had been, he had also restored a part of her—the
part that Joe had destroyed with his betrayal. She wanted
to thank him.

"Brooke, we have to talk."

He sat on the edge of the tub. She raised one foot and
brushed her toe across his trouser-clad knee. "I do my
best thinking when I'm in your arms."

He didn't smile. "That's what I want to talk about.
I—"

"Thank you," she interrupted.

"What?"

"Last night, when you held me and touched me, you
made me feel like a whole woman."

"But you are. You're the most perfect woman I know."

She shrugged. "I didn't feel especially perfect." She
drew the washcloth across her breasts. "In fact, I've
spent the better part of the last three years feeling like
a failure."

He frowned. "I don't understand."

She looked away. This was harder than she had thought.
Perhaps telling him about her most embarrassing and
shameful moment would best be done clothed, not sitting
naked in a bathtub.

"Tell me," he prompted. He leaned forward and
dropped one hand into the water until it brushed reassur-
ingly against her calf.

"I was engaged to a man several years ago."

"What?" He pulled his hand back and wiped it off
with a towel.

His shocked expression caused her to laugh. "You think you're the first one to notice my wit and charm?"

"I assume there's a point to this story?"

"Yes." She sighed. "He left me for another woman, just a week before the wedding."

"Oh, Brooke." Dalton knelt down beside the tub and stroked her face with his fingers. "I'm sorry."

"My brothers wanted to force Joe to marry me, but I didn't really see the advantage of that. I never believed that a loveless marriage was better than none at all. But later . . ." She drew in a ragged breath and pressed her cheek against his palm. "I saw her all the time. Her father owned the store where we did most of our shopping. She would taunt me about being abandoned. Then my older brother got married, and his new wife didn't like me much either. She complained about having an old maid in the house."

Tears slipped down her cheeks as she remembered the pain and humiliation. Dalton smoothed them away. "Hush. They'll never hurt you again."

"I know. That's why I wanted to thank you. If you hadn't agreed to teach me how to run the saloon, I might have had to go back. You mean the world to me."

His face was close to hers, his eyes dark with concern. A healing power flowed across the space that separated them and seeped into her being.

Slowly his expression changed to one of self-recrimination. "I should never have—"

She covered his lips with her hand. "Of course *we* should have. Haven't you figured it out yet? It was our destiny. You could no more escape me than avoid being born. Nothing can ever come between us."

She was so sure, he thought to himself. If only it were that simple. But it wasn't. He had to tell her that what she saw was an illusion. What she perceived as a future was merely a tantalizing glimpse of what could never be. It taunted him with its sweetness, but would always be just out of reach.

"Brooke . . ."

There was a knock on the door.

"Yes?" she called.

"Amanda Carson's downstairs to see you, Brooke. I done told her you was in the bath, but she says she'll wait," Elizabeth called through the closed door.

"I'll be right out."

"I'll tell her. And you git your hand out of that water, Dalton Reed."

He glanced at Brooke, and they both laughed like children caught with their fingers in the cookie jar. He held up the towel and wrapped it around her when she stepped out of the tub.

"I'll let you get dressed. Don't plan on coming down tonight."

"I won't."

"We'll continue this conversation later."

"Fine." She stood on tiptoe and kissed his cheek.

He walked to the door. How could he bear to turn her away? But then, it wasn't his decision. She was right about that. Their destiny had already been foretold. Unfortunately it wasn't the one she envisioned.

"You're certainly looking better than you were the last time I saw you," Amanda said as she stepped into Brooke's bedroom. "There's a bloom on your cheeks that would put a painted lady to shame."

Brooke laughed and hugged her friend. "I feel better, too." She led the way to the small table that Elizabeth had set up with a light meal. "But I'm more than ready for everyone to stop treating me like an invalid."

Amanda sat down and smoothed a napkin over her lap. "I'd take advantage of the situation, if I were you. I can't remember the last time I was spoiled and cosseted. The only way I could persuade my husband to let me visit you was to promise him that he could gamble downstairs."

Brooke served the savory vegetable soup. "You don't fool me, Amanda Carson. I've seen the way your husband watches you. He's madly in love with you and is probably terrified that you'll run off with some handsome cowboy."

"Is it true about Mrs. Prattly?"

"What?"

"That she's been arrested?"

Brooke laughed. "How do these rumors get started? No, she wasn't arrested. She . . ." She hesitated, not wanting to tell too much, yet wanting to stop the torrent of gossip that was sure to follow Edna's trip to the sheriff's office. "She had some information about Evan Jones. He had done some work for her in the past. I hope they find him soon."

"I'm sure they will." Amanda blushed and stared into her bowl. "*I* have some news of my own."

"Yes?"

"I'm . . . we're going to have a baby. Doc says it's due in late December."

Brooke reached across the table and squeezed the other woman's hand. "That's wonderful. You don't have any children yet, do you?"

"No. We've been married four years, and I was beginning to wonder if we'd ever be blessed with a little one."

"Sometimes these things take time."

"It certainly wasn't for lack of trying. Oh!" Amanda blushed and covered her mouth, her eyes wide. "I'm sorry. I shouldn't have said that."

Brooke laughed. "You're married. I somehow assumed that you and your husband might be intimate."

As she and her friend chatted on, a small part of Brooke's mind thought about the coming baby. Would she and Dalton conceive a child? she wondered. Her hand stroked her flat stomach. Was there already one growing inside her? She smiled at the thought, but then grew solemn. What would she do if they had made a baby? What if Dalton still wanted to leave? She would be ruined. But then, it couldn't be all that much worse than owning a saloon, she thought to herself. Could it?

Brooke stood by her window and watched the last customer leave the saloon. There was a murmur of voices and the sound of hushed footsteps as Elizabeth and Caleb climbed the stairs and entered their room.

Nearly an hour passed. She paced, sat on the bed, and paced some more.

Finally, when she was about to pull on her wrapper and go find him, she heard Dalton's step on the landing. He stopped outside her door. Her welcoming smile lingered for two more heartbeats, then began to fade. Before she could bring herself to cross the floor, he had entered his own bedroom and shut the door. The audible click of the lock being shot home caused her breath to catch in her throat.

The pain was too great for tears. Long after the moon had set, she huddled in the chair by the fireplace and stared at the ashes of the once raging fire.

Chapter 17

"Damned horse," Brooke muttered as she snapped the whip over the horse's haunches. The animal reluctantly abandoned its snack of grasses and stepped back onto the road. The buggy lurched over the rough terrain. She should have reached the Prattly ranch in about forty minutes. At the rate she was going, she'd get there by Sunday.

It had been almost a month since Edna made her confession. A month of wondering if they'd ever capture Evan Jones. A month of Dalton carefully avoiding any but the most businesslike conversation. Since their last glorious mating, they hadn't touched or laughed or kissed or even smiled together. Why? she longed to ask him. But whenever she tried to form the question, her courage failed her.

The pain in her heart was growing each day. Soon nothing would be left of her except a great gaping wound. She'd felt that she had to get away from the saloon or go mad. So she'd left a note for Elizabeth, telling her she'd gone calling on Mrs. Prattly.

The man at the livery stable had been reluctant to rent her a buggy at all but had finally given her the gentlest horse—or as Mr. Wilson had said, between spits of tobacco, "She don't even shoo away the flies that land on her back." What he had neglected to mention was that the mare was a bottomless pit that would eat half the greenery between the stable and the ranch.

The sun was already past its zenith when Brooke pulled up in front of the Prattlys' home. The two-story structure was even grander than she remembered. She stepped down and tied the horse to the hitching post. "I guess I know where you'll be."

The animal lowered its head and started to eat.

"I thought so."

She smoothed the wrinkles out of her gown and started up the steps. After knocking loudly, she hummed tunelessly under her breath. No one answered. That was odd, she thought. Nelly should have . . . She knocked again.

Nothing.

Brooke hesitated, then started to leave. She was at the bottom step when a feeling of apprehension drifted over her like a dusting of snow. She felt cold and wary. Something was wrong . . . very wrong.

After creeping back to the door, she tried the handle. It turned silently. The wide foyer was empty, but the sound of voices drifted out from the back of the house. She pulled the small gun from her reticule and moved slowly along the wall. A loud thump followed by a crash froze her in her tracks.

"Stop it," she heard Edna Prattly scream. "I'll give you the money. Just leave my things alone."

"You're mighty worried about your precious furniture, Mrs. Prattly. If'n I was you, I'd be a mite more concerned about myself. You may be a little old, but I'm not all that fussy about who I take."

Brooke swallowed the bile rising in her throat. She recognized Evan Jones's awful laughter. Gripping the derringer more tightly, she stepped into the room.

"Don't move," she yelled.

Edna was sprawled on the floor, the shock on her face almost comical. Brooke stepped forward instinctively. "Are you all right?"

"Look out, Bro—"

Brooke turned to her right and saw the door swinging toward her. She tried to jump away, but the heavy wood struck her side, sending the gun flying onto the floor and her head crashing into the doorjamb.

Dalton flipped a card across the table. It landed face up, exactly on top of the previous three he'd thrown. Despite his time in Horse Creek, his gambling skills were still up to par. He wouldn't have any trouble finding work on a riverboat . . . or maybe in Natchez. He had six weeks to make the decision, but something told him he wouldn't find his destination any more palatable then than now. Why did it have to be like this? he wondered.

A faint rumbling began in his mind. The sound was always the same: Joanna's laughter when he'd stared at the broken buggy, her skilled fingers pulling at his shirt, her taunts that she'd have him now . . . or after they were married, his angry promise that he'd see her dead first.

A life for a life, he told himself. Then the debt would be paid. What irony. By leaving he'd be free of the past, but forever lost to Brooke. But if he stayed, he'd dishonor all that her love represented.

"Care to join me in a drink, Dalton?"

Samuel Prattly stood in front of the table holding an unopened bottle of whiskey and two glasses.

Dalton nodded toward one of the empty chairs. "Suit yourself. What brings you to town? It's early yet."

"I had to get out of that house. Every time I see Edna I feel lower than the claws on a bear. I still can't believe what she went through for me. I never thought . . ." He sighed heavily and poured them both an inch of the amber liquid. "I guess I never did understand women, and I'm too old to start learning now."

"I'll drink to that." Dalton drained his glass in a single swallow.

Elizabeth scurried into the room. "Dalton, come quick."

"What's wrong?"

"Luke's here. He's got news of Jones."

She was still talking when Dalton and Samuel pushed past her and into the hall. Luke stood waiting, his hat in his hands.

"What happened?" Dalton asked.

"One of my men saw Evan Jones riding across my land. He was headed for the Prattly place. I brought you an extra horse."

Samuel pulled on his coat. "I left Edna home alone. Nelly has the day off today. I've got to get back."

Dalton was right behind him. "I'm coming with you. Brooke rode out to your place less than an hour ago."

"I'll get the sheriff," Luke said.

"If that man's done anything to . . ."

Prattly met his eyes as they walked out of the building. "You'll have to fight me first, Dalton. Jones is mine."

"Damn fool men," Lizzy complained, hugging her arms around her chest as she trailed behind. "Jes' git out there and then worry about who's gonna take Jones. Dalton, you bring that little girl back safe and sound, you hear?"

He swung into the saddle and gathered the reins together. "I promise, Elizabeth. I promise."

* * *

"Brooke? Brooke, can you hear me?"

"What?" She moaned softly, wondering who was pounding on the inside of her head. "Where am I? Edna, is that you?" She shut her eyes and tried to still the rapidly spinning room.

"You banged your head when Evan Jones pushed the door against you. Are you all right? You've been unconscious for almost fifteen minutes."

The surface she was lying on was hard and unyielding. Brooke struggled to sit up, but found her feet tied and her hands tightly bound. "What happened?"

"He tied us both up. He's planning to rob the place and then . . ." Her voice cracked. "I don't know what else."

"I heard you offering to pay him off."

"Pretty stupid, I know. That man will never be satisfied until he's got all my money. But I couldn't take a chance on him hurting you again."

Brooke risked opening her eyes. The room still lurched a little, but she could deal with that. They were in the parlor where Edna had entertained her when she'd come with the sheriff. Brooke was on her back, on the floor, her wrists tightly bound behind her. Edna was in a yellow overstuffed chair, her wrists bound together on her lap, her ankles tied to the legs of the chair. The tall bookcases had all been pushed to the floor and the corner cabinet was empty. From upstairs came the sound of someone moving rapidly from room to room.

"He's still hard at work looting my house," the older woman said grimly. "It took him some time to get us all tied up." She tried to smile but her expression was closer to a grimace. "You're not as light as you look."

"I hope he pulled his back out trying to carry me," Brooke said. She saw the rapidly swelling bump under her friend's eye. "I see you put up a struggle."

Edna shrugged. "I did my best."

"We've got to get out of here. Jones will never let us go."

Edna twisted at the bonds holding her wrists together. "I've been trying to loosen these, but they're too tight."

"Maybe I can do something." Brooke rolled onto her side. A hard object pressed against her thigh as she struggled into a sitting position. "I've got a plan," she said between gasps of air. "If I can just get close enough . . ."

She pushed up onto her knees and moved closer to Edna's chair. "I have a knife strapped to my leg. Try to get it out and cut my hands free."

Edna's dark eyes gleamed with excitement. She leaned as far forward as she could. "Yes. That would work. Turn a little this way. Can you help me lift your skirt?"

Brooke pulled the heavy fabric sideways and up, inch by inch. Her bound wrists made the movements awkward and slow. She felt Edna fumbling under the petticoat. Fear tightened in her chest; each breath was loud and labored.

"I've got it."

"Thank God." She turned her back and held out her hands. The ropes moved back and forth, digging into her wrists, but she bit back her cry of pain. Seconds later she was free.

After cutting Edna loose and untying the bonds at her ankles, Brooke slipped toward the door. Heavy footsteps from up above reassured her Evan was still busy. "It's clear. Let's go."

"Wait." Edna ran back and pulled open the bottom drawer of a cabinet. She pushed a button, and a small panel popped open. Inside was a gun. "We may need this. Come on, we'll go out the back."

They crept down the hall and through the kitchen. At each noise, Brooke flattened herself against the wall and prayed. By the time they'd made it down the back steps, she was afraid her heart was going to leap right out of her body. They paused by the flower garden. As she rubbed the raw marks on her wrist, she inhaled the scent of flowers. She felt as if she'd lived a hundred lifetimes in the last few minutes, but the world seemed unchanged.

"My buggy's in front," she said softly.

"No. We need to take two of the horses from the stable. If we use the buggy, Jones will catch up with us. Can't you ride?" Edna grabbed her arm and pulled her toward the stable.

"Astride?" Brooke shook her head as she ran along. "No, but this seems like a very good time to learn. I'll just—"

"You two weren't thinking of just running off without saying good-bye, now, were you?"

She froze at the sound of Jones's voice close behind. He'd caught up with them halfway between the house and stable. From the corner of her eye she saw Edna motion for her to turn around slowly and step away. Brooke nodded.

"Why, no, Evan. We were planning to—"

There was a gunshot, followed by Jones's startled scream of pain. The man dropped his weapon and clutched his thigh. "You crazy old woman. You almost hit me in the—"

"That's what I was aiming for, Mr. Jones. I'm only sorry I'm such a poor shot."

Brooke stared at the blood flowing from the man's wound. Her stomach twisted as the ground seemed to tip.

"Don't faint now," Edna said as she put a reassuring arm around Brooke's shoulder.

"I'm fine, really." She felt a smile touch her lips. "We make a hell of a team."

The two women were still laughing when they heard the sound of horses.

"Edna! Edna! Where are you?"

Samuel and Dalton, followed by Luke, the sheriff, and several other men, came riding around the house.

Samuel slid from his horse and raced toward them. "What happened? Edna, are you all right?" He pulled his wife into his arms and held her close.

Brooke watched the woman she now thought of as her friend tentatively return the embrace. She didn't know she was crying until Dalton handed her his handkerchief. Smiling her thanks without meeting his eyes, she turned to the sheriff.

"Jones tied us both up and ransacked the house. When we got loose, he came after us. Edna shot him. I think he might need a doctor."

"I assume you can handle this, Morgan?" Dalton asked.

"Sure. Sam, I'm gonna need to borrow one of your carriages to get Jones here back to town."

"Go ahead." Samuel led his wife into the house. "We'll be in tomorrow to give you a statement."

Dalton picked Brooke up in his arms. Before she could complain, he'd already started toward the buggy tied up in front. She wanted to protest; he had barely spoken to her in the last month, but the feel of him holding her so close was too wonderful to relinquish. Her anger and pain could wait until they returned to the saloon.

Brooke woke up with a start. The sleeping draft she'd taken had worn off, leaving her awake and trembling from the memory of what had happened at the Prattlys'.

The ride home was mostly a blur, as was Elizabeth's gentle concern. The doctor had arrived, examined the bump on Brooke's head then told her to rest.

Now, in the crystal hour of morning when the world was hushed and still, waiting for the dawn, she remembered the look on Dalton's face as he'd carried her to her bed. There had been sadness and great longing . . . and resolution. He'd made his decision.

She rose and pulled on her robe. Stepping carefully to avoid the boards that creaked, she crept down the stairs. A light shone from under the office door. The scent of a cigar lingered in the hall, and she knew who was sitting in the room.

"Why aren't you in bed?" He spoke without turning around.

Brooke paused in the doorway, staring at the back of Dalton's head. His boot-clad feet rested on her desk, and one of the ledgers was open on his lap.

"If I'd known you were planning to go over the accounts, I would have come down sooner to help," she said.

He shut the book. "You've done a fine job. The business is doing well."

She moved into the room and around to her chair. "Thank you. Why are you up? It's very late."

He curved his lips into a smile that didn't quite reach his eyes. "I've been thinking about my life. It's an interesting exercise. You should try it sometime."

"Dalton, talk to me." She sank heavily into her seat, a wave of melancholy threatening to engulf her. "You've been avoiding me for weeks. I don't know you anymore. We don't talk, we don't touch, we aren't . . . close."

His eyes met hers, then darted away. The rigid set of his shoulders warned her that something was terribly wrong. She was suddenly cold. Please, God, she thought, don't let him leave me.

Dalton lowered his feet to the floor. "I've been unfair to you, Brooke. I've taken everything you've offered and repaid it with betrayal."

If his words hadn't frightened her, the hollow expression in his eyes would have been enough to cause her heart to stumble a beat. Their bleak emptiness was worse than any anger could have been. She saw twin reflections of herself, but nothing else, as though the very core of him had ceased to exist.

"But we love each other. You told me you loved me. Were you lying?" Her voice quavered, and she hated herself for showing weakness.

"No. Of course not. I never imagined I would meet anyone as fine and beautiful as you."

"Then I don't understand. What's wrong?"

He drew in a deep breath, then exhaled it. She wanted to run away, to cover her ears so that she couldn't hear what he was about to tell her. Pain cut through her. A knife twisted in her stomach, slicing her into tiny pieces that could never be whole again.

"I'm still leaving."

"Why? What have I done?"

He laughed harshly and without humor. "You? Your crime is loving me. My crime is twofold: allowing you to enter my life at all, and"—he swallowed and stubbed out the cigar—"that which keeps me from you. I can't stay with you because I am not the man you believe me to be."

She stood up and pounded on the desk. "Damn you, Dalton Reed. Stop playing word games with me. You are a master at them, I'll grant you that. Tell me straight out! Tell me what you've done!"

Her voice rose with every sentence until her cries echoed in the tiny room. When they had died, the silence expanded the small space until she felt they were alone in the vastness of time.

"I once killed a woman."

She heard what he'd said, but the enormity of his confession was so far beyond anything she had imagined that she found herself unable to grasp the meaning. He had to be lying. Dalton wouldn't hurt anyone, especially a woman. There had to be a mistake.

"What do you mean?" She had to force the words out past her stiff lips as she lowered herself slowly to the edge of the chair.

He gripped the desk until his knuckles whitened. Tendons stood harshly outlined, and his fingers trembled with the force of his hold. But his face was blank, his eyes carefully hooded.

"There was a girl, when I was growing up. Her name was Joanna. Her family wasn't wealthy, but they were well respected in town. She set her cap for me when we were both quite young. It didn't seem to matter that I detested her. She was determined to marry a Reed son and live in the big house on the corner." He glanced at Brooke and then away. "One afternoon, when we were both sixteen, Joanna and her sister came over in their father's buggy. She said she had something important to show me. I didn't want to go with her, but my mother insisted."

Brooke felt jealousy course through her until the dark emotion filled her with anger. Just the thought of his being with another woman . . . But she tried to ignore the feelings and concentrate on his words.

"I'll never forget that. 'Dalton,' Mama said, 'when a lady invites you out, it's impolite to refuse.' Only

Joanna was no lady. After I got into the buggy, she headed toward the far side of town, where she dropped her sister at the dry goods store. Joanna told me she had to deliver some preserves to a friend of the family's. I was so angry at her, I didn't notice where we were, or how late it was getting. About twenty miles outside of town, a wheel came off the buggy. While I was trying to fix it, she unhitched the horse and turned it loose. I was shocked, but Joanna . . . she only laughed. Said she'd finally gotten what she'd always wanted. She taunted me, saying we were going to be man and wife forever, so I might as well have my way with her now." His fists clenched tight. "I didn't touch her. I just walked away without saying a word. Eventually, she followed. It was a long walk, and we didn't make it back until the next morning."

He brushed his hands over his eyes as if to block out the memory. But Brooke pictured the scene all too clearly. Two sets of frantic parents, the whispers, the accusations.

"The families said we *had* to get married. Joanna was willing. Hell, she'd already made out a guest list. But I refused. I flat out said no. Nothing had happened between us, and I wasn't about to spend my life tied to some girl I didn't like simply because she'd loosened a buggy wheel."

He was silent for a long time, lost in painful memories that Brooke could only imagine. "Did you marry her?" she asked finally.

"No. When I told my mother I was leaving, she said I was besmirching the family name. I still remember the look in her eyes when I told her I wasn't going to ruin my future because of something as elusive as honor. You couldn't see it or touch it. How important could it be? So

I left. Ran off, like a thief in the night."

He was eating himself up with pain. She could feel it radiating from him, a swirling blanket of agony that had scored him with hundreds of wounds too small to see, too deep to heal.

"What did you do?"

He shrugged. "I hitched a ride on a railroad car as far as the Mississippi River. Then I stowed away on a riverboat. An old man found me. He was a gambler. The best I've ever seen. Took me on as an apprentice and taught me everything he knew." Dalton's lips curved into the first genuine smile she'd seen on him in weeks. "I still miss him. Before he died, he told me I had to go back and make things right with my family. He said that in the end that was all that really mattered. I knew he was right. I'd been thinking about it myself, for some time. In the four years I'd been gone, I'd grown up and learned about things like respect and honor. So I went home."

His voice sounded distant, as though he were speaking through water. Some sounds were amplified, others muted, until everything blended into a harsh discord. Apprehension prickled along her spine.

"To Joanna?" she asked.

"She was dead. Two days after I left, she took her father's gun out of his desk drawer and killed herself."

Brooke drew in a breath, but the much-needed air didn't seem to fill her lungs. Suddenly Dalton's feelings and actions were so very clear. In her innocence she had assumed that once she knew the secret, the solution would be clear. She knew now that knowledge was simply the beginning of the problem. Nothing between them had really changed.

He leaned back in his chair. "*I* remember the look in her eyes when I told her I was leaving. *I* remember how she cried and begged me not to abandon her to her shame. *I* remember how I walked away without looking back."

She couldn't bear to watch the man she loved in such torment. She rose from her seat and circled around the desk, then dropped to the floor by his feet. "You mustn't continue to blame yourself, Dalton."

He shook off her comforting touch. "Who else is there? I knew Joanna wasn't like other girls. I should have known what my leaving would do to her. I killed her. Don't you see? I murdered her as surely as if I'd pulled the trigger myself."

Long after he'd left the room and her legs had grown cold and cramped, Brooke continued to crouch on the floor. Dry sobs racked her body, the wheezing gasps cutting through the morning air. Joanna hadn't only killed herself with that bullet. She had killed Dalton as well.

Dalton stood in his bedroom and stared at the open carpetbag, then kicked it back into the armoire. Running away would accomplish nothing, he reminded himself. It sure as hell hadn't helped before. He had a month and a half left in Horse Creek. How difficult could it be to get through that short a period of time?

He walked to the window and stared out into the street. The sun was setting, and the sounds from the saloon floated up through the floorboards. The next six weeks weren't the problem. It was the few seconds it would take to say good-bye to Brooke. It was the time after that.

His life stretched on endlessly. A great desert to be crossed one day at a time, one step at a time. And at the end there wasn't a reward. No Holy Grail or great wealth of knowledge. Simply an ending, and the pain to prove he'd earned the rest.

He heard Brooke leave her room and walk down the stairs. He wanted to go after her and tell her how sorry he was. But the words would be inadequate. She had heard the story of his shame; there was nothing left to say. Drawing the draperies closed, he drew in a breath. He had a business to run. No matter what else had happened between them, he owed that to Brooke.

Late that evening Brooke carried the cash box to her office. As she passed the gambling room, she saw Dalton seated alone at a table. He was shuffling a deck with one hand. To a stranger, he would have looked fine. But her eyes saw past the blank facade. His poker face was simply a mask that no longer fit. Lines of pain ran from his nose to his mouth, and a muscle twitched just below his right eye.

"You're up late," she said.

He froze. The deck split in two. "So are you."

"I have an excuse. I slept most of the day."

"How are you feeling?"

"Better, thank you." This polite conversation was worse than the silence, she thought.

She set the money box on the floor and walked into the room. Drawing a chair close to his, she tried to smile. "Are you angry with me?"

"For what? The correct question is Why haven't you thrown me out?" He glanced at her. "Don't I make you feel uncomfortable?"

"Dalton . . ." She tried to touch his arm, but he pulled away. "I still love you. I'm sorry about what happened, but it was such a long time ago. You were only a boy."

"I was old enough to kill her."

"But you didn't." She leaned closer and cupped her palms around his jaw. "She killed herself. You're not to blame. A stronger woman would have survived. She would have found work or moved to another city to live with relatives. I'm not saying running away was right, because it wasn't. But that was a long time ago. You're a different person now, a grown man who *is* honorable."

He pulled away from her grasp and stood up, his back to her. "Honorable? Don't even say the word. Is it honorable to have run away a second time?"

"What do you mean?"

"After I found out about Joanna, I left again. There was no reason to stay. My return to the fold was an exercise in futility. My parents asked me to remain in Boston, but I knew they were only being kind. There was nothing for me there. I would be a constant reminder of the dishonor I had brought to the family."

"You've never been back?"

"No."

"And you don't write?"

"No."

"So they don't know if you're dead or alive."

He shrugged his shoulders. The movement was stiff, as if a great weight rested on his back. Her soul cried out, longing to ease his wretchedness, but she had no relief to offer him except her words. They were feeble bandages to stem the blood flowing from such a bottomless and ancient wound.

She rose. "Dalton Reed, you are the noblest man I know."

His softly muttered curse indicated that he didn't agree.

Wrapping her arms around his waist, she leaned her head against his back. "It's true," she said. "You've been kind to me since the moment we met. You protected me on the train. You took me to Margaret's rather than have me spend the night in a less than respectable hotel. You've helped me with the saloon. I wouldn't have made it without you."

"What *about* all I've done for you? Do you want to talk about what I've taken from you?" He turned to face her. His hands squeezed her upper arms until his fingers dug into the tender skin with a pressure that would mark her for days. "I've taken your only chance at ever marrying a decent man. At least I left Joanna a virgin."

Dalton had expected her to shrink from his words, but her green eyes flashed defiantly. The smooth line of her jaw was clenched tight, and he read the stubbornness in her stance. Some part of him, separate from the horror of his past, admired her spirit. She always challenged him, he thought. He'd miss wondering which of them was going to win.

"I told you before that I don't believe in marrying for convenience," she said. "I would only be interested in marrying a man I loved. And right now he's standing in front of me. A pigheaded fool, too stupid to realize the past is over. You have a life to live, Dalton. Live it with me. Let me love you until we're both too old to do anything but rock on the front porch and complain about our grandchildren. I know you care for me. I see the passion burning in your eyes when you touch me. Everything you do is filled with love for me. Don't deny us both because of something that happened a long time ago. Don't condemn me to repeat the tragedy Mattie was forced to endure."

Her pleas were a gunshot to his gut. "I wish I could be what you need," he said hoarsely.

He let go of her arms and held his hands out in front of him, the palms up. She reached out to touch him, but he warned her away with a quick shake of his head. "You can't see it, but I can."

"What? What do you see?"

"Blood. Joanna's death remains on my conscience and on my hands. As much as I love you, I have nothing to offer."

Brooke could have understood anger. She would have let him rage until he was weak with exhaustion, then comforted him. She could have understood pain. Tears would wash away the sorrow and begin the cleansing. But she couldn't react to nothing.

And that was what she saw in his face. A shadow or two flickered across his features; a muscle twitched in his cheek. But his eyes were as dark as a bottomless pool. They pulled in all the light in the room and reflected none back. She couldn't see inside to his soul. There was no longer anything to see.

"Oh, Dalton. Don't do this, I beg you." She clutched the lapels of his jacket and rested her head on his chest. "I will do anything, say anything. But don't leave me like this."

"I'm staying until the fall."

"That not what I meant." Tears coursed down her face and dampened his vest. "You've already left me, in your heart."

She waited for him to say something. A small denial, a word of comfort, but he was silent. When her tears had slowed enough that she thought she could find her way, she stepped back and left the gaming room.

The staircase to her room had never seemed so steep. Her heart was heavy; the extra weight made each step a mountain. When at last she reached the landing, the few feet to her door seemed like a vast uncharted plain. Elizabeth stepped out of her room and called to her. Brooke turned and looked at the her.

"I was wonderin' if you'd . . . What happened?"

"I . . . nothing."

"But, child, you look as if your best friend just passed on."

She tried to smile, but her muscles wouldn't cooperate. "Yes. That's exactly what happened."

Elizabeth took her arm and helped her into her room. Once on the bed, she pulled the coverlet over Brooke's shoulders. "I'll bring you some tea, dear."

"I'll be fine, Elizabeth. I just need a few minutes to recover." She closed her eyes. "You see . . . it was nothing."

Chapter 18

"Brooke . . . Where are you?"

Suzanne's call echoed throughout the wooden building. Her voice was filled with excitement. Brooke hurried out of her office and into the saloon. "What is it? Are you all right?"

Suzanne grinned and waltzed across the room. Her blue eyes glowed with an inner light, brighter than any fire. "He's done it."

"Stephen Bolt?" Brooke asked, crossing the room to her friend's side.

"Oh, I couldn't believe it when I heard the words. I thought I'd made the whole thing up. But he asked me—to marry him. *Me*. A girl with a past. Oh, Brooke. I never thought I could be so happy."

She found herself caught up in one of Suzanne's enthusiastic backbreaking hugs. "I'm glad for you," she gasped as she tried to catch her breath.

Suzanne released her and collapsed on the edge of the stage. "I couldn't've done it without you. I'm hopin' you . . ." She looked down and swallowed. "Will you stand up with me? We're to be married in the spring."

Brooke sat next to her. "I'd be honored. And I'm very pleased for you. Stephen is a wonderful man."

"Yes. He's so handsome and generous and thoughtful and—"

"Enough." Brooke laughed. "You'll be nominating him for sainthood, soon."

She winked. "No, I don't think so. I want him to warm my nights as well as my heart."

As Suzanne continued to chatter about her future, Brooke tried to push away the feeling of envy that pressed against her soul. The young woman deserved a fine husband and family but . . . *I do too,* a little voice whispered in her head.

She looked out the saloon window and stared at the leaves on the trees. They were turning brown and drifting to the earth. It was fall. Where had the time gone? It seemed just an hour ago that she had boarded the train in Nebraska, and now Dalton was almost ready to leave. He'd be gone by the middle of October, and she wasn't any closer to persuading him to stay than she had been back in the summer.

She'd remained in her room and cried for hours after he rejected her. The next morning, she'd dressed and gone downstairs. He had tried to apologize, but she'd told him not to bother. If he chose to live his life alone, she wouldn't try to change his mind. She had hoped to see disappointment in his eyes, but had seen only relief. After several false starts, their days had settled back into a familiar pattern of working together. Eventually they had returned to their friendly teasing, but they were careful never to touch.

She longed for him until every part of her body ached. Her nights were restless, her days long. But she didn't beg him. She'd done that once, and it hadn't worked. Pride was all she had to sustain her. That and the memory of their brief time together. There hadn't even been a child to comfort her.

Long after Suzanne had left, Brooke sat in the empty saloon imagining what should have been.

Dalton leaned against the door and watched Brooke in her office. He thought about stepping in to see her, but held back. He didn't have anything to say. There was no business to discuss, no mistake to tease her about. And telling her that he was slowly dying from wanting her wasn't part of their agreement.

The last five weeks had been a new form of deadly torture. To see her, to talk with her, but not to touch her . . . he couldn't imagine a worse fate, except that of not being with her at all.

The warm September had given way to a crisp October. He would be gone before the snow had a chance to build up. Maybe Natchez, he thought. Or France. It didn't matter. Nothing mattered anymore, except the emptiness eating away his soul.

I'm doing the right thing, he reminded himself. But being correct didn't make being without her any easier. He wished he could forget the past and stay with Brooke.

Dalton pushed himself away from the wall and walked into the saloon. A familiar figure sat at one of the tables. Everything about the man set Dalton's teeth on edge. He picked up a bottle of whiskey and strolled over to greet him.

"Franklin. Mind a little company?"

If Arthur's apprehensive stare was any indication, he did mind, greatly. But he only nodded at the other empty chair.

"I suppose you're here to pick up Brooke. Are you going to take her driving?"

Arthur tugged at his tie, as though his collar was too tight. "I rented a buggy, yes."

Dalton grunted, then set two glasses on the table. He filled each with two inches of amber liquid and pushed one in front of the law clerk. "I'm leaving in a few days." He took a deep swallow, enjoying the burning sensation in his throat.

"Yes. I know." Arthur made no move to touch his glass. "I'm sure Brooke will miss you. She's very fond of you, I think."

Dalton stared at the pale man and wondered if he had the stomach to continue with the charade. But he knew it was necessary for Brooke's future. She was the only one who mattered.

"I expect you to take good care of her when I'm gone."

Arthur coughed nervously. "I'll, um, do my best."

Dalton leaned forward until his nose was inches from the younger man's. "If I hear otherwise, I'll come back and cut your heart out. Do I make myself clear?"

Sweat beaded on Arthur's upper lip. "Yes. I understand."

Dalton heard Brooke's soft step in the hall. He picked up the bottle and glasses and carried them to the bar. She walked straight to Arthur without glancing in his direction.

Brooke smiled as the law clerk rose from his seat. "I'm sorry to keep you waiting, Arthur. I lost track of the time."

"It's quite all right. The buggy is out front. Shall we go?"

She tucked her hand into the crook of his arm, all the time aware of Dalton's dark eyes following their every move. She wanted to say something to him, to tell him that Arthur was a comfort, a simple convenience that made her feel less alone. But she said nothing. Not even good-bye.

"Back to the meadow?" Arthur asked as he turned the carriage around.

"That would be nice. Although I doubt there are any flowers left from summer."

They drove along in companionable silence. Their outings were a familiar part of her life now. She no longer questioned their purpose or meaning. No doubt Arthur would declare himself, one way or the other, but she didn't care about that. For now he provided her with some semblance of normalcy. With Arthur she could pretend she was back in Philadelphia being courted by one of her older brother's friends. During these brief respites there was no saloon to worry about, and no gambler.

Arthur stopped the buggy in the field and helped her out. The ground was bone dry underfoot and the grasses were brown. Most of the flowers had faded away, leaving only the golden rabbit bushes to dot the countryside.

They made their way to their usual tree. Brooke sat with her back pressed against the hard scratchy bark. "I imagine this will all be covered with snow soon," she said.

"Yes." Arthur lowered himself down next to her. "The winter comes early and stays late. But you'll make it through. We all do." He hesitated. "That is, if you're planning to stay?"

His pale blue eyes were troubled, she thought as she looked at him. He sounded overly anxious to know her plans. She wondered why. She had come to enjoy Arthur's company, but she wasn't sure how he felt about her. At times he seemed to like her, as a friend, but he'd never again tried to kiss her or declare deep feelings.

Not that she minded, she thought as she toyed with a

ruffle on her dark blue gown. There was only one man
in the world for her . . . if he would only realize that they
belonged together. "Yes. I'll be here. I've been going
over the books. We do a surprising amount of business
in the winter."

He shrugged. "The ranchers all try to come to town
when the weather's good. And Horse Creek is big enough
that we keep the road pretty clear. There's not all that
much to do in the snow here."

"I figured that. I've ordered about a hundred new
books for the literary society. If nothing else, the ladies
can always read."

Arthur stretched out on the ground, supporting himself
on one elbow. He smiled tentatively. "I have some good
news."

She raised an eyebrow. "Tell me."

"Edward Gannen is taking me on as a partner. He's
going to hire another clerk to do my job and allow me
to start handling law cases."

She leaned forward and squeezed his hand. "You must
be very happy. That's quite a step up for you. I know
Edward has a lot of relatives in California and plans to
retire there. Soon you'll be the only lawyer in town."

Arthur stared at the grass. "I'm also getting a large
increase in wages. I've arranged to have a house built,
across town from the saloon."

"The local builder must be very busy." Just last week
Stephen Bolt had mentioned that he was having a couple
of rooms added on to his house by the church. He'd be
needing the extra space when he married Suzanne in the
spring.

"Brooke, I . . ." Arthur cleared his throat.

The odd expression on his face caused her stomach to
clutch into a tight knot. She prayed that he wasn't going

to say what she thought he might.

"Would you do me the honor of becoming my wife?" His blue eyes watched her intently. "I'd prefer that you didn't run the saloon, but I do understand your reluctance to sell your inheritance. I'd be willing to overlook your ownership if someone else took care of day-to-day business." He coughed. "That is, if you'll consider my proposal?"

Oh, God. Why now? she thought as she stared at him. She didn't know what to say. A firm refusal hovered on her lips, but she couldn't bring herself to say no. She didn't love him, but then, he hadn't said anything about love.

But you don't believe in marriages of convenience, a little voice in her mind whispered. This is different, she answered silently. This could be her one shot at respectability. She'd be a fool to refuse him out of hand.

Brooke clearly recalled Suzanne's happy face when the former dancer announced her engagement. Everyone had said that the minister wouldn't forgive her past. But he had. And they loved each other. Perhaps if she waited, she would find the same type of man.

But she already had. Dalton Reed was her true mate. There wouldn't be anyone else for her, ever. How was she to make her empty life bearable? His time was almost up. The six months would end on Sunday.

"Why?" she asked finally.

He blinked several times. "Excuse me?"

"Why do you wish to marry me, Arthur? You hardly seem overcome by emotion."

"I . . . You . . . That is, you're very beautiful, Brooke. And I've always been . . . fond of you." He stared intently at the ground. "We both have need of a place in society. You can't deny you want to belong."

Now it was her turn to avoid his glance. When had
Arthur Franklin become perceptive? Or had she been so
blinded by Dalton's light that she'd failed to see the law
clerk as a man?

"Arthur, you honor me with your proposal. I must
ask your indulgence and tell you that I will give you
an answer on Sunday." After Dalton had left.

"I understand."

He sat up and leaned toward her. This time she knew
what he was planning and held her ground. His mouth
brushed hers once, twice; then he rose and offered her his
hand. She pressed her fingers to her lips, trying to recall
the sensation. The kiss had been so brief, and yet it had
spoken volumes. There had been no fire, no spark . . .
no feeling at all.

"Well, what do you think?"

Brooke stared at the hat Mrs. Gilmore was holding.
The brown felt was accented by three red feathers. "It's
quite lovely and very daring."

The small woman caressed the soft feathers with her
index finger. "I know, but when I saw it, I couldn't resist.
Sometimes I think Amanda orders hats from Cheyenne
just to tempt me. I must have a talk with that girl."

Brooke bit back a smile. She knew for a fact that
Amanda did indeed order the oddest hats she could find
in the millinery catalog. And every time they came in,
Mrs. Gilmore hemmed and hawed and bought them
all.

"Did you hear about Arthur Franklin?"

"What?" Brooke nervously sipped her tea. He couldn't
have said anything about the proposal, could he?

Mrs. Gilmore arched one thin eyebrow. "Come, child.
Don't be coy. I know the two of you went riding together

last week. He must have told you about Mr. Gannen taking him on as a partner."

"Oh, that. Yes, he did mention it. I was very happy for him." She nibbled at a piece of Elizabeth's cake. "It's quite an opportunity, don't you think?"

"So, have you set the date yet?"

"Date?"

"Brooke! It's not like you to be obtuse. When are you and Arthur getting married?"

"I don't . . . Oh!" The question shouldn't have been a surprise. Mrs. Gilmore knew everything about everybody, but Brooke hadn't been prepared to discuss the proposal. "I haven't said yes yet."

The older woman smiled softly. "I know how you feel about your gambler, but men like him don't settle down. Inconsistency is in their blood. I tried to warn you on the train, but . . . Marrying Arthur is the sensible decision."

"Maybe I don't want to be sensible."

"Perhaps being sensible is all you have left." Mrs. Gilmore smiled kindly, then set her cup on Brooke's desk and gathered her purchases together. "I must be getting home. A couple of friends are coming over later this evening. We're working on a quilt for one of the ladies in town." She walked to the door, then paused. "If you need . . . anything, I'm here for you. You know that, don't you?"

"Yes, I do."

Brooke tucked the bank receipt into her reticule and walked back toward the saloon. Already the clouds chasing across the sky looked heavy and cold. It would be snowing before the month was out. The Wyoming winter was right on time.

Time . . . She'd never thought of it as a living breathing beast, but now she knew it to be her enemy. Without time, she could hold on to this day forever, keeping Dalton by her side, knowing he must leave, but able to put off the inevitable for an eternity.

She entered the saloon and walked straight into the gaming room. He sat at the same table, in his regular seat, forever practicing. She grew tired just watching him.

"I've make the last deposit," she said.

He looked up. His dark eyes gave nothing away. No small flicker betrayed his thoughts. She could almost hate him for that. Each morning she saw the desolation in her own face, the sadness in her smile. Perhaps one day she'd learn to wear the mask as well as he did.

"Thank you, Brooke."

She twisted the cord of the reticule. "When do you . . ."

The cards fell to the table as he stood. "I'm leaving on Sunday morning."

She'd known what the answer was before she asked the question, but that didn't stop her heart from collapsing upon itself. "That's three days from now. When were you going to tell me? Saturday night? Or were you just planning to drop a note on my pillow?"

"Brooke, don't. Please—"

She cut him off with a harsh laugh. "You've got it all wrong, Dalton. I believe I'm supposed to be the one making the impassioned plea." She placed a paper on the table between them. "Here's the draft from the bank. I'll leave the books out so you can check my figures."

He shook his head. "I don't need that. I trust you, Brooke."

She looked away. "And I trusted you."

* * *

On Saturday the last customer left shortly before midnight. Brooke said good night to Elizabeth and Caleb. When the older couple had left the saloon, she walked behind the bar and picked up a bottle of brandy and a glass. Nasty stuff, she thought as she poured herself a generous serving. She drank it down in three long gulps, then coughed and choked for several minutes.

By the time she had recovered her composure, a warm glow burned in her stomach and radiated to her feet and hands, caressing everything in between with liquid heat.

She had chosen her dress tonight with great care. The pale blue silk buttoned up the front. The bodice was cut lower than her other gowns; the fabric barely concealed her nipples. Each pleat was individually boned, so there was no corset underneath. There wasn't anything underneath.

Tomorrow was the Sunday. Dalton was leaving, and she had to give her answer to Arthur Franklin. But she had one last night to live before she was condemned to a life without love. One more night to make memories that would warm her during the cold Wyoming winter.

She walked into the gaming room and closed the door behind her.

Dalton looked up from the deck he was shuffling. "I thought you'd already gone upstairs. It's late."

"I know." She moved to the table and took the seat next to him. The dark round wood reflected the chandelier. "I thought you might like to play a game or two of cards."

She wanted him. Dalton read it in the fire blazing in her green eyes. Answering embers within him exploded into life.

Send her away, he told himself. Touching her now would only cause the leaving to be more difficult.

He passed her the deck.

She faced him; a slow, knowing smile curved her lips in an expression that was as old as time. He would willingly partake of all that she offered. A last hour of passion together—in the morning, he'd pay whatever price was necessary.

She pulled two pins from her hair and dropped them on the table. The click of metal striking the wooden table was unnaturally loud in the quiet room. As she shook her head, the artfully arranged curls tumbled down around her shoulders, dressing her in a cape of reddish-brown silk. His heart started beating faster, causing the ache in his groin to throb with more intensity.

She shuffled the cards, then dealt them each two. "What shall we wager?" she asked.

"I leave that up to you." His voice was hoarse with desire.

She glanced up at him, then back down at her cards. "Not money. That's so . . . vulgar between friends. Perhaps a small forfeit?"

He nodded, unable to force sound past the tight muscles in his throat.

She smiled again, then fanned herself with her hand. "I find it very warm in here, don't you?"

He clenched his jaw as she unfastened the first three buttons of her gown. The fabric gaped, revealing the full curve of her breasts; the secret hollow between was in shadow. The tips of her nipples were still hidden, but he could see the place where her creamy flesh darkened to a sweet pink. With each breath, the cloth clinging to her body trembled, as if it might slip off the turgid peaks. He licked his lips as he remembered the exact taste of her skin. She would smell of lilacs flavored with honey.

"A kiss," she said softly.

"The bet?"

"Yes. The loser must kiss the winner."

"Where?" He barely ground out the word.

"Anywhere the winner chooses."

Dalton glanced at the table. Two ordinary playing cards lay before him. A one-way ticket to heaven or hell. No, he corrected himself. Tonight with Brooke would be heaven. Hell would wait until dawn.

He turned over his cards. "Twenty."

She smiled and flipped up hers. "Twenty-one."

Dalton couldn't recall when losing a hand had brought him such a feeling of relief. He stood up and removed his jacket, then slipped off his vest. "I'm ready."

She rose to her feet, swaying slightly. He reached out a hand to steady her. Her mouth opened slightly, and he watched as her tongue darted out, moistening her lips. He lowered his head to hers, his body aching for her passionate warmth.

"No." She pushed against his shirt. "That's not where I want you to kiss me."

He straightened up and waited. She undid two more buttons and parted the fabric of her bodice. "Here."

He bit back a groan. She pointed to the deep valley between her breasts. The place where a man could feast for days and never sup his fill.

He stared at her for so long that Brooke was afraid he was going to refuse. The brandy had worn off, leaving her trembling and embarrassed by her boldness. But this was her last chance to convince Dalton that they belonged together. It had taken every ounce of her skill to cheat enough to deal Dalton the twenty and herself the twenty-one. She couldn't guarantee who the next winner would be. Somehow she had hoped a single hand would be enough.

Just when she was about to step away, the backs of his fingers brushed against the top of her breasts. She felt as if someone had taken a candle and burned a trail across her skin. When he lowered his head, she held her breath, waiting for the moment his lips would touch her. Her heart paused and then she exhaled. The hot moist pressure of his tongue stroked the side of her breast until he pushed the cloth aside and tenderly toyed with her nipple.

Pleasure exploded in her belly with the suddenness of a gunshot. Her legs grew weak.

"Dalton, love me," she pleaded as she clung to him.

With a single movement, he lifted her up so that she sat on the gaming table. He moved between her legs searching, rubbing, but the yards of her dress prevented any intimate contact.

He looked into her face, his eyes dark coals blazing with desire. "I'm sorry," he said as he clutched her bodice and ripped it open. Buttons flew everywhere, bouncing on the table and floor before skittering into silence.

"You're not . . ." He cleared his throat. "You're not wearing a corset."

"I know." She shrugged out of the dress. The fabric pooled at her waist, leaving her bare to his gaze. "Tell me you love me, Dalton."

He gripped her shoulders and bent her back until she arched up, offering her breasts for his pleasure. "Until the day I die," he murmured against her body.

His lips explored her from throat to waist. Leaning back as she was, she could do nothing but allow him to caress her at will. He licked her hard nipples, then blew softly on the moist peaks, causing her to grind her hips against his groin, seeking relief from his exquisite punishment.

Their lips joined in a kiss. It had been so many weeks that she'd been afraid her imagination had embellished their mating. But the tasting and dueling of their tongues was more sensuous than she remembered.

When he had divested himself of his clothes, she stood up and slid out of her dress. His eyes widened. "Were you walking around all evening without—"

She smiled. "Yes."

He pulled her against him, the hard evidence of his desire pressed against her belly. "I'm shocked." He kissed her with maddening thoroughness. "And delighted."

But his tongue between her lips only fueled the fire raging between her legs. She reached down to stroke and tease him into cooperation. He grasped her buttocks and raised her until she sat on the table. The cool wood was a delicious contrast to his hot chest pressing against her breasts. His satin chest hair tickled her nipples.

When he hovered over her, impatiently pressing against her moistness, she touched his face. "Have you ever—"

"No. I've never made love on a gaming table before." He plunged into her. "I won't be able to play cards again without thinking of you."

She smiled, then closed her eyes and gave herself up to the pleasure spiraling within her body. The steady strokes brought her closer to fulfillment. She clutched him tightly to her, feeling his muscles contract and release with each movement. And even as her breathing quickened and the rhythmic pulsing deep within her pushed her toward her peak, she felt the moisture welling up behind her closed eyelids. Sadness and ecstasy wove themselves together like fine linen until she couldn't distinguish one from the other.

When her release finally came, she opened her eyes. Dalton's features were blurred by tears, but she saw the matching sorrow and joy etched in his handsome face. When he cleaved to her in that final thrust, she prayed his seed would take root.

They lay together, her dress spread below them on the shiny wood. His slow breathing told her he'd finally found rest. Night after night she'd listened to him pace in his room. After tomorrow there would be only silence.

Her head lay on his shoulder, one of his arms curved around her waist. Her hair was still damp from her tears.

Pulling herself up, she brushed her fingers against his face. He stirred slightly, but didn't awake.

"I love you, Dalton Reed." She kissed his lips. "Why can't you see the truth? You didn't kill Joanna, but by leaving now you're killing me."

He slept on. She slipped into his shirt and slid off the table. Only the dawn would tell if he really understood what their love was all about.

Chapter 19

Dalton stirred restlessly, then reached out for Brooke's warm, willing body. His hand encountered only the cold silk of her gown. With the suddenness of a flash flood, the memories of the previous evening swept around him. The taste of her sweet skin lingered on his tongue. The picture of Brooke, her head thrown back in final release as pleasure mingled with sorrow, was forever implanted in his mind.

He moved off the table and stepped into his trousers. The chill of the morning made him shiver, but he welcomed the discomfort. It distracted his mind from the date. The six months were up . . . today.

As he gathered her dress in his arms, he noticed the buttons scattered on the table and floor. The hint of a smile tugged at his lips. She'd always met him more than halfway. There was strength in Brooke Tyler . . . and character. It took a special woman to travel west and carve out a life for herself in a wild town. But she had found her place, and here she would stay. If only he could do the same.

Dalton walked into the office and dropped the dress on her desk. Faint noises came from the kitchen. Lizzy was already up and starting breakfast. None of that would change. When he was gone, they would continue without him.

He dropped the buttons into a dish and turned to leave. The pull was strong. The very walls of her office exuded a force, as if attempting to persuade him to stay. Slowly he moved back to Brooke's gown and picked up one of the pearl buttons, then squeezed the shiny jewel in his fist. A small token of all that had passed between them. She probably wouldn't even know it was gone.

The stairs were steeper than he remembered, the landing higher. Her door was closed tightly against intruders, but he wasn't even tempted to knock. The accusation and sadness in her green eyes would be more than he could stand.

He stepped into his room and stripped off his clothes. After washing quickly, he dressed with care. The dark pants were clean and recently pressed. As he smoothed the neat center crease, he wondered how long it would take to erase every trace of Lizzy's hard work. The vest he chose was of green and gold brocade, one of Brooke's favorites.

He paused in the act of tying his tie. Footsteps moved down the stairs. Each soft footfall was like a blow to his heart; the pain increased as the sound grew fainter.

He crossed to the window and stared out over the town. There was a dark patch on the street where spilled water had frozen in the night. Soon the buildings would be covered with a light dusting of snow. How would Brooke survive the winter? Would she be alone or would she marry that pasty-faced law clerk?

His fingers toyed with the coins in his pocket, then removed a flat disk and the pearl button. He stared down at the poker chip he'd stolen from the train. He knew now that it could never truly match the color of Brooke's eyes, but it was close enough. When the wanting got too raw, he could stare at it and remember.

The two objects nestled in his palm; desolation gripped his soul. There should be something more tangible to take with him. He had two-thirds of the money the saloon had earned, but in his mind, that didn't count. When he left, there'd be no permanent record of his time in Horse Creek. Nothing remained, nothing except these two small tokens. It wasn't a hell of a lot to show for six months of a man's life, he thought grimly. It wasn't a hell of a lot to show for the love of a woman like Brooke.

Brooke folded the dress and set it neatly in the corner, then gathered the buttons into a twist of paper. Soon she'd have to explain the damage to Lizzy and ask her to repair it, but not just yet. She needed time to commit all the details of last night to her memory.

He was leaving. She knew that as surely as she knew her name. Their time together had done nothing to change his mind. If he had decided to stay, he would have swept into her room and told her the news. Instead, he had crept silently past her door like a thief in the night. There was to be no happy ending.

She drew in a deep breath and waited for the sadness to fill her. There was only the sunlight filtering through the office window and the smell of coffee on the stove. A strength rose up in her, bringing with it a strange but welcome numbness. She had survived Joe's abandonment; she would survive this day. Dalton had taught her to be strong. He had taught her to believe in herself. Even his leaving couldn't take that away.

"Br-Brooke?"

She looked up and saw Arthur Franklin standing awk-wardly in the hall outside her office. It was Sunday. He had returned for his answer.

"Come in, Arthur." She indicated the empty chair. "Please, have a seat. You're here early."

"I wouldn't have imposed, but I met Elizabeth on the street and she mentioned you were already up and about." He cleared his throat. "If this isn't a good time . . ."

His once pale face was flushed with color and beads of sweat clung to his brow. A painfully new black suit clung to his frame, outlining broad shoulders. He looked every inch the respectable lawyer he would soon be.

"This is a fine time," she said.

He sat in the chair. "I'm sure you're aware of why I'm here. Before you give me your answer, I want to tell you that if you needed longer to consider, I would be agreeable."

Pale eyes met hers. She couldn't read the expression. Was he hoping she'd say yes or no? The floor above her head creaked and was followed by the sound of a drawer slamming shut. She swallowed against the sudden tightness in her throat. Dalton was leaving.

"No. I can tell you my decision."

She looked at Arthur. He could give her everything she needed. She'd have his name, a place in the com-munity, an independent income from the saloon and the money left from Mattie's bequest. In time, she would come to care for him . . . and he for her. With all that she'd learned, he would find pleasure in her bed. Dalton would be able to leave with a guilt-free conscience. It was the practical solution to all their problems.

Brooke rose from her seat and walked around the desk. She stepped close to Arthur, her full skirt settling between his knees. One hand cupped the smooth line of his jaw, the other, the back of his neck. Slowly she kissed his cheek.

"I'm honored," she said softly. "But I must decline to accept your proposal. I don't believe in marriages of convenience. In time you will find a woman you love, Arthur. And you must wait for her." She stepped back.

Arthur stood up and smiled sadly. "He's staying, isn't he?"

"Who?"

"Dalton. He's decided to stay. I understand. It's always been him. Before, when I thought he was leaving, I had hoped . . ."

She touched his arm. "Dalton's upstairs packing his bags."

"What?"

The faint outrage in his voice made her smile. "The stage pulls out in an hour."

"So you'd rather be alone than . . ." Arthur drew in a deep breath. The lines of his body stiffened as if he'd been slapped. "I see."

"No, you don't see. This isn't about Dalton at all. It's about you and me. You deserve better. You deserve a woman who will need you. How many years would you sit across from me and wonder if I was thinking about Dalton?"

"I hadn't thought of it in quite those terms." He paused. "I see your point."

"I'm glad. I hope we can still be friends."

"Of course."

She smiled. If nothing else, she could count on Arthur to behave like a gentleman.

"It's not . . ." Arthur cleared his throat and looked away. "If it's because he took . . . I mean, if you're holding back because there were liberties . . ." He coughed. "I would be willing to overlook . . ."

"Liberties?" She hated the blush she could feel climbing her cheeks. Did everyone in town know she and Dalton had . . . "That's not the reason I can't marry you."

Arthur looked doubtful. Anger clouded his pale eyes. "If you're sure?"

"I am."

"Well, thank you for your candor. I must be going." He planted his wide-brimmed hat on his head and walked away. His step was forceful and stiff. When he reached the hall, he pulled the door shut with a firm thud. He was upset, she told herself. But he'd get over it.

Who would have thought Arthur Franklin would be willing to overlook "liberties"? she thought with a smile. He'd seemed ready to defend what was left of her rather tattered honor. It was unnecessary, but very sweet.

Dalton closed the carpetbag and looked around the room. Nothing remained to show that he'd lived there for six months. The highboy was empty, the bed stripped of blankets. He shrugged on his jacket and adjusted the collar.

Rapid footsteps thundered on the stairs. He reached for the door, but before he got there, it was flung open and a very flustered, very red-faced Arthur Franklin stormed into his room.

"I'll have satisfaction," the clerk panted as he pulled off his coat.

"Franklin, I'm not in the mood for theatrics." Dalton picked up his bag and started for the door.

"Sir, you have dishonored a lady."

Dalton sighed. He didn't have time for this right now. The stage was leaving in an hour and he still had to say good-bye to Brooke. "Listen, Franklin, I don't know what you're talking—"

He sensed the punch before he actually saw the fist moving toward his face. Stepping back quickly, he jerked his head to the right. The blow crashed into his chin.

The impact was harder than he'd expected. The bag fell to the floor. He scrambled to maintain his footing as his body crashed into the highboy.

Dalton tasted the blood in his mouth and rubbed the injured area. "Dammit, man, what was that for?"

Arthur adjusted his vest. "I told you. I mean to have satisfaction. You have dishonored Miss Tyler."

"She told you that?"

"It wasn't necessary. Now will you fight like a man or must I again prove my intent?"

The angry gleam in Arthur's eyes would have been comical if Dalton's head hadn't been throbbing. What the hell kind of day was it turning out to be? The law clerk stepped forward purposefully. Dalton sidestepped quickly, grabbed the outthrust arm, and twisted it behind the clerk's back. Arthur yelped as his shoulder stretched painfully.

"There will be no more talk of satisfaction. Do you understand?"

"No!" Arthur gasped. "I'm not afraid of you."

And he wasn't. Dalton felt a flash of surprise. Fistfight or duel, the law clerk would be bested. They both knew that. Yet here was Arthur, defending Brooke at the risk of his own life.

Dalton glanced at the carpetbag resting on the floor. One handle was bent from a run-in with a train door. Water stains patterned the far side. He'd bought that piece of luggage on his way out of Boston thirteen years before. It symbolized every mistake he'd ever made. And here he was—running away again. Hadn't he learned anything?

For all his fine talk of honor and duty, he was turning his back on the only decent thing in his life. Brooke loved him with all the fierceness and loyalty contained in her generous heart. She gave and gave until the well was dry, then dug down deep and gave some more. He didn't deserve her . . . but how in God's name was he going to let her go?

Everything about him was a fraud. He was supposed to be the cool-thinking gambler, but Arthur Franklin was more of a man than he would ever be. The realization left a bitter taste in his mouth.

He released Arthur. "I won't fight you."

"I demand—"

"Satisfaction. Yes, I know." He stared at the carpetbag. It was time for the running to be over. It was time to put the past to rest. The debt was paid.

He turned to Arthur. "You win."

The law clerk's mouth dropped. "What?"

"You win this round, my friend. But I'm afraid the final victory is mine."

Brooke paced in her office. The pink satin gown whispered with each step. How much longer was he going to linger upstairs? she wondered. The stage would depart in less than a half hour. Did he mean to leave without saying good-bye?

For the hundredth time she silently recited her farewell speech. It had, she hoped, just the correct amount of strength and humor. She wanted Dalton Reed to remember her with love and regret, not pity.

At last she heard his slow, measured tread on the stairs. Smoothing her hands over her skirt, she stepped into the hall.

"Dalton, I . . ." Her voice failed as she took in the curious expression in his eyes. It wasn't the sadness or longing she had wanted to see, but something else. An expression she'd never seen before. She cleared her throat and began again. "I'm going to be fine. I'm not going to try to talk you into staying. I've said as much as I can."

"Brooke, wait, I—"

"No. Let me finish. I'm stronger than either of us knew. And that's because of all you've taught me. I love you. I always will. But as much as I want and need you, I know I can survive on my own."

She brushed her fingers against his vest, savoring the nubby texture. From there she moved her hands up to the smooth cotton of his shirt, then to the sensual satin of his hair. He studied her for three long heartbeats, then lowered his lips.

So this is what it feels like to die, she thought. His mouth clung to hers, expressing without words all the feelings in his heart. Never before had she been so sure of his love for her. Never before had she been so happy . . . and so sad.

She pressed harder on his mouth, and he winced.

"What on earth?" She touched his lips. "My God, you're bleeding. What happened?"

He smiled softly. "Someone showed me the error of my ways."

A light flickered in the smoky depths of his eyes. His heart thudded in his chest. She could feel the accelerated beat. Hope, smaller than a seed of grain, took root inside and began to sprout.

"Dalton?"

He touched her face, her hair, then rested his hands on her shoulders. "You'll never be able to make a go of this place on your own," he said gruffly.

"I will, too."

"Not if you continue to stack the deck the way you did last night. You're a lousy cheater."

"You knew?"

"Yes." His grin flashed white against his skin.

"Then why did you—"

"Because I needed one more night with you."

She drew in a ragged breath and looked away. "And this is where we say good-bye?"

His fingers forced her chin up. Their eyes met. "No. This is where I tell you I need all your nights. I love you, Brooke Tyler. Will you marry me?"

She couldn't have heard him correctly. "What? Why did you change your mind? I don't understand."

He brushed her lips with his thumb. "You don't have to understand anything except that I love you. Will you marry me?"

"Oh! Yes. Yes. Yes!" She punctuated each word with a kiss.

"Ouch."

"Poor man. Come on. We'll put some ice on that lip."

He drew her toward the stairs. "Later. First there are a few details I'd like to become reacquainted with."

Brooke drew back in mock surprise. "In the middle of the morning?"

"I don't know a better time."

She wrapped her arms around his waist and squeezed. "I'll go anywhere with you."

"Even to Boston in the spring?"

She glanced up at him. "To see your family?"

He nodded.

"Of course. But we may have to wait until next fall."

"Why?"

She touched her hand to her stomach. "I have a feeling about last night."